THE ENCHANTED EXCHANGE

Jennifer Erxleben

Acknowledgments

Great big thank you hugs to my husband, Scott Hartman, and stepson, Andrew Hartman, for having the patience to read drafts of my novel along the way. Knowing romcoms aren't quite their cup of tea, but still receiving positive feedback that they couldn't put it down, gave me the encouragement I needed to keep going.

I began this novel after watching one of my favourite Christmas movies, The Holiday, and had no idea that it would lead to the many adventures my two beloved female co-leads, Maria and Heather, would experience. Hope you enjoy the escape!

Dedication

I would like to dedicate this book to my parents, Helmut and Ligia, whose own love story began on a beach in Acapulco in the early 1960s.

About the Author

Jennifer Erxleben was born and raised in Waterloo, Ontario. She is a proud, second-generation Canadian who has leaned into her German and Colombian roots to weave a romantic and heartwarming story full of adventure and hope.

Table of Contents

CHARACTER LIST

SCHMIDT FAMILY & FRIENDS

Heather Schmidt: Co-protagonist (early 40s) who owns My Sweet Addiction in the town of Munich
Pam Fischer: Heather's best friend (40s) who owns a deli in the farmers' market
Martha Weber: My Sweet Addiction's shop manager
Charlotte: Heather's tuxedo cat
Vanessa: Part-timer
Sara Schmidt: Heather's younger sister (late 30s) who lives in Montreal and is married with two kids
Lars Borgen: Famous baker
Laura: Book editor

RODRIGUEZ FAMILY & FRIENDS

Maria Rodriguez: Co-protagonist (mid-30s) who is a marketing/advertising executive for Suavolino and lives in Boca Bonita
Alonso Garcia: Maria's estranged husband (early 40s) who is an investment banker
Yolanda Rodriguez: Maria's mother (late 50s) who owns a skincare line called Suavolino
Jorge Rodriguez: Maria's father (late 50s) who is a successful plastic surgeon
Abuelita: Jorge's mother (79) who came to live with them after her husband passed away

Sofia Perez: Maria's best friend (mid-50s) who runs a chain of health food stores called Pura del Sol with her husband Kevin

Gloria Delgado: Maria's older cousin (early 40s) who is Chief Sales Officer for Suavolino and is married to Nick

Jack Cardona: The Rodriguez family's chef (early 40s)

Gabriel Rodriguez: Maria's older brother (early 40s) who works as a cameraman for the Nicolás Pérez food travel show

Carlos Ramirez: Gabriel's boyfriend (late 30s) who is the location scout for the show and his co-pilot

Olivia Rodriguez: Maria's daughter (18) who wants to be a mechanical engineer

Oliver Torres: Olivia's new boyfriend (18) who wants to be an environmental engineer

Bianca Johnson: Olivia's best friend (18) who wants to be a pediatrician and is dating Oliver's best friend JC

Juan Carlos (JC) Juárez: Dating Bianca (18), is Oliver's best friend and wants to be an architect

Josephine Juárez: JC's mother (late 40s) and is a lawyer

Arturo Juárez: JC's father (60s) and well-respected judge

Carmen Juárez: JC's sister (mid-20s) who is dating Dylan O'Neil and is in law school in Boston

Breanna: The Juárez family's housekeeper (30s)

Max: The Juárez family's Chocolate Lab (8)

Mila Moreno: Carmen's childhood frenemy (mid-20s)

Logan: Mila's latest boyfriend (late 20s)

MÜLLER FAMILY & FRIENDS

Brian Müller: Heather's ex-boyfriend (late 30s), Phil's younger brother and artist

Phil Müller: Brian's older brother (early 40s) who is a weathercaster in Miami

Ursula Müller: Mother (mid-60s) and is married to Klaus

Klaus Müller: Father (mid-60s) and is married to Ursula

Martin Weber: Klaus' friend (60s) who is part owner of the Regal Winter Fair

MUNICH
FRIDAY, DECEMBER 20

"Can you grab the milk out of the fridge?" Martha Weber, the shop manager, yelled over at Heather.

Heather Schmidt, the shop owner, peered into the fridge and realized there was only one carton of milk left for the hot chocolate they were serving customers. It was a few days before Christmas, and the small town of Munich was getting busier by the day. My Sweet Addiction was packed. She cursed herself for not noticing sooner that they were running low on milk, but then again, she'd been so preoccupied lately. She took out the last carton and closed the fridge door.

"Last carton. I'll go to the store," she whispered in Martha's ear, "don't worry, I'll be quick."

"No rush," Martha reassured her.

Heather went into the back room, grabbed her purse, and put on her red puffy parka that went all the way down to her knees. She squeezed her way through the lineup of customers in the middle of her German bakery and chocolate shop, all the while smiling and wishing them Merry Christmas. She hummed along to "White Christmas" by Michael Bublé that was playing over her wireless speakers.

As she stepped out onto Main Street, the cold briefly took her breath away. A surprise after the cozy warmth of her shop. There were couples, families, and locals strolling along the quaint, European-like streets. During the winter months, Munich was touted as Christmas Town by journalists, and the townspeople worked hard at keeping this beloved nickname. Every year, the streetlamps were adorned with festive wreaths, and white lights were strung along the rooftops, twinkling hello.

Since it was a short, one-hour drive west of Toronto, it was also listed as one of Ontario's top ten tourist destinations, which meant people visited from all over, all year round.

On the main strip of town, there were other bakeries like hers (although hers was the only one that also offered edibles), home décor shops, antique shops, toy and gift shops, pubs and diners, and a gigantic, year-round market called Munich's Market where you could find pretty much anything and everything; while on the outskirts of town, there were Christmas tree farms, horse ranches offering trail rides, quaint inns and wineries, and of course, the Regal Winter Fair. All to say, there were a zillion things for tourists to happily spend their money on.

It was no secret that the shop owners on Main Street had a friendly competition to see who could decorate their shopfronts the most creatively for Christmas. At the beginning of November, Heather and Martha had found a mannequin and dressed it up as Will Ferrell's character, Buddy the Elf, from the movie, "Elf", and then had surrounded him with pyramids of white rumballs that looked like snowballs. They'd printed "The best way to spread cheer is to buy chocolates for all to share" on a poster and had hung it up in the top left-hand corner of the window. Then they'd spent a considerable amount of time creating miniature chocolate molds for a rosy-cheeked Santa, his hefty sleigh of toys and a team of spry reindeer. They'd carefully hung the chocolate mold at the top right-hand corner of the window. She was admiring their handiwork when she saw a familiar and unwelcome reflection in the window.

She turned around and locked eyes with her ex-boyfriend, Brian, who was standing on the opposite side of the street. He was wearing a lumberjacket over black snow pants and a down-filled aviator hat. He was carrying a bouquet of red roses and dodged a car as he crossed the street to come over to her. He was short and stocky, and his mass of sandy blond curls was bobbing under his hat.

"Wait, Heather, please!" Brian yelled as he tried to catch up to her.

She gave him the middle finger and made sure she looked tall and confident as she strode away using all of her five foot, nine-inch frame. She had long legs that gave her an elongated stride, making quick work of reaching the convenience store. Her body type was what people would describe as sturdy. She could feel her long, blond ponytail swing as she turned and opened the convenience store door.

"Good afternoon, Heather!" Peter greeted her in his usual friendly manner as she stepped inside.

"Hi, Peter. Running low on milk," she said quickly as she picked up a grocery basket from the stack by the door.

"The town does seem busier this year," he remarked mundanely as he turned his attention back to the newspaper he was reading.

Brian entered the store, nodded at Peter, and then rushed to follow Heather as she passed the metal aisles filled with canned goods and disappeared into the back of the store where the refrigerated section was.

"I thought I made it clear we're done," Heather's tone was cold, and she didn't bother to look back at him as she opened the fridge door, "just leave me alone!"

"But I miss you so much," Brian said as he danced around, trying to get Heather to look at him.

"But I miss you so much," Heather mimicked back, finally looking at him with her intense blue eyes as she placed four cartons of milk into her basket.

"I fucked up. I'm an asshole."

"Yes, you are."

"Okay, that was fast. You didn't have to agree that quickly. Literally, this is the only thing I've done wrong since we've been dating. No, wait, I take that back. I haven't done anything wrong because nothing's happened. You know, I think you're really blowing this whole thing out of proportion." Brian was starting to get frustrated.

"Oh, really? How so?" Heather stopped and gave him an inquisitive look while impatiently tapping her foot.

"Um, well, I needed someone to pose for me, and she happened to be free. You know how important this art show is to me," Brian mumbled.

"She's free, alright," Heather said sarcastically.

"I swear, nothing is going on between us. Nothing happened! I'm an innocent man!"

Heather responded slowly, her freckled nostrils flaring. "Uh-huh. So ... the fact that I saw a text from you telling Elsa that you liked her birthday suit and that you wanted to try it on ... meant nothing."

Brian's face turned white. "Yeah, but nothing's happened. Please, these are for you. I want you," he said as he tried to place the bouquet of roses in Heather's basket, but she managed to dodge them, and they fell to the floor.

"Well, um … okay, so, I'm a flighty, flaky artist. I regret everything. Please, think of how much fun we've been having together. I know we can work this out. I'm never going to talk to her again." Brian's hands were flapping in the air, causing his down-filled aviator hat to keep falling over his eyes, so that he had to keep pushing it back up. She would've thought it was endearing if she wasn't so mad at him.

"Oh, I can think of a few more choice names … You're a lying sack of shit, a scumbag, a peckerhead … The smallest of men in so many ways –" Heather yelled, looking him up and down with disgust.

"Hey guys, the town is packed with tourists. Some of them could come in here at any minute. I can't have this kind of language going on in my store," Peter pleaded with them from the front of the store.

Heather stomped on the roses and shoved herself past Brian, the basket swinging as she made her way to the front of the store.

"My apologies, Peter, but someone doesn't understand the concept of a break-up," Heather said as she placed the cartons of milk on the counter one by one for Peter to scan.

Brian picked up the flattened roses off the floor and joined Heather at the front of the store.

He half-smiled at Peter and said, "I'm sorry, Peter, it won't happen again," and then looked sorrowfully at Heather, "I'm not giving up on us."

Heather rolled her eyes as Brian left the store.

"I didn't realize you guys weren't together anymore," Peter remarked.

"Yeah, it just happened," Heather said with irritation.

"Well, you know Sally and I are here for you if you need anything." Peter gave her a sympathetic look.

"Actually, Peter, I'm going to make a quick phone call," Heather said grimly.

"Of course. I'll keep your milk right here," Peter nodded.

Heather handed Peter her credit card and pulled out her phone from her purse. She wanted to call her best friend Pam Fischer, who owned a deli in the indoor-outdoor farmers' market, called Munich's Market.

"Hey, girl," Pam answered happily.

"You're not gonna believe this … He followed me to the corner store and tried to give me another bouquet of roses," Heather's words tumbled out of her mouth.

"Well, I mean, they are just flowers," Pam said matter-of-factly.

"Blooming hell! That's not the point. The point is, he won't leave me alone. He's driving me crazy!" Heather whined.

"What? He's harmless. Besides, that's not a long drive," Pam teased.

"I'm ignoring that … What I meant was that the next time he tries to give me flowers, I really don't know what I'm capable of!" Heather's voice was getting loud again.

"Woah, okay. I'll come over tonight after I feed the fam, and we'll figure out a plan. Gotta go. Love ya," Pam said and then added in a stern tone, "Stay calm."

"Yeah, yeah," Heather put her phone back in her purse. Thinking to herself that Pam had forgotten what it was like to date someone, spend time getting to know them and trust them, and then have that trust taken away in an instant. And that just because an apology came in the form of flowers, didn't mean she had to accept it.

"Take care of yourself," Peter said as he handed her credit card back and the grocery bag with the cartons of milk in it.

"Thank you," she managed to say, calming herself down with a few deep breaths.

When she opened the door to leave, she looked up and the street and was relieved to see that Brian was gone.

As she walked back to her shop, she thought back to when she'd first met Brian in August. She'd been bent down, lacing up her hiking boots, when a pair of very shapely, slightly hairy, and somewhat tanned legs stood in front of her on the gravel parking lot. She'd stood up to see a stocky man dressed in grey cargo shorts, a faded blue polo shirt, dark Oakley's, and a Buffalo Bills baseball cap over a mass of sandy blond curls.

He was new to her hiking group, and she immediately liked the way he carried himself. Brian and some of the other newbies had been introduced to the group, but as they'd headed out for the hike, he'd personally re-introduced himself to her again as Brian Müller, and they'd kept talking during the two hours they'd hiked the trail.

He'd told her that he was a portrait artist but loved making sculptures out of scrap metal the best. He'd said that he was a free spirit and loved travelling to new places and learning about new cultures. It helped to inspire ideas. But every few months, he'd come home, back to his parents' house to recharge, which was where he was staying. That's when they realized they'd gone to the same high school together, but because he was four years younger than her, they didn't remember each other. She'd also learned that his older brother was her age, but he'd gone to a different high school, so their paths had never crossed either. He'd told her that he was getting ready for a new fall exhibit at the art gallery in town, and he'd love it if she'd come when it opened in a few weeks.

After that, they'd kept hanging out. She'd visit him at the shed he rented from an elderly lady out in the countryside where he could weld, hammer and make as much noise as he liked without any complaints.

He'd invited her over to his parents' house for a few Sunday dinners, where he'd make some type of roast with vegetables and potatoes. His parents were always warm and welcoming though she'd observed that his mother seemed tipsy quite often. She'd met his older brother a handful of times, and she'd been surprised at how polar opposite the two were in looks and personality.

Brian had come over to her house to watch her as she made her baked edibles, carefully measuring and mixing everything so that each tiny delicacy was consistent. She'd always excelled at math in school. It was her golden rule to never indulge in edibles herself because she wanted to stay focused on the business, and focused on making sure her customers knew they could expect the same high-quality taste and the same high every time they bought her products. It gave her satisfaction knowing that she was also helping neighbours deal with all sorts of health problems like anxiety, depression, sleeplessness, and menopause thanks to some of her products.

But she'd broken that golden rule with Brian. They'd indulged a few times in edibles, which had led to them running around her house naked and ended with Brian slowly dripping and licking chocolate off her body. She'd even let him sketch her lying naked on the bed despite not liking the fact that someone could accidentally see the sketches.

She'd never let herself act so freely in her life. She had to credit him for bringing out the sensual parts in her that she'd never even known existed. She'd felt safe with him and thought they were happy.

She'd found out otherwise when he'd been over at her place cooking her dinner in early December. He'd gotten up to get some more wine from the fridge when his phone, which was sitting on her kitchen table, had dinged. The name Elsa had popped up on the screen, and she'd asked him what that was about. He'd said that it was nothing, Elsa was posing for him, and they were confirming the time. But then she'd realized that the text read, "Can't wait for you to try on my birthday suit." So, before he'd been able to stop her, she'd grabbed the phone, run into the living room, and scrolled through the endless flirty texts between Brian and Elsa.

She'd been so shocked that she'd told him to get the hell out of her house. At first, she'd responded to his constant texts by saying they were done. She'd lost her trust in him. When the texts hadn't stopped, she'd told him to fuck off, but that only made her feel the hurt and anger all over again, so she'd started ignoring the texts, which was why he'd started showing up at her shop with flowers. He'd also started sending her drunken texts saying, "You're so sexy", which she'd misread as "You're so easy", until she'd noticed that the "a" and the "s" were right beside each other on the keyboard and he'd probably meant to type "sexy".

MUNICH
FRIDAY, DECEMBER 20

Pam had walked over to Heather's house around nine o'clock, and they were now sitting at Heather's Formica kitchen table that was carefully covered with a white embroidered tablecloth she'd bought at one of the Mennonite stalls at the market. It was a vintage chrome table that had matching red and green floral-patterned chairs.

Pam lived four doors down from Heather on a wide street lined with a mix of hundred-year-old maple trees and towering pine trees. The neighbourhood was made up of homes built in the mid-1800s, and Heather's house was yellow-bricked with a peaked shingled roof adorned with pretty white trimming.

They were sitting on the vintage chairs while drinking Doppelbock beers, and Heather had put out a bowl of salt and vinegar chips. Pam was blond like Heather but not quite as tall and a bit heavy-set.

"What am I going to do, Pam? I'm so distracted. I'm finding it hard to focus," Heather covered her face with her hands, "I feel so stupid for falling for him. I really liked him. I guess I was fooling myself into thinking it was anything but a bit of fun. But now, he's pissing me off."

"I was thinking that maybe it's better for now if you get out of town for a while?" Pam looked at her with hope.

Heather felt the anger swell up inside of her, "why should I leave? He's the one who should leave me alone! And look, he sent me more texts tonight."

Heather went to pick up her phone to show Pam but incurred a look that Pam normally reserved for one of her teenage kids when they misbehaved.

"Blooming hell! I'm not running away," Heather stomped her foot.

"Don't think of it as running away. Think of it as giving yourself a well-deserved holiday. A mental health break?" Pam's voice sounded higher than usual.

"Hmm hmmm," Heather murmured, the anger slowly subsiding.

"Just think of the upside. You could get away and not have to worry about running into him. And he wouldn't get to bother you anymore," Pam said encouragingly, "I mean, you could go somewhere warm?"

"Hmm, hmm. That'd be nice. But seriously, you know I'm stretched thin. I can't afford to go on a trip," Heather's voice sounded strained.

"I thought you'd say that. So, before you say anything else, hear me out. I saw this reality show where people exchanged houses. They just packed a suitcase and left. They didn't have to plan anything, and they had the pleasure of experiencing someone else's life for a little while. Think about it. You wouldn't have to pay for anything but travel expenses," Pam pointed out.

"Oh, like that Christmas movie 'The Holiday' with Kate Winslet? I love that movie! I was so happy when she finally stuck it to that schmuck!" Heather scrunched up her face.

"Whatever. I think it's a great idea," Pam said, dismissing Heather's comment.

Heather gave her a skeptical look, "well, I suppose leaving all this behind would be nice. But exchange houses? Do you mean like I trade my house with a stranger? Some stranger would stay in this house?" She waved her hand around.

"Listen, both couples had an awesome time, and they experienced things they never would have otherwise. This way, you wouldn't be in some strange city all on your own. And don't worry, I'll be here making sure whoever exchanges with you takes care of your house," Pam had practiced all the points in her head and hoped it was coming out right.

"What about my shop? I can't leave it during our busiest time!" Heather exclaimed.

"But you have Martha. She can handle it. And she has Vanessa. Aaaand ... What if we asked the person who exchanges with you to help out?" Pam smiled at her, knowing there was nothing Heather could say against that.

"Boy, you've really thought all of this through, haven't you?" Heather eyed Pam.

"Yep," Pam said satisfactorily as she grabbed some chips.

"Okay, say I go through with all of this. Where do I even start?" Heather was beginning to feel overwhelmed and took a large swig of her beer.

"Don't worry. We're going to do this together. First, we have to take amazing pictures of your house and then post them online. Which is going to be easy because your house is already amazing," Pam pretty much sang the word 'amazing.'

"This could be kind of exciting. I get to live someone else's life for a little while. You know what, let's do it," Heather felt her spirits lifting.

"Great, let's get started," Pam took out her phone, "first, pictures of the outside."

They walked to the front hall where the cubbyhole under the stairs served as a front hall closet. Heather grabbed her red puffy parka, and Pam grabbed her matching blue one they'd bought together at the nearby outlet mall.

"I've been so distracted, I haven't had a chance to decorate my house for Christmas," Heather said while looking around.

"Don't worry. Your house has enough Christmas charm on its own," Pam touched Heather's arm.

They went out the front door and down the porch steps. As they stood on the sidewalk, Pam took pictures of the front of the house. Heather peered over Pam's shoulder to see what the pictures looked like. Her yellow-bricked house did look pretty. There was a thin layer of snow on top of the boxed evergreens that lined the curving flagstone path that led to her front steps. The wide front porch with her two rattan chairs and small table looked inviting, as did the white screen door with its floral pattern. It was all what had drawn her to the house years ago.

When they were happy with the pictures, Pam said, "Okay, inside pictures now."

Heather ran to her upstairs closet and took out two large pillows with snowflake patterns from a plastic bin marked "Christmas," and fluffed them up. She rested them on the two red upholstered loveseats that faced each other, separated by a short-legged Pine coffee table. She'd also found her German candle arch and placed it in the middle of the coffee table. Pam took some pictures of the loveseats from the hallway so that the red-bricked fireplace was noticeable in the background.

Her adjacent dining room contained an oval table with four chairs and a matching Oak hutch that she'd taken from her parents' house. She opened the drawer of the hutch, took out four red placemats and a sterling silver candle holder, and then motioned for Pam to take pictures.

They stepped into the kitchen with its clean white appliances, pine cupboards, and green laminate countertop. Heather set her coffee maker and air fryer just right, and Pam took pictures from different angles.

They went up the creaky wooden stairs and took pictures of her small bedroom with its Queen-sized brass bed that took up most of the room. It had been carefully covered with a flowery white linen bedspread and matching pillowcases.

They walked over to the bathroom and hesitated.

"I'd always meant to renovate it to something more modern," Heather felt embarrassed by its pink décor, "it looks like from the fifties."

"Ah, don't worry about it. It tells a story about the house," Pam's attempt at a positive spin came out flat.

"Maybe don't take any pictures," Heather said, and Pam nodded.

Pam was about to open the door to the next bedroom when Heather stopped her.

"No, no. That's my office where I keep all of my baking supplies and special things," Heather said.

"Oh, right," Pam snorted, "the town's legit drug dealer."

"Very funny … And, did you just snort?" Heather teased and Pam nodded, embarrassed.

They entered the third bedroom just off the stairs, where there was a light brown couch and matching ottoman across from a fifty-one-inch television that had been mounted to the wall.

"I'm so jealous of this couch," Pam ran her hand along the top of the couch, feeling its soft leather before taking pictures from different angles, "I think we're done."

"Great, let's create my profile," Heather said as they walked back down the creaky stairs and towards the kitchen.

Heather brought her laptop over to the kitchen table. Sitting side-by-side, Heather watched with anticipation as Pam typed in house exchange and scrolled through their options.

Pam picked one of the options and read the reviews aloud, "house was infested with cockroaches … Pictures must've been of some other house … Didn't tell us her unemployed ex lived in the basement."

Pam looked over at Heather's worried face. "Okay, so not those. Don't panic. Let me refine our search to top ten."

"Yeah, not very encouraging. Click on that one," Heather said as she pointed to one called "The Enchanted Exchange".

Pam read the company's "About Us" section aloud. "Safe, secure home exchange. Voted best home exchange company by our clients five years running for the Readers' Choice awards. Well, this one certainly sounds way better."

"It does. Read some of the reviews," Heather nudged her.

"Oh here, this one. Best experience of our lives. House was as described and stunning. Another review ... Have become great friends with the owners and have agreed to keep exchanging houses every summer," Pam read out loud.

"Way more promising," Heather admitted.

"Are we actually doing this?" Pam asked.

"Yes, you've got me all excited now!" Heather exclaimed.

Pam pushed the laptop over to Heather so she could start creating her profile by entering her email address and creating a password.

"Oh look, it's asking me to upload a police clearance, so they know I'm not a criminal. That's a good thing! And I happen to have one!" Heather exclaimed.

"You had a background check done? When was that?" Pam was puzzled.

"When I volunteered with Brian at that kids' art camp for that week in August," Heather said as she pulled up the PDF of her police clearance from a folder marked Government Papers.

"Oh right, I remember that," Pam nodded.

"Yeah, there was a heatwave that week, and we were outside teaching the kids how to paint landscapes, but the paint kept melting. Brian ended up passing out from heatstroke because he was standing in the sun for too long," Heather explained as she uploaded the PDF to the site.

"He passed out?" Pam smirked, "I'm pretty sure you've never told me that story. And you're scared of a guy who passes out from standing in one place for too long?”

“Well, he was kind of embarrassed about it … And I didn’t say I was scared of him! I said I didn’t know what I was capable of! Besides, I’m tired of him chasing me around … Oh, it says here we have to create a 200-character description of my house. What should I say?” Heather looked over at Pam in dread and pushed the laptop back to her.

“How about we start with … Quaint, century-old home,” Pam started typing.

“Oh yeah, people eat that shit up,” Heather grinned.

“And then, how about … Looking for a clean…No wait, tidy resident for the holidays,” Pam continued typing.

“Oh yes, love it. And then maybe … in Munich, a quaint, no, we said quaint already, how about a warm and welcoming town known as Christmas Town,” Heather said satisfactorily.

Pam continued typing.

“Read it back to me, please,” Heather asked.

Pam finished typing and then read it aloud: “Quaint, century-old home looking for a tidy resident for the holidays in Munich, a warm and welcoming town known as Christmas Town,” Pam squinted at the character count listed in tiny font at the top of the screen, “that’s a 131-character count, so we’re good. Anything else you want to add?”

“Nope, it’s getting late. We should start uploading the pictures,” Heather looked at the clock on her stove. It was nearing ten o’clock.

“Wait, the form is asking if you have pets and if your house is pet friendly,” Pam pointed out.

As if on cue, the sound of tiny feet jogged towards them. Pam looked down and saw that Heather's tuxedo cat was looking at them with curiousity.

"Oh, maybe we can take a cute picture of her!" Pam leaned down to pick up Charlotte, but the cat stopped, arched its back, and hissed, "eek! Okay, maybe not. When did she get so testy?"

Heather was laughing, "She's getting old. She's not always in the mood to be picked up. Isn't that true, Charlotte?" Charlotte responded by curling her long black tail into the form of a question mark and exited the kitchen.

"Um, okay, so what do we say? I mean, we kind of have to say you have a cat in case someone's allergic," Pam pointed out.

"Just say yes to having a cat, and no to pet friendly. Charlotte would not like it if someone brought their pet here," Heather said and then remembered what Pam had said about her shop, "do we need to add in something about helping out at my bakery?"

"No, I'd wait and see who responds. Feel them out," Pam suggested.

"True. Don't want to attract any crazy chocoholics," Heather made a crazy face, "and we're definitely not telling them about the edibles part. Never know how people react to that."

"Or thinking they're going to get some free highs!" Pam chuckled.

Pam began uploading the pictures from her phone to Heather's laptop. Once they were uploaded, they deleted the ones they didn't like, added the good ones to Heather's profile and entered a short description for each.

"I think that's it. Ready?" Pam asked as the mouse hovered over the Done button.

"Nervous," Heather half-smiled and then nodded.

Pam hit the Done button, and Heather's profile went live.

"Thanks so much, Pam. This may sound strange, but I think it's exactly what I need right now. I guess we'll see who ends up picking my house!" Heather exclaimed.

"I'm sure it'll be someone very lovely," Pam reassured her.

Heather closed her laptop and unplugged it from the wall socket.

Pam picked up her half-empty beer and shook it, "oh, I'm taking this one for the road."

Pam put her heavy winter parka back on, and they waved goodbye. After Heather closed and locked the front door behind her, she went back into the kitchen, finished up her own beer, and turned off the lights.

Then she went back upstairs to get ready for bed, knowing full well that she wouldn't sleep a wink.

BOCA BONITA
SATURDAY, DECEMBER 21

Miles away in Boca Bonita, Florida, Maria Rodriguez was watching as her husband packed up his black Mercedes-Benz with suitcases of his belongings. He'd just told her that with their daughter now being settled at college, he could finally live the life he wanted. That he was bored with her. He was tired of pretending that he still loved her. That he'd met someone else, and they'd fallen in love. He couldn't face another fake Christmas with her family. It was just past three in the morning and her husband, Alonso, was sneaking off in the middle of the night like the rat he apparently was.

"Why are you leaving me all alone?" After all the crying and screaming, her voice was hoarse, and the words came out like a raspy whisper.

"Oh, my darling, you're never alone. That is the problem," Alonso announced bitterly.

"Why are you doing this to us?" Maria whispered.

"Nice, blame it all on me," Alonso said as he quietly closed the trunk. His tall, thin shape moved elegantly through the garage as he made his way to the driver's side door. The moonlight slid through the small garage door windows and bounced off his Rolex. They were trying to move as quietly as they could so as not to wake up the neighbourhood.

"Well, you're the one leaving," Maria pointed out.

"You know it's never been right between us," Alonso said defiantly.

Maria opened her mouth to say something else and then closed it, feeling that the conversation had been going around in circles for a while now and that she'd said enough.

As Alonso opened the driver's side door, he turned to look at her. "Let's get one thing straight. I don't want anything from you or your family."

"Where are you going?" Maria imagined him running into the arms of some voluptuous blond.

"I'll be staying at the Ritz in Miami," Alonso said nonchalantly, "I've left my house key on the dresser."

Maria nodded, now imagining him tap dancing with this voluptuous blond to the song "Putting on the Ritz" by Taco.

She was exhausted and couldn't watch anymore. Besides, there was nothing left to say, so she left the garage and came back into the house. She heard the garage door grind open and then grind back down, shutting him out and them in.

In the kitchen, her grandmother, whom everyone called Abuelita, was using a molinillo spoon to stir hot milk in the chocolatera pot on the gas stove in their white marbled kitchen. The lights from the chandelier above the kitchen island twinkled. Maria went over and gave Abuelita a sideways hug.

"Ay, mi Amor," Abuelita said, gently patting the top of her dark, glossy hair.

"Ay, Abuelita. Qué vamos a hacer?[1]" She whispered.

"Pobrecita mía. Pero, no te preocupes, todo saldrá bien[2]." Abuelita whispered back.

---

[1] What are we going to do?
[2] My poor little girl. But, don't worry, everything is going to be okay.

After a few minutes of hugging, Maria said. "I think I'm going to text Sofia and let her know I'm not up for playing tennis."

Abuelita nodded, and Maria moved away from her embrace. She picked up her cellphone from the kitchen island and walked into the high-ceilinged living room. They had picked this house because it was so beautifully laid out with its welcoming flow and high ceilings. Now the house suddenly seemed so cold and vast, while she felt so small and vulnerable. It felt like anything could fall from that high ceiling and land on her tiny body that was barely over five feet tall.

She lowered herself onto the white sectional couch. She grabbed her white faux fur pillow and hugged it, leaning her chin on it. The gas fireplace was flickering along the wall in front of her. She continued leaning on the pillow as she texted her best friend, Sofia, to say that she was sorry, but she wasn't going to be able to play tennis tomorrow, or rather today. Her phone immediately rang.

"Maria! Is everything okay? Why are you texting me at this hour?" Sofia Perez yelled into the phone.

"Hi, yes, well, no. Not really," Maria wasn't sure what to say, "Alonso's leaving." Maria suddenly felt her world tilt and her body grow heavy. She sank further into the pillow.

"Leaving? What do you mean, leaving? Like, going on a trip?" Sofia asked.

"No, like leaving leaving. He says he's bored with me," Maria said quietly.

"That man is crazy. You're anything but boring." Sofia was appalled.

"So, I thought," Maria said and then added quietly, "he's met someone else."

"That bastard. No, you know what. You're better off without him. He's done you a favour."

"What do you mean?"

"He's never treated you right. You know that. He doesn't deserve you."

"We've had our ups and downs, but I never thought he'd leave me."

"Think of it this way. You can be free now, too, to do what you want," Sofia was quick to point out.

"Free?" Maria whispered.

"Yes, free," Sofia repeated.

"You know what, you're right. Why am I so upset? I should be happy he finally ripped off the band-aid," Maria said.

"Well, I don't know if you should be happy. I wouldn't go that far," Sofia said, frowning.

"Maybe I should go away," Maria began to perk up.

"But isn't your brother coming home? And Olivia?" Sofia asked, now regretting her previous words.

"Yeah, but maybe just for a few days, and then I'll be back," Maria began imaging her big escape.

"And what about tonight? You'll be missing your mother's company's Christmas party!" Sofia reminded her, trying to backtrack.

"I'm definitely not in the mood for that!" Maria said defiantly.

"I guess not?" Sofia said, not too sure what Maria meant by that.

"I think this is a great idea." Maria's mood was shifting upwards.

"But wouldn't it look like you're running away?" Sofia pointed out.

"What? No. I'm taking time for myself," Maria frowned.

"What about your mother? She'll freak out if you leave." Sofia was beginning to worry that she'd talked Maria into something very hasty.

"Maybe," Maria said, knowing her mother would most definitely freak out.

"Not maybe. Yes. She will," Sofia reminded her.

"Yeah, but she'll get over it. Besides, I'd just be proving her right." Maria knew her mother thought she was always too impulsive.

"Well, where would you go?" Sofia asked.

"I don't know. Somewhere totally different. Where I've never been," Maria said satisfactorily.

"Ah, somewhere where you're not you. Where nobody knows your family," Sofia said, beginning to see the upside.

Maria looked over at Abuelita, who was pouring milk into their favourite set of mugs with the funny-looking cartoon birds on them. One of the birds had its right claw resting on top of an egg with the words "Ruffle my feathers and prepare to be scrambled" printed on it, and the other mug had a colourful Parrot with the words "Parrot after me: Yes, dear." printed on it.

Maria looked at the clock on the stove as it neared three-thirty in the morning, "wait, why are you up this late?"

"Just wait until you hit menopause in a few years' time, my dear. Then you'll know why. Sweating one second, shivering the next," Sofia complained.

"Eek, sorry to hear that," Maria shrank away from the phone.

"You know, I saw this reality show where couples exchanged houses. It looked kind of fun," Sofia said, trying to remember the name of it and then giving up.

"What are you talking about? That sounds crazy!" Maria exclaimed.

"No, I'm serious. They just packed a suitcase and went to stay at each other's houses." Sofia was proud of her idea.

"So, like, they come live at my house, and I go live at theirs?" Maria scrunched up her nose.

"Yes, exactly."

"Ah, I get it. I wouldn't even have to think about it, plan anything. I could live someone else's life for a little while." Maria was starting to warm up to the idea.

"Exactly. Now you're getting it." Sofia felt proud of herself.

"Wait ... Isn't that like the movie 'The Holiday' with Cameron Diaz? I love that movie! So romantic! Oh my gosh, I knew you were my best friend for a reason!" Maria teased. "You know, I always felt the way Alonso and I met was like a meet cute. Gosh, Jude Law is so hot."

"Whatever, you're going off-topic. Just do it." Sofia demanded crankily.

"Okay, okay ... What site do I go on?" Maria asked, still dreaming of Jude Law.

"Just search house exchange. Something's bound to come up. My work here is done. Yuck, I need to change out of my silk pajamas again. And Maria, he'll realize his mistake and beg to come back … And you'll show him," Sofia said ruthlessly.

"That I will," Maria said solemnly as she hung up the phone.

Maria grabbed her laptop off the glass coffee table in front of her and brought it onto her lap.

"Abuelita, venga[3]," she said as she patted the seat beside her on the couch. Abuelita made her way over, carrying the two mugs of hot milk, each with a teaspoon of honey.

Maria opened up her search browser and typed in "Top ten house exchange sites." Abuelita peered over her shoulder, and several sites that had high ratings popped up.

"Oh mira, este sitio se llama El Intercambio Encantado[4]." She told Abuelita.

"Now, where do I want to go?" She had no clue and then noticed a "Most Recent Posts" button and clicked on it.

They spent a few minutes scrolling through some of the newest listings until they arrived at a picture of a quaint-looking, yellow-bricked house in Canada in a town called Munich. As she read the description and looked at all of the pictures of the house, a feeling of déjà vu swept over her, as if the house had already chosen her long ago.

"This is it. This is the one," Maria said breathlessly. "Gosh, it's been so long since I've spent Christmas surrounded by snow."

---

[3] Abuelita, come
[4] Oh look, this site is called The Enchanted Exchange.

She pictured the last ski trip their family had taken to Aspen four years ago and remembered how absent Alonso had been even then.

As she clicked onto the page, she said, "Oh, it's asking me to create a profile first."

Maria spent a few minutes creating her profile.

"Oh look … I can send her a message through the chat. But it's four-thirty in the morning, she might not be up? Am I crazy for doing this?" Maria asked and Abuelita shook her head, no.

Maria nodded and typed into the chat bar:

Hi Heather,

My name is Maria, and I live in Florida. Your house looks so lovely. Is it still available for a house exchange? I would like to leave as soon as possible. Does that suit you?

Thanks,

Maria

Back in Munich, Heather was indeed up as she was always at the bakery by five in the morning. And, truthfully, she hadn't slept at all. During the night, she'd been tempted several times to go back downstairs and delete her profile.

Heather was wondering to herself if everyone in town would think she was crazy? On top of it all, how could she leave Martha and Vanessa to run the bakery on their own, even with the possibility of help from some stranger?

She was absent-mindedly stirring milk into her coffee when she heard a ding from her laptop sitting on the counter beside her. She leaned over and saw a message waiting for her in The Enchanted Exchange's chatroom. She looked at it in disbelief and brought her laptop over to her kitchen table and sat down. She read the message, felt a flutter of joy, and began typing.

Back in Florida, Maria saw that the message she'd sent had been marked as read and watched as three little dots danced up and down, indicating that Heather was typing.

She tugged at Abuelita's arm and yelled, "She's up! She's up!"

Heather's message appeared in the chatroom:

Hi Maria,

Thank you so much for the compliment. Yes, my house is still available for a house exchange. The town of Munich is just outside of Toronto, and I think you would love it here. As I said in my description, people call it Christmas Town. I would like to leave as soon as possible as well, so that sounds perfect! It's just me on my own. Whereabouts in Florida, are you?

Thanks,

Heather

Maria translated the message for Abuelita and wrote back:

Hi Heather,

This is such great news! I live in Boca Bonita, 33-00 Pelican Way in Palma Royale. I'll leave my car at the Fort Lauderdale airport for you to use. I just have one thing to add. I live with my grandmother, so you'll be sharing a house with her, but there's plenty of room. She doesn't speak much English as we're Colombian. I hope that's okay?

Thanks,

Maria

Heather read the message and looked up Colombia to find out what language they spoke.

Spanish! Then she searched the address and was completely shocked by the statuesque endlessness of the house. It had been designed in a beautiful rose-colored stucco with white trimmings underneath a wave of terracotta roof tiles. There were what seemed to be endless turrets and delicate white shutters announcing beautifully arched windows, some with Juliet balconies. She was in love.

Heather wrote back:

Hi Maria,

I love grandmothers! We'll get along just fine! Maybe I'll learn some Spanish. ☺ I have to say your house is stunning and looks quite a lot bigger than mine. Are you sure you want to stay in my tiny little house?

And I, too, have one favour to ask. I own one of the German bakeries in town called My Sweet Addiction and am leaving during our busiest time. If you could go by the shop once in a while and help out during the day, I would be ever grateful. My shop manager Martha is very capable of running it while I'm away, but she'll need help serving customers as we only have one other part-timer.

Thanks,

Heather

P.S. I have a cat named Charlotte, but she's very independent and won't bother you.

Maria read the message and translated it with delight to her grandmother. Maria began thinking about how much fun that sounded. So romantic! And the total distraction she needed. She opened another browser window to start looking up flights.

"¡Qué maravilloso![5]" Abuelita said, replacing her earlier concern with happiness.

Maria wrote back:

This is wonderful news! I would love to help out at your bakery. (And I love cats.) As for your house, I love it. It's exactly what I need right now. You don't have to worry about a thing. I will look after your house and your shop. We have a family business, so I know all about customer service. You can come here and enjoy the warmth of the sun. My friend Sofia can show you around, and if you like to play tennis, you can go to the club with her.

While Heather had been waiting for Maria to write back, she'd been looking up flights as well and found one of the last seats on a non-stop flight to Fort Lauderdale. She'd run upstairs and found her passport in the top drawer of the little desk in her office. She thanked her lucky stars that she'd had to renew it last year when she'd flown to Amsterdam, where she'd taken an edibles-making course.

Heather wrote back:

Perfect! I've found a flight for this afternoon. Like Sofia, my best friend Pam will take care of anything you need. She lives four doors down from me on the same street. Tell your grandmother I'm looking forward to meeting her! I'll leave my truck at Toronto Pearson airport for you in short-term parking with the key under the driver-side wheel well. Never played tennis, but what the heck, there's a first time for everything! Mine and Pam's cell numbers are …

---

[5] How wonderful!

Maria had been praying that there would still be flights available. Thankfully, she found one that left in a few hours and started booking it right away. Maria wrote back:

Found a flight too! Tell Martha I'm on my way! I'll leave your name at the front gate. My cell is …

Heather didn't understand what Maria meant by front gate, so she simply wrote back:

This is crazy, but it's going to be a fun adventure!

Maria wrote back:

Agreed! ☺

BOCA BONITA
SATURDAY, DECEMBER 21

With the help of Abuelita, Maria had managed to escape without anyone suspecting a thing. They'd packed her suitcase quickly and quietly and had placed it in the trunk of her car before the sun came up.

Earlier that morning, she'd dressed in her tennis attire (leaving her wedding rings in a box on her dressing table), and had said goodbye to her mother, Yolanda, who always came over around seven. With her tennis bag over her shoulder, Maria pretended she was going to her usual tennis match, but instead, headed out for her ten o'clock flight. She'd heard her mother asking Abuelita where Alonso was and saw that Abuelita pretended not to hear.

She'd told Sofia about the ruse so that she wouldn't accidentally mention that they hadn't played tennis. She'd also told Sofia about the picturesque town she was going to and the German bakery she was going to help run. Sofia thought it was an excellent idea and said not to worry about anything, that she would look after this lady, Heather, so well she'd understand the meaning of *mi casa es su casa.*

She'd parked her Alfa Romeo in the short-term parking lot and then left her keys and instructions with a pimply-faced, teenaged valet. When she'd entered the airport, rolling her luxury suitcase behind her, she'd gone straight to the women's washroom. From her tennis bag, she'd pulled out and changed into a cream-coloured cashmere sweater and beige linen pants, put on her chocolate leather jacket, and exchanged her tennis shoes for knee-high brown leather boots.

During the flight, she'd researched the town of Munich, and everything she'd found out backed up Heather's claims. She'd even looked up Heather's German bakery, My Sweet Addiction, and was slightly surprised at the edibles part. She'd never tried any drugs in her life, but as Heather had pointed out, there was a first time for everything, she'd giggled to herself. She'd also learned that many of the homes in Heather's neighbourhood were built in the late 1800s. She'd been fascinated as most of the homes in her neighbourhood were maybe ten years old.

She'd basically kept her mind busy and away from any despairing thoughts about Alonso. She'd told herself that there'd be plenty of time to figure all that out without the threat of getting emotional in front of strangers. And then, she'd fallen into a deep, much-needed sleep.

Now, she felt the plane tilt, waking her up.

The pilot's voice floated throughout the cabin, "Ladies and gentlemen, please bring your seats upright. We're making our final descent into Toronto Pearson airport. The temperature is a balmy minus twenty-three Celsius. That's minus nine Fahrenheit for the Americans on board. We thank you for flying with us and wish you a very Merry Christmas."

From the look on the stewardess' face, Maria could tell it wasn't the first time the pilot had told that same stale joke. But really, he must be joking, she thought to herself. How could it be that cold? What had she packed? She couldn't really remember; it was all a blur. She'd thought that what she was wearing was fine, but by the looks of the other passengers in their huge, ugly coats, she wasn't so sure.

When she'd first boarded the plane, the man next to her had taken one look at her height and had immediately offered to help put her tennis bag in the above-head compartment. He was quite tall and seemed to barely fit in his seat, but he was wearing a bulky black winter coat over a blue dress shirt and jeans, so she couldn't quite tell if he was big or if it was the size of the coat.

"You have to fill out your declaration form." The man pointed to a form that had been placed in her lap.

She took a pen out of her purse and quickly filled it out.

When it was their turn to take their luggage down from the above-head compartment, he once again said to her, "Allow me, please."

"Thank you." Maria smiled.

"I didn't want to disturb you during the flight. You looked pretty busy. And then, you, uh, fell asleep," he said as he brought down her tennis bag.

"I appreciate that. Yes, I had a lot of research to do." Maria took the bag from him, and then he brought down his own carry-on.

As they departed the plane, the man towered over the pilot as he said, "thank you."

"Thank you," Maria echoed, and the pilot nodded back.

The two of them were now walking side by side down the gangway.

The man turned to her and grimaced as he said, "And I appreciate you pretending not to recognize me."

"What?" Maria was confused and looked at him properly, taking in his blue eyes and thick blond hair. He was good-looking enough to possibly be a celebrity, but not one she knew of anyway.

"I don't know what you're talking about," Maria shrugged.

"You don't?" He was surprised.

"No." Maria shook her head.

"You really don't?" He sounded skeptical.

"No, I really don't," Maria emphasized her words.

"Oh God, then please forget what I just said," he looked uncomfortable.

"Oh no, my friend, once you say something like that, you can't go back," Maria teased, "especially since we're trapped in this gangway and will probably be stuck together in the customs lineup for the next hour or so."

He sighed loudly and asked, "Have you watched the news lately?"

"The news? No. Why?" Maria asked as they reached the escalator that would take them down to customs.

"Ah well, I'm a weathercaster for a Miami news station, and you know that tornado that touched down a few days ago at that golf course ... Well, I was covering it live when ... Um ... When an ... When an alligator fell from the sky straight down onto the pathway ... Right beside me," he stammered.

"You're kidding," Maria eyed him, not quite believing the story. "What did you do?"

"Well, I'm not proud of this, but I sort of freaked out," he said as he made a shameful face.

"No way. A big guy like you? Scared of a little alligator?" Maria was trying not to laugh.

"Yes, way. I've become quite popular." His face was reddening.

"Okay, I have to see this for myself. What's your name?"

"Um, just type in 'Phil Miami weathercaster'. It'll come up." Phil hung his head in shame.

Maria took her phone out of her purse and saw that the voicemail symbol was showing. She ignored it and began searching for 'Phil Miami weatherman freak out video'. She was rewarded with several hits and opened up one of the videos.

When the video started up, she heard, "this is unusual tornado activity for Miami this time of year, and I just want people to know… THUD…" a dark shadow fell super-fast from the top of the screen and landed on the pathway beside Phil.

"Whaaaaa … whaaa the fuck … Whaaat the fuck!" Phil was flailing his arms and running in one spot like a cartoon character, too panicked to actually move. "Is that, is that?" He pointed at the alligator, started to run one way, and then changed his mind and tried to run another, but still kept running in one spot.

The alligator shook its head, looked a bit dazed, and then slowly crawled away in the direction of the cameraman, who started screaming and running. The video was now a dizzying mix of pathways, feet, and alligator. The cameraman eventually dropped the camera, abandoning it on the grass. Maria was laughing so hard that she was almost crying. Other passengers standing in line were looking at them in amusement.

"I was sitting beside a celebrity the whole time and didn't know it," Maria chided.

"I'm so glad I could provide some entertainment," Phil said as pretended to bow.

"Wow, so you're escaping Florida. Fleeing for your life," Maria teased.

"Very funny. Although maybe there's some truth to that ... I kept coming into work and finding toy alligators on my desk. But no, I'm going home to visit my parents for Christmas." Phil was smiling sheepishly.

"Where's that?" Maria asked curiously as they continued their way towards customs with their passports and documents in hand. To their dismay, the line looked quite long.

"Munich," Phil said, and Maria looked up at him in surprise.

"Get out of here!" Maria exclaimed as she lightly slapped him on the arm.

"No! Not the one in Germany! It's about an hour and a half from here," Phil explained quickly.

"No, no. I know that," she gave him a do-you-think-I'm-stupid look, "it's just that ... That's where I'm headed."

"What? Why are you going there? You look like you belong somewhere exotic," Phil complimented her.

"Well, I don't know about that, but now that I know you're a full-blown celebrity, I don't mind telling you. I've exchanged houses with a lady named Heather, who owns My Sweet Addiction, a local bakery. We're exchanging houses for

Christmas. And... isn't Munich known as Christmas Town, so that's kind of exotic?" Maria explained, smiling.

Phil's face went white as he quietly said, "well, that's an unfortunate coincidence. Just my luck."

"What do you mean?" Maria gave him a puzzled look.

"She didn't tell you why she was leaving town?" Phil asked, emphasizing the why.

"No, we met on a house exchange site just this morning." Maria furrowed her eyebrows.

"Geez, that's uh, kind of hasty but understandable on her part. Well, apparently, I'm terrible at keeping secrets, so why not keep going? Truth be told, I know Heather ... She was dating my younger brother, Brian, and things didn't end well. That's kind of the other reason why I'm coming home," Phil explained glumly.

Maria thought about Alonso's words and felt the hurt coming back. "Trust me, I know all about things not ending well. I'm Maria, by the way. Pleased to meet you, Phil."

She held out her hand and he gently shook it.

"A pleasure to meet you, as well," he said as he gave her a big goofy grin, "and don't worry, I don't plan on spilling the beans about you and Heather. I won't tell anyone about your house exchange situation."

"I'm sure Heather will appreciate that." Maria smiled and thought to herself that she really was about to live this other person's life. A strange coincidence but an interesting one so far. Besides, what harm could come of getting to know Phil? It would be nice knowing at least one other person in this new town.

At that moment, one of the customs officers waved them over, assuming they were together.

MIAMI
SATURDAY, DECEMBER 21

Alonso had checked into the Ritz-Carlton in Miami and was now lying comfortably on the King-sized bed in the suite he'd booked. He'd changed into his purple Nike tracksuit and was channel surfing while he waited for Josephine to join him.

He was trying to keep himself calm as he knew she was going through what he'd just gone through with Maria. Josephine would be telling her own husband that she'd met someone else and would be leaving them. He was feeling confident that she'd know to handle herself as she was a high-powered lawyer in Miami.

He continued flicking through the channels until he stumbled upon a young girl hip-hop dancing in front of a panel of judges. Alonso stopped and stared at her. She looked so much like Maria had at that age.

His mind somersaulted back to when they'd first met. They'd both been attending the same dance competition in Miami. He'd been in the lobby on the pay phone (back when they had pay phones) with his back turned to her while she was waiting to use the phone to call her mother. He'd kept hearing little sighs of impatience, so he'd finally turned around to tell the person to back off and find another phone, but then he saw how gorgeous she was and he'd managed to stammer that he'd be done soon. Maria thanked him but had a similar look of surprise on her face. He'd known she'd felt the instant attraction too.

Later that day, after Alonso and his dance partner had finished their routine in a cumbia competition, he'd been walking back to the dressing room to change out of his purple and silver dance outfit when he felt a light touch on his arm. He turned around, and there she was again, tiny and fit.

She'd told him that it was her first time attending an all-weekend dance competition and had been mesmerized by the way he moved. He'd told her that it was his last competition as his parents wanted him to move on from "all of this nonsense" as they called it now that he'd graduated with an MBA in finance and was expected to focus on his career as an investment banker.

She'd told him how her mother had refused to let her study dance and that she'd just started her first year at Florida State studying marketing, and that nobody knew she was in Miami for a dance competition. Her whole family had thought she was at some women's empowerment conference. They'd both laughed at that.

He thought back to those first few months with Maria. She was high energy and spirited, and he loved taking her out dancing, showing her off in front of other men. And that was just it; it was only supposed to be a fling. He'd been planning on breaking up with Maria the night she'd told him she was pregnant.

He'd felt they'd been forced to get married. Everyone had been disappointed in them. Even he'd been disappointed in himself. From the very beginning, he'd felt they had nothing in common other than dancing, which had been taken away from him anyway. The first time he'd met her mother, Yolanda, she'd interrogated him about his career and what his goals were. He'd been completely turned off.

It had been a very long one-night stand that should've ended months ago. He'd wanted to have time to build his career before having kids, so he'd mentally checked out. He knew what he'd done was wrong, having immersed himself in work and never being around long enough for them to become a close-knit family.

And now, here he was, disappointing everyone once again.

When he'd met Josephine, he knew he'd met his true soul mate. The one he'd been looking for all these years, and he didn't want to wait any longer. His favourite quote from "When Harry Met Sally" summed it up: "When you realize you want to spend the rest of your life with somebody, you want the rest of your life to start as soon as possible."

MUNICH
SATURDAY, DECEMBER 21

After Heather had finished exchanging messages with Maria and then booking her flight, she'd barely had any time left to get ready. She'd quickly called Martha and told her about her plans, asking her if she could handle things for today until Maria could help out tomorrow. Martha had been completely understanding and told her not to worry. She'd told her to go have fun and get away from all of this hogwash.

Then she'd called Pam and told her amid screams of joy how she'd lucked out and was exchanging houses with a lady in Fort Lauderdale who seemed to be loaded and lived in a mansion and was a member of some tennis club! Pam had almost abandoned her own family and left with Heather, but then reality set in.

The only phone call Heather hadn't made that morning was to her sister, Sara. She knew that her sister was planning on going to her in-laws for Christmas, so she wasn't too worried about it. Heather had decided she'd call her sister from Maria's car once she arrived in Florida.

In a continued flurry of activity, she'd found her pink carry-on, rolled up enough tank tops, T-shirts, capris and shorts (she'd learned that by rolling instead of folding, they didn't wrinkle) for a week, and then placed them inside. The only thing she didn't have was a nice, suitable bathing suit. And then she'd realized that she'd have to check her carry-on if she brought shaving supplies. Why waste time waiting for luggage? She'd buy a razor down there. She wanted to get outside and enjoy the fresh air as soon as possible. In her little desk, she'd found an envelope containing several U.S. Dollars, leftover from her trip to San Francisco.

Deciding to dress comfortably for the plane ride, she'd slipped into her capri jeans, a pink tank top, and white sneakers. As for her long, blond hair, she went for the usual, and pulled it into a ponytail. Grabbing her laptop, she unplugged it and placed it, along with a light jacket and a sunhat, in her large, over-the-shoulder purse.

Looking around the house, she'd decided to put the white Formica tablecloth in a drawer to prevent any food stains from getting on it. She'd filled up Charlotte's water bowl and added some food to her other bowl. Charlotte had eyed her with fake disinterest from one of the chairs where she'd been curled up.

When she'd been all packed and ready to go, she'd stood by the front door trying to decide whether she should bring her red puffy parka or not. What would she do with it on the plane? She'd probably have to sit on it and then end up with a backache. But it's so cold, what if she got into a car accident during the hour-and-a-bit drive to the airport and had to wait in the cold by the road? Then she'd realized she could just leave it in the truck for Maria, who probably didn't have a suitable winter coat to wear.

Thankfully, she'd made it to the airport without incident and then through luggage inspection just in time to make her flight. When she'd boarded the plane, most of the passengers already had their heads buried in their devices, headphones blasting.

Last year, she'd used a free language app to learn a bit of Dutch for when she'd gone to Amsterdam. This time, she'd decided to spend the better part of the three-hour flight learning a bit of Spanish. She'd always found learning new languages a good mental challenge and discovered that Boca Bonita, the city where Maria lived, meant "pretty mouth" in Spanish.

She'd also set herself up with a cross-border plan, so she could text and talk without running up major charges, unlike those fools you hear about on the news. She'd ordered a ham and cheese croissant from the menu, which had satisfied her before taking a quick nap.

Now, the soothing voice of the pilot was floating throughout the cabin.

"Ladies and gentlemen, we're making our final approach to Fort Lauderdale airport, and we ask that you bring your seats to their upright positions. The current temperature is twenty-four Celsius, that's seventy-five Fahrenheit for the Americans on board, and from all of us, we wish you a very Merry Christmas, and thank you for choosing to fly with us."

Heather had the window seat, so she slowly pushed the window shade up and watched the cars as they sped along the interweaving highways that snaked below. She was relieved to notice how much smaller Fort Lauderdale airport was compared to Toronto Pearson, which meant she was less likely to get lost.

When it was her turn, she tugged her carry-on down from the above-head compartment, squeezed her way up the aisle, and then nodded at the pilot as she exited the plane and entered the gangway.

After she'd slowly made her way through customs, she was pleased to discover that the airport was well-marked. She was able to easily follow the short-term parking signage that led her to a set of automatic doors.

As soon as she exited the doors, the gentle evening air was a warm welcome. It confirmed that she'd definitely made the right decision and that the warm, sticky ocean air, plus the vitamin D from the sun, was exactly what she needed. She used the crosswalk to make her way to the open-air parking garage, and then approached the valet.

"Hi there, I'm Heather. I'm looking for a set of keys that Maria Rodriguez left for me this morning." She showed him here I.D. as she smiled at the pimply-faced, teenaged boy.

"Hi, ma'am. Yes, they're right here." The boy leaned over and unhooked a set of keys from the wall. "Parking's already been paid for. The car is parked in spot C4. Safe drive."

"Thank you!" She smiled as she took the keys from him.

When she arrived at the spot, she stopped short. She couldn't believe that she was looking at a shiny, red sports car. She had to take a picture of this! Knowing how terrible she was at taking selfies, she took a picture solely of the car and sent it to Pam.

Pam wrote back immediately: *Woah! Fancy! What is it?*

Heather did a quick search and found out that it was an Alfa Romeo Giulia Quadrifoglio. She wrote back: *Alfa friggin' Romeo!!* ☺

Pam wrote back: *Holy crap!! Have fun, drive safe. So jealous! xoxo* ☺

Once she put her carry-on in the small trunk, she pressed the red start button, and the car revved up. She looked at the digital dashboard and started pressing buttons until she found the settings that allowed her to adjust the seat and mirrors and turn on the much-needed air conditioning. Then she grabbed her phone to dial her younger sister's number.

Before dialing, she paused and bit her lower lip as she thought about how their parents had been killed just over two years ago on the way back from an Oktoberfest event. She remembered how the police had told her that they'd been following a tractor trailer as they exited the off ramp of the highway when the trailer had lost control and jack-knifed in front of them. She'd imagined the rest. How they'd most likely had nowhere to go and had crashed right into it.

Her sister, Sara, had long before moved to Montreal with her husband where they'd eventually had two kids. She'd come back to Munich for the funeral and afterwards, she'd stayed on to help pack up and sell their family home. The death of their parents had been an extremely difficult time for the both of them. They still felt tremendous pain at the loss as they'd been a very close-knit family. She would never forget the moment her sister turned to her on the day of the funeral and had sorrowfully whispered, "I guess we're orphans now."

Pushing the memory away, Heather dialed Sara's cell number.

"Hey, sis." Sara said as she picked up on the third ring. Heather could hear children's screams in the background, "Hey, did I call at a bad time?"

"It's always a bad time. Ignore it," Sara lamented.

"Got it. So, I have some surprising news ... I'm going to be in Florida for Christmas!" Heather exclaimed.

"Florida? No, Phoebe, you're not bringing your Hallowe'en costume. I already told you that! Sorry, we're in the middle of packing. We're leaving for Ottawa early in the morning." Sara sounded stressed.

"I wanted you to know where I was. I just landed, and it's gorgeous here!" Heather could barely contain her excitement.

"What made you go there?" Sara asked amid more children's screams.

"Well, it's Brian. He's still not leaving me alone." Heather had told her sister all about the breakup, and she'd sympathized with her.

"That little peckerhead!" Sara said, and then Heather heard Phoebe yelling "peckerhead" over and over again in the background. "Honey, no, don't say that! Greeeaat!"

"Sorry about that." Heather was laughing.

"That's all I need," Sara sighed.

"Anyway, I needed to get away for a while." Heather was now trying to wrap up the conversation as quickly as she could so she could get going.

"I understand. I wish there was something I could do," Sara empathized.

"There's nothing anybody can do. Please don't worry about me. Have a nice Christmas with your in-laws and focus on family time," Heather said quickly.

Sara let out another big sigh.

"And, Sara, you should totally let Phoebe bring her Hallowe'en costume. That picture you sent of her dressed up as a pirate was adorable. I'm sure everyone would love it!" Heather exclaimed.

"Shhhh. Don't say that. Maybe you should come visit us in February. We can do Carnival?" Sara suggested.

"Would love that. By the way, you'll never guess what kind of car I'm sitting in right now. I'll send you a pic." Heather texted the picture of the car to Sara.

"Wow … that's one sweet ride. Whose is it?" Sara blurted.

"It's a long story, but with the help of Pam, I've exchanged cars and houses over Christmas with a lady named Maria who lives in Fort Lauderdale. So, this is her car." Heather was hoping Sara wouldn't judge her harshly for her quick decisions.

"You struck it lucky. She must be loaded." Sara sounded genuinely happy for her, and Heather was relieved.

"Yeah, and get this, she's Colombian, so I learned a bit of Spanish on the plane," Heather explained happily.

"Wait a minute. She's Colombian? And she lives near Miami? And she happens to be super rich? Did she mention why she's so rich?" Sara sounded worried.

"She said she ran a family business. Blooming hell! You don't think…" Heather's voice trailed off.

"Did you just exchange houses with a drug cartel family?" Sara sounded even more concerned.

"What? No, it can't be. I think we're jumping to conclusions and being a bit stereotypical. I chatted with her. She sounded really sweet." Heather scoffed it off.

"Anybody can sound sweet. Did she say what their family business was?" Sara lectured.

"No, everything happened so quickly. I didn't have time to ask. But I'm headed to her house right now, so I guess I'll find out. I'm sure everything will be fine. I used a highly recommended website. And I mean, I'm kind of in the drug business myself. Maybe I can expand my business!" Heather joked, trying to minimize the situation.

"Haha, very funny. Well, be careful. If you see anything strange, get out." Sara instructed.

"I think we're making assumptions. I mean, would someone in the drug cartel business invite a total stranger to live in their house? Nah, doesn't make sense," Heather said, trying to sound nonchalant.

"Text me as soon as you get there and let me know if you get any weird vibes. And Heather, remember to keep that temper of yours in check," Sara continued with her lecture.

"Will do. Love to y'all," Heather said as she rolled her eyes.

"Love you!" Sara yelled into the phone, and they hung up.

Heather scrolled through the digital display screen, found the GPS settings, saw that Maria had her street address already programmed under Home, and hit Start.

Thinking that music says a lot about a person, she turned on the radio to hear what Maria was listening to and the energetic beat of Latin pop filled the air as she backed out.

Ah, she's fun, Heather smiled to herself.

The first thing Heather noticed as she made her way out of the airport and onto the highway was how colourful everything was. The sun splashed orange and yellow stripes across the blue sky and the gangly palm trees happily swayed their vibrant green leaves in the warm breeze.

After about an hour, she exited the highway and arrived in the city of Boca Bonita. As she drove through the city, she observed that many of the strip malls she passed had terracotta roofs similar to Maria's, and their outdoor patios were filled with couples and families enjoying themselves.

She was definitely looking forward to doing that once she'd settled in, she thought to herself. She wondered how Brian would react once he found out she wasn't going to be around for Christmas. Despite Pam's promise not to say anything, she knew the small-town gossip mill would make its way to him. Whatever, she wasn't going to waste any more time worrying about him or his stupid flowers. Blooming hell! Now she had flowers on the brain as she noticed a flower shop in one of the strip malls and decided to stop and buy some fresh-cut flowers for Maria's family. She turned into the parking lot and parked the car near the shop.

"Bienvenido[6], what can I help you with today?" A Latin-looking lady in her early thirties asked as the

____

[6] Welcome

door jingled, announcing Heather's entrance into the brightly lit shop.

"Hola[7], I guess I'd like a bouquet that says thank you," Heather said, shrugging.

"Well, lucky you, I have this lovely bouquet right here that's just perfect." The lady pointed to a beautiful bouquet that was a mix of pink roses, lavender carnations, and violet daisy poms.

"Yes, that would be most appreciated," Heather agreed, and the lady picked up the bouquet and took it to the front counter.

"Would you like me to put it in a vase?" The lady asked.

"Yes, that would be lovely," Heather said and then added hesitantly, "muchas gracias[8]."

"This one?" The lady pointed to a shapely glass vase that had a pinkish sheen.

"Yes, I think so," Heather said, realizing how weird it felt to be picking out a gift for someone she hadn't even met yet.

The lady nodded and packed up the vase in a sturdy carton, wrapped it in cellophane, and then tied it together with a pink ribbon.

After Heather paid and returned to the car, she carefully placed the wrapped vase on the floor of the passenger's side seat. Back in the driver's seat, she exited the strip mall and returned back onto the main street. Soon, GPS told her that she was to turn left in five hundred yards. As she approached the turn, she noted the lavish entranceway announcing the community of Palma Royale.

---

[7] Hello
[8] Thank you

She slowed down and stopped the car just outside of the front gatehouse. Ah, now she understood, front gate as in this. After a few minutes, a guard stepped out of the doorway of the gatehouse.

"Hi, there! I'm Heather Schmidt. Maria Rodriguez said she was going to leave my name with you." She smiled at the elderly gentleman who was dressed in a beige uniform and holding a clipboard.

"I.D.," he demanded, without smiling.

Heather was offended by his gruffness, but then reminded herself that he was simply doing his job and who knew how his day was going. She opened up her wallet and handed him her driver's license, which he took, and then scanned the clipboard with his finger.

"I'll open the gates for you," he said as he handed back her driver's license and ducked inside the front gatehouse.

Heather rolled the car through the gates and into the boulevard. GPS told her to keep going straight, and so she passed countless beautiful homes similar to Maria's. Man-made lakes were peppered throughout, and she wondered if there were alligators living in them. The community was lush with colourful vegetation, from its perfectly manicured lawns to sky-high palm trees and vibrant flower beds. Eventually, GPS told her to turn right and then left and that the house was coming up on her left. She slowed down, and the luxurious house she'd seen online was now looming in front of her, breathtaking and intimidating all at once.

She parked the Alfa Romeo beside a royale blue Porsche 911 that was sitting in the driveway. She decided she'd introduce herself first before bringing her carry-on inside. She put her large beige purse over her shoulder and carefully picked up the vase of flowers and practiced saying, "mucho gusto de conocerte.[9]"

As she approached the ornate French doors, she could hear a woman screaming in a language she assumed was Spanish. And then she realized there were several screaming voices.

Heather hesitated, not knowing what to do. What were they screaming about? Should she leave and come back another time? Or was this a totally crazy idea, and the screaming was a sign that she should run for the hills and find a hotel?

No, she told herself, she was doing this no matter what. Maria sounded lovely, and she was looking forward to meeting Sofia. This was a commitment she'd made to Maria. And to herself. Besides, how would it look if she bailed, and Maria stayed? But then again, what if they truly were a drug cartel family?

She leaned into the door to try and hear what was being said – not that she'd understand anyway, she chuckled to herself.

The door abruptly swung open, and she almost fell inside. A Latina woman who was immaculately manicured from head to toe stood before her with a glass of white wine in her hand. She was wearing a brightly patterned floral sundress, a turquoise necklace, and sparkly sandals. She had big, dark eyes and long eyelashes, and there were a few well-placed beauty marks on her cheeks. Her dark hair was long and wavy, falling a bit past her shoulders,

---

[9] Nice to meet you.

the front bangs partially kept back in a hair barrette.

The woman pretended not to notice that Heather had been trying to eavesdrop.

"I thought I heard Maria's car. Here she is, Yolanda! Hi Heather, I'm Maria's friend, Sofia." She looked at the vase Heather was holding, set her wine glass down on a nearby mirrored console, and held out her hands for it.

"Hi, yes, I'm Heather. I brought these flowers for Maria's grandmother. Um, I hope I'm not interrupting anything," Heather said hesitantly as she handed the vase over to Sofia.

"Oh no, don't worry. Yolanda was just expressing her delight at having you here," Sofia said sarcastically.

"Ha! I know it's a very impulsive thing we've done here, but everyone's going to have to just deal with it," Heather declared.

"That's the attitude! I am going to love hanging out with you," Sofia said as she leaned in and air-kissed Heather on both cheeks, "that's how we say hello the Colombian way."

"Amazing, I'll remember that," Heather said as she heard a male's voice say that he was done with this nonsense and was going to take a quick swim before it got too late.

"Please come in and meet everyone!" Sofia said brightly as she opened the door wider.

They made their way into the white-marbled kitchen where the female half of the Rodriguez family had gathered to wait for Heather's arrival. Three women sharing similar features were standing side by side, leaning against the kitchen island. Heather told herself that she wasn't going to be intimidated.

Looking around the house, Heather was a bit startled at how much white and grey there was: white furniture, white walls, white counters with grey marbling, stainless steel appliances, and grey flooring. After passing through the colourful neighbourhoods, it felt a bit sterile. And yet, at the same time, it looked lived in. A bit messy? She also noticed a tall white Christmas tree with twinkling blue lights in the corner of the living room.

Sofia placed the flowers on the kitchen island and then pointed to the first woman, "Heather, I am pleased to introduce you to Yolanda, Maria's mother."

"Mucho gusto de conocerte[10]," Heather said hesitantly.

Yolanda smiled stiffly back at her, with her arms remaining crossed. "Hola," she said as she eyed Heather up and down and loudly whispered, "que gordita[11]."

Yolanda was tall, elegant, and wearing what Heather could only guess was a designer dress and gorgeous jewelry that heightened her elegance to a whole other level. She had high cheekbones and dark sparkling eyes. Her hair was slicked back into a Spanish bun that made her eyelashes look even longer. Heather was beginning to feel pale and frumpy.

"This is Gloria, Maria's cousin." Sofia pointed to a curvaceous woman with thick, luscious hair and a

---

[10] Nice to meet you.
[11] What a fat one.

beauty mark on the right side, above her full lips. She was wearing a well-fitted, red party dress and an obvious push-up bra, making Heather feel slightly uncomfortable as to where to look.

"Hello," Gloria said politely.

"And this is our Abuelita … I've made her adopt me," Sofia said as she smiled and walked over to the kitchen island and put her arm around a petite woman wearing a powder-blue pantsuit that looked elegant on her, and her warm smile lit up her face. Her highlighted, softly curled brown hair was expensively cut and shaped into a bouffant, adding a bit of height to her small stature. Examining all of the ladies together, Heather noted that they all seemed to have tightened facial features, as if they'd all recently had Botox injections.

Abuelita admired the flowers, whispered something quietly in Spanish, and Sofia translated, "she says thank you for the beautiful flowers."

"De nada," Heather said, remembering how to say you're welcome, and Abuelita smiled back.

"Maria's father, Jorge, went for a swim. You can meet him later," Sofia continued with her introductions, "we're also missing Olivia, Maria's daughter. She's in Key West with her friends until Christmas Eve. And Gabriel, Maria's brother, who'll be here tomorrow, maybe."

"How long are you staying in my daughter's house?" Yolanda demanded to know, and Heather was taken aback by the abruptness of the question.

"Well, Maria and I kept our tickets open-ended. But honestly, please... You don't need to worry about me. I will treat her house with total respect. And you don't need to entertain me. I'm very independent.

I'm sure you're upset that Maria left. I have no idea why she left, but I'm sure she had a good reason," Heather explained, feeling defensive.

"Hmm, mmm, and what was your reason?" Yolanda probed her again.

Heather was beginning to see why Maria wanted to leave so badly. This woman was insufferable.

"I don't see how that's any of your business," Heather said bluntly.

"You're staying in my daughter's house. It is my business," Yolanda barked back.

"No, I really don't think so." Heather was getting angry.

"Well, I have one rule. I don't want to see any boys being brought in and out of my daughter's house while you're staying here," Yolanda said icily.

"What are you talking about? I would never do that! But then again, you have no right to tell me what to do! Who do you think you are?" Heather yelled back.

"This is my daughter's house!" Yolanda yelled.

"And I will treat it with the utmost respect, like I said!" Heather's face had gone red.

"And I don't want to see a single scratch on her car!" Yolanda yelled.

"You know, I can see why your daughter wanted to get out of here in such a rush! You're —" Heather began.

Sofia jumped in. "Let's leave it at that. Heather and I better get going, or we're going to miss happy hour."

"I need to get my carry-on from the car," Heather said huffily. She was feeling angry and confused.

Weren't Latinas supposed to be warm and welcoming?

"Of course! I'll go with you!" Sofia said a little too excitedly.

"Sure." Heather stomped towards the ornate French doors.

Once they were outside, Sofia grabbed Heather's arm and whispered, "Please, don't let Yolanda ruin your trip here. It's not personal. It's family stuff. I promised Maria that I'd make sure you have a wonderful time and that's exactly what I'm going to do."

"Maybe I should stay in a hotel." She hadn't come to impose on a family. Surely, they knew that?

"No, no, please stay here. Yolanda just needs a bit of time. Maria would be upset if you left," Sofia said.

"If you're sure," Heather said in a clipped tone.

Heather clicked the key fob, and the trunk popped open.

"So, where are we going?" Heather asked flatly, thinking to herself that when Pam had convinced her to do this, she'd made it sound so easy.

"There's a great Mexican restaurant in The Mercado. Do you like Mexican food?" Sofia asked softly.

"Yes, I do. Thank you so much for doing this," Heather said gratefully.

"My pleasure. And just so you know, I said that bit about happy hour, so we'd have an excuse to leave right away. But trust me, by tomorrow Yolanda will be fine. Her bark is worse than her bite," Sofia reassured her.

"Let's hope so." Heather gave Sofia a half-smile.

TORONTO
SATURDAY, DECEMBER 21

Back in Toronto, after Maria and Phil had made their way through customs and picked up her suitcase from baggage claims, she'd asked him how he was getting to Munich, and he'd said by cab. She'd explained that Heather had left her truck for her and he'd given her a protective look while declaring he was definitely doing the driving.

Now, they were making their way through the terminal. Phil had both his carry-on and her suitcase rolling behind him.

As they headed towards a set of automatic doors, Phil said, "get ready."

"For what?" Maria was confused.

"The cold. Here, put this on. It'll help," he said as he tugged out a Buffalo Bills toque from his coat pocket and offered it to her, "our internal body temperature is regulated by a part of our brain, so it's important to keep it covered."

She looked at it in horror and exclaimed, "I'm not wearing that!"

"Trust me. You'll need it." He shook it towards her, gesturing for her to take it. A couple pushing a cart piled high with suitcases flew past them, triggering the automatic doors to open. Biting, cold air blasted through the terminal.

"Ay, ay, ay! What's happening!" Maria shrank back.

"Told ya! Will you take it now?" Phil shook the toque towards her again.

Maria stared at the toque and finally grabbed it, carefully tucking her shiny, dark hair underneath it.

"Nothing to worry about. You look fabulous. Your first experience in Canada and it's as a Buffalo Bills fan, go figure!" Phil looked at her with a warm smile.

"No, that's not it. I'm actually a die-hard Dolphins fan, but que sera," Maria said playfully as she walked through the doors, "and by the way, you are such a nerd."

Phil looked at her and nodded, smiling as he mumbled, "huh, and you keep getting more and more fascinating."

He caught up to her and motioned for her to tuck in behind him so he could try to shield her from the headwind. They crossed the street in hunched-over shapes and cringed as the bitter gusts knocked their breaths away. They entered the parking garage, where they finally had a bit of reprieve from the cold wind, and made their way to the elevator, both muttering curse words.

"I can take my suitcase back now." Maria held out her hand for it, and Phil relented.

Maria pressed the "up" button and then stamped her feet to try and warm them up. When the elevator arrived, they got on, and Maria pressed level number three.

"You weren't joking," Maria said as she shivered violently.

"Nope. I am one with the weather, you know," Phil said in a serious tone.

"Yes, and weathermen are never wrong," Maria teased.

"You know, when people make jokes like that about weathercasters, we call on the weather Gods to teach them a lesson," Phil smirked, and Maria laughed.

"Can I ask what you do?" Phil asked.

"Ah, we have a family business. We sell skincare and beauty products," Maria explained.

"Well, that explains why you look so … Oh, um, sorry, just realized how cheesy I was about to sound," Phil trailed off.

"No, go ahead. I want to hear it." Maria eyed him, smiling.

"I was going to say radiant, but then I realized I'd sound like a television commercial." Phil was blushing again.

"Haha! I think that's a nice compliment. Thank you." Maria smiled warmly.

Phil smiled back. The elevator stopped, and the doors opened. Phil kept the elevator door open with his right hand as she pushed her rolling suitcase out the door first and then twisted it beside her as she stepped out of the elevator. Phil pulled his carry-on behind him.

"Look for G5," Maria said.

"This way," Phil pointed to the next row over, "I can see the truck."

When they arrived at the spot, Maria grabbed Phil's arm in alarm.

"Oh my gosh, what am I looking at?" She said as she stared at Heather's huge black pickup truck that towered above her.

The parking garage was jam-packed and the truck was nosed in between an SUV to its the left and a sedan to its right.

"It's an F-150, a Ford. You'll be nice and safe driving this one. It can plow through anything," Phil stated.

"If I can get in!" Maria declared.

"Don't worry, it has a step. I can show you. But, where are the keys?" Phil asked.

"Heather said she'd tape them underneath the front driver-side wheel," Maria explained.

"Sounds like Heather," Phil nodded.

They both stared at the space between the SUV and the truck. The SUV had been parked so close to the truck that they were surprised the side hadn't been scraped.

"What an asshole," Phil said gruffly.

"Looks like I'll be getting the keys," Maria sighed.

"So much for warming the truck up right away," Phil muttered.

Maria set aside her suitcase and squeezed herself sideways between the two vehicles, up on her tippy toes and arms up in the air. The tips of her boots scraped the black slushy ground as she slowly made her way in between the two trucks, not wanting to dirty her coat from the sides of the trucks. Her whole body was shaking from the cold.

The wheel well was within her reach, so she searched around for the set of keys with her left hand, while her right hand held onto the truck for support. She could feel grease getting onto her fingers. Tears started forming in the corners of her eyes from the cold. When her hand eventually touched the keys, she pulled on the tape but her hand shot back in response to sharp pain, and she realized her fingers were brittle from the icy-cold. Feeling frustrated, she tried to blow on her hands to warm them up, but it did little. She told herself to ignore the pain and tug harder.

"You can do it! I believe in you!" Phil yelled, sensing her frustration.

After a few minutes, the tape finally released, and she pulled the keys out.

"Got 'em!" She held them up for Phil to see.

Her nose had started to run, and she quickly wiped it with the back of her hand in embarrassment. She tiptoed slowly back to where Phil was standing and handed him the keys, blowing on her hands again, trying to warm them up.

"Well done. I kind of wished I'd filmed that," he said as he grinned at her.

Maria was enjoying Phil's sense of humour. "Haha! Then I'd be all over the Internet. You know what we have to do, right?"

"What's that?" Phil looked at her in confusion.

"Write ASSHOLE in big letters on their back window," Maria grinned.

"I see, a little bit of revenge." Phil looked over at the SUV's back window and was happy to see it was dirty enough to get the job done. "I like your thinking."

They took turns scrawling the letters onto the back window – Maria jumping up each time to reach the window – and then stood back for a second to admire their quick handiwork.

"Perfect. I think they'll get the message," Phil said, "now, let's turn this truck on and get the heat going."

"I can't feel my fingers anymore, and yet they hurt. How's that possible?" Maria kept rubbing her hands together and blowing on them, but soon gave up.

"I'll get you warmed up," Phil said as he unlocked the truck with the key fob and opened the passenger-side door.

There, on the passenger seat, was Heather's orange winter parka.

"Oh look, Heather left her winter coat for you! It's probably cold but try it on anyway," Phil said as he handed her the parka.

"How nice of her!" Maria took the parka from Phil's hand and started to put it on, realizing too late that it was draping down around her and falling onto the slushy cement floor. Phil was lifting the luggage into the back seat and didn't notice.

"So, how ridiculous do I look now?" Maria was laughing and thinking if only Sofia could see her now. "You know what, take a picture of me. I want to send it to Sofia. She'll love it!"

Phil turned around to look at Maria and burst out laughing.

"Sorry, I shouldn't laugh, but yes, you do look very Canadian. Hiding every possible body part from the cold is what we do around here, and that coat does the most excellent job," Phil teased, and then asked, "Who's Sofia?"

"She's my best friend down in Boca Bonita, where I'm from, but my parents are Colombian," Maria explained.

"You'll have to tell me all about that when we get inside the truck," Phil said quickly.

Maria took her phone out of her purse and handed it to Phil. She wrapped the orange parka all around her, re-adjusted the Buffalo Bills toque, and smiled for the camera.

"Your friend is going to have a good chuckle at that," Phil said as he took the picture, "now for another interesting challenge. I'm going to have to get in through the passenger side door."

"How tall are you, anyway?" Maria looked up at him.

"I'm 6'5. And yes, I could stand to lose a few pounds," he said as he patted his belly.

"I think you look great. You have nothing to worry about," Maria reassured him.

"You're very kind." Phil smiled.

He stepped up into the cab and sat down on the passenger seat. Grunting, he lifted his butt up and over the middle console and onto the driver's seat. He folded and lifted his left leg clumsily over the console, hitting the ceiling with his knee, getting it slightly stuck, and then grimaced as he pushed and squeezed his left leg down so it would fit under the steering wheel and repeated the process with his right leg. As he grimaced, Maria cheekily wondered if she was witnessing his sex face.

"Voilà." He said, pretending it had all been so easy.

"Yeah ... Voilà ..." Maria couldn't stop laughing. She couldn't believe how different Phil was from Alonso. In the short time they'd known each other, Phil had shown himself to be funny, warm, and encouraging. Whereas Alonso would've been telling her to hurry up and find the key while absent-mindedly scrolling through his phone. They'd pretty much stopped talking to each other altogether when their daughter, Olivia, went off to college last September.

"Maria ... Hello? You need to get in the truck, or you're going to turn blue and wreck that beautiful complexion of yours." Phil woke her up from her thoughts. He had turned on the truck, blasted the heat, and turned on the heated seats while she'd been daydreaming.

"Dios mío[12]. Oh, I see the step!" Maria took off Heather's parka to prevent it from getting dirty, scrunched it up, and handed it to Phil, who placed it in the back. With her hands free, she used the step to climb into the truck and then pulled herself in using the door handle.

"Now, that was a voilà," Maria teased and then leaned into the back of the truck, grabbed the coat, and slid it onto her lap, intending to use it as a blanket.

Phil looked over at her, "I've put the heated seats on too. We'll warm up soon. But as a very professional weathercaster, I just need to say one more thing before we go ... MOTHERFUCKER IT'S COLD!"

Maria covered her face with the coat and yelled into it. "¡DIOS MÍO!"

Satisfied, he backed up the truck, and they exited the parking garage, making their way onto the off-ramp for the highway. The first thing Maria noticed was how grey everything was. Grey sky, grey highway, and grey buildings. No wonder there were so many grey-haired snowbirds in Florida.

---

[12] My goodness

"So, tell me about yourself," Phil said once they'd both somewhat stopped shivering.

"What do you want to know?" Maria smiled.

"Everything," Phil said happily.

"Um, okay. Well, as you know, I'm Colombian. My parents immigrated to Florida before any of us were born. My dad is a plastic surgeon and opened up a practice in Miami. My mother started a skincare line. Her company is called Suavolino. A blend of suave and remolino. Her products are sold all over," Maria began proudly.

"Plastic surgery and skincare? Two things I know nothing about. But I do know it's called a portmanteau when you combine two words together to create a new one," Phil chuckled.

Maria eyed Phil and then continued, "Let's see … I'm the youngest. There's my brother Gabriel, who is a cameraman for a reality show, he's seven years older than me, and then there's my cousin Gloria who's five years older than me, who we've kind of adopted. Her parents sent her here from Colombia to go to college."

"Impressive. Go on …" Phil was intrigued by her story.

"When Gloria graduated from business school, my mother asked her to join the company, and she did. She's worked her way up to Chief Sales Officer and managed to have four kids along the way," Maria giggled.

"Four!" Phil exclaimed.

"I know! Me … I never thought I'd be a part of the business. I wanted to go to dance school, but my mother wouldn't let me, so I agreed to study marketing, but then I got pregnant and had to drop out." Maria said a little sadly, remembering how her mother had told her that dance school was a waste of time; and more explicitly, was for whores.

"Woah, okay, that's a lot for me to digest. Dance school?" Phil looked over at her quizzically.

"Yes, I know. Tough business to be in. I wanted to be a dancer and then eventually a choreographer. I always thought it would be fun to choreograph music videos. But instead, I got married young and had a baby," Maria explained, trying to keep her tone light, but feeling a bit sad inside.

"How old is your baby now?" Phil asked hesitantly.

"Olivia? She just started college, studying engineering. She's on a mini vacation with her boyfriend for a few days in Key West, which is why I was able to escape," Maria explained.

"So, when you say you married young. Are you still married?" Phil asked, trying to sound casual about it.

"Turned out not to be such a great idea, if you know what I mean," Maria answered.

"Yep, certainly do. You said you were going to send that pic to your friend, Sofia. Who is she?" Phil was ecstatic to learn that Maria was single.

"Oh, she's lovely. We're like sisters from another mister," Maria joked warmly.

"Haha! How so?" Phil asked.

"Well, she's quite a bit older than me, and yet we clicked right away the first time we met. After that, we became inseparable. When she was still working, we'd go to conferences together. Now, we play tennis, go shopping, sometimes go dancing ... We're there for each other through thick and thin," Maria explained.

"All the important stuff," Phil smiled.

"Exactly," Maria nodded.

"So, what do you do for your mother's company?" Phil asked.

"Well, I decided to accept the fact that we have a family business. It'd be silly if I wasn't a part of it. And besides, no one was going to hire a college dropout. It made my mother so happy when I joined. I started out at the bottom, of course," Maria explained.

"Sure, I guess that makes sense," Phil frowned, not quite agreeing that she should have started at the bottom of a family business.

"You know, I'm very proud of my mom for building up the business," Maria said.

"Of course, you are," Phil nodded, "but you must enjoy it?" He asked, not quite believing her reluctance.

"To answer your question, yes, I do enjoy it. Now. But you know, when I first started, I thought skincare was boring. If you can believe it," Maria teased and Phil chuckled, "over time, my mother gave me more responsibilities and trusted my instincts. I've shown her that my ideas work. Now I'm in charge of marketing, which also includes advertising," Maria explained, failing to mention that sometimes her and her mother wouldn't see eye to eye and would have screaming matches in the boardroom.

"Do you get to mingle with celebrities?" Phil asked.

"Not really. I wouldn't exactly call the actors in our commercials, celebrities. But I can let you in on a little secret. I'm hoping to work out a deal with Rubia Lopez. You probably don't know her," Maria grinned, leaving out the fact that she'd carefully approached her mother on Friday about "refreshing" the packaging of their youth-targeted skincare line to the face of the young pop singer, Rubia Lopez.

She'd explained to her mother how focus group testing had shown that the singer would bring in tremendous star power. She'd managed to skirt around the issue that this would mean Yolanda's face would no longer be needed for that skincare line. Despite her sound arguments, her mother had been hurt and had loudly expressed her dissent.

Yolanda had emphasized to Maria that she wasn't going take the advice of a college dropout, to which Maria had pointed out that it was precisely because of the advice of a dropout that they'd become so successful. Afterwards, Maria had been so upset that she hadn't told anyone about what had happened. And was happy to be missing her mother's Christmas party.

"Sure, I've heard of her, but can't say I listen to her music." Phil was impressed.

"Well, it's still in the works. But I'll have you know; I'm going to make it happen. Just like how I arranged product placement in a movie last year. Definitely one of my biggest accomplishments." Maria decided to have fun impressing Phil with some of her more recent achievements.

"Really? Would I know the movie?" Phil asked, smitten by her charisma.

"Not sure. The movie was called 'The Ideal You'. We chose specific skincare products to be displayed in the lead actress's bathroom throughout the whole movie. So, every time she went into the bathroom, you'd see them," Maria explained.

"That's so cool! I think my mother may have seen that movie," Phil said, wondering how many times the actress would have had to go to the bathroom in order for moviegoers to notice the product and then remember it.

"Sales of that product line increased by twenty-two percent!" Maria bragged.

"Oh! That's impressive!" Phil was happy to hear that it had worked out so well for Maria, but didn't really know if twenty-two was a good number or not. "So, how did you learn to do all of this if you never finished college, if you don't mind me asking?"

"I read a lot. Like, anything and everything. Books on marketing, advertising, consumer behaviour, brainstorming techniques ..." Maria explained, happily.

"That makes sense," Phil smiled.

As they continued their journey, Maria rearranged Heather's coat around her body and leaned further back into her seat.

"And how come Gabriel didn't join the business or become a plastic surgeon?" Phil felt he was being nosy but didn't care, he loved hearing about her family, and he loved the sound of her voice.

"He can't sit still. He would hate being stuck in an office," Maria thought proudly of her elusive older brother who always had to be onto the next adventure.

"Kind of like my brother ... the 'not being stuck in an office' part," Phil empathized.

"He became a pilot when he was quite young. He's had his own Cessna 172 since forever, but the reality show upgraded his training to include jet certification. They needed a pilot to get the crew back and forth from all of the different places they visit. So, now he flies some type of jet. He's flying back home to Florida for Christmas, from wherever they are right now in South America," Maria explained.

"Which reality show does he work for?" Phil asked politely. He wasn't a reality show kind of guy unless it had to do with food.

"Have you seen Nicolás Pérez's food travel show? He's part of the crew on that one." Maria admired her brother for going off and doing what he loved.

"Oh, I love that show!" Phil happily knew the show.

"It is such a great show, isn't it? Each episode delves into more than just the food," Maria pointed out and Phil nodded.

"Okay, one more question and I'll stop being so nosy," Phil said, poking fun at himself.

"Haha! Why don't we say naturally curious," Maria teased and then stared out at the darkness that surrounded them. She noticed they were no longer on a highway, but rather on what seemed to be a hilly country road. "Where are we?"

"We're almost there. About twenty more minutes," Phil said cheerfully.

"So, what was your last question?" Maria asked happily.

"The Dolphins, huh?" Phil jokingly scolded her.

BOCA BONITA
SATURDAY, DECEMBER 21

After Heather and Sofia had returned to the house with Heather's carry-on, they'd ignored Yolanda, who had been sitting on the couch with Gloria and Abuelita, their backs to the door anyway. Sofia had taken Heather to a bedroom that Maria had agreed could be Heather's for the duration of her stay. Heather had been shocked at the size of the room. It seemed to be the size of her whole main floor and then some.

Sofia had then said she'd wait outside for their ride and that she'd come back for her car tomorrow. (It had turned out that the royal blue Porsche 911 parked in the driveway was hers.)

Heather had texted her sister Sara to tell her that Sofia was lovely and to stop worrying. Then she'd texted Pam and told her a bit about what had happened, saying that Maria's mother, Yolanda, was a nightmare. Pam had sent a text back, reminding her that she was there to get away from stress, to ignore Yolanda, and to mind her temper.

She'd quickly freshened up in her ensuite bathroom, which had a huge walk-in shower and a window that overlooked the pool, where she'd noticed a well-tanned man in a blue bathing suit doing laps. Her anger had slowly subsided as she changed into a fresh pair of patterned capris and a coral tank top.

Now, after waiting in line for about ten minutes at the restaurant, they were being led to a table under one of the many heat lamps in the bustling outdoor patio of La Gordita.

"Bienvenido a La Gordita," the hostess said, gesturing to one of the tables and placing flamboyant menus down on the table. "Your waitress will be here soon."

"Gracias," Heather said as they sat down on two metallic chairs that were surprisingly comfortable.

Heather looked around and noticed the beautiful glowing lanterns hanging from the edges of the restaurant's terracotta roof. As she looked at the signage, she realized the restaurant was called the same name Maria's mother, Yolanda, had pretended to whisper to Gloria while looking disapprovingly at Heather. She didn't recall learning the word gordita from the language learning app.

"Sofia, what does gordita mean?" Heather tried to ask casually.

Sofia had also overheard Yolanda and felt bad, so she evaded the question by explaining, "It's a stuffed tortilla. They make tortillas here."

"So, Yolanda basically called me fat." Heather was hurt but not surprised.

Sofia cringed and said, "No, it's a term of endearment, like ... filled with love."

"Pretty sure that's not how Yolanda meant it," Heather frowned, "anyway, changing the subject. Have you ever been to Mexico?"

"Yolanda thinks anyone who weighs over a hundred and twenty pounds is fat. But yes, a few times over the years to all-inclusive resorts in the Mayan Riviera with my family. We love it. Have you?" Sofia asked.

"No, never. I've always wanted to," Heather said wistfully.

"But you've travelled to other places?" Sofia asked.

"I have! I took a chocolate-making course in Amsterdam last year, which was a mind-blowing experience. And I've been to San Francisco to check out the incredible bakery scene there," Heather explained, reminiscing at the happy memories.

"Lucky you!" Sofia grinned.

"So, you're married with kids?" Heather asked.

"Yes, three kids. Two grandkids. One marriage, so far," Sofia smirked and Heather laughed.

Sofia paused, lowered her voice, and mimicked Yolanda, "Heather, tell me why you are here in my daughter's house!"

Heather began to see the comedy in the situation and guffawed, replying back just as seriously, "I am here to rape and pillage your family!"

They were both giggling when the waitress came over to introduce herself.

"Hi, sorry to interrupt the fun. I'm Andrea, and I'll be looking after you today." She was blond, perky, and wearing a short black dress. "Welcome to La Gordita. Have you decided what you'd like to drink?"

"Do you like lime margaritas?" Sofia asked Heather.

"Of course!" Heather thought of the hot summer days spent in Pam's backyard, enjoying a pitcher of margaritas while watching the kids swim in the pool. In Heather's opinion, each season had its own set of weather-appropriate drinks.

"Perfect, then we'll have two lime margaritas on the –"

"Rocks!" Heather finished Sofia's sentence.

"Exactly! When it's all mixed up like that in the blender, I get an ice cream headache," Sofia explained as she mimicked the motion of a blender with her hands.

"Me too! And no salt on the rim," Heather requested in amusement.

"It just gets in the way!" Sofia yelled appreciatively.

"Exactly! And ends up all over your lips!" Heather chuckled.

They looked at each other and started giggling again.

"You two look like you're gonna have a fun night," Andrea grinned at them. "Normally, I'd get your drink order first and then come back for your food order, but happy hour is almost over. Would you like to order two margaritas each? It's two-for-one margaritas and two-for-one tacos."

"Amazing!" Sofia said.

"I feel like I'm living the dream," Heather said as she looked at the patrons around them and noticed how nicely tanned everyone was. They all had that same polished look that Maria's family had, and yet everyone was dressed casually. Many of the women either wore colourful sundresses or tanks and capris with sandals, whereas the men mostly wore polo shirts with dockers or knee-length shorts and canvas shoes. And yet, everyone looked ... glossy.

"Well, enjoy the feeling. That's what you're here for." Sofia smiled and then asked, "is it okay if I order some scallop ceviche for us to share?"

"Yes, please!" Heather looked at the menu and wanted to try everything, but went with her all-time favourite, "I'd like the fish tacos, please," she told the waitress.

"How would you like your Grouper cooked? You have the choice of steamed, deep-fried, or blackened," Andrea asked.

"Definitely blackened," Heather said enthusiastically.

"I'll have the shrimp tacos," Sofia said.

"I'll be back with your drinks." Andrea smiled as she wrote everything down and left.

Heather noticed that on the other side of the cobblestoned street, a band was getting set up to play on an outdoor patio of what looked like an Italian restaurant.

"You have to see this! Maria sent me a photo!" Sofia was giggling as she held up the phone for Heather to see.

"Haha! She looks adorable! I left that coat for her. I didn't realize she was so short ... Oops sorry, don't tell her I said that. Where'd she get the toque?" Heather asked.

"I don't know. All she says is that she met someone on the flight, and he's from Munich too," Sofia shrugged.

"Really? That's a strange coincidence." Heather had a sinking feeling she knew exactly who it was.

At that moment, the waitress came back with a tray filled with two margaritas in artisan glasses, complimentary bowls of housemade tortilla chips and guacamole, and the scallop ceviche. She set everything carefully down on the table. They waited until she left to resume their conversation.

"Heather, I may be just getting to know you, but I have a good feeling about you. I promised Maria that I'd be here to look after you and that's exactly what I'm going to do. Maria's my best friend in the world. Don't worry about Yolanda. As I said, she's all bark and no bite. She'll calm down. Let's make a toast to your new adventure. Salud is how we say cheers in Spanish, so … ¡Salud!"

"¡Salud!" Heather repeated as they clinked their margarita glasses together.

After she took a sip, Heather murmured, "delicious."

"The best," Sofia agreed as she savoured the flavour of the lime in her mouth.

"Listen, Sofia. I appreciate your words. They mean so much to me. You have no idea. And, just so you know, I asked my best friend back home, Pam, to look after Maria and make sure she has everything she needs."

"Maria mentioned something about that. Does Pam work with you?" Sofia asked.

"Nope, she has her own deli in the farmers' market," Heather began explaining, "we grew up together in Munich, a few doors down from each other. It's a small town, so all the locals pretty much know each other."

"You mean, know each other's business," Sofia smirked.

"Exactly," Heather smiled, "which is why I kind of want to ask who Maria ran into. I probably know them. Is that okay?"

"Yes, for sure, that would make sense. I can text her back and ask," Sofia said as she picked up her phone and texted Maria. They waited a few minutes, but there was no response. "I'm sure she'll text back soon."

"No worries. How do you and Maria know each other? Did you go to school together?" Heather asked.

"Actually, no, we met through her family business. Maria's quite a bit younger than me. My husband and I ran a chain of health food stores and Maria's mother, Yolanda, wanted to sell her all-natural skincare line in our stores. We said, yes, because it was a no-brainer. It was actually one of their salespeople who contacted us and who we dealt with, so I didn't meet Maria until their company Christmas party a few months later. In fact, that's where Yolanda and Gloria were off to tonight. They're having their annual Christmas party. My daughter is going," Sofia explained.

"Oh, that's why they were so dressed up," and pushed up, Heather thought to herself and then asked, "what are their parties like?"

"Always lavish. They usually rent a banquet hall at some ritzy hotel. I remember at that first party, we arrived late because we'd been at another party that night, so people were already kind of tipsy. We'd made it just in time for dessert, and afterwards, the dance floor opened up. I wanted to check my makeup before finding and introducing myself to Yolanda, but on my way to the bathroom, I overheard a lady yelling at someone in Spanish, telling them that they'd better go sit down and to please stop making a fool of themselves.

"I remember turning around to see who was yelling and saw this stunning, petite girl in a ruby red gown with a belly out to here," Sofia held out her hand so that it was almost touching the table and then continued with her story, "she was pregnant with Olivia, and her mother was embarrassed that she was dancing in front of all those important people with such a big belly. But Maria didn't care, she just laughed and told her mother to stop bothering her, which Yolanda did in a huff.

"I'd changed my mind about going to the bathroom and introduced myself to Maria instead … We ended up dancing all night." Sofia's face was glowing at the memory.

"I bet you two tore up that dance floor!" Heather teased.

"I don't know about that, but we had fun! She may be quite a bit younger than me, but we instantly clicked," Sofia smiled.

"Maria must be a really fun person. I mean, she drives a friggin' Alfa Romeo for crissake! And her mother, Yolanda, has a skincare line?" Heather chuckled to herself. So, not a drug cartel family like her sister Sara had feared, and it sounded like Yolanda's bark has always been fierce, despite Sofia's protests otherwise.

"I guess she didn't get a chance to tell you much about herself? Her father's a plastic surgeon. At first, Yolanda's skincare line was only sold in her husband Jorge's practice, but then some high-profile celebrity clients started buying and endorsing it on social media. That's when Yolanda put Maria in charge of marketing and advertising," Sofia explained.

"Good for her," Heather said, happy to hear that Maria did understand business as she'd said she did.

"She's so incredible at it. It's because of her that their products were placed in a movie last year," Sofia continued.

"A movie?" Heather was startled.

"Yes, 'The Ideal You'. Have you heard of it?" Sofia asked.

"I saw that with my friend Pam! So, Maria's an all-round badass!" Heather exclaimed happily. She decided not to mention that she didn't quite remember the product placement, however, she did remember the movie being wildly entertaining.

"It was definitely one of her biggest accomplishments," Sofia smiled.

"Sounds incredible, but it must be hard working with a mother like that?" Heather cringed.

"Oh, Yolanda isn't always like that. She was just having a bad night."

"If you say so. Is that why Maria left?"

"It's more complicated than that, but yes, sort of." Sofia answered vaguely.

Heather decided to respect Maria's privacy and not push for more answers. "What does Gloria do? Did you say she's Maria's sister?"

"Not Maria's sister, her cousin. She's Chief Sales Officer," Sofia explained.

"Geez … None of you go half-ass on anything, do you?" Heather teased.

"Haha! I guess not!" Sofia laughed.

"And wait, you said you ran a chain of health food stores … as in the past?" Heather asked.

"Well, yes, after building up our business for over twenty years, our three kids officially took it over this past year," Sofia said with a wide, proud smile on her face.

"Wow, so you're retired. Salud to that!" Heather lifted her glass.

"Thank you! ¡Salud!" Sofia echoed.

"Oh! Our waitress is coming," Heather said as they clinked glasses and then drained them.

Andrea arrived at their table carrying a tray filled with their tacos and small serving bowls overflowing with additional toppings of shredded cheese, sour cream, and pico de gallo. She carefully placed the items down on the table and put the two empty margarita glasses back on her tray. The table was now very crowded.

"Is everything okay here?" Andrea asked, eyeing the untouched appetizers.

"Oh, yes, everything is fine. We're just getting caught up with each other," Sofia explained.

"Glad to hear that," Andrea said, and they noticed a look of relief flood over her face. "Let me know if you need anything else ... Or want me to take something away. I'll be back with some fresh margaritas."

"That'd be great. We're all good otherwise," Sofia reassured Andrea.

Once the waitress was out of earshot, Heather asked, "what was that about?"

"I have no idea. She must be new. I've never seen her before," Sofia shrugged and then took a scoop of the scallop ceviche using one of the freshly made tortilla chips. As it crumbled in her mouth, she added, "so messy, but so good."

Heather followed her lead. "Wow, so fresh," she said as she wiped the corners of her mouth with the cloth napkin and then added some shredded cheese and pico de gallo to her three tacos that sat upright in a metal taco holder.

"You built up a whole chain of health food stores? And have three grown kids who are willing to take it over! How'd you manage to do all of that? I barely have time for anything else after running my shop!" Heather exclaimed.

"Well, yes, it was a lot of hard work, long days, and weekends, but we worked really well together as a family," Sofia said.

"What's the name of your chain?" Heather asked.

"Oh! That was a challenge. We wanted to give our business a name that evoked health, nature and purity, but so many of those words and sentiments were already taken. So, we chose to give it a Spanish name, Pura del Sol. And, believe it or not, we started out in a small kiosk in a mall … only selling vitamins! And now we sell all types of health food, nutritional supplements, and beauty care products. And have chains all over the southern States!" Sofia explained, happily.

"Amazing!" Heather smiled.

"I'm one of the lucky ones who has a husband who is very supportive, no matter how crazy my ideas are," Sofia giggled.

"Ha! That is so true. Having support is key. If you don't mind my asking, how did you two meet?" Heather asked.

"Not at all. We met in the first-year of business school in Tampa. He'd asked to borrow my notes because he'd missed a few classes because his grandmother had died. Of course, I didn't believe that story. I thought he'd just skipped class. I warned him that I'd taken short-hand in high school and that all my notes were in short-hand, but he didn't quite understand. When I saw him a few days later, he admitted that he couldn't read a single thing I'd written. He asked me to teach him short-hand," Sofia laughed.

"That's a wonderful story! And his grandmother?" Heather asked.

"Turned out she really had died. His family had sent him here from Mexico City to study and he'd gone back for the funeral," Sofia explained and then asked, gently, "and what about you?"

"A supportive husband? I haven't been so lucky. I thought I would've met someone by now, but nope," Heather paused and then continued, "well, I recently had someone, but it turns out he wasn't mine to have."

Heather shrugged and took a big bite of her taco. The blackening spices danced in her mouth, and she wanted to keep eating. She'd had Mexican food before, but never like this.

"Sorry to hear that. Is that what made you come here?" Sofia asked tenderly as she ate some more of the ceviche.

"Yes," Heather answered, not wanting to say more.

"The rest is yours," Sofia said, pointing to the last of the ceviche.

"Thank you." Heather gladly finished the ceviche.

At that moment, Andrea came back with fresh margaritas and set them down on the table.

"Here you go, ladies. Enjoy," Andrea smiled as she placed the empty plates on her tray, which gave them a bit more room at the table.

"I just have to say. These are the tastiest tacos I've ever had in my life. Everything's so fresh," Heather said to Andrea.

"That's so nice to hear. Do you mind if I ask if you could post your compliments on our site?" Andrea asked.

"Of course! But why are you asking? I have to confess that my husband and I come here at least once a month, and it's always so busy," Sofia said.

Andrea looked uncomfortable and then bent down and whispered, "you didn't hear it from me, but people have been posting negative comments about us on social media. But honestly, we think it might be the new Mexican restaurant that just opened up over there. Actually, if you're a regular, you must know her. It was Tonya. She opened up her own place about a month ago. Again, we're not sure, but we think she may be posting fake comments."

"That's sneaky … And rude." Heather said.

Sofia reassured Andrea, "don't worry, dear, we'll write some glowing comments. It'll be fine."

"Thank you so much," Andrea said with relief and then left.

Once Andrea was out of earshot, Sofia said, "well, that explains why she looked so worried earlier. I can't believe Tonya would do such a thing. I'm shocked. Tonya was always so nice to me. She was one of the reasons why I came here so often. Funny she never told me she was going out on her own."

"Some people just have no morals. Trying to cut down someone else's business just to build their own," Heather frowned.

"That's definitely not the way to start a business," Sofia pointed out.

"You know what we should do? Go on Tonya's restaurant's site and write our own fake nasty reviews about her restaurant," Heather said angerly.

"No! Definitely not. What we need to do. Or, rather what I need to do is visit her restaurant and see if this is really true or if something else is going on," Sofia said, "let's give her the benefit of the doubt before jumping to conclusions."

"I guess," Heather reminded herself to calm down, "anyway, I can see why you come here so often. I mean, why cook when you can do happy hour with food like this!"

"Do you enjoy cooking? I find that people either enjoy cooking or baking. Not many enjoy doing both," Sofia remarked.

"That's so true. I'm a baker, obviously, and no, definitely not into cooking. Brian, my ex, did all the cooking, actually. He'd have dinner waiting for me when I'd have to work late or was too busy to even go shopping for groceries," Heather said as she thought about that last dinner he'd made for her right before everything had fallen apart.

It had been her favourite ... Veal schnitzel, normally served plain with lemon wedges, but she liked it the Italian way, where it was loaded with tomato sauce and mozzarella cheese. She'd only gotten to eat half of it before the evening was spoiled.

There were a few more minutes of silence as they indulged in their tacos. The upbeat sound of Latin pop music rang out from the speakers, and they both swayed unconsciously to the music.

"Um, Sofia, where's the best place to buy a few pieces of clothing? Nothing too expensive."

"Oh, definitely the Calico Outlet mall. I can take you if you like?"

"No, that's okay. I don't want to trouble you."

"No trouble at all. I love shopping!"

"Haha! Not me. I stay as far away as possible from malls. As you can probably tell."

"Ah, you're fine. You just need a bit of primping and prodding."

"Primping and prodding? That doesn't sound very enjoyable," Heather smirked.

"What do you need to buy, exactly?" Sofia asked.

Heather blushed and said, "actually, I need a bathing suit."

"Ugh, that's the worst. I hate trying on bathing suits," Sofia rolled her eyes.

"Me too. I always look so pale and lumpy in those awful changeroom mirrors." Heather was dreading the whole experience.

"I know! Why can't the lighting be softer like at strip clubs, and why can't the mirrors be like those funny ones at the circus … Only, they make you look skinny!" Sofia exclaimed.

"Riiiight? Those changerooms turn us into gorditas," Heather said cheekily, "and, how do you know what the lighting is like in a strip club?"

"I haven't always been the saintly mother of three," Sofia smirked, "anyway, I think we both look fabulous!"

"Salud to that!" Heather said, and they clinked their glasses.

"By the way, do you have a favourite beach?" Heather pondered.

"I do, but I like shopping and action, so I go to Fort Lauderdale beach. But you might prefer quiet?"

"Yes, someplace I can just sit in the shade and read."

"Okay, then you'll want to go to –" Sofia's phone dinged, and she looked to see who it was. "Oh! Maria's written back. She says to say sorry to you that it was an accident –"

"I have a feeling I know what she's going to say next," Heather muttered under her breath.

"— that the guy she met on her flight is Phil, Brian's older brother. And don't worry, he's not going to tell his parents or Brian about you leaving," Sofia explained.

"So, yeah, Brian's my ex. What a strange coincidence," Heather murmured as she picked up her margarita and took a sip. So much for not talking about miserable topics, she thought to herself. She was relieved to hear Phil wasn't going to say anything and wondered how much he knew.

"Do you want to talk about it?" Sofia asked gently, noticing the worry on Heather's face.

"I really don't, but kind of do," Heather sighed, "I wanted to keep our conversation light and fun, but maybe it's better if I just get it out in the open and maybe even off of my mind."

"It's up to you," Sofia said softly.

"Well, here we go … Here's my story." Heather sat back in her chair and looked at Sofia. "I love hiking and have been a part of a hiking group for years. In August, a new guy, showed up, Brian. I thought he was cute, and we ended up talking the whole time during that two-hour hike. He made me laugh, and I liked that he's artistic. He creates sculptures out of scrap metal and paints portraits. I felt we had something in common, a connection, you know, because I treat my baking like artwork. I try new techniques, new designs …"

Sofia nodded, and Heather took a few breaths.

"We hit it off and started hanging out pretty regularly. Oh, and he's four years younger than me, which I guess I should've known better. Guys do not mature at the same rate as girls. That's a definite fact." Heather gave Sofia a serious look.

"They do not." Sofia shared the look.

"I mean, we hung out a lot. He was so sweet. He loved dirt bike riding, and he actually found an old dirt bike for me and spent hours fixing it up so that I could fit my legs around it. We'd go on these wild rides in the woods, up and down hills. One time he'd built this obstacle course deep in the woods. I was too scared to ride it, so I watched as he went up and down the hills. But on one of the turns, he lost control and crashed his bike so badly. It was terrifying to watch but somehow, he didn't break any bones. His bike was a mangled mess. Took a couple of hours to push our bikes back home." Heather remembered how angry she was at Brian for being so stupid.

"I went to his parents' house once in a while for Sunday dinners that he'd cook. You know, isn't that supposed to be a good sign, meeting the family? Anyway, a few weeks ago, I saw some texts between him and this lady named Elsa. She was going to pose nude for him for this art show that's coming up over the holidays," Heather continued.

"You were okay with that?" Sofia looked a bit shocked.

"Yes, I was." Heather felt like she was having an out-of-body experience for confessing all of this to a stranger who was quickly becoming a friend.

"And you trusted him?"

"Completely ... Stupid me."

"What did the texts say?"

"That he liked her birthday suit, and he wanted to try it on."

It took Sofia a minute to realize what that meant. "Creative, but inappropriate."

"Yes, I mean, blooming hell, it really hurt, you know, and there were more texts. She said she was looking forward to him trying it on. He insists nothing's happened, and nothing's going to happen and wants me back. You know, the usual crap, I made a mistake ... Blah, blah, blah. He's tried giving me flowers so many times, and he won't stop texting me." Heather was getting wound up and chugged the last of her margarita.

"What do his texts say?" Sofia asked, slightly alarmed at this behaviour.

"The same stuff, that he's sorry, he made a mistake, he wants me back," Heather explained.

"Okay, so nothing hateful. Nothing threatening?" Sofia asked.

"Oh, no, no. Nothing like that. He's harmless," Heather said, shaking her head.

"Just making sure," Sofia said.

"Here, I can show you a few of his texts," Heather offered and scrolled through her phone.

Sofia took the phone and looked at the texts.

"Yeah, you're right. They seem harmless. Do you want him back?" Sofia asked gently as she handed the phone back.

"No," Heather said obstinately.

"That's a pretty quick answer," Sofia eyed Heather.

"Do you miss him?" Sofia asked.

"Yes, but I'll get over it," Heather said.

"Are you sure?" Sofia asked.

Heather took some deep breaths and looked around her. Everyone looked so happy and in great moods.

"You know, I think I just need to take a break from all of that drama … My thoughts keep going around in circles. Like, what did I do wrong? Why wasn't I enough? But then, I get angry and think, no, it has nothing to do with me. You know, he told me when we first met that he couldn't stay in one place for too long, that he had to keep moving, that he'd travel around and then come back to his parents' house to recharge. So, maybe I made him stay in one place for too long and he acted out, rebelled against it by being a bit reckless with this Elsa woman," Heather sighed.

"You know, sometimes people tell us exactly who they are right from the beginning, but we're too smitten at the time to listen," Sofia looked steadily at Heather.

"Blooming hell, I really need a break from feeling like a total fool," Heather exclaimed.

"Heather, you're not a fool," Sofia said softly.

Heather gave her a half-smile. "Thank you. But, let's get back to having a good time. Maria seems like a fun girl. I listened to her Latin music in the car. What do the two of you usually do for fun?"

"Are you asking me to take you dancing?" Sofia grinned.

"I think I am," Heather grinned back.

"Done! Let's go tomorrow night," Sofia said happily.

MIAMI
SATURDAY, DECEMBER 21

It was now past dinner time, and Alonso's patience had worn out. He hadn't heard from Josephine, and she hadn't answered any of his texts. He was pacing back and forth in his lush hotel room, his mind racing through possible scenarios.

He jumped when his cellphone finally rang.

"Hello!" He yelled a little too loudly into the phone.

"Hi," Josephine whispered back.

"Where are you? Why aren't you here yet?" Alonso demanded to know.

"Just give me a minute to explain. I'm so sorry about this. I saw your texts. I wasn't able to answer them. My husband didn't take the news very well and ended up having an anxiety attack, which I thought was a heart attack, so I called an ambulance, and we're still at the hospital," Josephine explained quickly.

"But you're still coming, right? You know he doesn't deserve you," Alonso pleaded.

"I can't leave him like this," Josephine whispered.

"No, no, no ... This can't be happening," Alonso felt sick to his stomach.

"I'm so sorry. I just can't," Josephine whispered.

"Which hospital are you at? I'm coming," Alonso pleaded.

"No! Please don't. It'll only make things worse," Josephine begged.

"I love you," Alonso said vehemently.

"Love you too," Josephine whispered back.

"We had this all planned out," Alonso begged.

"I know, but how could we know this would happen?" Josephine whispered in desperation.

"But we're still flying out to Paris tomorrow, right?" Alonso pleaded.

There was a long pause before Josephine finally answered.

"I really don't know. I'm sorry, I don't know what to say," she said quietly.

"Oh God, no. Please don't do this," Alonso begged some more.

Josephine didn't say anything.

"But you said it was an anxiety attack, not a heart attack. Why do you still have to stay at the hospital?" Alonso questioned.

"I don't know. Because of his age, I guess. They want to keep an eye on him. They're running some tests. Alonso, I really have to get back," Josephine whispered.

"I love you so much. We deserve to be together," Alonso declared.

"I know, I know … I love you too. I'm so sorry. I'll call you when I have better news," Josephine whispered and then hung up.

In desperation, Alonso threw his phone onto the King-sized bed where it bounced a few times. He plunked himself down at the edge of the bed, vigorously rubbing his face with his hands.

This was not how he'd imagined things going. He'd known it would be a hard day, and that's why they'd booked their flight to Paris for Sunday and not today, in case things should go wrong, but he'd never imagined this scenario.

As his frustration subsided, he realized that he had to do something to remind Josephine of why they'd decided to tear apart two families. And, he had to do something quickly, as he was terrified, he could lose her forever.

He thought about how it always made her laugh whenever he'd burst into song in the shower after they'd made love in secret. Grabbing his phone off the bed, he began searching for romantic songs on YouTube, and "You're the Inspiration" by Chicago came up.

> *You know our love was meant to be*
> *The kind of love that lasts forever*
> *And I want you here with me*
> *From tonight until the end of time*
> *You should know everywhere I go*
> *Always on my mind, in my heart*
> *In my soul, baby …*

Perfect, he'd film himself singing it, and then send the recording to her.

MUNICH
SATURDAY, DECEMBER 21

Phil had insisted on driving Maria home, saying that he could walk to his parents' house from Heather's, so they were now pulling into Heather's driveway on a quiet suburban street.

"So, here we are," Phil said satisfactorily.

The yellow-bricked house twinkled under the stars. "It's exactly like her photos. So pretty, especially with all the snow," Maria said as she unbuckled her seatbelt and went to open her passenger door.

"Please, allow me," Phil said as he got out and walked around to open the passenger door. He held out his hand for her to grab as she stepped down and landed softly on the snow.

"It's been so long since I've seen snow." She noticed that the temperature was quite different from the airport. The bitterly cold had vanished and had been replaced by a fresh feeling of breathing in crisp, clean air.

"I'm so glad I did this," Maria said as she looked up at Phil. They were still holding hands.

"Me too," Phil mumbled, "um, let me get our stuff from the back."

"Thank you," Maria said as they clumsily let go of each other's hands, and then she moved out of Phil's way so he could grab their luggage.

With Heather's parka and her tennis bag in hand, Maria followed Phil as he pulled the luggage along the flagstone pathway that led to the front porch.

Maria admired the pretty screen door and rattan chairs while she held it open for Phil as he unlocked the front door. He set his carry-on down on the front porch and brought her suitcase inside.

"Well, thank you for everything," Maria said as she hung Heather's coat and her tennis bag over the knob of the staircase and then turned back to Phil as he waited by the door.

"My pleasure," Phil said to her, but stared at her lips.

On impulse, Maria said, grinning, "I can think of some other pleasures."

At that, Phil leaned into Maria, and they gently kissed. They meant to stop kissing but couldn't pull themselves apart, and soon it became apparent that Phil wasn't going home to his parents' house any time soon, so he quickly pulled his carry-on inside the house and closed and locked the front door.

They pulled off their coats and dropped them onto the floor as they kept kissing passionately. Phil's back started aching from leaning down, so he decided to pick Maria up, and she responded by wrapping her legs around his waist. He carried her like this into the living room, and she unwrapped her legs as he gently set her down on the loveseat.

"You're so beautiful. So sexy. So sweet," Phil whispered. "And you laugh at all of my stupid jokes."

"Just the cheesy ones," Maria joked.

"I've never met anyone like you," Phil said as they both could tell where the moment was heading.

"I've never done anything like this before," Maria told the lie that everyone knows is a lie but pretends isn't.

"But you are single?" Phil stopped moving and then asked, "there's not some burly guy who's going to come bursting through the door?"

"Oh! No, I'm separated. Like, since this morning." Maria held up her hand where Phil could see the white circular band left by her bare wedding finger.

"What?" Phil stood back and looked at her in surprise.

"It's a long story," Maria shrugged.

"Are you sure you want to go through with this?" Phil asked as Maria unzipped her boots and placed them on the hardwood floor.

"Yes, never been more sure. But do you have protection?" Maria asked casually.

"Oh God, no, I don't. Didn't think anything like this would happen to me. Like, ever," Phil said as he ran his hand through his thick, blond hair.

"Maybe Heather has some," Maria suggested, and prayed she was right.

"I'll go check," Phil offered and ran into the miniature bathroom next to the cubbyhole, but saw that it only had a pedestal sink and no cupboards.

He threw off his boots and galloped up the creaky stairs. After opening a few doors, he found the second bathroom and took a few steps back in surprise at the amount of pink, never having taken Heather for a pink décor kind of person, and then quickly resumed his search. He rummaged through Heather's cabinets and found a strip of condoms. Before pocketing them, he swiftly checked the expiry dates to make sure they were still good, and was thankful that they were. As he left the bathroom, on impulse, he grabbed the floral towel that was hanging from the rack and began making his way back downstairs.

Bounding back down the stairs, Phil yelled, "found some!"

When he reached the living room, to his delight, he saw that Maria had closed the curtains to the front bay window and had taken off her clothes. She was standing on top of the loveseat in a lacy red bra and underwear. He blushed as he drank in her incredibly toned body.

"I thought I'd save us some time," she said mischievously.

"Oh, and you're trying to make it easier on my back, I see," he smirked.

Maria watched with curiousity as Phil walked over to the opposing loveseat and flung out a towel. It billowed and landed crookedly on the loveseat. He threw the strip of condoms on top.

"What's the towel for?" Maria was puzzled.

"I thought we could, you know, sit on it. So, we don't leave any 'DNA evidence'," Phil said, using air quotes. "Not that we're planning on committing a crime or anything ... other than the crime for looking so good."

"Haha! Are you always this cheesy?" Maria giggled. "But good thinking, now it's your turn," Maria instructed as she waved her hand towards his shirt and pants as if to magically make them disappear.

Phil eagerly unbuttoned his blue dress shirt and threw it onto the ground, then unbuckled his belt and unzipped his jeans, pulling them down before remembering he was wearing his Buffalo Bills boxer briefs.

"Wow, you really are a fan," Maria laughed.

"Oh geez, sorry. I forgot I was wearing these." Phil tried to cover them up with his hands.

"I like them. They're cute. Turn around," Maria ordered, grinning.

Phil felt silly, but turned around, and Maria checked out his butt.

"Definitely cute," Maria said as he faced her again.

"Now, it's your turn," Phil said.

"To do what?" Maria asked.

"To turn around," Phil grinned.

"Oh! Sure, why not." Maria laughed as she twirled for him.

"Damn, you're sexy." Phil was impressed. "How often do you work out?"

"Enough," she said and then satisfactorily noticed his boxers were bulging a bit more.

He began tracing his fingers along her shoulders, lightly down her sides, and circled around her taught waist. They kissed some more, and then Phil picked her up, and she wrapped her legs around his waist once again. This time, they could feel the heat coming off each other's bare skin.

He carried her around the coffee table and over to the other loveseat and sat down on top of the towel. Maria straddled herself around his waist.

"Are you enjoying yourself, so far?" Phil whispered into her ear and his breath tickled her neck.

"Mmmm Hmmm," Maria murmured.

He began kissing her behind her tiny ears, along her neck and back to her mouth. Maria felt herself shiver, and her hands moved from his shoulders to the sides of his face to his blond hair, where she grabbed handfuls of it with delight. Her body began moving back and forth rhythmically, grinding herself against his groin, and she could feel it standing straight up against her belly.

"Are you ready?" Maria murmured.

Just then, they heard a cry.

"What was that?" Phil asked.

Maria looked over Phil's shoulder and saw Charlotte staring at them.

"Oh, it's Heather's cat. I forgot about her," Maria said, wondering if the cat was getting ready to pounce on them.

"Is she going to attack us? What's she doing?" Phil sounded worried, not being able to turn his head far enough to look.

"No, I don't think so. She's just staring at us," Maria said, hoping she was right.

"Okay, good," Phil said with relief. "As for the answer to your question, I'm so ready."

They unfolded themselves from each other, stood up again, and wiggled off their underwear, both taking quick peeks at one another's bodies. Maria unhooked her bra and let it drop to the floor.

Phil sat back down on the loveseat and grabbed the strip of condoms, ripped one open, and rolled it on. Then he held onto the sides of her hips and guided her back down onto his lap. She took a deep breath and slowly lowered herself onto him, pushing him gently inside of her.

Maria felt all the anger and hurt from that morning melt away, and the only thing she could feel was him inside of her. Phil was lightly kissing her nipples and it sent shock waves down her body. She could feel herself getting wetter. She closed her eyes and tilted her head backwards. She gave in to the pleasure and began moaning.

She could feel herself getting closer to climaxing and grabbed tightly onto Phil's shoulders, their bodies rocking back and forth, both of them working up a slight sweat.

Her body was now moving up and down so fast that it was only a matter of time. When she ultimately came, it rippled through her insides, her stomach convulsing from the power of it. Her tight convulsions pushed Phil over the edge, and he came a few seconds later. He cried out as if in anguish, and his body hunched forward when he finished.

"Wow," Phil said, panting.

"By the way, that was your sex face back in the parking lot when you were trying to get in the truck," Maria pointed out, giggling.

"Is that why you were looking at me with such lust back then?" Phil chided.

"Haha! My gosh, that was only a few hours ago." Maria felt herself being pulled back into the present.

"Strange. It seems a lot longer," Phil pointed out.

"Crazy. It does to me, too," Maria nodded.

There was a bit of a pause, and then Phil said as he looked down at himself, "um, I really should go to the bathroom, sooner rather than later."

"Oh! Of course!" Maria giggled.

She unwrapped her legs from around him and he draped the floral towel around his waist as he stood up. He was making his way to the bathroom when a loud ringtone set to the tune of "Thunderstruck" by AC/DC rang out.

"Wow," Maria raised an eyebrow at him as she began gathering up her clothes.

"That's my cell. What can I say? It's a solid tune," Phil tried to say nonchalantly, but was blushing.

"Hmm hmmm." Maria murmured.

"It's probably my parents wondering where I am." Phil explained.

"Oh, right," Maria said, nodding.

Phil hesitated, then decided it was best to go to the bathroom first.

"I'll call them back when I'm ... You know," he said as he made his way to the tiny downstairs bathroom.

"Yeah, good idea," Maria said distractedly, as she couldn't understand why her bra was nowhere to be found.

While Phil was in the bathroom, she decided to see if there was a robe in Heather's upstairs bathroom. She ran to the bathroom and was slightly startled at the amount of pink, as she would've definitely remembered it from the pictures, but was thankful to discover a fluffy white bathrobe hanging on the back of the door. She wrapped it around herself and returned to the living room where she saw that Phil had put his underwear back on and was tugging his phone out of his jeans' pocket, ready to dial.

"Hi, you guys called me?" He said when someone picked up. "Oh yeah, sorry, everything's good. I happened to run into a friend on the plane, and they gave me a ride back ... Yes, that's right ... I was just about to walk home from their house ... Yeah, like ten minutes." Phil hung up and rushed to explain, "sorry, it's not you. It's just easier this way. You know, with the whole Heather and Brian thing."

"I totally get it," Maria thought about her own escapades this morning and sympathized.

"Look, I would love to see you again. What are your plans?" Phil asked almost shyly.

"Well, I promised Heather I'd help out at her shop. I was planning on going over there tomorrow morning and staying until early afternoon," Maria explained.

"Why don't I text you around two and see if you can get away for a late lunch at the farmers' market?" Phil asked as he finished putting his clothes back on and grabbed his parka off the floor.

"That sounds lovely," Maria smiled at him.

"Hand me your phone, please," Phil asked, and Maria pulled it out of her purse and gave it to him.

Phil typed in his cell number. "Now you have my number," he said as he handed it back to her.

Maria texted him a heart emoji, "and now you have mine."

He put his parka back on, and they kissed one last time by the door.

"Oh! Your hat!" Maria giggled as she tugged it out of her coat pocket and handed his Bills toque back.

"Of course!" Phil smiled as he pulled it on over his head, "see you tomorrow!" Phil waved as he walked down the front steps, pulling his carry-on behind him.

"See you," Maria smiled, noticing that the toque suited him nicely, and then closed and locked the front door. Amazing, she thought to herself, she couldn't wait to tell Sofia how wonderful Phil was.

She picked up her phone and funnily enough saw that there was a text from Sofia saying that she was out for dinner with Heather, and they wanted to know who the stranger was that she'd met from Munich. Okay, definitely, not the time to tell Sofia about what just happened. She texted back:

Tell Heather, I'm sorry, it was a coincidence. The guy I met is Phil, Brian's brother. Don't worry, he's not going to say anything about Heather swapping houses with me.

She decided to avoid listening to her mother's voicemail messages and sent her dad a text instead:

Hola papá, todo está bien. No te preocupes. Estoy en Canadá y la casita es muy bonita. xoxo[13]

Maria gathered up the rest of her clothes, although her bra still was missing, and walked towards the kitchen to get a glass of water. When she entered the kitchen, she realized there was the smell of something cooking. She dropped her clothes onto the kitchen table and walked over to the slow cooker that was plugged into the wall. There was a trickle of steam coming out of the small hole in its glass lid, but condensation had built up on the inside, so she couldn't quite see what was giving off a mouth-watering aroma.

She lifted the lid and picked up the wooden ladle that was lying on the spoon rest beside it. Giving it a stir, she realized it was a chicken stew made up of potatoes, carrots, and peas. She hadn't planned on eating, but it smelled so delicious. She unplugged the slow cooker, so it would cool down by the time

---

[13] Hi dad, everything is okay. Don't worry. I'm in Canada and the tiny house is very pretty.

she finished eating and could be stored in the fridge. She opened a few cupboards before finding blue ceramic bowls and then searched for the cutlery drawer. That's when she noticed the note held to the fridge by a magnet that read: "~~Breakfast~~ Coffee is the most important meal of the day." A woman after my own heart, Maria smiled to herself as she took the note off the fridge so she could read it:

Hi Maria,

Welcome! I thought you might be hungry after a long day of travelling, so I brought over some chicken stew. Please make yourself at home. I'm here if you need anything. Heather is very grateful that you're okay with helping out at her shop for a few hours a day. She wanted me to let you know that her shop is open from 8 a.m. to 4 p.m., but if you could come around 10 a.m. that would be very helpful. The manager's name is Martha, and the part-timer is Vanessa.

I look forward to meeting you!

Pam

Maria felt relieved that these women seemed genuinely nice and welcoming. As she spooned some of the chicken stew into the ceramic bowl, she thought about how much she was truly looking forward to helping out at the shop. It would be something quite different from what she'd ever experienced before. Besides, how hard could it be?

As she sat down, she examined the shiny Formica table with its red and green floral-patterned chrome chairs and tried to imagine what kind of person Heather was. From the furniture she'd seen so far, she obviously valued antiques. The décor in her house was warm and welcoming. Yes, it was a tiny house, but everything in it felt like a big hug.

She'd seen Heather's picture on her shop's website, and she was a freckled blond with a warm smile, pretty blue eyes and big cheekbones. In Maria's opinion, Heather would have to be quite self-sufficient to run her own bakery and definitely creative but also meticulous. She wondered about the edibles part, was Heather into that, or was it just a business opportunity?

She took a spoonful of the stew and it melted in her mouth. It was rich in flavour and the chicken was moist. She could hear her mother's voice in her head, *a moment on the lips, a lifetime on the hips.*

"Mother," she whispered, "I'm in a very cold country and I need all the fat I can get right now, so go away."

She wondered what explanation her mother was providing about her absence from the Christmas party and then wondered what had made Heather want to get out of town and away from Brian so badly? What had happened between them? Maybe she'd find out more details from Sofia. If Heather was out with Sofia for dinner, they were definitely drinking margaritas, so the stories would spill. She hoped Sofia wouldn't tell Heather too much about Maria's own disastrous marriage.

She'd always known Alonso hadn't really been in love with her, so she'd given him space. Never questioning where he was or what he was doing. And eventually she learned to go off and do her own thing as well. She wondered who this other woman was and how they'd met. She knew she had no right to judge Alonso harshly as she'd given him permission long ago to fulfill his needs. And really, her family shouldn't be that surprised, as they'd all known, but pretended not to, that her and Alonso had been living separate lives. And honestly, her family should be grateful that he'd finally left and didn't want anything from them.

Sofia had said that he'd done her a favour. Well, she guessed he had. It'd given her the chance to meet what seemed to be a wonderful guy who was cute and funny; and to boot, it appeared they worked well together when they had to figure stuff out.

She could definitely say this was not going to be like the flings she'd had on her business trips. From how she felt right now, she really liked him. There was a fun connection between them and she was looking forward to spending time getting to know him better.

When she was done eating, she opened up the cupboards to look for a glass storage container. When she found one that was big enough, she spooned the food into the container and placed it in the fridge. She was alarmed at how empty the fridge was as it only had a jug of milk, a store-bought container of half-eaten potato salad, and a beer caddy with three beers in it. She washed out the slow cooker and let it dry on the dish rack.

Exiting the kitchen, she returned to the front hall where she placed her tennis bag around her right shoulder and then lugged her suitcase sideways up the narrow stairs to Heather's bedroom. When she got to the doorway, she saw that the tuxedo cat had curled itself on top of Heather's bed, and on top of her missing bra.

"You little devil," Maria said as she entered the room and set her suitcase down on the floor.

She placed her tennis bag on the edge of the bed and then noticed a book sitting on the bedside table. Out of curiousity, she picked it up and scrutinized the cover. There was a picture of a handsome, middle-aged man with a ruby-coloured goatee smiling widely at the invisible camera. He was wearing a chef's coat and hat. The book's title was "Into the Oven with Chef Lars Borgen: 1001 Creations for the Professional Baker." She put it back down on the table.

She leaned down and began petting Charlotte's head. The cat purred and then rolled onto her back, begging for a belly rub.

"Ay, no, you're a sweetheart," Maria whispered into the night.

BOCA BONITA
SUNDAY, DECEMBER 22

Heather was sitting on one of the stools at the kitchen island, nursing a hangover with a black cup of coffee that she'd poured from a carafe. She'd showered but hadn't dried her hair, so it was hanging in a wet ponytail. She'd barely managed to pull on a pair of jean shorts and a dark blue tank top without feeling like she was going to topple over. They'd stayed out until late, drinking margarita after margarita. This was not the first impression she'd wanted to give Abuelita, so she'd kept apologizing over and over again, but Abuelita just kept rubbing her arm and repeating "pobrecita", which Heather knew meant, "poor thing".

"Tienes el corazón roto, sí?" Abuelita asked her now. She was wearing a light pink pantsuit that looked and smelled like it had just come from the dry cleaners.

"I have heart broken?" Heather slowly deciphered. "Oh, I have a broken heart. Yes, sí."

"Bueno, no te preocupes. El sol y el mar te recupararan."

"Not to worry, the sun and the sea will heal me. Okay, I can take that. Gracias, espero que sí[14]."

Abuelita patted her hand and motioned to the backyard lanai, where the pool was. Heather followed Abuelita, walking gingerly so as to not spill her coffee. She thought they were going to sit down on the comfy-looking rattan furniture facing the

---

[14] Thanks, I hope so.

pool. Instead, they walked past the furniture and exited the lanai through its screen door to the left.

They entered a covered porch that ran along the entire back wall of the house, and as she stepped into it, she realized it was pretty much another entire kitchen, but an outdoor one. There was a sleek rectangular dining table with enough seating for twelve people in matching chairs. Just past the dining table was a long bar made up of grey-toned stone slabs topped with a grey-specked granite countertop.

Behind the bar was a tall Hispanic-looking man in a short-sleeved chef's jacket who was cutting up tropical fruit. His dark wavy hair was parted to the side, and an elaborate tattoo was snaking out from under his right sleeve and wound around his muscular bicep. She guessed he was in his early forties.

"Heather, you meet Jack," Abuelita said, smiling.

"Hello, Jack," Heather said shyly.

"Hello, Heather." Jack smiled at her, and she noticed he had the kind of smile where you could see both rows of teeth. It was a lovely smile.

All around him was more cookware: a huge stainless-steel fridge, a double grill BBQ, a pizza oven, sinks, blenders, and a Big Green Egg smoker. Next to the bar was another seating area with sofas and a massive flat-screen TV mounted to the wall.

"I hear you aren't feeling that great this morning," he said with no sign of an accent, "I'm going to make you something that will help."

"Oh, no. You really don't have to do that," Heather protested.

"I know I don't have to. I want to." Jack said kindly as he finished cutting up fruit and ginger and threw the pieces into a sturdy-looking blender. He added in almond milk, opened a jar of green powder and spooned some of it in, and then turned on the blender.

"What's the green powder?" Heather yelled over the noise as she noticed Abuelita discreetly making her way back to the house. The sound of the blender was drilling into her head, and although she was grateful, she hoped the noise would stop soon.

"It's spirulina. Very good for you," Jack yelled back.

"Oh yeah, I've heard of it. So, Abuelita told you I wasn't feeling well?" Heather yelled again, she felt she had to lean into the bar so he could hear her better, and as she did, she realized he was a few inches taller than her.

She put her coffee mug down on the counter, noticing that it had "One wrong look and you're toast" written on it with a funny-looking cartoon bird sporting a mohawk. The bird was standing on top of a piece of toast that looked well beyond burnt.

When Jack finally stopped the blender, he inspected the consistency, and Heather prayed he was happy with it. To her relief, he looked satisfied and poured it into a highball glass, adding in a stainless-steel straw and then handing it to her.

"You should know that Yolanda, Maria's mother, comes over here every day, very early in the morning, around seven. I make the ladies their breakfast. You're lucky she didn't come by this morning ... They were out late last night at their Christmas party," Jack explained.

"Oh dear, so Yolanda comes over here every morning? Maria didn't tell me that. The only thing she told me was that she lived with her grandmother." Heather was starting to feel irritated.

"We all love Abuelita," Jack said, smiling.

"Yolanda was pretty overbearing last night. Can't be easy having a mother like that." Heather took a sip of the smoothie and enjoyed its taste.

Jack cocked his head to the side, but didn't say anything.

"I'm so embarrassed. I never drink that much," Heather sighed and took another sip of the smoothie.

"Just make sure you're up before seven, and it'll all go smoothly," Jack nodded.

"Speaking of smoothly ... This smoothie is delicious. Where does Yolanda live again? I know I was told last night, but it's all kind of hazy." Heather was still feeling disoriented.

"Right across the street," Jack grinned again.

"Blooming hell, really?" Heather groaned, "well, I'm used to getting up early, so I should be able to be up and out before she gets here. As long as Sofia isn't planning on taking me to Margaritaville every night."

"Is that what happened? Ah, I love Sofia. She's the best," Jack smiled warmly.

"Yes, she really is," Heather smiled.

"She's an easy person to warm up to," Jack nodded.

Heather smiled and then decided to prod Jack a bit more. "Listen, I have to ask, was there a reason why Maria wanted to leave so quickly? Normally I'm not this nosy, but I kind of feel like I need to know

... Now that I know I could run into Yolanda again while I'm here," Heather said, leaving out the rest of the sentence that was running through her head: *and to help avoid a repeat of last night.*

"I don't know anything about that," Jack said as he began cleaning up the messy kitchen area.

"But you must know something?" Heather asked, realizing that there was truly only one reason why a married woman would leave her family at Christmas.

"You two really exchanged houses without even knowing anything about each other? You just went ahead, and did it?" Jack asked, avoiding the question again.

"Yeah, I know it seems impulsive. Single and running away from my problems!" Heather lifted her glass in a lazy cheer.

"Single, eh? Good to know," Jack winked.

"And not looking." Heather pretended to glare at him.

"We'll see about that," Jack grinned.

"You know, I think the drink is working. I'm starting to feel better," Heather said, giving up on getting more information and then realizing she was actually telling the truth about feeling better.

"You sure it's not the company?" Jack winked at her again.

"Ha!" Heather smiled back at him. "By the way, I have a feeling you know more than you're telling me."

"Ah, I'm just the lowly chef."

"Doubt that."

"Loose lips sink ships."

"Case in point." Heather finished the drink, placed it on the bar, disappointed she wasn't going to get any information from him, and started to ramble, "well, it was really nice meeting you, and thanks for the drink, but I need to get out of your hair, so you can get on with your day, and I should probably get on with mine now that I'm feeling better, thanks to you. I guess I'll see you around."

"Well, I am the chef, so yes. What time do you want breakfast tomorrow morning to avoid you-know-who? Have you ever had arepas?"

"Ha! But no, you really don't have to –"

She was interrupted by the screen door opening and slamming shut, and a boisterous voice filled the air.

"Jack!" The voice yelled.

Jack's face lit up and Heather enjoyed that bright, full smile again. She looked over to see two men approaching.

"Gabriel! Welcome home, buddy!" Jack yelled back, waving.

Jack moved from around the bar, and the two men gave each other big bear hugs.

"Looking good, big fella," Gabriel said as he slapped Jack on the back and then pointed to the young man standing behind him, "this is my boyfriend, Carlos. He's my co-pilot and does the location scouting for the show."

"Hello!" Carlos gave a salute and then dug his hands back into his pockets.

"Hey, Carlos," Jack waved and then turned to Heather, "and this is Heather."

Gabriel put out his hand, and she leaned down to shake it. She noticed that he had the darkest of eyes and that his man-bun, though dark, was greying, and that his red T-shirt over well-fitting black jeans was slightly frayed.

"I'm Maria's brother. And yes, I've heard all about you," Gabriel said, smirking.

"Oh, really?" Heather could only imagine what types of things Yolanda was saying about her.

"So, how long are you staying?" Jack asked Gabriel.

"A week or so?" Gabriel's answer was more like a question. "We'll see how the family drama plays out."

"I just made Heather a smoothie. Would you guys like one?" Jack asked.

"Oh yeah, that sounds grand. Carlos, Jack's smoothies are like miraculous cures to whatever's ailing you," Gabriel said enthusiastically as he looked over at Carlos.

"Sounds fantastic!" Carlos said, and they both made themselves comfortable on the bar stools.

"Heather, why don't you stay a bit longer?" Jack asked casually.

Heather hesitated, not sure if she was interrupting a bro-thing or if Jack really wanted her to stay. And then, as if to make the decision for her, the screen door opened and slammed shut again. This house was like a revolving door, she thought to herself.

"Heather!" Sofia called out. She was wearing another floral dress but with flip-flops this time.

"Oh, hiya Sofia!" Heather was relieved to see her.

"Oh, you're not ready," Sofia sounded disappointed.

"What do you mean?" Heather was confused.

"I said I was going to treat you today," Sofia was explaining, but as she listened, she could also overhear a muffled side conversation between Jack and Gabriel. Something about having the goods ready for the drop-off. And then she thought she overheard Jack say everything was set to go, but Sofia kept talking, so she wasn't too sure what exactly she'd heard.

"...and I told you I was going to take you to the salon today," Sofia was explaining, "and that I would pick you up at one."

"What are you talking about?" Heather asked.

"You told me how everyone looked so glossy and that you could never look like that," Sofia teased.

"Oh, blooming hell! I totally forgot!" Heather dimly remembered repeating the word "glossy" over and over again to Sofia.

"You know what, you're fine. They're going to gloss you up, anyway!" Sofia grinned.

"Haha! Yes, now I remember. Okay, let me grab my purse, and we'll go!" Heather yelled, "nice meeting you guys!"

"¡Ciao, bella!" Jack yelled as Heather and Sofia left through the screen door of the lanai.

When they were out of earshot, Sofia said, "well, I see you've met Gabriel and Chef Jack."

"Yeah, you'll have to tell me all about that dynamic," Heather said as she grabbed her purse off the couch, wondering what in blooming hell she'd just overheard.

Abuelita was at the stove stirring something in a pot, and Sofia went over and gave her a big hug and a kiss.

"Mi amor[15]," Abuelita said, warmly.

"Heather y yo vamos a salir. ¿Nos vemos más tarde?[16]" Sofia murmured.

"Sí, sí. Diviértete [17]." Abuelita said, smiling.

They left the house, hopped into Sofia's blue Porsche 911, and headed for the salon.

"I'm so sorry if I was too much last night," Heather said, cringing.

"Too much? My gosh, no. You were a blast!" Sofia was laughing.

"Honestly?"

"Yes, honestly," Sofia reassured her.

"Phew, okay. So, what's going to happen at this salon? Are they going to pluck me like a chicken?" Heather teased.

"That's a strange expression, but yes, I suppose so!" Sofia laughed, "and it's on me, so don't even think about paying. I told Maria I'd look after you, and that's exactly what I'm doing."

"Thank you, that's very generous of you," Heather felt a little awkward that Sofia had planned all of this because of her comments last night. She'd definitely have to buy Sofia some sort of present in return.

"So, what do you think of Jack?" Sofia asked, coyly.

"He's definitely not hard on the eyes. And he's nice, he made me a smoothie for my hangover," Heather blushed.

---

[15] My love.

[16] Heather and I are going out, we'll see you later?

[17] Yes, yes, go have fun.

"Oooh, that was sweet of him. And Gabriel?" Sofia asked.

"Oh, I barely talked to him. He arrived thirty seconds before you did."

"He's a great guy, but between you and me, he gets away with whatever he wants," Sofia pursed her lips.

"By his parents?" Heather asked, wondering what exactly he got away with and if it had something to do with what she'd overheard.

"By his mother, whereas Maria has to fight for everything," Sofia announced.

"I see. But don't we all?" Heather blurted.

"Sure, but siblings should be treated fairly," Sofia pointed out.

"I guess in an ideal world," Heather shrugged.

"So, I have to ask," Sofia went on, "this Phil guy, Brian's brother, is he a good guy?"

That morning, Sofia had received Maria's texts telling her what had happened between her and Phil. Sofia was a bit taken aback that Maria was up to her old tricks – despite her claims that this time things were different. She felt slightly responsible as she'd given Maria the idea for the house swap. And then the text had gone on to ask Sofia to try and find out what had happened between Heather and Brian, to which Sofia had simply responded with an "ok" as she didn't quite know what else to say.

"Well, I've only met him a few times, but he seemed nice, so I hope so," Heather replied.

"Me too," Sofia nodded.

"He's a weatherman for some Miami news station," Heather explained, "and I remember him being super tall."

"Really? How would that work? Maria's super tiny, like barely over five feet," Sofia frowned.

"What work?" Heather looked over at Sofia, her alarm bells ringing.

Sofia realized what she'd said and tried to backtrack, "oh, I don't know why I said that."

"Hmmm hmmm," Heather said doubtfully and then added, "I thought Maria was married?"

"No, I never said that."

"You said she has a daughter. I assumed that meant she was married," Heather said, realizing by Sofia's reaction that she was right, Maria was running away from her marriage.

"I guess I forgot to mention that she's going through a separation," Sofia explained hastily, not wanting to reveal that it had only been one day.

"Okay," Heather frowned, wondering what exactly had happened between Maria and Phil in just one night, "is that why she left?"

Sofia pursed her lips, "yes."

Heather nodded, confirming her thoughts and feeling badly for Maria, knowing she was escaping because of Yolanda, "well, in that case, I can look him up for you, if you want?"

"Sure," Sofia nodded, mad at herself for letting Maria's indiscretion slip.

After a few seconds, Heather's search for Phil Müller brought up a video that started to immediately play. Phil's voice echoed throughout the car, "this is unusual tornado activity for Miami this time of year, and I just want people to know ... THUD ..."

Heather screamed and threw her phone onto the car floor. Sofia jumped in response. There were muffled sounds coming from the phone on the floor.

"There was an alligator!" Heather yelled.

"What are you talking about?" Sofia looked down at the phone, and Heather bent down to pick it up. All Heather could see on her screen was a dizzying mix of feet and grass. Heather hit pause and looked over at Sofia.

"Should I hit replay?" Heather asked as she composed herself.

"No! No more screaming! Wait until I'm parked," Sofia exclaimed.

"Good idea," Heather said and then asked, "by the way, what's the deal between Jack and Gabriel? I would've thought with all the travelling Gabriel does that they wouldn't be all that close?"

"Gabriel is grateful that Jack's here looking out for Maria," Sofia explained.

"Now I get it," Heather nodded.

"And trust me, Maria and I know that Jack keeps Gabriel informed of everything that goes on and make sure he only knows what he needs to know," Sofia smirked.

"Haha! Good for you!" Heather chuckled, completely understanding, and then thinking to herself, so much for the whole "loose lips sink ships" motto.

As they maneuvered their way through the packed parking lot, Sofia noticed a white Cadillac sluggishly backing out of its spot. She put on her turn signal so no one would steal the spot, and they waited in silent agony as the Cadillac backed itself out, one jerky movement at a time.

Once they were parked, Heather took out her phone again and asked Sofia, "ready? I promise not to throw the phone down this time."

Sofia smiled, "ready."

Heather hit play, and once again, Phil's voice echoed throughout the car, "this is unusual tornado activity for Miami this time of year, and I just want people to know ... THUD ... Whaaaaa ... whaaa the fuck ... Whaaat the fuck!"

When the alligator appeared, they both screamed.

"Is that an alligator?" Sofia asked in disbelief.

"I told you!" Heather yelled.

Heather and Sofia watched in horror as Phil flailed his arms and ran in one spot like a cartoon character.

"Is this for real?" Sofia started giggling.

"Well, I guess that answers your question. He seems like a ... Well, a softie." Heather said as she burst out laughing.

"More like a scaredy cat," Sofia joked.

After the video stopped, memes started popping up on her phone.

"Oh! There are memes!" Heather exclaimed.

"Memes? Of what?"

Heather was laughing hysterically. "Of cartoon caricatures of Phil in a dress shirt and pants ... Posed in a mid-run stance!"

"No way! What do the captions say?" Sofia screamed in delight.

Heather read the memes aloud: "'I'd say see ya later, alligator. But I can't seem to move my legs.'; 'When I run. I run hard. But, like, in one spot.'; 'I'd give ya the weather report, but I gotta run.

Eventually.' Looks like this just happened last week! I wonder if Maria knows about this!"

"Oh, I have to find out!" Sofia yelled in between laughs.

Sofia texted Maria:

Did you know your lover boy is all over the Internet? He's a meme!

Sofia's phone pinged, and she read Maria's text out loud, hesitating on the last part. "She says 'Yes, I know he's a celebrity! Didn't know about the memes. Going to meet up with him for lunch at the farmers' market later. Tell Heather her shop is an absolute dream. Did u ask her?'"

"What does Maria want you to ask me?" Heather asked, confused.

"Um, she wanted to know what happened between you and Brian," Sofia cringed.

"Let me think about this," Heather said, realizing that she shouldn't be surprised.

Sofia waited while Heather thought about it.

"I got it. Tell her that I realized he was too young for me. I don't want her to know about this other woman just yet. It's too embarrassing," Heather explained.

"Fair enough," Sofia said, nodding.

Sofia typed back to Maria:

He was too young for her. Says met Phil a few times and was nice. U have our blessing. Xo

Sophia's phone dinged, and she read Maria's note out loud, "she says, 'Phew! Thanks so much. Lots of customers. TTYL' Well, we've done our duty."

"You know, you're a really good friend," Heather smiled warmly at Sofia.

"Right then, let's get plucked!" Sofia said cheerily, hoping she was making the right decisions as to the half-truths she was telling, and then wondering how she was going to keep track of them all.

"Ha! Let's do it!" Heather sang back.

They jumped out of the car and made their way out of the parking lot and onto the sidewalk of the strip mall. They passed a grocery chain, a smoke shop, a breakfast place, and then the blinking neon sign of the salon came into view: Sphynx Spa & Nails.

Sofia opened the door, and Heather followed her inside. The foyer was spacious and lushly carpeted in a light grey. There were a few oversized upholstered chairs in the waiting area, and the blond girl behind the front desk looked to be quite young.

"Hi, Jodi. I have an appointment for one-thirty for me and my friend Heather," Sofia said to the girl.

"Good to see you, Sofia. Yes, it's all set for you gals. I'll let them know you're here. Please take a seat." Jodi pointed to the chairs, and they sat down next to each other and waited.

"So, how does this work?" Heather was feeling a bit overwhelmed by what was about to happen.

"We're going to get waxed first, and then we'll meet back in the salon where we'll get our manicures and pedicures. And, if you want them to do your hair, go for it." Sofia quickly explained.

"No, that's not what I was asking. I mean, you know, down there." Heather pointed to her privates.

"Wait … is this your first time getting waxed?" Sofia looked at her in surprise.

Heather blushed, "yes, how does it work?"

"You're asking if it hurts?" Sofia laughed.

"Yes," Heather nodded.

"Like a son of a bitch," Sofia grinned.

"Great," Heather sighed.

A tall woman dressed in a white nurse's uniform entered the waiting area.

"Hi, Sofia. And you must be Heather. Welcome. Please come this way," the tall woman said.

"Hi, Britney. Thank you."

Sofia grabbed the door from Britney, and the two of them followed her down the white-paneled corridor that had the same lush carpeting as the waiting area.

Britney opened one of the pristine white doors along the hall, "Heather, you can go in here and wait. Please take your pants and underwear off and wrap yourself in the gown that's there for you on the table."

"Yup, thank you," Heather said as the door closed behind her. She looked around the room, and it felt very clinical, like she was about to get a pap test. She took off her clothes and wrapped the gown around her waist. She tried to pull it down, hoping it would provide some privacy, but it wouldn't fall past her knees.

The gown bunched up even higher as she sat down on the table, and when she tried to pull it down again, it made a loud ripping noise, but she couldn't quite see where the rip was. She sighed and crossed her legs, wondering how much more uncomfortable things could possibly get. She waited impatiently until the door finally opened, and a petite blond girl wearing a similar uniform to Britney's entered the room.

"Hi Heather, welcome to Sphynx Spa & Nails," the girl said in a soothing voice, "I'm Dolores."

"Are you serious?" Heather blurted before she could stop herself.

"Sorry?" The girl looked confused.

"Uh, no, nothing. That's … that's my mother's name," Heather lied, trying to backtrack, realizing too late that the girl was way too young to know Seinfeld, let alone the highly memorable name-rhyming episode that her mind had immediately sprung to. "Lovely name."

"Oh, thank you. Please lie back and make yourself comfortable while I get everything ready for you," Dolores said calmly.

"Okay." Heather tried to scoot backwards.

As the girl mixed and heated up the solution, Heather reminded herself to take deep breaths – in and out to keep herself calm, and Dolores noticed.

"Are you okay?" Dolores peered at her, concerned.

"It's my first time," Heather confessed.

"Oh, thank you for telling me. You have nothing to worry about. I've been doing this a long time," Dolores comforted Heather, "please lie all the way down."

Heather nodded and tried to lie down onto the plastic examination table, but it felt like she could fall off at any moment.

"Here, do you mind if I position you better?" Dolores asked.

"Sure," Heather hesitated.

Dolores bent down over top of Heather, grabbed underneath her arms and tried pulling her over to the right. Heather could feel Dolores' breasts pressing up against her, and her breath was tickling her neck.

"Sorry," Dolores apologized but kept pulling until she'd moved Heather what seemed to be less than an inch.

Dolores sighed, "I guess that'll have to do."

She went back to mixing her potions.

"Now, would you like me to do a G-string, a bikini, or a Brazilian? With a Brazilian, I can leave a landing strip if you like?" Dolores explained.

"What's the difference?" Heather had no idea what Dolores was talking about and definitely didn't want to look like a child down there.

"Well, with a Brazilian, I wax everything, and I mean everything. But I could leave a small strip of hair from here to here." Dolores touched her as she demonstrated, and Heather unexpectedly felt even more vulnerable.

Dolores continued, "if you're going to be wearing a G-string or regular bikini, I wax only the hair that would normally show outside of your suit."

"I'm not sure," Heather mumbled.

"I can also do different designs. I'm one of the few estheticians who can offer unique vajazzle designs like the American flag, pretty stars or hearts. Clients tell me that it's improved their sex life tremendously by having pretty designs," Dolores explained.

"Huh, I've never heard of that before." Heather wasn't quite sure if she believed Dolores. "Is it permanent and can I still go swimming?"

"It's not permanent and you can definitely go swimming. You know, from what I'm seeing, I think

I can wax what's here into a nice triangular shape
that would be super pretty with a tiny vajazzle heart
at the top right corner. Do you want to try that?"
Dolores suggested.

"Sure, why not." Heather unexpectedly found
herself giggling.

KEY WEST
SUNDAY, DECEMBER 22

For the past few hours, Maria's daughter, Olivia, had been thoroughly enjoying snorkeling the lukewarm waters of Key West. She was completely immersed in the experience and had lost track of her friends.

The ocean lapped itself around her body, tickling the insides of her ears as she peered through her mask down to the ocean floor below. With her arms resting at her sides, she gently flicked her fins every once in a while, as she floated along the top of the water. She could feel the heat of the sun beating down on her back as she marveled at a school of yellow and black-striped sergeant majors she'd been following as they flitted among the majestic reefs.

All of a sudden, the school of sergeant majors alerted to a nearby danger and quickly dispersed. Olivia turned to see what had spooked them and jolted in surprise at a barracuda lurking behind her. They'd been told by the captain that this could happen, and they'd taken off all jewelry as a precaution. It turned out that barracudas could mistake shiny jewelry for an injured fish and launch into attack mode. They'd also been told to remain calm and ignore the barracuda. They'd lose interest and move on once they'd satisfied their curiosity; and that they rarely attacked. Easier said than done, she thought to herself, as she felt her body grow tense in anticipation.

The barracuda swam up and looked straight at her. It took all of Olivia's strength not to freak out as she stared at the ugly-looking creature.

After what felt like a lifetime, the barracuda finally flicked its tail and left. Olivia kept watching the barracuda until it was far, far away from her.

She was startled once again when a hand lightly touched her back, but was relieved to see the friendly face of her boyfriend, Oliver, appear before her.

They both lifted their faces out of the water and began treading in place to stay above the surface. The desperate cries of seagulls rang out high above them. Olivia lifted up her mask and snapped it onto her forehead, and then spat out her snorkel. Oliver did the same.

"Hey babe, you did great. I was keeping an eye on you, ready to fight it off," Oliver smiled reassuringly at her.

"That scared the shit out of me. I'm shaking. I think I'm ready to pack it in after that," Olivia said.

"Totally get it. Our snorkeling time's up anyway. Captain Waters is going to take us to a park where we can have lunch. Bianca and JC are already back on the boat," Oliver said.

Olivia nodded and then felt a sudden adrenaline rush course through her body from the encounter.

"Race ya to the boat!" She yelled as she snapped her mask and snorkel back on, and then propelled herself towards the boat. She also felt the sudden need to get out of the water as quickly as possible.

"Heck no, I'm not leaving you alone after that," Oliver yelled as he put his gear back on and caught up to her.

Olivia watched as Oliver made strong strides alongside her in his red swim trunks, and she thought how lucky she was to have met such a sweet, funny guy.

She'd met Oliver just over a month ago at a mixer for first-year engineering students, where they'd been introduced, and had immediately giggled at how similar their names were.

After he'd gotten her number and taken her out a few times, he'd announced that it was time she met some of his friends and had set a date to meet at a local pub. She'd said great and that she'd bring her best friend, Bianca, to which he'd happily agreed.

And, to their delight, Bianca had hit it off with one of Oliver's friends, Juan Carlos, who they affectionately called JC, which had then led to them planning a mini trip during Christmas break for just the four of them.

They'd been fortunate enough to be given the okay to stay at JC's parents' vacation house in Key West. His mother had generously told them to make use of it since they'd be working over the holidays. And then, his mother had asked JC what he wanted for Christmas, and he'd said a full-day outing on the water with his friends.

His mother had been delighted with the idea. She'd chartered a powerboat which came with a captain who would take the four of them snorkeling in the morning and swimming with the dolphins in the afternoon.

JC's vacation house had turned out to be a dreamy, all-white beach house with hand-crafted pillars and vaulted ceilings. There was a galley kitchen that appeared rarely used, a cozy living room with enough decorative pillows to build a fort, and a floating spiral staircase that led to three upstairs bedrooms. Outside, there was an outdoor dining table that sat under a pergola and overlooked a narrow pool.

As Oliver and Olivia approached the back of the powerboat where the ladder was, she could see Bianca happily chatting with Captain Waters under the hard top. Bianca had confided in her earlier that day that she thought the captain looked a lot like the rugged actor, Kevin Costner. JC was sitting on one of the white swivel chairs in his wet swim trunks, lazily scrolling through his phone. He'd put his Bad Bunny concert T-shirt back on and had a Tommy Hilfiger beach towel draped around his shoulders.

Before climbing back onto the powerboat, they helped each other remove their flippers, after which Oliver threw all four of them over the side of the boat and could hear them clunk onto the floor. Then they took off their masks and snorkels and threw them onto the boat as well.

Oliver climbed up the ladder first and then held out his hand to help Olivia up. Once aboard, he grabbed Olivia's brightly patterned beach towel from the bench and wrapped it snugly around her. He then hugged her tightly and began rubbing her back.

Captain Waters whispered something to Bianca and then leaned down to grab all of the snorkeling gear off the floor so he could put it in a bin near the bow of the boat. Bianca moved to sit down on the other swivel chair beside JC.

Captain Waters began getting the Tipsy Wahoo ready for take-off.

"Are you okay?" Oliver asked quietly, putting his arms around her. She'd gotten her short stature from her mother and sturdy chin from her father.

"Yeah, I'll be okay," Olivia murmured.

Finally putting his phone away, JC exclaimed, "wow, that was amazing!" He took a swig of water from his tumbler, oblivious to what was happening between Oliver and Olivia.

"I know. I felt like I was in some sort of magical aquarium," Bianca mused, oblivious as well.

"It really was ... Until I was almost eaten by a barracuda just now," Olivia said shakily.

"Are you serious?" Bianca squeaked.

"For real?" JC was equally shocked.

"Yeah, I saw the whole thing. A barracuda came right up to her," Oliver nodded.

"It looked right at me," Olivia shuddered.

Captain Waters overheard what was being said and paused his work to ask, "are you okay?"

Olivia nodded, "it was quite unnerving, but I'm okay."

"She did everything you told us to," Oliver said proudly.

"Glad to hear that," Captain Waters nodded and then resumed his work.

Olivia noticed that Bianca had rearranged her blond hair into a messy bun on the top of her head and had put on her orange sarong dress.

"I'm okay. Let's get cleaned up for lunch," Olivia suggested.

"Good idea," Oliver nodded.

Olivia lifted the lid of the bench and rummaged through her duffle bag until she found her pink sarong dress. She slipped it on over her head and wriggled it over her black bikini. She found her gold-coloured Ray-Bans and put them on while Oliver dried himself off with his tropical beach towel. He pulled out his white tank top that had "Siesta Key" printed on it and yanked it over his head. Olivia tugged the black elastic hair tie from her tangled hair and rearranged it back into a slightly smoother ponytail. Lastly, they shoved their feet back into their flip-flops.

"The boat's ready for take-off, so I'd ask y'all to sit down and put your life jackets on again, please," Captain Waters drawled in his North Carolina accent as he finished bringing up the anchor.

Obediently, all four of them grabbed their life jackets and zipped them up. Oliver and Olivia placed their duffle bags back into the bench, closed it, and sat down.

"Now, when we get there, I'm going to need somebody's help docking the boat. Any volunteers?" Captain Waters looked at them.

"I've only done it once or twice, but I'd be willing to help," Oliver volunteered, smiling.

"Good," Captain Waters smiled.

The deafening roar of the engine started up as Captain Waters carved the powerboat through the clear blue waters. The salty air whipped around them, echoing in their ears and stinging their skin.

They reached the park in no time, and the captain slowed the powerboat down as they approached the small marina where several other powerboats and jet skis had already been docked.

"Well, here we are. Oliver, can you please drop the bumpers?" Captain Waters asked.

"Sure, can." Oliver jumped up from his seat and ran about, quickly flipping all four bumpers over the sides of the boat.

Captain Waters expertly maneuvered the boat backwards into one of the slips.

"Oliver, I need you to jump out of the boat and onto the dock," the captain ordered and Oliver did as he was told.

"I'm throwing you what's called a spring line. Don't do anything yet. Just hold it steady and don't let it fall in the water." The captain explained as he threw him the nylon spring line.

The captain continued his instructions, "keep holding that rope. I'm going to throw you the bow line, and you'll need to tie it to that hook," the captain pointed to a dock cleat near the bow of the boat.

"You'll need to make a knot like this," the captain showed him how to make a simple cleat knot. He held it up so Oliver could see it, then undid it in one stroke and threw Oliver the rope.

Oliver grabbed the rope and practiced the knot first. He held it up for the captain to see, and asked, "Like this?"

"Yep, you got it," the captain nodded.

Oliver undid it and then bent down and tied the bow line to the dock cleat near the bow of the boat.

"Now, you'll need to tie the rope I first gave you to that hook over there," the captain pointed to a dock cleat near the stern of the boat, "make the same knot. Just angle it away from the bow of the boat and towards the stern."

Oliver did as he was told.

"Now, last one, this is the stern line, and you'll need to attach it over there," Captain Waters said, pointing.

"Here?" Oliver pointed to a dock cleat near the stern of the boat.

"Yep."

Oliver tied the last of the ropes.

"You're a quick learner." The captain pulled at the ropes, testing each one of them.

"Yay, Oliver!" Olivia beamed.

"Well, that's all there is to it. You guys can jump off the boat. And it's up to you if you want to take your bags with you or leave them here. I can lock the bench," Captain Waters offered.

"We'll take them with us," Olivia said, and the rest of them nodded in agreement.

They grabbed their bags, and one by one, they jumped off the boat and onto the dock. They watched as Captain Waters stepped onto the dock and tested the ropes once again, adjusting them ever so slightly. He jumped back onto the boat and grabbed the cooler.

He motioned for JC to grab the cooler from him, "here, put this on the dock for me."

JC lifted it over the gap between the boat and the dock. He wobbled a bit with the awkwardness of the weight, and the cooler thudded heavily down onto the dock.

"Geez, what's in here?" JC asked.

"Lunch," Captain Waters smirked as he jumped onto the dock, and JC grimaced.

The captain pulled the cooler easily behind him as the four of them tailed him up the dock until they reached the sandy shore and began walking up the beach. Captain Waters pointed towards a boardwalk to their left and they trudged through the sand over to it. The boardwalk took them over the remnants of the beach, which quickly disappeared below them and was replaced by a shallow river. Soon, lush mangrove trees flanked both sides of the boardwalk as they continued onwards.

After a while, a majestic park came into view with countless trees providing shade to clusters of brightly coloured picnic tables. There were families and couples spread about the area, all enjoying the break from the hot, noon-hour sun. They stepped off the boardwalk and onto the cool, patchy grass. They eventually found an empty picnic table and claimed it by piling their bags on top of its benches.

"Looks good to me," Olivia said, noticing that each oval picnic table had a small grill stationed beside it.

"So, why's your boat called the Tipsy Wahoo, anyway?" Bianca asked.

"Because that's what we're having for lunch. Freshly caught this morning," Captain Waters explained as he set down the cooler.

Oliver took a football out of his duffle bag and whipped it unexpectedly at JC. The ball hit him in the stomach, and he stifled a groan.

Recovering from the hit, JC yelled, "It's on!" and whipped it back at Oliver. The boys ran over to a nearby empty grassy spot and began tossing the ball back and forth.

"Well, I guess that means you two are helping me with lunch," Captain Waters said as he placed a cloth bag on the picnic table, "you'll find cutlery and plates in there."

He went over to the grill, scraped it, and began lighting it up, "help yourselves to something to drink in the cooler."

"Thank you," Bianca said.

Olivia began setting the table for five with the blue plastic plates and cutlery she'd found in the bag. Bianca lifted the lid of the cooler to find something to drink but instead found the Wahoo. She brought it over to the captain. He carefully unwrapped the filets and placed them on the grill. They began to sizzle.

"Smells good. What'd you put on them?" Bianca asked him.

"I marinated them in a little bit of olive oil, some fresh lemon and lime juice, a bit of paprika, and then for a bit of a kick, some spicy tequila." Captain Waters explained as he flipped the fish onto the other side.

"Where'd you learn to cook?" Bianca asked.

Olivia tuned them out as she began rifling through the cooler to see what else was in there. She found a six-pack of flavoured sparkling water and put it on the table. Then she pulled out store-bought containers of garden salad, cut-up fruit, and pasta salad. She ripped the packaging off each container, added the dressing to the garden salad, and then snapped the lids back on to keep out the bugs and placed them in the middle of the picnic table.

"Lunch is ready!" Captain Waters yelled.

The boys stopped throwing the football and ran over to the picnic table. Oliver shoved the ball back into his duffle bag.

"Ladies, first," Oliver motioned for the girls to go ahead.

One by one, starting with the girls, they brought their empty plates over, and Captain Waters used the spatula to flip the filets onto them. Once everyone had been served, he closed the vents to let the grill burn out.

They filled their plates with salads before sitting down on the benches. Bianca and JC sat together on one bench, and Oliver and Olivia shared the other. Captain Waters sat on the third.

"This fish is delicious. I've never even heard of Wahoo before," Oliver complimented the captain.

"Thank you. It's one of my favourites because it's a hard fish to catch," the captain said.

"Why's it so hard to catch?" Oliver asked.

"Because it's a loner, and it's fast," Captain Waters explained.

"Kinda like you," Bianca joked.

"Hey, would you quit flirting with him?" JC chided, and Bianca stuck her tongue out at him. "Besides, a good-looking guy like you is probably married."

The captain shrugged and kept eating with a smirk on his face. Ignoring each other, JC began scrolling through his phone with one hand as he ate with the other. Watching JC, Olivia realized she hadn't checked her phone in hours, so she pulled it out of her duffle bag and saw that there was a text message from her mother, Maria.

"Okay, this is weird. My mom sent me a text message this morning saying, 'Hi, my darling, don't worry, everything's ok. Had to go on a last-minute trip. As long as it's okay with your friends, stay as long as you like. Will explain later. xo,' What the heck does that mean?" Olivia kept looking down at her phone, frowning.

"Okay … when parents say not to worry. You know what that means, right?" Bianca furrowed her eyebrows.

"To worry," Olivia nodded.

"And don't tell her about the barracuda!" Bianca yelled.

"No way!" Olivia agreed.

"Why is that weird?" Oliver asked.

"I mean, my mom travels for work a lot, but she would never go away over Christmas," Olivia explained.

"Yolanda would kill you guys if you weren't home for Christmas," Bianca pointed out, and Olivia nodded.

"Well, text her back and ask what's going on. I'm sure there's a reasonable explanation," JC said optimistically.

"I guess," Olivia bit her lower lip and simply texted back: Hi mom, hope ur ok. Xo

She thought of texting Yolanda, but then changed her mind.

"What about your dad? Wouldn't he know what's going on?" Oliver asked.

"Ah, my dad's probably working," Olivia explained, not wanting to divulge too much personal information and thinking how invisible she always felt around her dad. The last time they went skiing in Aspen, four years ago, she remembered looking around at other families and finally realizing that there was nothing normal about them. Fathers were teaching their kids how to ski and joking around with them. Her dad had barely spent any time with them, and when he had, he'd been on his phone. Business calls, he'd claimed. How could her mother put with that all these years?

"Everything's going to be okay," Oliver reassured her, but Olivia felt a knot forming in her stomach.

"It's going to be okay, and whatever it is, we're here for you," Bianca reassured her.

"Thanks, guys. I know you are," Olivia nodded, but continued to worry.

"Sometimes parents just need a bit of space, too," Captain Waters observed.

"Yeah, you're right." Olivia nodded.

"How do y'all know each other?" Captain Waters asked Oliver.

"Um, JC and I both had the same guitar teacher, and we'd run into each other in the waiting room, and then we kinda just started hanging out. Olivia and I are studying engineering at Miami State. We met at a school mixer about a month ago?" Oliver jostled Olivia, who was still staring at her phone.

"Why engineering?" The captain asked Oliver.

"I love building shit. My parents have an engineering firm. My dad would take me to the office on Saturdays when I was little, just the two of us, and I loved looking at the miniature models or sometimes blueprints of stuff they were gonna to build. It's just cool, you know?" Oliver explained.

"What about you? Are your parents' engineers too?" Captain Waters looked at JC.

"Nah, my mother's a lawyer, and my father's a judge. I'm going to be an architect." JC explained, embarrassed by how pretentious it all sounded, and resumed scrolling through his phone.

"And you two?" Captain Waters pointed at Bianca and Olivia.

"We met at STEM camp. I know it sounds nerdy. I don't remember this, but my mom told me that when I was really little, if I got a doll as a present, I'd get so disappointed that I'd throw it into the pool. When I was old enough to make my own birthday or Christmas wish list, I'd ask for building sets," Olivia giggled, and the captain raised an eyebrow.

"Do I need to be worried?" Oliver chuckled.

"I'm going to be a pediatrician," Bianca announced.

"You bet you are, babe. You're going to be the best," JC said quietly into her hair, kissing her on the ear.

"Thanks, babe," Bianca smiled at JC and then asked, "what about you, Mister Captain Waters?"

"Grew up in the Carolinas and then after the navy, moved here to Key West for the so-called simpler life, and all that," the captain explained.

"So ... you're married?" Bianca eyed the captain.

"Been married three years. We have a two-year-old daughter," he smiled.

"Geez, took you a while to get married," JC chided, "that's not going to happen to me."

Captain Waters shrugged and then explained, "as I said, I was in the navy."

"That does explain a few things," JC said with a hint of sarcasm.

"Where were you stationed?" Oliver asked.

"Oh, you know, here and there," the captain answered vaguely.

"And it's pure coincidence that your last name happens to be 'Waters'? That's just weird," JC pointed out.

"There are weirder things," the captain shrugged.

"You know, I was thinking, my mom had me when she was my age. I can't imagine having to give up all of this stuff ... School, travel, friends ... I mean, that's what she had to do, right? I don't think I'd have it in me to do that," Olivia said quietly.

"Took a lot of courage," Oliver nodded.

"Seems like she did a lot of things right," the captain observed.

"Both Bianca and I had strong moms who raised us," Olivia said shyly.

"Yeah, but your mom was lucky she had your dad ... I know, I know ..." Bianca said as she received a "yeah right" look from Olivia, "and your grandparents, Yolanda and Jorge. My mom was young too, but she had nobody," Bianca explained, stopping herself from adding that Olivia's mother's family also had money, so it was not quite the same thing; whereas, she lived with her mom in a mobile home and the only way she'd been able to attend STEM camp was by fighting hard for one of the five spots they reserved for underprivileged kids every year.

"Both of your moms did a great job raising the two of you, from what I can see," Captain Waters remarked.

"Thanks," Olivia smiled.

"Don't ever take what your moms did for you for granted. Trust me, I realize now how much work it is raising a kid," Captain Waters said.

“We won’t,” Bianca half-smiled at the captain.

“You’re good kids,” Captain Waters nodded adamantly.

MUNICH
SUNDAY, DECEMBER 22

It was Sunday afternoon and Maria was helping out at Heather's German bakery. With its comforting smells of steaming hot chocolate and warm baked goods right from the oven, she was thoroughly enjoying herself. And yet, she found herself distracted as she kept glancing at the door in anticipation of Phil taking her to lunch. The shop manager, Martha, had been fine with her leaving at three, so she'd let Phil know.

Earlier that morning, as she'd made her way into the shop, Maria had giggled at the "Buddy the Elf" window display. The shop manager, Martha, had turned out to be a no-nonsense, efficient leader who took charge and showed her the ropes in just a few minutes. The part-timer, Vanessa, was a quiet high school student who spent time on her phone when she wasn't helping customers. When Maria had mentioned this to Martha, she'd brushed it off by saying Vanessa was in charge of all their social media accounts.

Curious about the edibles side of the business, she'd asked Martha that if she wanted to try one for the first time, which kind would she recommend? Martha had pointed to the brownies, so she'd bought two and put them in her purse, figuring it was a safe way to experience what all the fuss was about.

Working at the bakery had proved trickier than she'd thought as it was a constant parade of customers. On top of the constant bustle, she quickly realized that she had to memorize the display cases backwards since the baked goods faced outwards towards the customers who then shouted out the names of the goods at the top of their lungs.

She was pulled back into the present as a customer shouted and pointed to the last poppyseed cake. She twisted her body sideways into the display case and grabbed it. As she twisted her body back up and out of the display case, she was relieved to see Phil's tall shape finally fill the doorway.

Even from afar, as she was boxing up the treats for the customer, she could see that he was sporting a big, goofy grin on his face as he entered the shop. She also noticed he was carrying a fuchsia parka as he manoeuvred his way towards her through the crowded bakery.

"Hi!" He yelled as he got closer, just as Maria handed the boxed up treats to the customer.

"Hi!" Maria yelled back, beaming at him and noticing he was wearing the same large winter coat as yesterday over a flannel shirt and dark jeans. She'd dressed in one of the outfits she normally reserved for her family's ski trips: dark wool pants and a cream-coloured cashmere turtleneck with a silk camisole underneath.

"Martha, this is Phil. Phil, Martha." Maria did the introductions.

"Hi, Phil. Nice to meet you." Martha smiled and nodded.

"Likewise," Phil said to Martha, "right, so is it okay if I take Maria to lunch?"

"Yes, of course! Everything's under control," Martha said, despite the long lineup of customers.

As Maria took off her apron, Phil said, "I got this coat from my mum. That coat you had on yesterday is definitely not warm enough, and Heather's coat was way too big, so I think this'll be more your size and keep you warmer."

"Wow, that's so nice of her." Maria was touched.

Phil made a strange face and then handed her the down-filled coat so she could put it on.

"It fits," she said happily.

"It suits you," Phil gazed at her, and she gazed back.

"Well, you two better get going before the farmers' market closes," Martha said, breaking the spell.

Maria snapped out of it. "Oh, right!" She grabbed her purse from under the counter and then asked Martha, "is it okay if I leave my leather jacket here?"

"Yes, of course. Now, go!" She ordered.

"The farmers' market is pretty close by, so I thought we could walk. Is that okay?" Phil asked, and Maria nodded.

As they walked down Main Street, Maria noticed what a difference having a proper winter coat made. Sure, she was still colder than she'd ever been in her life, but she was no longer shivering, and she could walk without hunching over. She also noticed that the town had become even busier than the day before, and in fear of losing Phil, Maria grabbed his hand.

"How did you get to the shop this morning?" Phil smiled at the ease with which she'd simply grabbed his hand.

"I walked. Very quickly."

"I imagine so."

"Wow, what a difference this coat makes. So much warmer. I thought you weren't going to tell them about me," Maria asked, slightly hoping he'd told the truth.

"Oh, I didn't. I kind of took it without asking. She hardly wears it. I knew it would look great on you," Phil explained.

"Oh, she's not going to be upset if she finds out?" Maria felt disappointed that Phil hadn't told the truth. "And, what if we run into her at the farmers' market?"

"Nah, she's at home helping Brian get Sunday dinner ready," Phil said casually.

"You're not going to spoil your appetite by eating so late, are you?" Maria teased, but feeling a bit hurt that she hadn't been invited to Sunday dinner.

"You haven't seen how much I can eat," Phil grinned, and then led them into the farmers' market.

A sign with big red letters that read "Willkommen zu Munich Farmers' Market" loomed above them as they walked through the double glass doors. They were greeted with jolly Christmas music playing over the loudspeakers.

"So, where are we eating?" Maria asked. She'd thought the crowded streets were bad, but this was ten times worse. They had to walk sideways in order to pass through the crowds.

"It's my favourite delicatessen in the entire farmers' market. Have you ever tried bratwurst?" Phil asked with a backwards glance, his grip tightening around her hand as they pushed their way along the narrow concrete pathway that divided the stalls, cafés, and restaurants.

"Brat-what?" Maria yelled.

"Ha! I knew it! You're going to love it. Oh wait ... You're not vegetarian, are you?" Phil asked in a sudden panic.

"No way!" Maria yelled.

"Great! Then here we are," Phil said as they approached a delicatessen with a tidy sign that read "König House".

There were white plastic tables set atop of a small area of artificial grass that was cordoned off by stanchions. Beyond the seating area was the deli, with its long glass counter filled with every kind of deli meat imaginable. Behind the counter were men and women in butcher's outfits working hard at filling orders that were coming in fast.

Draping their winter coats onto the back of their chairs, Phil and Maria sat down at one of the last remaining tables. It had a table marker on it.

"Ah, lucky number thirteen," Phil remarked sarcastically as he sat down on a plastic chair that looked kid-sized beneath him.

"Does that mean I'm not getting lucky tonight?" Maria teased.

"Well, I wouldn't give one little piece of plastic that much power," Phil teased back.

Maria watched as a tall, lanky boy dressed in a butcher's outfit came over to their table carrying two paper plates that were filled with something she couldn't quite make out, but had toothpicks sticking out of them.

"Willkommen," the boy said as he placed the paper plates in front of them, "please enjoy these samples, and I'll come back to take your order."

When he left, Maria asked, "isn't there a menu?"

"Yes, on the chalkboard over there, but I think you'll really like the smoked bratwurst. It's a garlicky, smoked pork that has nice herbs like cloves and marjoram. It's this one," Phil said as he pointed to one of the round pieces of sausage on her plate.

Maria looked down at her plate and counted three huge chunks of sausages, which in her mind was pretty much like having lunch before even having lunch.

"What's this one?" Maria pointed to a piece of sausage that was a dark red colour.

"I don't think you want to try that particular one," Phil warned her.

"Why not?" Maria asked, curiously.

"You really want to know?"

"I really want to know."

"It's blood sausage."

"It's what? You mean, like … Are you serious?"

"Well, yes, it's made out of blood. I mean … if that's your way of telling me you're, in fact, a vampire. You know, if Sookie and Bill could make it work, I guess we can figure it out," Phil teased.

"Now you found me out. I was hoping to wait until at least the third date to bite you," Maria teased back.

"Haha! In all seriousness, let's get back to the very serious task at hand of trying the smoked bratwurst," Phil said.

They both picked up their pieces using the toothpicks, and while Maria gently placed the meat in her mouth, Phil gobbled his up. As Maria bit into it, the casing satisfactorily cracked open, and its savory flavour mixed with the sweetness of the pimento flooded her taste buds.

"Impressive. I thought it would taste fatty, but it's very flavourful," Maria remarked.

"I may be a weathercaster, but I also know my meat," Phil said and then blushed at how that sounded.

"Well, I'm glad you do." Maria giggled and then looked at the people around her and began to wonder if she was going to gain twenty pounds in the time that she was here. "You know, I pretty much did all of the talking in the truck yesterday, so I'm thinking, it's your turn. You need to tell me about yourself, mister," Maria teased.

"You know, I kept thinking the same thing ... When is this girl going to stop talking. Me, me, me," Phil teased back.

"Very funny," Maria eyed him, "I'm serious. I'd like to know a bit more about you."

"Well then, let's figure out our order first, and then I'll spill the beans," Phil teased, "do you want to try the third one?"

"Well, I was kind of wondering what it was." Maria looked down at the chunk of white sausage.

"It's Weisswurst. It's made from minced veal and pork back bacon. And it's seasoned with parsley, lemon, mace, onions, ginger, and cardamom," Phil easily explained.

"I'm kind of impressed by your sausage knowledge," Maria giggled.

"It's an important skill I use to impress the ladies," Phil grinned.

Maria grinned back, picked up the chunk, and daintily took a small bite. She was surprised at how soft it was and that it didn't have the same complexity of flavours as the bratwurst.

"I think you're right. The bratwurst is the winner ... or the wiener," Maria said and then rolled her eyes at her own bad joke.

"Oh boy," Phil said, shaking his head, "moving on, you now have the choice of adding sauerkraut, red cabbage, or potato salad to your plate. And you can have it on a bun or no bun."

"Geez, so many choices. What does red cabbage taste like?" Maria asked.

"It's pickled but not vinegary like sauerkraut. It's kind of crunchy and sweet," Phil explained.

"That sounds delicious. I'll have a side of that and make it no bun." Maria decided.

"Do you like beer?" Phil asked.

"A veces[18]," Maria said, moving her hand side to side, remembering Phil had told her he'd learned a bit of Spanish from working in Miami.

"We can order half glasses then. Do you like bitter or sweet?" Phil asked.

"Definitely sweet."

And with that, Phil waved the boy over.

"Yes, what can I get for you?" The boy asked, ready with a pen and pad of paper.

"We'd like two half glasses of Hacker-Pschorr Kellerbier to drink. And to eat, the lady would like the bratwurst with no bun and a side of red cabbage." Phil paused as the boy wrote it down.

"As for myself, I'd like the bratwurst on a bun with sauerkraut on top and a side of potato salad. And I'd like three packets of mustard, please," Phil said and then turned to Maria, "is one packet good enough for you, Maria?"

---

[18] Sometimes.

"Yes, of course!" She exclaimed.

The boy nodded and took their paper plates away.

"You really like your mustard," Maria observed.

"It brings out the flavour of the meat," Phil explained.

"If you say so," Maria said skeptically.

"You said you wanted to ask me questions, so shoot away," Phil said.

"Well, first of all, why do you live in Miami and not here with your family?" Maria asked.

"Umm, aren't you the same person who swore like a trucker in Heather's ... well, truck ... last night?" Phil teased.

"Yes, I get it. The weather sucks. But don't you miss your family? And don't they ever ask you to move back?" Maria was so close to her family, even though they drove her crazy at times, she could never imagine moving so far away from them.

Before Phil could answer, the boy came by again with their beers in small glasses and set them down on the table.

"Thank you," Phil said to the boy as he left and then answered Maria's question, "no, they don't. They know I enjoy my life in Miami and that I'm happy. That's all they want for me. Is to be happy. Besides, I'd never want to be a weathercaster here, reporting on winter storms, no thanks."

"So, you prefer tornadoes," Maria teased.

"Ha! Touché. Now, let's cheers," Phil grinned.

Maria yelled, "¡Salud!" at the same time that Phil yelled, "Prost!" and they laughed.

Maria took a tiny sip and set it down while Phil took a big swig that pretty much emptied the small glass.

"Yummy! Tastes like caramel and honey! I had no idea beer could taste like that." Maria felt happy and relaxed.

"I thought you'd like it."

"So, 'Prost' is the same as 'Salud'?"

"Yes, it is."

"I'll have to remember that. Your parents ... Do they pressure you to get married? Or have you been married before?" Maria asked.

"Geez ... I thought these questions were going to be like where did you go to school? What did you have for breakfast?" Phil joked.

"Hey, I don't fool around. Well, apparently, sometimes I do with perfect strangers," Maria teased.

"Yes, that was quite fun last night, wasn't it?" Phil smiled warmly at her.

At that moment, the boy brought over their food on recyclable paper plates and placed them on the table, along with some wooden utensils.

"I'm also leaving the bill with you. When you're ready, you can pay at the cash register." The boy pointed to the cash register by the deli counter and then ripped the paper from his pad and left it on the table.

Maria noticed that Phil inspected his plate of food before saying "thank you" to the boy. She looked down at her own plate, and it looked and smelled delicious. She pulled open the packet of cutlery and brought a forkful of the cabbage up to her mouth and ate it.

"Wow, yes, the red cabbage is just as you described. So yummy!" Maria exclaimed happily as she began cutting the sausage into medallion-like pieces.

"You'll want to dip the pieces into the mustard." Phil pointed to her packet of mustard.

"I like to eat my food without too much sauce. It's full of sugar. Do you want it?" Maria picked up the packet.

"Sure, why not?" Phil took the packet from Maria and added it to his already completely concealed sausage.

Satisfied, he lifted the whole thing up and took a huge bite. When he looked back at her and began chewing, there was a dollop of mustard on his chin, and some of the sauerkraut began falling out of his bun and onto the paper plate.

After he'd managed to swallow his huge bite, Phil sheepishly said, "I'm beginning to realize that this is not date food." He then wiped his chin with his napkin.

"The way I eat it, it is," Maria said as she daintily placed a piece of the sausage into her mouth with her fork.

"Yes, I can see that," Phil said as he watched her slide the fork out of her mouth.

"So, have you ever been married?" Maria asked, liking the way Phil was looking at her.

"Well, yes," Phil swallowed hard, "twice, actually. The first time to my high school sweetheart, Clara. We divorced when I was offered a job in Miami. She didn't want to leave Munich, so that was that. We didn't have kids, which made it a pretty easy divorce," Phil shrugged.

"And that was how long ago?" Maria asked.

"Geez, almost twenty years ago."

"And the second marriage?"

"I met Sara in New Orleans while I was covering Hurricane Katrina."

"And what happened there?" Maria asked, wondering if Phil realized that all of their names rhymed.

"She left me for our cameraman," Phil sighed.

"Oh! That must've been a shock," Maria frowned and Phil shrugged, "so, no one else after Sara?"

"Oh, I've dated here and there, but nothing serious." Phil thought it best to leave out that his mother was constantly pressuring him to get married again, and have kids.

Phil and Maria ate in silence for a while, both finishing off their plates of food. Phil had scraped some of the sauerkraut off his sausage to make it more manageable to eat.

"Do you and your brother get along?" Maria asked.

"We're very different. There's a bit of an age gap between us too, but not quite as big as between you and Gabriel. But yes, we do get along in our own way."

"I see. How much of a gap?" Maria asked.

"He's four years younger than me. Not for lack of trying on my parents' part, apparently. So, they were beyond happy when Brian came along. They've totally spoiled him. And now, he seems to float through life."

"He's not a respectable weatherman?" Maria teased.

"Ha! Not anywhere close to that. He's actually a super-talented portrait artist and sculptor. He just can't seem to focus on the business side of things. He's kind of immature, to be honest. So, I wasn't surprised to hear that he'd messed things up with Heather."

"Do you know what happened between them?" Maria asked.

"Not really. I wanted to talk to him about it last night, but he gave me the look of death when I tried to bring it up. And this morning, he wasn't awake yet. All I know is that she broke up with him out of the blue. I'm assuming he did something stupid."

"You keep saying that," Maria pointed out, "is he really that much of a trainwreck?"

"Not so much a trainwreck. More like reckless. Here's a story for you. My dad comes from a generation of farmers. So, growing up on a farm, we were expected to help out. In fact, that's where my interest in weather patterns comes from," Phil explained.

"Ah, that makes sense. What did your father grow?" Maria asked, picturing a tall, adolescent, shirtless Phil lifting hay in overalls. His muscles flexing and shiny from sweat.

"The sweetest of vegetables. All organic," Phil explained and then continued with his story, "we always hired seasonal workers to help out. When Brian was a teenager, he'd hang out with them late at night, drinking around the campfire. My parents knew but never did anything about it. Anyway, I guess one night, Brian and the workers heard mooing from the dairy farm next door. And for some foolish reason, Brian decided to brag that he could ride a cow like a horse. And I guess bets were placed," Phil sighed.

"No!" Maria exclaimed.

"Brian hopped the fence into the neighbouring farm and tried to grab onto a cow to ride it. Well, not surprisingly, the cow wasn't too thrilled and began mooing really loudly. It had been grazing with a herd of other cows, and the poor thing was so scared that it jumped about, creating a stampede, which of course, woke everyone up. The farmer called us, screaming over the phone, 'Get your dumb ass son out of my farmyard before I get out my shotgun'," Phil said, imitating a grumpy old man's voice.

Maria couldn't stop herself from laughing at this horrifying story. "You have to be making this up."

"I swear, it's a true story." Phil held his hands up in the air, claiming innocence.

"Your brother does sound reckless. He's lucky he didn't get trampled to death." Maria had never heard a story like this before.

"Yeah, no kidding!" Phil exclaimed.

"Other than almost getting squashed by an alligator, how many near-death experiences have you had?" Maria asked.

"What a strange question," Phil frowned.

"I've almost died ... Wait, no, this is about you, not me," Maria caught herself.

"No, now I'm curious. What were you going to say?" Phil prodded her.

"Um, okay. I've come close to death; I'd say about five times." Maria held up her left hand, showing all five fingers.

"That many? That seems like an awful lot. Are you a thrill-seeker or something?" Phil looked at her in awe.

"What? No! It's just that things happen," Maria tried to explain.

"Give me an example then," Phil dared her.

"Calm down there, mister," Maria teased.

She paused, thought about it, and then said, "I know which one I'll tell. I almost died white water rafting."

"See … You are a thrill-seeker." Phil felt satisfied with himself.

"You think so? I loved white water rafting. I'd already gone three times before and I was never scared. Always looked forward to going. But then, that fourth time, we went to a new place. What we didn't know was that there'd been a heavy rainfall, which had led to heavy flooding. We were in our late teens, our senior year, and invincible –"

"And didn't watch the weather channel," Phil teased.

"Didn't know the weather channel existed," Maria laughed, "anyway, the crew that was looking after us … We only found this out afterwards … Took us down a river that had been closed off, marked as too dangerous because of the heavy rainfall. The water was higher than normal and the rapids were fast. They'd already nicknamed that section of rapids the 'washing machine', but now it was much worse."

"So, you went through the 'spin cycle'," Phil observed.

"Yes! The minute our raft hit that section of rapids … we didn't stand a chance. The strength of the current shoved our huge raft downwards, folded it in half like a taco, and dragged us down into the spin cycle. We were all wearing life jackets and yet we were still a tangled mess of feet, legs and arms, fighting for our lives to get back up to the surface of the water. I'll never forget that horrible feeling of not knowing if I was going to make it up to the surface." Maria paused to catch her breath.

"Those seconds felt like forever, but eventually, I managed to push myself up to the surface, to grab some air before the current dragged me back down into the spin cycle again. I remember thinking ... this is it. I wasn't even going to get to live my life. I was tumbling through the water with no control over where I was going. I've always been a strong swimmer and I'd always assumed I'd be able to fight a current, but there was no way. You can't fight a current that strong.

"And then, all of a sudden, everything went still around me. I looked around and realized that I'd made it out. I was now on the other side of the rapids and was floating underwater in a part of the river that was calm. I looked up and saw dark shapes shimmering above me. So, I began to swim upwards and was nearing the top, when all of a sudden, I felt myself being dragged backwards and upwards through the water, breaking the surface. My head was above water, but my body was still submerged."

Phil gave her a quizzical look.

"You see, when you go white water rafting, there are guides who follow the rafts in kayaks in case something like that happens. I got lucky that one of them saw me and grabbed the handle at the back of my life jacket and dragged me up to the surface. He dragged me alongside his kayak all the way to the beach and basically threw me up onto the shore. I felt like hugging him, but had no energy and couldn't move, and he had to leave right away to go rescue others, anyway. I used the last of my energy to crawl onto the beach and sat there in a state of shock. It was one of the strangest and scariest things I've ever experienced. I finally looked around and noticed that other rafters were sitting on the beach beside me. All of us were just staring into the distance. In shock." Maria had a haunted look in her eyes.

"What an intense experience, especially at such a young age," Phil sympathized.

"The thing is, I haven't been able to put my head under water ever since," Maria admitted.

Phil was feeling a deeper connection with Maria. "I'm so sorry you had to go through something like that."

"Gosh, I hadn't thought about that in years," Maria said shyly.

"I'm glad you shared it with me," Phil said sympathetically.

"Thanks, Phil. Why don't we talk about you again? But no more death. Um, when did your dad sell the farm?" Maria asked.

"Okay, sure, we can do that. I guess about five years ago? That's when they bought a house closer to town. It's just north of Heather's house."

"What's Heather like?" Maria asked.

"I only met her a handful of times at my parents' house for Sunday dinners. She seemed very nice, maybe a little uptight and serious. Very opposite from my brother, so I was surprised they were together, but then again, they say opposites attract.

Or maybe balance each other out? I guess I was hoping that because she runs such a successful business, she'd teach Brian some things, but that didn't happen. Don't repeat this, but Brian told me once that she has a bit of a temper."

"A temper?"

"Yeah, that she gets angry, quite easily."

"Oh! That won't go over well with my mother at all. I wonder how many fights they've gotten into already," Maria contemplated.

Phil looked at Maria with amusement.

"Not that ... I want Heather to get into a fight with my mother ... Sorry, that came out wrong." Maria realized she'd sounded a bit petulant.

Phil shrugged and said, "no worries, I get it."

They stared at each other in silence for a while.

Phil opened and closed his mouth a few times as if to speak and then finally said, "look, I know we said we'd keep this quiet between us, and with two failed marriages, I try not to introduce my parents to everyone I date, but screw it. Come home with me to my parents' house for dinner. The farmers' market is going to close soon, and my mum asked me to get some wine from the Italian lady."

"Really? Don't you have to ask your mother first if it's okay?" Maria was so happy, she felt like dancing.

"Nope, we'll just surprise them. And it's not my mum you have to worry about. My brother does most of the cooking and he always makes enough to feed an army. Not that you eat like an army ... In fact, you eat quite little, don't you?" Phil observed.

"I watch what I eat," Maria said defensively.

Phil rested his hands flat on the table, palms up, and began wiggling his fingers, motioning for Maria to put hers on top of his, which she happily obliged. He began to gently rub her hands as he asked, "you do want to come to my parents' house with me, right?"

Maria felt the warmth of his hands and whispered, "kiss me."

Phil leaned across the tiny table, and they kissed. As luck would have it, the song "Christmas is All Around" was playing through the loudspeakers above them as they kissed.

"I guess that means, yes?" Phil asked goofily.

"Yes, and thank you so much for lunch," Maria said, smiling.

They both stood up, put their winter coats back on, and then stacked their plates and threw them into the recycling bin. Maria waited by the exit as Phil walked over to the cashier to pay for the two of them. They held hands once again as they made their way down and around the rest of the stalls and cafés.

Maria tugged at Phil's hand, "hey, do you know where Heather's friend Pam's deli is? I wouldn't mind thanking her for the dinner last night."

"What dinner last night?" Phil asked.

"Oh! I didn't tell you! After you left, I went into the kitchen for a glass of water and there was a slow cooker filled with chicken stew. It was delicious."

"Wow, that was nice of her."

"I know! So, do you know Pam and where her deli is?"

"I've actually never met Pam."

"Oh wait ... I have her cell number," Maria said as she let go of Phil's hand, scrolled through her phone and tapped on Pam's name.

It rang twice before Pam answered.

"Maria! Hi!" Pam's voice resonated loudly through the phone.

"Hi, Pam! Thank you so much for the dinner last night," Maria said.

"No trouble at all. It was from a big batch I made for the family. How was your first day here?"

"Great. That's why I'm calling. I'm at the farmers' market and wanted to come by and say hi."

"You are? Do you know where my deli is?"

"No, I don't."

"Where are you right now?"

Maria looked over at Phil for help and whispered, "where are we?"

"Tell her we're on our way to the Italian wine store. She'll know," Phil reassured her.

"We're on our way to the Italian wine store," Maria repeated.

"Oh, perfect! We're three north of it," Pam said.

"Great! See you soon!" At that, they both hung up.

"She's three north of the Italian wine store," Maria repeated.

"We just need to keep walking then." Phil held out his hand, and Maria grabbed it.

They quickly made their way past coffee shops, seafood counters and pizzerias, and then Maria spotted a German bakery. She stopped abruptly in front of it and lost her grip on Phil's hand as he kept walking ahead. Phil was bewildered at the loss of

Maria's hand and turned back to see where she'd disappeared to.

"What's going on?" Phil shouted over the top of people's heads.

"I'm not showing up empty-handed to your parents' house! I want to bring a dessert!" Maria shouted back.

Phil squeezed his way back to her and said, "you really don't have to."

"Yes. I do. I've been taught to never show up empty-handed," Maria declared, and Phil shrugged.

Maria looked at all of her options and asked, "What does your mother like?"

Phil glanced at the counter and saw a freshly baked apple strudel that looked delicious.

"The apple strudel!" Phil pointed at it.

"I'd like the apple strudel, please!" Maria instructed the shopkeeper.

He wrapped it up for her and then took her credit card. After she paid, she put the strudel in her purse, and they continued onwards through the crowds until Maria spotted a shop selling boots, and she stopped abruptly once again.

"What now?" Phil asked, confused.

"I need proper winter boots!" Maria yelled over the crowds as she wandered into the shop.

"True, you do. But wait …" Phil leaned down and whispered in Maria's ear, so the shop owner wouldn't hear, "things are cheaper at the outlet mall. I was planning on taking you there tomorrow."

"Oh, that's nice of you! But I kind of need them now. I mean, we're going to walk to your parents' house, right? And then after dinner, I'll have to walk back to Heather's," Maria pointed out.

"Ah, you're right. Let's take a look," Phil relented.

Maria meandered around the shop while the elderly shop owner watched her with little interest. She found a pair of brown, faux-fur boots that she liked the look of and then read the tag that was attached to them. She was relieved to read that they were waterproof, but then was shocked to read that they were insulated against temperatures as cold as -25°C/-13°F.

"Is this for real?" Maria showed the tag to Phil.

"Oh yeah, but don't worry, we're looking at a mild winter this year," Phil reassured her.

"Boy, can't take the weather out of the man," Maria laughed and then turned to the shop owner, "can I please try on a size six in brown?"

"True, but I'm a weathercaster, not a weatherman. There's a difference ..." Phil was about to explain the difference, but then realized Maria was focused on her new boots.

The elderly shop owner nodded and looked through his sparse shelves until he found a size six and brought the box over to her. Maria sat down on the tiny bench, unzipped her knee-high leather boots, and carefully placed them on the floor beside her. She opened the box, unwrapped them and slid her feet into the thick, faux-fur boots. She stood up and walked around the shop, feeling their comfort and warmth.

"They're perfect. I'll take them. In fact, I'd like to wear them right now," Maria said as she began placing her own boots into the box and then handed her credit card over to the shop owner.

"They suit you. Now you're starting to look like you belong here," Phil smiled at her.

"Not so exotic?" Maria teased.

"Damn, you're still exotic, trust me," Phil teased back.

After Maria paid for the boots, they continued their quest towards the wine store. Maria spotted it right away as it had an Italian flag draped over its entranceway. An elderly lady who had a bit of hunched back looked at them from behind the counter, and a big smile spread across her face. She was wearing a red knitted sweater that complemented her olive complexion.

"Filippo! Benvenuti![19]" She said in Italian as she enclosed Phil's hands in hers.

"Come stai, Isabella[20]?" Phil asked in Italian.

"Molto bene[21]," Isabella answered, smiling.

"My mum would like me to bring home two bottles of pinot grigio, per favore," Phil explained jovially, having reached the end of his limited knowledge of Italian.

"I 'ave some very good wine for you to take to your moder. But first, who is dis lovely young lady?" Isabella asked in a thick, Italian accent, peering at Maria.

"Oh, pardon my manners, this is Maria." Phil waved for Maria to join them.

"Nice to meetchu. Where are ju from?" Isabella inquired.

"Lovely to meet you as well! I'm Colombian, but I live in Miami," Maria explained sweetly.

"How marvelous! Like Filippo!" Isabella smiled broadly.

---

[19] Philip! Welcome!
[20] How are you, Isabella?
[21] Very well.

Maria nodded as Isabella guided Phil over to a rack of wine and pulled two bottles off the shelf.

"Actually, I'd like to buy a couple of bottles as well," Maria said hesitantly.

"Of course! What would ju like?" Isabella asked.

"I'd like to buy a thank you wine for Pam, who owns the deli three north of you. Do you know her?"

"Sí, sí! Her deli is one of dee best. Here, come, dis one," Isabella said as she pointed to a bottle of cabernet sauvignon.

Maria picked it up, read the description, and thought it sounded delightful. "Yes, perfect. I'll take two!"

As they were paying for the wine, Isabella looked at them and said, "you two ... Very good for each other. Dese tings, I know."

Phil blushed and Maria smiled.

"That's very kind of you. Thank you," Maria said.

"Sorry to 'ear about Header and Bryan," she said to Phil, patting his hand.

"Thank you?" Phil mumbled, as he didn't quite know what to say and wondered how she knew.

Phil's hands were now full as he was carrying Maria's big bag with her no-longer-weather-appropriate boots in one hand and the wine in the other, so they could no longer hold hands as they left the store and headed north towards Pam's deli. Maria counted as they passed each stall.

"One, two, three. Here we are!" Maria exclaimed as they found themselves standing in front of Pam's deli.

All of the workers were busy packing up the deli counter for the evening. Maria noticed a short, wide lady with her blond hair pulled into a bun covered by a hair net and figured it was Pam.

"Pam!" Maria shouted.

The woman looked up, and her eyes lit up with delight.

"Hi!" Pam waved to them as she left the counter and walked over to them.

Pam held out her hand to shake Maria's, but Maria was already leaning in enthusiastically to give her an air kiss on both cheeks, which meant Pam bumped her hand into Maria's stomach, and they both stepped back, laughing.

"Here, this is how we say hello in Colombia," Maria giggled as she air-kissed Pam.

Pam didn't quite know what to do, so she simply patted Maria's back. "Well, thank you."

"I'm so happy to finally meet you," Maria said eagerly, trying to ease Pam's obvious discomfort. "This is Phil."

Phil and Pam nodded at one another.

"I wanted to give you this bottle of wine as a thank you for the dinner you left for me last night." Maria took the wine from Phil and handed it to Pam.

"Oh, you didn't have to do that! But thank you!" Pam said happily. "How are you finding everything here?"

"Heather's house is lovely! I had a very nice time helping out at her bakery today. It's all been fantastic. But I don't want to keep you. I know you're super busy. I'm sure we'll see each other again," Maria said, politely.

"Actually, I was going to text you when I got home tonight. We're having our annual drop-in on Christmas Day from three to whenever the last person leaves, which is usually Heather," Pam chuckled at the last bit, "but it would be terrific if you and Phil could come?" Pam had only intended to invite Maria, but now felt she had to include Phil.

"Yes, we'd love to! That's so kind of you." Maria was surprised at the invitation, and then realized she was being presumptuous and turned to Phil, "oh, you're okay to come too, right Phil?"

"Yes, should be." Phil was also surprised at the invitation, wondering how awkward it was going to be.

"We'll see you on Wednesday," Maria said as they left.

Pam watched them leave, went back around the deli counter, and picked up her phone to text Heather:

Hi Heather! Just met your Colombian visitor and Phil, and wow, she's quite the looker. Seems lovely. All good here.

Pam put her phone away, knowing full well that she wouldn't be the one looking after Maria while she was here.

BOCA BONITA
SUNDAY DECEMBER 22

After surviving her first waxing experience, Heather had met up with Sofia back at the salon to have their lashes, hair, and nails done. Afterwards, they'd returned to the car so they could head to the outlet mall.

Once they were in the car, away from the judgemental ears of other customers at the salon, Heather had finally been able to tell Sofia about the vajazzling experience, and how she'd felt no pain during the waxing.

Sofia had been shocked at both sets of news and had admitted that she'd never even dared to try vajazzling, but admired Heather's courage. She couldn't believe that Heather had felt no pain during the waxing and was upset to learn that she'd been going to the wrong girl this whole time. And then, she'd repeatedly asked Heather if she was sure the girl's name was Dolores, because she was definitely going to book with her next time.

Afterwards, they'd finally arrived at the outlet mall where Heather could look for a bathing suit.

Now, Heather and Sofia were at the bathing suit store, trying to pick out ones that would be the most flattering for Heather's body type.

"How about this one?" Sofia held up a black, v-shaped one piece that had laces around the bust area.

"Oh, wow, that's sexy. I don't think I've ever worn anything like that in my life," Heather said.

"Well, I think it's time." With that, Sofia added it to the growing pile.

Heather looked at the pile. "I'm going to start trying them on; otherwise, we'll be here all day. Cross fingers there's at least one that looks good."

"I think we've picked out some good ones. I'll be right here," Sofia said as she pointed to a chair stationed nearby.

Heather nodded and then entered her changeroom, locking the swinging door behind her.

She was startled at her reflection in the full-length mirror. Her hairdresser had cut her long hair quite short. It was now resting just above her shoulders. She hadn't had it styled like this in years. The hairdresser had also added layers of soft highlights so that her hair looked sun kissed. Whatever product the hairdresser had gently rubbed into her scalp had given her hair a healthy sheen and removed all signs of fly aways. She looked down at her fingernails, which were now painted a soft pink with matching pink toenails. She'd never had fake eye lashes in her life, so she'd chosen more subtle ones, but they were now longer than usual and curled upwards.

She looked ... glossy. And admittedly, she kinda liked this version of herself.

Choosing from the pile of bathing suits, she picked up the turquoise one-piece that had a discreet blue-on-blue diamond pattern around the bust area and a control top tummy. As she picked it up, she thought about how she'd been trying to convince Brian to go to an all-inclusive resort in Mexico in January. It would've been her first beach resort trip. She'd thought she'd be buying a new bathing suit for that trip, not a trip by herself to Florida. Well, his loss, not hers.

She flipped off her shoes and then yanked off her jean shorts, dark blue tank top, bra and underwear as quickly as possible. Standing fully naked in a changeroom was a very uncomfortable feeling for her – especially now that she was waxed and vajazzled. She peeked at herself and thought how right she and Sofia were, these mirrors and lighting made one look horrible. In her mind, saw a lumpy, translucent, and too-tall-of-a-middle-aged woman. The small vajazzle heart looked somewhat garish in this lighting.

Sighing, she squished herself into the turquoise, one-piece bathing suit, trying to push any extra parts of her inside of it. She pulled the portion around her butt as far down as she could.

It looked okay, she guessed.

"I'm coming out," Heather announced, flatly.

"Ready," Sofia replied.

She pushed open the swinging changeroom door and walked into an open area where there was a tri-fold mirror.

"That looks fabulous on you!" Sofia exclaimed, her eyes looking her up and down.

"You think so?" Heather wasn't so sure.

"Yes, God's honest truth. It does. You have to add that to the 'yes' pile, but try on the next one." Sofia beamed at her.

Heather went back inside the changeroom and picked up a conservative, striped one-piece. She put it on but immediately knew it was terrible.

"Not even going to show you this one. It's awful," Heather said.

"Gotcha," Sofia said.

Heather picked up a few of the others and changed her mind about even trying them on. She hesitated as she reached for the sexy, black, one-piece that Sofia had picked out for her. She slowly put it on. This time, she didn't announce her entrance and quietly came out of her changeroom.

"Ta-da," Heather whispered.

"Wow, you look stunning. Your boobs look amazing. The guys on the beach are going to have to hide their enthusiasm," Sofia giggled.

"Is it too much?"

"It's definitely sexy."

"But I really only need one bathing suit," Heather pointed out, trying to stay frugal.

"Do you? Why don't you get the turquoise one for the beach and this one for more adult opportunities?" Sofia suggested.

"Adult opportunities? What does that even mean?" Heather teased.

"You know what I mean! Ah, I think I've been a parent and grandparent for too long! I mean for more private times," Sofia blushed.

"Private times?" Heather chuckled.

Afterwards, as Heather changed back into her clothes and then paid for the bathing suits, she realized that she was looking forward to wearing them instead of completely dreading it.

KEY WEST
SUNDAY, DECEMBER 22

After their morning of snorkelling, Captain Waters had dropped off Olivia and her friends at a nearby dolphin sanctuary, promising to come back for them in a couple of hours.

Before entering the water, they'd been told to take a shower to get rid of any oils or perfumes, and then had followed the rest of the instructions – to not jump or splash and to let the dolphins come to you.

Right off the bat, Olivia had bonded with a particularly peppy dolphin named Pippa. She was petting its smooth head as it chattered happily at her.

"This whole day has been surreal," Bianca said as she floated by Olivia on her back.

Pippa gave Olivia a kiss on the cheek and then nudged her, which the instructors had told her meant that the dolphin wanted Olivia to hang onto her fin so that she could take her for a spin. Feeling exhilarated, Olivia grabbed Pippa's fin, and the dolphin once again propelled her through the water.

"This is amazing!" Olivia yelled as she felt the current drive up against her body. "Where are the boys?"

"They went to shower," Bianca said.

"I didn't even notice them getting out of the water. I think I'm in love," Olivia giggled as she gently clung to Pippa.

One of the instructors stood up and made a hand gesture, meaning their time was up. Pippa understood the gesture and slowed down to take Olivia over to the ladder.

Olivia gently patted Pippa's head one last time and was rewarded with a final kiss. Bianca came up behind her, and they exited the water together. Grabbing nearby towels, they wrapped themselves up and headed towards the changerooms.

"Have you heard from your mom?" Bianca asked as they walked the concrete path towards the changerooms.

"Nope," Olivia said worriedly.

"I'm sure she just needs some space, as the captain said," Bianca remarked as they entered the women's changeroom and then made their way to the shower area.

"I'll call her when we get back to JC's place," Olivia said as she turned on the water and then entered her shower stall.

When they were done showering, they walked back to the women's change area where they'd stored their clothes in lockers.

"How's it going with you and JC?" Olivia asked as she put on her undergarments, yoga pants, and cropped sweatshirt.

"He's a great guy," Bianca said as she changed into skinny jeans and an oversized sweatshirt, and then began fixing her makeup in the mirror.

"I sense a 'but' coming on," Olivia frowned.

"Haha. Yeah, to tell you the truth, I think I'm going to have to break up with him."

"Why's that?"

"He's always on his phone."

"Okay," Olivia said skeptically.

"I need to be with someone who doesn't need to be on their phone all the time," Bianca shrugged.

"Yeah, but everyone's always on their phone, all the time." Olivia pointed out, and then thought about her own father, who was on his phone, all the time, even during important moments. Maybe Bianca did have a point.

"On top of that, he's just so happy-go-lucky. Like no matter what, he thinks everything's going to work out," Bianca explained.

"And that's a reason to break up with him?" Olivia frowned.

"Yes, it's annoying. Trust me, I've learned that bad things can happen at any moment," Bianca explained in a serious tone, "I just can't be with someone who's so optimistic, all the time."

"Well, I'm sorry to hear that," Olivia said, wondering what was so wrong with being optimistic.

When they exited the changeroom, they saw that Oliver and JC were already waiting for them inside Captain Waters' jeep; Oliver in the passenger seat and JC in the back. As they climbed in, they could sense something was wrong.

"I don't know how to say this exactly, so I'm just going to say it. JC got a text from his mom saying that his dad is in the hospital, but not to worry, it was an anxiety attack and not a heart attack, and that she'll let him know more in a bit," Oliver said as JC kept his head bent downwards, texting.

Bianca gave Olivia a "told-you-so" look and Olivia's stomach sank.

BOCA BONITA
SUNDAY, DECEMBER 22

Heather was waving goodbye from Maria's front door as Sofia sped off in her Porsche.

After having paid for the bathing suits, they'd visited several clothing stores to buy an outfit for Heather to wear dancing. She'd also snapped up a few discounted sundresses and a pair of silver sandals for half price. The plan was for Sofia to pick Heather up in a rideshare later that night.

Heather entered her designated bedroom and emptied her shopping bags onto the bed. She sighed at the thought of Pam's promise that she wouldn't have to spend any extra money.

Wanting to wear a new outfit that matched her glossed up look, she changed into one of her new sundresses. She took the rest of her purchases into the bathroom and gave them a thorough washing. Glancing out the bathroom window, she couldn't help but notice how serene the backyard looked. The pool water was gently lapping back and forth, making a quiet slapping noise against the sides of the pool. Feeling grateful, she decided she would order something for dinner, sit by the pool and continue reading the wildly entertaining novel she'd started months ago on her reading app.

A part of her was still in disbelief about everything that had happened. Just forty-eight hours ago, she'd been wearing her orange parka and dodging Brian.

Now, she was showing more skin than ever in this spaghetti-strapped, sunflower yellow sundress and standing in a bedroom decorated with a beach motif. Over the bed hung a scenic print of a sunset descending over voluptuous sand dunes with the words "Beach Happy" splashed across it, which intentionally or not on the artist's part, made her think of Pharrell's song "Be Happy".

She looked at herself in the dresser mirror. The sundress was designed to hug all the right places and hide all the so-called wrong places. Happy with how she looked, she slid her feet into her silver sandals. She put her cellphone into the dainty over-the-shoulder purse that Sofia had picked out for her — instructing her to get rid of the big purse that looked like a diaper bag and would scare off any potential suitors.

As she made her way out of the bedroom and towards the back patio, she saw that Jack was in the kitchen, transferring a sheet pan loaded with baked white fish, peppers, and onions onto a serving platter.

"¡Hola, mi amiga! You look beautiful." Jack stopped what he was doing and looked at her in admiration, smiling.

Heather blushed. "Thank you."

"So, what are you up to now? I'm making dinner for the family. Everyone's at Yolanda's house across the street if you would like to join us," Jack suggested.

"Oh, that's so sweet of you, but I think I'll postpone the criticism and judgment for another night," Heather joked.

"Don't be like that!" Jack laughed.

"My plan is to order something for dinner and sit by the pool. Sofia's picking me up in a couple of hours, and then we're going dancing. But why are you making the fish here if they're all over there?" Heather asked.

"Yolanda doesn't like the smell of baked fish in her house," Jack explained.

"Wow, so she stinks up Maria's house?" Heather exclaimed.

Jack laughed. "I understand Maria's mother can be a bit much at times."

Heather wanted to say more, but taking her sister Sara's advice to watch her temper, and Pam's advice to just have fun, she settled for an eye roll.

"Why not save your money? I can make up a plate for you. There's plenty," Jack suggested.

"Hmmm … I did spend a bit of money buying new clothes today," Heather agreed.

"Have you ever had tamales?" Jack asked, excitedly.

"No, never. What are they?" Heather asked.

"Ah, you'll love them. I'm going to bring this platter over to the family, and then I'll be back with a plate of food for you." Jack winked at her.

"Sounds good," Heather smiled, thinking to herself that he sure did wink a lot.

"There's some Chardonnay and Rosé in the fridge. Help yourself," Jack said as he finished snapping the cover onto the platter of fish.

"I'll get the door for you," Heather said as she walked over to the front door and opened it for him.

"Gracias," Jack said as he carefully balanced the platter in his hands.

"I'll leave the door slightly open for you, so you can easily get back in," Heather said as she gently shut the door half-way.

She walked back into the kitchen, peered into the fridge and found a bottle of Rosé nestled in the door shelving. After opening a few drawers, she found a corkscrew and then snooped through a few more cupboards until she found a floral, plastic goblet. She happily uncorked the bottle, filled her goblet to the top and was going to put the Rosé back in the fridge, but then changed her mind and decided to bring it with her.

Heather pushed open the sliding door, leaving it open behind her for Jack, and entered the lanai. As she stepped outside, she noticed the evening sky was beginning to darken, and the air was cooling down. A fresh breeze rustled through the palm trees.

Feeling relaxed, she exited through the lanai's screen door, entered the outdoor dining area, and sat down on one of the sturdy dining table chairs. Then she started to wonder what a tamale was. What had she just agreed to eat?

She took a long sip of wine, picked up her phone, and looked up "tamale". Her search results showed that it seemed to be slow-cooked meat, either pork or chicken, mixed with corn, and it was either wrapped in a corn husk or a banana leaf and then steamed. She figured that it sounded pretty good.

Leaning back into her chair, she clicked on her reading app and scrolled through to the amusing novel. But before she could start reading, a message from Pam popped up on her screen telling her that she'd just met Maria and Phil and that she seemed lovely.

Heather wrote back to Pam:

Happy to hear. I knew she'd be a lovely person!

She realized that Pam had never seen her with hair this short or even this glossed up.

She held the phone away from her, high up at an angle, and then tried hitting the capture button but couldn't quite reach it. On her second attempt, she yelled "Cheese!", hoping the voice command setting would kick in and take the picture for her. Nothing happened. Frustrated, she brought the phone down in front of her and looked down into the camera. She fiddled with the angle until there was no sign of a double chin. Satisfied with how she looked, she smiled and hit the capture button. As she sent it to Pam, she realized it was the first time she'd ever taken a selfie. She chuckled to herself, thinking that now that she was so glossed up, she was becoming vain. At least she hadn't done duck lips. Her phone immediately dinged.

Pam's message read:

Wow!! You look absolutely gorgeous! Stunning! Like a supermodel!

Heather wrote back:

Sweet of you to say! xoxoxox

She decided the nice thing to do would be to text Maria and make sure everything was okay. She'd been so focused on her own issues that she'd forgotten Maria must be going through her own stuff, too.

Heather texted:

Hi Maria, I heard you've met Pam and wanted to check-in. Hope you're having a good time.

But then, she second-guessed herself. What if it sounded like she hoped Maria was having a "good time" with Phil? She didn't want Maria to think that Sofia had let it slip about what had possibly happened in just one night between the two of them. Heather deleted the last sentence and changed it to: *Hope everything is going well.*

She got an immediate response from Maria:

Hi Heather, I'm having a lovely time. Your house, bakery, everything, it's all great. Exactly what I was looking for. I hope you're having a wonderful time too.

Heather thought it best not to mention what had happened between her and Yolanda, so she wrote back:

Glad to hear that. Yes, I'm having a wonderful time with Sofia. You're lucky to have such a great friend.

Maria wrote:

Yes, she's the best. Gotta run, have a nice evening.

Heather wrote:

Thanks, you too!

Then she texted her shop manager, Martha:

Hi Martha, how did it go today? Is Maria helping out okay?

Martha wrote:

Maria's doing great, but I need to tell you something before you hear it through the grapevine. Mrs. Franklin ate an oatmeal pot cookie by accident.

Heather wrote:

What? Little, old Mrs. Franklin? You're joking, right?

Martha wrote:

Nope, not joking. That's the one. Who we've never ever heard laugh. Ever.

Heather wrote:

Wound tighter than a tootsie roll. Well ... did it make her laugh?

Martha wrote:

Oh, yeah. Made her laugh. And sing.

Heather wrote:

Sing? What did she sing?

Martha wrote:

Girls just wanna have fun LOL

Heather wrote:

Good for her!

Martha wrote:

She ordered some 'of the same' cookies to go.

Heather wrote:

Really? And, she was there with her church group?

Martha wrote:

Oh, yeah! 😄 You're not upset?

Heather wrote:

Not at all! She deserves a bit of fun!

Heather was giggling uncontrollably at this piece of gossip and realized that in the past, she would've tried to find out exactly what circumstances had led to Mrs. Franklin accidentally getting a pot cookie, but at this point, being down here in Florida, so far away from it all, she really didn't care.

As if to test her patience further, a new text came in from Brian saying that he was going to miss her at Sunday dinner. She took a deep breath and decided to ignore it like the others and that's when she heard Jack tapping on the screen door, so she set her phone down and walked over to open the door for him.

Jack gave her a toothy smile as he set the two dinner plates down onto the dining table, proudly pointing out, "here we have the tamales and some baked tilapia with peppers and some steamed rice."

"Looks delicious. Thank you so much," Heather said, still slightly giggling from Martha's texts.

Jack pulled out two sets of cutlery from his pockets and placed one set in front of Heather and the other beside his plate of food. He sat down on a chair beside Heather, pulling an unopened beer out of his pocket and twisting it open.

"Yolanda won't be upset if you're spending time with me?" Heather asked and then immediately regretted it.

"Ha! Not at all. I made a special drink for her tonight; she's in her happy place." Jack winked again, and Heather chuckled.

She began unwrapping one of the tamales he'd given her. It was hot, so she had to keep blowing on her fingers. When she finally managed to open it, she looked down at a glistening, greyish lump. She took a sip of wine.

"By the way, thank you so much for this morning. Your smoothie really helped me get over that hangover," Heather said, smiling at him.

"Sounds like you might need another one tomorrow morning as well," Jack smirked.

"Yeah, probably," Heather guffawed as she filled up her goblet once more.

Hesitating, she took a tiny forkful of the tamale and placed it in her mouth. The texture was mushy and slightly unpleasant, but then its savory flavours reached her palate.

"Oh wow, that's actually quite good!" Heather said in surprise.

"You sound surprised," Jack teased.

"It's just that I've never had anything like this before," Heather explained.

"I do have a surprise for you!" Jack exclaimed as he took out his phone.

"What? You barely know me. How could you possibly have a surprise for me?" Heather teased as she took another forkful of the food.

"Hey, I'm good at picking up on things. I like to think I'm a pretty observant guy," Jack said confidently.

"Who keeps his lips sealed." Heather raised an eyebrow.

"Ha! True enough." Jack smiled at her.

"What's the surprise?" Heather took another sip of wine.

Jack smirked, "answer me, yes or no. You have a crush? ... Admiration? ... For a certain famous baker?"

Heather gave him a puzzled look. "You couldn't possibly mean Chef Lars Borgen?"

"That's the one," Jack confirmed proudly.

"How in blooming hell did you figure that out?" Heather was shocked.

"If I'm being honest, it was quite easy. I looked up your shop's website and saw that you mention him as one of your biggest role models." Jack grinned, not revealing that he was also impressed by the fact that she'd won Readers' Choice awards a few years in a row and had won Best New Bakery.

"Okay, score one for Jack. What about him?" Heather beamed.

"He's going to be calling us in 3, 2, 1 ..." Jack's phone started ringing, and he answered the video call.

"Hey, buddy! Thanks so much for calling. Really appreciate it. Here's my good friend, Heather, who is a fellow baker and a huge fan." Jack shifted the phone so that Heather was included in the video.

Heather flushed with excitement and flashed a big smile into the camera.

"Hiiii! Sorry if I'm about to come across as a dorky fan ... Jack sprung this video call on me literally just now ... So, I'm just going to say it ... I love love love all your recipes .... But especially the one for chocolate chip skillet cookies. I make it all the time and must confess it's a bestseller ... Although now that I'm thinking about it, I probably shouldn't be telling you this ... You're going to start asking for a cut. Blooming hell, I have a big mouth!" Heather yelled, laughing into the phone.

Chef Borgen was howling with laughter at Heather's confession.

"Heck no ... My recipes are out there for a reason. And I'm flattered to the core that such a beautiful woman as yourself is making them. I would love for you to come visit my test kitchen tomorrow. Would you like that?" Lars asked in a loud, booming voice.

"Are you serious?" Heather gaped at him.

"I'm dead serious," Lars chuckled. "If Jack says I should meet someone, I listen to him."

"Well, I'm playing tennis with Sofia in the morning. I could come by after lunch?" Heather was shaking with excitement.

"Sounds like a plan. I'll text you the details. See you tomorrow!" And with that, Lars hung up the phone.

Heather looked at Jack in awe.

"Can I hug you?" Heather asked.

"Yes, of course!" Jack laughed.

They both stood up from the table, and Heather gave him a big hug.

"Thank you so much! This is amazing! You're amazing!" Heather couldn't contain her excitement.

"You're very welcome. I wanted to do something nice for you because of the whole Yolanda situation." Jack smiled warmly, having heard the story of what had happened during Heather's arrival at Maria's house.

"How do you know Lars? From the food industry?" Heather asked.

"Heck, no. We go to the same tattoo studio," Jack smirked.

"Haha! Cool. Well, it seems like I have a lot to thank you for ... dinner, this introduction ..." Heather gushed.

"Ah, my pleasure. What's your number? Put it in my phone and then I'll send it to Lars," Jack asked as he handed over his phone, and Heather typed in her number.

Feeling exhilarated, Heather quickly ate some more of her dinner, had a couple more sips of Rosé, and then said, "Thank you so much for everything again."

"You're welcome. Would you like dessert?"

"Thank you, but no. I should start getting ready. I'll see you tomorrow?" Heather gave him a big smile.

"Yes, for sure," Jack nodded.

Heather reached for her plates, but Jack jumped in, "nope, I got it. You go."

"Thank you again," Heather smiled and then made her way back to her designated bedroom.

Once there, she decided to text Sofia. Her hands were shaking with excitement as she wrote:

Hi Sofia! When will you be here?

Her phone dinged, and Sofia's message read:

30 minutes?

Heather wrote:

Perfect! See you then. I have news!!

She brushed her teeth, fixed her make-up, and changed into the blue pleather pants and sparkly tank top that Sofia had helped pick out for her.

As she waited outside on the driveway for Sofia, she could hear the low murmur of voices and music coming from Yolanda's house across the street. A few minutes later, a black sedan pulled into the driveway, and Heather slid into the backseat with Sofia.

"Hiya!" Heather said excitedly to both the driver and Sofia. The driver nodded hello.

"Hola," Sofia said as they leaned in and air-kissed each other on both cheeks. "I've told the driver to take us to the main entrance of the barrio and then we can pick a place once we get there. But, what's your news?"

"I'm still in shock. I'm going to meet my idol, Chef Lars Borgen! Thanks to Jack!" Heather pumped her arms up and down with joy.

"Wow, that's amazing! I told you Jack was a lovely guy," Sofia beamed at her.

"You did!" Heather smiled.

"I have some interesting news, too. I talked to Tonya and she completely denies leaving those nasty reviews about La Gordita restaurant," Sofia explained.

"That's a relief! But I wonder who's doing it, then?" Heather frowned.

"I'm glad we didn't jump to any conclusions. By the way, you look absolutely beautiful," Sofia said.

"So do you. Oh! I have a present for you!" Heather rummaged through her small purse and found the gift card she'd secretly bought for Sofia at one of the clothing stores they'd visited that day. "I wanted to thank you for organizing my makeover."

As Sofia took the gift card, she said, "you shouldn't have, but thank you."

"Electric" by Katy Perry was playing over the car stereo, and to the driver's amusement, they sang along, despite being slightly out-of-tune:
"In the dark when you feel lost
Wanna be the best but at what cost?
If you're gonna stay here
Nothing's ever changing, no
Big world, gotta see it all
Gotta get up even when you fall
There's no point in waiting —"
"Don't want to interrupt the outstanding karaoke, but we're here, ladies," the driver chuckled as he slowed down to a stop at the side of the road.

Heather peered out the window and saw that they were stopped at the entranceway to a cobblestoned, pedestrian-only area where there were restaurants and bars all festively decorated with Christmas lights.

They thanked the young driver and got out. Standing on the cobblestoned street, they looked around and noticed a line up outside one of the clubs. Near its front entrance were strobe lights crisscrossing each other and casting strands of purplish light up into the night sky.

"Let's go there." Sofia pointed towards it.

"Looks promising," Heather agreed.

They joined the lineup and were happy that the line moved pretty quickly and they easily made their way into the club after showing their I.D.

Once inside, it was quite dark and they only managed to catch glimpses of clubgoers' faces thanks to the neon strobe lights that roamed sporadically about the place. The dance music was thumping loudly, and they realized they would have to shout in order to hear each other.

"Let's get a drink!" Heather yelled.

Sofia nodded, and they pushed their way over to the shiny bar.

"What should we get?" Heather hollered.

"Cosmos?" Sofia suggested.

"Yes!" Heather happily agreed and then turned to the bartender. Holding up two fingers, she yelled, "dos Cosmos, por favor!"

The bartender nodded at her in acknowledgement as he finished up with another customer. Heather leaned against the bar and continued to look around. The dance floor was packed and bordering it were several lounge areas where people were sitting and chatting. She was relieved to see the crowd was a mix of all ages, although most of them looked Latin. She noticed a pack of girls leaving a nearby sectional sofa and nudged Sofia.

"Quick! Go get those seats! I'll bring the drinks over!" Heather yelled.

Sofia nodded and elbowed her way through the crowd to the empty sofa where she spread herself out in an effort to save enough space for the two of them.

Knowing time is money when it comes to making drinks, the bartender finished making them in record speed, and Heather gave him a healthy tip. Holding the drinks up high so they wouldn't get knocked over, she hip-checked her way through the crowd to the sofa, handing one of the drinks over to Sofia and then plopping herself down beside her.

"¡Salud!" They yelled as they clinked glasses.

Heather watched in angst as two middle-aged, blond men wearing brightly coloured golf shirts and khaki shorts meandered over and sat down across from them. The two men stared at them uncomfortably. Heather noticed their dark tans had left them with reverse raccoon eyes from where their sunglasses had been. One of the men smiled at them.

"Greetings," he yelled in a strange, thick accent, "I'm Nathan, and this is my brother, Noah."

"Hello. I'm Sofia and this is Heather. Can't quite place your accent. British?" Sofia asked.

"We're from down under," Nathan explained.

"Down under where?" Sofia was confused.

"Haha! Made ya say 'underwear'," Nathan laughed.

Heather and Sofia cringed.

"You have to excuse my brother. Can't take him anywhere," Noah yelled.

"What? Can't take a joke?" Nathan chided.

Heather rolled her eyes, and Sofia pursed her lips.

"We're from Australia. You two from 'round 'ere?" Noah asked.

"Just visiting for Christmas." Heather kept her answer as short as possible.

"Visiting from whereabouts?" Noah asked.

"A town near Toronto, Canada." Heather pronounced the city like most Canadians do, as Trawno.

"Never heard of it." Noah shook his head.

"Sorry, Tor-ron-tow," Heather enunciated.

"Oh, righto. What'd you call it before?" Noah asked.

"Trawno," Heather said, embarrassed.

"Trahna," Noah tried to mimic Heather.

"Yeah, that's it," Heather lied.

"Isn't it freezing there?" Nathan asked.

"Well, yes. It can get really cold. Like, minus twenty-five Celsius. Oh, um." Heather picked up her phone and yelled, "hey, Google, what's minus twenty-five Celsius in Fahrenheit?"

There was complete silence.

"She can't hear me," Heather explained.

"Oh, we go by Celsius, too," Noah said dismissively.

"I see my friends have arrived," Sofia said swiftly.

Heather was confused and then realized Sofia was giving them a polite out, so she added, "nice to meet you."

"Righto. Nice meeting you ladies," Noah said, and Nathan gave them a wave.

Sofia and Heather picked up their Cosmos and wandered through the crowd.

"We didn't come here to talk about the weather!" Sofia yelled into Heather's ear. Or underwear, Heather smirked.

"Let's finish these and go dance!" Heather yelled as she pointed to their Cosmos.

The enthusiastic rhythm of the Latin music was catching. Sofia nodded, and they drained their Cosmos. They set their empty glasses at the edge of the bar and shoved their way through the tightly packed dance floor while purple and blue strobe lights flashed about erratically. "Timber" by Pitbull was playing.

"Wait a minute! Let's do a shot first! I need some more liquid courage!" Heather yelled as a waitress with a tray of shots hanging around her neck approached them.

"How much?" Heather yelled.

"Two dollars a shot! It's Sex on the Beach!" The girl yelled back.

Heather gave her a ten-dollar-bill and yelled, "Four shots, please! Keep the change!"

The girl waited as Sofia and Heather downed two shots each, returning the empty glasses to the tray. She smiled and continued onwards.

"Okay, ready!" Heather yelled as she started to dance, trying to follow the moves of the other clubgoers around her.

"You're doing great, but you have to move your hips more!" Sofia yelled.

"Like this?" Heather tried to shake her hips back and forth.

"Yeah, kinda. Here, let me get behind you and move you. Is that okay?" Sofia asked, and Heather shrugged.

Sofia snuggled up behind Heather and put her hands on either side of Heather's hips.

The Pitbull song ended, and "Hips Don't Lie" by Shakira started up. Sofia guided Heather, and they were both moving in unison to the beat of the music. A few clubgoers whistled at them.

"You got it!" Sofia yelled.

At that, Heather turned around and faced Sofia. They danced in perfect tandem, both smiling and working up a slight sweat.

The song ended, and Heather yelled, "let's take a break!"

"Sure, let's get another Cosmo!" Sofia yelled back.

They exited the crowded dance floor and jostled their way back to the bar again, just as the DJ began to make an announcement.

"Ladies and Gentlemen ... Welcome to our annual Mr. Claus contest! The men have been busy backstage getting ready for you! Please join us as they put on a show just for you! At the end of the show, you'll vote for the best Mr. Claus! Put your hands together and make some noise!" The DJ's voice boomed and echoed around the room.

"Looks like we picked the right place after all!" Sofia giggled.

At that, the dark blue velvet curtain that had been hiding the stage behind the dance floor lifted to reveal a lineup of young, bare-chested men sporting red, shiny thongs and Santa hats. The DJ began playing "It's Raining Men".

MUNICH
SUNDAY, DECEMBER 22

Brian was wandering the upstairs hallway of Heather's house. He was desperate to find her. He opened the door to her bedroom to see if she was in there. It was empty. Disappointed, he kept walking down the hallway. He opened the door to the bathroom, and its pinkness vibrated at him, hurting his eyes, so he immediately closed it.

He continued walking down the hallway. It felt like he'd been walking for hours. He kept putting one foot in front of the other, but the door to the second bedroom seemed to be floating farther and farther away. He was getting tired and decided to stop and have a rest. He slid all the way down to the floor and leaned his body sideways against the stairway railing, and then he closed his eyes.

When he opened his eyes a few minutes later, he found himself sitting sluggishly on the floor in the second bedroom. Heather's pantry room. He heard some scuffling noises and saw that Heather was standing in front of her wire shelving with a clipboard in her hand. She was naked under her sunflower yellow apron and was wearing fuzzy slippers.

Brian opened his mouth to speak, but she held up a finger to shush him. He jumped as a mouse ran by his foot and he briefly wondered where Charlotte was. Heather continued to ignore him and kept checking things off her clipboard.

Disobeying her orders, he opened his mouth to speak again, but this time, no sounds came out. He knew he had something really important to tell her, and was frustrated that he couldn't get the words out.

He noticed a shadow pass by, and when he looked up, he saw Elsa's face floating outside of the bedroom window. She was wearing a smug smile that spread from ear-to-ear across her face.

There was a knock at the door.

Not now, there's something I need to say, Brian thought angerly.

The knocking got louder.

Frustrated, and with all his might, he tried to yell "go away" but ended up jolting himself awake. He instantly realized he wasn't in Heather's house after all, but was in his own bed, covered in sweat.

"Brian! It's time to get up! Your brother's going to be here soon! It's the least you can do!"

It was his mother who'd been knocking at his door.

"Yeah, yeah, getting up!" He yelled back, disgruntled.

MUNICH
SUNDAY, DECEMBER 22

Phil had shoved all of their purchases into the big bag that held Maria's leather boots, so that they could stroll along the snow-covered streets, hand-in-hand. Some of the sidewalks were shovelled, and some were not. For fun, Maria occasionally piggy backed onto Phil's back, and he easily carried her across the snow-laden sidewalks. When they reached a particular driveway, Phil slowed down and stopped.

"Here we are!" He exclaimed excitedly.

Maria kissed him gently on his cheek as she slid down from his back and quietly dropped onto the pathway.

"This is my parents' house!" Phil raised his arms and presented Maria with a Bavarian-style house that had a silver Mercedes SUV parked in its driveway.

"It's gorgeous," Maria whispered.

"Yes, much better than the old farmhouse we grew up in. I swear it was haunted," Phil shivered.

"Haha! What do I need to know before we go in?" Maria said, realizing she probably should've asked sooner.

"Truth be told, Mum is going to love you. Actually, Pop will too. Can you handle being so well liked?" Phil smirked, leaving out the fact that his mother would probably be planning their wedding by the end of the evening.

"I can handle that," Maria laughed.

"But can you do me a favour, for now? Can we just tell them we know each other through, uh, mutual friends and ran into each other on the plane?" Phil asked shyly, gently grabbing both of her hands.

"Why?" Maria asked, confused.

"Because I just don't want my parents to, you know, judge you because of my past mistakes," Phil explained shyly.

"Okay, and what about your brother?" Maria asked.

"Yeah, and maybe don't mention you're staying at Heather's house," Phil said, cringing.

Maria stopped smiling and dropped his hands.

"So, basically, you're telling me to lie to your parents about everything the first time I meet them?" Maria exclaimed, slightly exasperated. "Then where am I staying? Why am I here?"

"Yeah, I think maybe the vaguer, the better. Just say you're here visiting a friend," Phil suggested.

"You know, maybe I should go back to Heather's. I don't think this is a good idea, after all. As you said, we're probably rushing things," Maria said, frustrated.

Phil realized his mistake and interjected in a panicky voice, "no, no, no. Forget what I said about my mistakes. Do it for Heather instead. Remember, she doesn't want Brian knowing she's swapped houses with you? ... But let me go in first."

"Fine," Maria relented, hazily recalling what she'd promised Sofia and Heather.

Phil stamped his boots on the outdoor welcome mat to get rid of the excess snow, and Maria followed suit. Phil opened the heavy wooden door and entered the foyer.

"Hello! I'm home!" Phil yelled into the vast foyer and then turned to Maria, "here, I'll take your coat." Phil's face turned to panic as he remembered Maria was wearing his mum's coat.

His mum yelled from the kitchen, "Phil! I got the strangest phone call today from Mrs. Hubert. She said that she saw you at the farmers' market with some young hottie who sounds like she's way out of your league –" His mother stopped mid-sentence as she entered the large foyer, her smirk turning to surprise at the sight of Maria.

"Mum, this is Maria," Phil said, trying to hide his discomfort at what his mother had been saying.

"Nice to meet you … Is that my coat?" Ursula gave them a puzzled look as she dried her hands on a dish towel.

"Nice to meet you, too. And yes, it is. I really appreciate you lending it to me. I kind of came here in a hurry," Maria said as sweetly as she could.

Ursula gave Phil a what-have-you-gotten-yourself-into-now look and then turned back to Maria with a bright smile.

"Oh, my pleasure. You must be the gorgeous girl Mrs. Hubert was telling me about. My coat suits you," Ursula greeted her brightly.

She was a short, slim woman who had the same lovely blue eyes and thick blond hair as Phil. Her hair was cut short with layers stylized into soft peaks around her pretty face. She was wearing a white, cotton blouse with the collar popped up, over a pair of slim jeans. A floral apron was tied around her waist.

Maria's instinct was to air-kiss Ursula on both cheeks, but after Pam's obvious discomfort, she changed her mind and held out her hand to shake Ursula's, to which Ursula responded by swatting it away with the dish towel, and then opened her arms up to give Maria a warm embrace.

"Don't be silly. Come here, girl," Ursula said, smiling.

As Maria fell into the embrace, she enjoyed the delicate, floral scent of Ursula's perfume.

"I hope it's okay that I invited Maria to dinner. We, uh, know each other through mutual acquaintances and, uh, happened to run into each other on the plane. I wanted Maria to experience Brian's cooking!" Phil said, giving Ursula his best puppy dog eyes.

"Oh, my goodness, yes, of course! The more the merrier! This is perfect because there's been a slight change in plans. Your father and brother are watching TV in the basement, if you want to join them. Maria, come help me in the kitchen," Ursula said, taking control of the situation.

Phil looked startled and was about to say something, but Ursula gave him a don't-you-dare look, and he shut his mouth.

"I'd love to," Maria said, recognizing that something wasn't quite right.

"Oh, Mum, here are the bottles of pinot grigio you asked me to pick up," Phil said as he took the bottles out of the bag and handed them to her.

"Thanks, darling," Ursula smiled as she took the wine.

Ursula waited while they took off their coats and boots and tucked them away in the large front hall closet. Maria took out her phone and the small apple strudel, and then put her purse and the big bag at the bottom of the closet.

"I didn't want to come empty-handed, so I brought you an apple strudel," Maria said as she presented the box to Ursula.

"My favourite! Very sweet of you, Maria. Bring it with you into the kitchen," Ursula instructed.

"I'll see you in a bit," Phil said as he stood at the top of the stairs, both of them wanting a goodbye kiss, but not wanting to do so in front of Ursula. Instead, Phil gave Maria a clumsy wave as he descended the stairs to the basement.

"Yep, see you soon," Maria said as she gave a tiny wave back and then turned to follow Ursula to the kitchen.

Maria and Ursula walked along the dark corridor, passing a family room with soft, chestnut-coloured furniture neatly arranged around a low coffee table. She noticed a large painting, most likely oil, of a farmhouse hanging on one of the walls and wondered if that was the farmhouse Phil had mentioned earlier. It did look kind of spooky.

They passed a dining room with a live edge table set for four and ultimately turned left into a spacious kitchen. Unlike Maria's white and stainless-steel kitchen, Ursula's was full of contrasts and colour.

Ursula put the wine in a mounted rack on the wall and motioned for Maria to put the strudel on the rich brown countertop beside the copper farmhouse sink. A mosaic backsplash framed the wall above the sink, and there were decorative copper molds carefully hanging in the space between the tall white cupboards and the ceiling.

In the middle of the kitchen, there was a huge rectangular island with the same rich brown countertop, and beyond that, there was an alcove with a white dinette that overlooked a screened-in porch.

"You have a beautiful home," Maria remarked politely. She felt the warmth of the décor and the care in which each piece had been thoughtfully put in its rightful place.

"Thank you," Ursula said as she inspected the bubbling slow cooker that sat on the kitchen counter by the stove. Happy with how it looked, Ursula picked up her martini glass, took a sip, and then exclaimed, "oh, where are my manners! Would you care for a cocktail?"

Maria blurted, "I'll have what you're having!"

"A gin martini it is, then," Ursula smiled and walked over to the bar cart that was set along the wall in the space between the kitchen and the dinette.

She picked up a stainless-steel shaker, gave it a quick jiggle, then removed the cap and carefully poured the contents into a fresh martini glass. Maria tried to take it from Ursula, but she wouldn't let her.

"Not yet. You need garnish," Ursula said as she put the drink down onto the kitchen island and opened the fridge door.

While Ursula was busy with the garnish, Maria noticed the wall art hanging above the bar cart. She read it silently to herself:

"Seven Rules of Life" was its title. Rule number one: Let things go. Never ruin a good day by thinking about a bad yesterday. Rule number two: Smile. It's okay to smile even when things are tough. Rule number three: Stay focused. It's okay to not have everything figured out because in time, you'll get there. Rule number four: Give it time. Time puts everything into perspective. Rule number five: Don't compare. The only person you should compare yourself to is the person you were yesterday —

"Here you go, dear," Ursula said as she interrupted Maria's reading, and handed her the drink.

Maria saw that it now contained a diamond-headed cocktail pick with five stuffed olives lined up and leaning against the side of the glass.

"Thank you," Maria tried to take a sip, but was taken aback by how strong it was.

"Too strong for you? I can add in some more vermouth, if you like," Ursula offered, half-smiling.

"Not necessary," Maria said as she tried again to take a sip. "May I ask, what kind of wood this is?" Maria put her glass down on the kitchen island and ran her hand over the countertop's rich texture.

"The countertops? They're made from black walnut trees," Ursula explained, her eyes twinkling, "very hearty trees that make for very solid, resistant-to-anything counters, if you know what I mean."

Maria thought she knew what Ursula meant, but wasn't about to go there. "I had no idea. It's so beautiful. We have boring, white granite countertops in my kitchen."

"In Miami?" Ursula asked as she sipped her martini.

"Near there. It's a city called Boca Bonita," Maria said, still marveling at the beauty of Ursula's kitchen.

"I'm guessing you don't know how to make spaetzle?" Ursula asked, abruptly changing the subject.

"Excuse me?" Maria was puzzled.

"You've never heard of spaetzle?" Ursula pointed to a doughy mixture sitting in a bowl.

"No, can't say I've ever heard of it. I'm Colombian, and my family, we kind of stick to our own kinds of food. But I'd love to learn about it. Your son taught me all about sausages, today." In horror, Maria realized what she'd just said. "I mean, at the farmers' market. The sausages at the deli in the farmers' market."

Ursula guffawed and winked at her, "yes, I'm sure he did."

Maria felt mortified and started tripping over her words. "My family, we eat mainly chicken, rice and vegetables. Jack cooks us healthy meals."

"Is Jack your dad?" Ursula asked as she ate an olive and then took another sip of her martini.

"No, he's ... our chef." Maria mentally kicked herself for letting this out; she always tried to keep their lives sounding as normal as possible.

"Chef? You own a restaurant?" Ursula asked, puzzled.

"No, he cooks for my family. We're all super busy and don't have time to cook," Maria explained, ready to take on any judgement or jealousy that followed when people found this out.

To her relief, Ursula looked impressed.

"How lucky! Just between you and me, Maria, I'm so tired of cooking. Actually, it's Brian who's been doing most of the cooking for the past few months, but he flaked out on me today. He promised that he was going to make this meal for Phil, and look ... here I am," Ursula said, pointing to the slow cooker.

Maria now felt bad for Ursula, which made new thoughts jump into her about Jack and how he and her brother Gabriel must be judging her hasty decision to leave home during Christmas. She tried to push these unhelpful thoughts from her mind.

Ursula continued, "which is why I'm so happy you're here! So, spaetzle is a German egg noodle. I would love to show you how to make it, if you like? It would be such a great help."

"I'm happy to learn." Maria tried to take another sip of the martini, but could only get it to her lips and had to set it back down because the smell of the gin was making her sick.

"I'm happy to teach! So, you're Colombian? What are you doing here? You must be freezing ... Ah, which is why Phil leant you my coat," Ursula said as she checked to see if the pot of chicken stock on the stove was boiling.

Oh no, here we go, the lies, Maria thought.

"A friend of mine asked me to come visit her for Christmas." Maria avoided eye contact as she told the lie.

"A friend? It's a small town; what's her name?" Ursula asked as she opened the fridge doors and began rummaging around.

"Oh, she just moved here a few months ago. That's why she was feeling lonely and asked me to come." Maria felt the lie suck her in deeper.

Ursula nodded vaguely and started cutting up the fresh parsley she'd taken out of the fridge. Steam began escaping from the covered pot on the gas stove. Ursula put on an oven glove, took off the lid, and placed it inside of the sink.

"Ready?" Ursula asked, looking straight at Maria with her ocean-blue eyes, and that's when they both realized that they were the same height.

"Yes." Maria smiled her pretty smile.

"Oh! You can step on the stool," Ursula said, pointing to a plastic stool set up in front of the gas stove.

Maria shrank back.

"There's nothing to be ashamed of. I use it all the time. You might burn yourself otherwise. Go on," Ursula urged her.

Maria slowly stepped onto the stool and waited for her next set of instructions.

Ursula picked up the stainless steel spaetzle maker and explained, "what you need to do is pour half of the batter into the cup part of it, and then you slide it back and forth along the grater, quickly, until all of the batter falls into the pot. Then you do the same with the other half."

"Are you sure you want me to do this? What if I do it wrong?" Maria was getting nervous.

"They're just noodles. There's nothing to mess up." Ursula smiled and firmly placed the spaetzle maker in Maria's hands.

As Maria scooped out the dough from the bowl into the spaetzle maker, Ursula continued to eat olives and sip on her martini.

"Only fill it up half-way," Ursula reminded her.

Maria nodded and saw that it had reached the half-way point, so she held it over the pot of boiling chicken stock.

"Slide the cup back and forth," Ursula encouraged her.

Maria began moving the cup back and forth across the grater as quickly as she could. At first, it was awkward to hold and kept getting stuck, but eventually she got the hang of it and the cup moved smoothly back and forth. Tiny droplets of dough were hitting and sinking into the hot chicken stock.

"There you go!" Ursula exclaimed happily.

When the cup was empty, she looked over at Ursula.

"Did I do it right?" Maria asked, feeling sweaty from the hot steam.

"You did great! You're a natural. Go on, do the rest," Ursula encouraged her as she topped up her own martini.

"I will, but I'm getting kind of hot. Is it okay if I take off my turtleneck? I have a camisole underneath," Maria asked.

Ursula shrugged, and Maria took off her turtleneck, folded it and laid it on one of the island chairs. She then repeated the same movements with the second batch in her beige silk camisole.

"Now give them a quick stir, and then we wait until all the little noodles float to the top. It takes about two minutes," Ursula explained as she handed Maria a spatula.

Maria took the spatula and gave the noodles a quick stir while Ursula set the timer for two minutes. Maria ate one of the olives from the toothpick in her drink and then bravely took a sip of her martini. Surprisingly, it went down a lot more smoothly. Ah, so that's the trick, Maria thought to herself, eat an olive and then take a sip.

"You've earned your place at the table. Well done, girl." Ursula smiled, and Maria beamed back.

"I must say, though, you're quite fit," Ursula remarked as she squeezed Maria's right bicep.

"Ah, thank you," Maria said, surprised at Ursula's brazenness. "I play tennis a few times a week," she explained as she put her turtleneck back on and then ate an olive before taking a few more sips of her martini.

"Good for you. Seeing as I didn't know you were coming; you'll need to set a place for yourself at the table. The dishes and placemats are in that cabinet," Ursula said as she pointed to the tall white cabinet on the other side of the fridge and then walked over to the slow cooker as it had started beeping.

Maria opened the cabinet door and found a stack of blue ceramic plates similar to Heather's. She pulled out a plate and a wine glass and then found a stack of beige placemats and pulled out one of those, too. While Ursula was busy turning off the slow cooker, Maria wandered into the dining room. She wasn't quite sure where to set herself up as there were only four chairs lined up around the table.

As if feeling her uncertainty from the kitchen, Ursula yelled, "set yourself up on the side where the stereo is. I'll get Phil to bring over a chair from the dinette."

Maria moved a place setting over a bit and then set up her placement, plate and wine glass beside it. She ran her fingers along the beautiful live edge dining table, admiring it. When she came back into the kitchen, Ursula was draining the noodles and placing them into a large, white serving bowl. A roast was resting, steaming hot on a white, oval serving platter with chunks of roasted carrots, onion, and broccoli arranged around it.

"Smells delicious. What kind of roast is that?" Maria said, admiring the platter.

"It's veal with a mushroom gravy. The trick is to sear it on all sides first and then slow-cook it. Brian taught me that. Having roasts is kind of our Sunday family dinner tradition," Ursula explained as she sprinkled the fresh parsley that she'd chopped up earlier over top of the roast.

"Phil told me about how you had a farm and grew vegetables?" Maria said, wanting to hear more about his childhood.

"Yes, we did. Please take this out to the table and place it on one of the trivets." Ursula handed her the steaming platter with the roasted veal and vegetables on it.

"The what?" Maria asked, confused by the word.

"The mats on the table," Ursula explained.

"Oh, that's what they're called. I just call them mats," Maria said as she brought the hot platter into the dining room.

"Well, you learn something new every day," Ursula sang out.

"That's so true! I learned a whole bunch of new things today," Maria said as she placed the platter onto the trivet. "Just this morning, I learned how to make hot chocolate and work the cash register at Heather's bakery –" Maria stopped mid-sentence.

Oh no, no, no. This can't be happening, Maria thought as her stomach sank.

Ursula came into the dining room with a puzzled look on her face, holding the bowl of spaetzle.

"What did you just say?" Ursula looked at her with curiosity as she placed the bowl of spaetzle onto the table.

The colour had drained from Maria's face.

"I'm so sorry. I can explain everything," Maria whispered, grabbing Ursula's arm.

"Okay, you better explain quickly before I call them up for dinner," Ursula whispered, leading Maria back into the kitchen.

Maria explained everything in one breath as adrenaline spread throughout her body. "I've exchanged houses with Heather for Christmas. We don't know each other. We met online through a house exchange site. She's staying at my house in Boca Bonita, and I'm staying at hers. Part of the deal was that I help out at her shop. In a strange coincidence, I met Phil on the plane over here, and we hit it off. We don't actually have mutual friends. He told me about Heather and Brian, but doesn't know what happened between them, and didn't want Brian to know about the whole house-exchange thing. I've been here since Saturday night."

"Thank you for telling me the truth. Finally! I knew there was something you weren't telling me. You could barely look me in the eye when you were talking about some imaginary friend," Ursula teased, waving a serving spoon at her.

"I'm so sorry. We didn't want Brian to get more upset than he already is," Maria pleaded.

"And that's why Phil was so late Saturday night. He was with you," Ursula's eyes sparkled. "I knew his story was fishy. I mean, who drives someone home but doesn't actually drive them home? That boy is terrible at making up stories."

"Ha! I really like your son," Maria blushed.

"And I can tell he really likes you, too. I could see it the moment you two walked in," Ursula smiled as she presumptuously topped up Maria's martini.

Maria thought she could see wedding bells dancing above Ursula's head.

"I know how protective Phil can be of his younger brother. And you must be very special to him because he never brings girls home anymore," Ursula confided.

"Yes, he told me a bit about his past," Maria said, trying to sound serious, but the gin was going to her head, and she sounded a bit too happy that Phil had a past.

"So, he did. And you? Are you divorced? A beautiful woman like you must have been married? Or are you still married … You little trollop!" Ursula teased as they both ate another olive before taking a sip of martini.

"Trollop! How dare you!" Maria laughed at Ursula's brazenness once again, "well, if you must know, you nosy woman, I'm separated. I have a daughter who just started college. Her name's Olivia."

"Well, in all seriousness, I'm so glad he's found you. I haven't seen him this happy in years," Ursula giggled.

"Ah, thank you," Maria said, turning pink.

"I guess we better call the boys up before dinner turns to rubber." At that, Ursula walked over to the cordless phone mounted to the kitchen wall and hit the intercom button.

It was picked up right away by Phil.

"Coming!" Was all he yelled.

"Would you like another?" Ursula asked, smiling.

Maria looked at her practically empty martini glass and thought, why not? It was going to be a weird night, so she ate the last olive, tipped back the glass and drained the final few drops.

"Yes, please," Maria nodded.

MIAMI
SUNDAY, DECEMBER 22

Josephine had seen Alonso's serenading video of him singing "You're the Inspiration" by Chicago and had called him back in a whispered hush to tell him that he could come to the hospital, after all, but that he better be discreet about it, or she'd kick him out.

Dressed in a pair of chinos and a purple dress shirt, Alonso was now walking down the hallway towards the waiting room Josephine had directed him to. When he found the allotted waiting room, he sat down in one of the low back armchairs and sent Josephine a text to let her know he'd arrived.

Not long afterward, he could hear the clicking of her heels echoing down the hallway. When she appeared in the doorway of the waiting room, Alonso noticed that she was nicely dressed in a silk blouse over black trousers, which complemented her height and straight posture. He wondered if the outfit had been chosen for his benefit, before she knew she'd be facing a hospital visit and not a hotel visit, and felt relieved that he'd changed out of his tracksuit before coming. At first, she looked harsh, then exhausted, and then she ran to him for comfort.

"I'm so glad you came. This is draining," Josephine said as Alonso wrapped his arms around her, and she nuzzled her head into his shoulder.

"I'm here now. You don't have to do this alone," Alonso whispered.

"Thank you."

"I love you."

"I love you, too."

"Do your kids know he's in the hospital?" Alonso asked.

"I told them he's had an anxiety attack and that I'd let them know more, soon," Josephine explained.

"So, they aren't here?"

"No, not yet. No need. This isn't the way I wanted you to meet them," Josephine sighed.

"Trust me, I know."

"Were you able to change our plane tickets?"

"I had to put them on hold for now, until we know when we can go," Alonso explained.

"I hope you're not mad at me, are you?"

"No, not at all."

"Okay, good, because I'm still a hundred percent with you. I just have to make sure he's okay, and then we can be together. You understand that, right?" Josephine looked into his eyes.

"Yes, of course, I do."

In that instant, they heard alarms coming from her husband's room.

"What's that?" Josephine jumped up.

"I think he's having another attack?" Alonso guessed, frowning.

"I better go!" Joseph yelled, panicking.

"I'm staying right here. I'm not going anywhere!" Alonso yelled after her.

Josephine nodded as she left the comfort of his arms and ran back to the hospital room, heels clicking away from him this time, and Alonso slumped back into his chair.

As he watched Josephine walk away from him in her shapely pants, he thought back to all those times he'd checked out her butt while she waited in line ahead of him at the coffee shop they shared at the bottom of their office building.

He'd finally been rewarded one day when she'd turned to him and smiled. It had been all he'd needed to summon up the courage to ask her out.

After which, it hadn't been long until they'd said the "L" word to each other. During one particularly heated rendezvous, they'd looked at each other and admitted they no longer wanted to sneak around and were fully ready to commit to one other.

MUNICH
SUNDAY, DECEMBER 22

Ursula and Maria could hear the loud stomping of three sets of feet climbing up the oak staircase.

"Smells delicious, Mum," Phil said as he entered the dining room and gave his mother a quick kiss on the cheek.

"Thank you, darling," Ursula said dreamily.

A short, stocky, elderly man entered the dining room directly behind Phil. And then a younger version of the man followed just behind him. They both had curly hair, but the older one's was thinning and graying, while the younger one's was thick and blond. They both were wearing heavy woolen sweaters over dark jeans. All three were carrying empty cans of German beer in their hands.

"Maria, this is my pop, Klaus, and my younger brother, Brian," Phil introduced them to Maria and then explained while emphasizing each word and nodding, "I was just telling them how we ran into each other on the plane over here on Saturday night and that you're here visiting a friend."

"Nice to meet you both. Thank you for having me. I truly appreciate it." Maria smiled politely, while wondering where the heck did Phil get his extraordinary height from?

"Let's get started before dinner gets cold. Phil, please go grab a chair for Maria from the dinette," Ursula said cheerily.

Phil nodded, grabbed the empty beer cans from his brother and dad, and went into the kitchen.

Klaus went over to the stereo system and turned on the radio. The song "Don't Worry, Be Happy" by Bobby McFerrin filled the room. Klaus did a little jig and then sat down at the head of the table. Brian sat down opposite Maria while she stood waiting for Phil to bring the chair over.

She noticed a pained look on Brian's face as he watched Phil bring the chair into the dining room. She wondered if he was thinking about Heather, seeing as she most likely came over for dinner, and this could be her chair that Phil was bringing over.

Ursula went back into the kitchen and brought out their martinis, placing one in front of Maria and the other at her end of the table, across from Klaus.

"Well, I see you gals have been having a bit of fun," Phil's eyes widened at the sight of the martinis. He placed the dinette chair to the right of his chair and motioned for Maria to sit down.

"Why, thank you," she giggled as Phil pushed the chair towards the table as she sat down.

"We've been bonding." Ursula glared cheekily at Phil. "Maria was very kind and helped me make the spaetzle."

"Very sweet of you, Maria, seen as someone flaked out," Phil said as he glared at Brian.

"Sorry, I just …" Brian began and then trailed off.

"Well, thank you, Maria, for helping Mum out," Phil said again, and Ursula gave him a stop-making-a-big-deal-out-of-it look.

"It was quite fun, actually. I've never made spaetzle before, let alone eaten it," Maria admitted.

"We'll be easy on you, then," Klaus said, winking.

"Alright, let's dig in. Ladies, first." Phil took his mother's plate, and knowing his mother's appetite, placed a light portion of veal and spaetzle on it and then a medium portion of vegetables, and handed it back to her.

"Thanks, honey," Ursula said as she took the plate from him.

Phil motioned for Maria to give him her plate.

"The same amount for me. I'm still full from lunch," Maria instructed, as the gin and olives milled about her stomach.

"Gotcha," Phil nodded.

He placed the same small portions for Maria on her plate, handed it back to her, then heaped large portions onto the men's plates, and sat himself down beside Maria.

"Where's the pinot grigio?" Phil asked, looking around the table.

"Sorry, I completely forgot about it! Why don't you go open it up, my dear," Ursula said as she sipped her martini.

Phil nodded and went into the kitchen. As the song "Bobcaygeon" by The Tragically Hip played over the stereo system, they all waited patiently as they listened to the tinkering sounds of Phil opening up a drawer and then popping open the wine bottle.

When he returned to the dining room, Phil asked, "who would like some wine?" and all four of them raised their glasses.

Once he'd filled up all of their glasses, Phil raised his and yelled, "kudos to the chefs!"

"Prost!" They all yelled together, clinking glasses.

"Oh, Maria, you know Prost?" Klaus was impressed.

"Phil taught it to me this afternoon. We had half a beer at the farmers' market. It was some type of beer named after a hacker," Maria explained happily.

Klaus chuckled, "you mean Hacker-Pschorr Kellerbier. That's a sturdy winter beer. Good choice."

Maria giggled at her mistake.

There was a bit of silence as everyone began to dig into their food. Maria put some spaetzle on her fork and placed it in her mouth. It was light and buttery. Then she tried some of the veal and vegetables. The veal was tender and practically melted in her mouth.

"Ursula, everything is truly delicious. Thank you for having me over for dinner last minute," Maria said, feeling quite warm and fuzzy from the martini.

"We're happy to have you," Ursula smiled brightly.

"So, you two ran into each other on the plane over here? And Phil tells me you're Colombian?" Klaus asked in between bites of food.

"Yes, my family is Colombian, but we live near Miami. And um, how we met … Well, it's a funny story, actually. The truth is, I recognized Phil from a video I'd seen." Maria told the lie so smoothly that she almost believed it herself.

Phil was nodding and smiling until it began to sink in as to what Maria was about to say and he began to shake his head vigorously back and forth, making cutting motions across his neck.

"A video?" Klaus asked.

"I recognized him because he's become somewhat of a celebrity." Maria concentrated hard on keeping a straight face, knowing that this story was the perfect distraction they needed from all the questions percolating in everyone's heads.

"A celebrity? Our Phil?" Klaus asked.

"Oh, you didn't know?" Maria mocked.

"You really don't need to tell them. It's not that big of a deal," Phil pleaded, his face starting to redden.

"Oh, I don't need to tell them. I can show them." Maria started to take her cellphone out of her back pocket.

"No cellphones at the table!" Phil shouted.

"We can wait until after dinner," Maria shrugged.

"Pop, she's a Dolphins fan! We have a Dolphins fan in our house!" Phil yelled, pointing at her.

"So sorry to hear this," Klaus jokingly consoled Maria.

"Mum, you have to stop her!" Phil yelled.

"No. There's something going on here and I want to know what it is." Brian demanded, looking back and forth between Phil and Maria, not realizing he was pointing out the obvious.

Ursula pursed her lips and pretended to scrutinize the cellphone-at-the-table dilemma.

"Fine. Just this once." Ursula conceded with a twinkle in her eye.

Maria clicked on the video and held her phone out for everyone to see.

"Wait. I need to put my glasses on," Klaus said as he rummaged through the front pocket of his shirt.

"Bring it closer. I can't see at that angle," Ursula instructed.

"Let me turn down the radio," Klaus said as he got up.

Maria paused the video and then repositioned herself so that everyone could see, and once everyone was happy, she hit play. The video of Phil's encounter with the alligator filled the room.

"Whaaaaa ... Whaaa the fuck ... Whaaat the fuck!" Phil was flailing his arms and running in one spot like a cartoon character, too panicked to actually move. "Is that, is that?" He pointed at the alligator, started to run one way, and then changed his mind and tried to run another, but didn't actually go anywhere.

Maria watched as all three faces turned from disbelief to horror to uncontrollable laughter. Phil covered his face with his hands, humiliated.

"When did this happen?" Klaus giggled.

"Last week," Phil groaned.

"Were you hurt?" Ursula asked in between laughs.

"Just my pride," Phil groaned again.

"Geez, and I thought being the talk of the town was bad enough. You're on the bloody Internet!" Brian chided.

"This is all over the Internet?" Ursula asked in disbelief.

"Yep, all over, and there are memes now, too," Maria said, unable to stop herself from saying more.

"What do you mean there are memes?" Phil asked hysterically.

"What's a meme?" Klaus asked.

"Those funny cartoons your friend Kurt sends you for your birthday, every year," Ursula explained, and Klaus nodded, remembering what they were.

While Phil hid like a turtle, his head fully tucked inside of his blue plaid shirt, Maria read out the captions that bookended the top and bottom of the cartoon caricatures of Phil in a mid-run stance:

"I'd say see ya later, alligator ... But I can't seem to move my legs." Maria giggled, "this one says: When I run. I run hard ... But, like, in one spot," Maria giggled again, "and last one ... I'd give ya the weather report, but I gotta run ... Eventually!"

They were all giggling except for Phil.

Brian was scrolling through his phone to see the memes for himself and said, chuckling, "oh look, it's become a thing! People are posting videos of themselves dressed up as Phil. They're running in one spot while presenting the weather!"

"My life is over," Phil mumbled into his shirt.

"Oh, honey, it's just a bit of fun. I mean, it brought the two of you together, didn't it?" Ursula winked at Maria.

Maria played along, "oh yeah, watching that video definitely endeared me to Phil. I saw him in a more vulnerable light."

"You see!" Ursula exclaimed as Phil slowly took his head out from under his shirt.

"Maybe that's what I need to do. Endear myself to Heather," Brian mumbled soberly into his plate of food, his enthusiasm fading.

Maria looked at Brian and gently said, "you know, if you want to talk about what happened ... Get a female perspective. I'm a good listener. I've helped my daughter and her friends through breakups."

"Thanks, but I don't really know you, so no," Brian mumbled.

"Brian! Don't be so rude!" Ursula scolded him.

"Sorry, Maria," Brian muttered to his plate.

"It's okay," Maria said softly.

"And, sweetheart, remember what the doctor said. You need to stop apologizing and focus on getting better. You're taking your meds, right?" Ursula was worried about the doctor's most recent diagnosis that Brian could have a bipolar disorder.

"Yes, Mum." Brian began to sob quietly.

Everyone shared uncomfortable looks, not knowing what to do until Klaus broke the silence.

"Brian, please stop it. That's enough already. You need to grow up and move on," Klaus said gruffly, which only made Brian sob harder.

Maria took a sip of martini she was now immune to and decided to lighten things up by asking, "how did you two meet?"

"Me and Ursula?" Klaus asked, and his shoulders began to visibly relax.

Maria nodded.

"I came to Canada when I was ten years old. We were sponsored to come here by my father's great-aunt, who had immigrated from Germany years earlier. There was nobody left back home. My parents had nothing. The four of us lived in one room in her farmhouse. I had an older brother." Klaus seemed to be lost in his own thoughts.

"Oh, Klaus, nobody wants to hear about those depressing stories," Ursula said, embarrassed.

"She wants to hear how we met. She needs context. It wasn't on some fancy plane ride with Internet videos. Life was hard, and you had to be tough," Klaus explained.

Everyone stayed silent. Even Brian's sobbing subsided.

Klaus continued, "Ursula's life was hard, too. You were orphaned during the war, and a couple from Canada adopted you. You lived in Guelph for a while, and then you moved here to Munich the summer you turned fourteen, and I turned sixteen. I saw you riding your bicycle down Main Street. And I remember thinking, who rides a bicycle in a white sundress and sandals?"

Ursula smiled alluringly at him.

Phil looked at his mum with admiration and murmured, "impressive."

"I followed you home one afternoon on my own bicycle, to see where you lived and then came back the next morning – after I'd done my morning chores around the farm, of course – and rang the bell," Klaus continued nostalgically.

"Kinda stalkery, but also very gutsy of you, Pop." Phil gave him a nod of approval.

"Who answered the door?" Brian asked, gaining more interest in the story.

"Her mother answered the door. I introduced myself and said that I was Klaus from the Müller farm and was wondering if I had permission to take her daughter into town for a milkshake," Klaus said proudly.

"And what did she say?" Brian asked.

"Well, hang on a second; let me finish. I went on to tell her my intentions were completely respectable, and I would have her back by two that afternoon because I had to be back at the farm for the rest of my chores," Klaus continued.

"What did she do?" Phil asked.

"She chuckled and said not in a million years and slammed the door in my face," Klaus guffawed.

"I've never heard this story before," Brian murmured.

"Me neither," Phil said, confused, "did you know, Mum?"

Ursula gave him a cheeky half-smile.

Klaus continued, "well, I always wanted to get to the good part when I did actually take her out for that milkshake, but I think you two need to know that nothing comes easy."

"I think we already know that, Pop," Phil said soberly.

Brian muttered something indistinguishable under his breath.

"So, how did you end up meeting and going for that milkshake?" Maria prodded.

This time Ursula spoke, nostalgically, "when school started, I noticed him in the hallways. He was tanned and fit from all that farmwork. I know a good thing when I see one."

"Ugh, Mum." Phil was embarrassed.

"One day, I was riding my bicycle home, and I hadn't realized that one of the tires was slowly going flat until it was too late," Ursula shrugged.

"And I came to the rescue," Klaus said satisfactorily.

Ursula gave Maria a private look that told her it was no accident, and Maria shot back a look of approval.

Klaus continued, "your mother was way out of my league."

Maria noticed Phil cringe at the expression.

"Her father was a lawyer. I was just a farmer. And yet, it'll be our forty-fifth wedding anniversary this year," Klaus raised his glass, "couldn't have asked for a better partner in crime."

"Love you to the moon and back," Ursula said, her eyes shiny with happy tears as she picked up her wine glass.

"Prost!" They yelled all at once, smiling and lifting up their wine glasses.

"Here's to those who wish us well, and those who don't can go to hell," Brian muttered, and they all shared confused looks. "Heather would've gotten it."

"Hopefully, I'm not stirring the pot, but where does Phil get his extraordinary height from?" Maria's words came out slightly slurred.

"Is that your polite way of asking if I think it was the postman or milkman?" Klaus chuckled. "No, no. Ursula's father was quite tall."

"From what we can tell from some old photos I have of my parents, Phil's the lucky one who inherited his height," Ursula said sadly.

"Pop's older brother died in a dirt bike riding accident," Phil blurted.

They all looked at him in surprise, and Phil felt the need to explain, "Maria and I were sharing near-death experience stories at lunch."

"My brother was a bit wild. He rode that dirt bike like a bat out of hell. So no, I wouldn't call it an accident. And I wouldn't call it a near-death experience. He did die trying to jump over some old, empty oil drums, like he was Evel Knievel. He'd lined them up on their sides, one after the other. He'd already made the jump over five of them several times. But this time, he wanted to do six. I tried to talk him out of it, but he was so stubborn.

Broke his neck. He was eighteen." Klaus' eyes were misty.

"I'm so sorry," Maria said while quietly thinking that no wonder Phil thought the farmhouse was haunted. It probably was.

"Well then, that's where Brian gets his wildness from. I was telling Maria about the time Brian tried to ride the neighbour's cows." Phil said, now regretting that he'd brought up his uncle's death.

"I'd forgotten all about that!" Ursula exclaimed, "We were so worried and mad, all at the same time."

Brian started to chuckle, "I'd convinced myself and those workers that I could ride it like a horse! And I almost did!"

"Yeah, right." Phil rolled his eyes.

"Is the farm still there?" Maria asked.

"After my great aunt passed away, my parents took over, and then we took over and built a good life for ourselves," Klaus reminisced and then started to get upset, "but look at how things are now, developers buying up farmland left, right and centre. There's not going to be any farmland left anymore. That's where things are headed."

"Yeah, but Pop, didn't you sell the farmland to some developers?" Phil pointed out.

Klaus grunted.

"And your adoptive parents?" Maria looked at Ursula.

"Oh, they moved to Osoyoos, British Columbia, when my dad retired, but they've passed on ... A few years ago," Ursula waved her martini glass around.

"It's just us," Klaus murmured.

"We were hoping we'd have grandkids by now. But between these two boys, it doesn't look like that's ever going to happen. Although now that you're in the picture, Maria, maybe there's hope!" Ursula teased, her words rushing together.

"Not the time, my dear," Klaus scolded her.

Maria smiled and said, "it's okay, Klaus. I have a daughter, so I know what it's like. First, you worry they're going to make you a grandparent too soon, and then you worry they won't soon enough."

"You got it. Well, on that note, I think it's time for dessert. Maria, will you help me, please?" Ursula said lightly.

"Yes, of course," Maria said as she picked up the platter with remnants of veal, thinking to herself that having another kid was the last thing on her mind.

Everyone began piling their empty plates on top of each other, so they could be easily brought into the kitchen.

"Maria brought apple strudel from the market," Ursula explained as she drained her martini glass.

"You can come back any time, Maria!" Klaus exclaimed happily.

"Aw, thanks, Klaus," Maria smiled.

In the kitchen, Maria placed the platter on the island.

"How do you want me to wrap this up?" Maria asked, pointing at the veal.

"I have some Pyrex in this drawer down here," Ursula pointed with her foot to a drawer at the bottom of the kitchen island.

Maria took out the Pyrex container and began filling it up with the leftover roast and vegetables, accidentally dropping a few pieces on the countertop.

"Well, that was a trip down memory lane. You certainly know how to divert a conversation," Ursula teased.

"Ah, I may be slightly tipsy," Maria giggled.

"I do hope that you and Phil will carry on when you get back to Miami," Ursula confided as she topped up their martini glasses.

"I'm glad to hear you say that. I really like Phil, and you, your whole family. Even Brian," Maria joked, and then wondered about Ursula's ambiguous comment about Brian taking his medication.

"Ha! By the way, I never asked what you do for a living. What keeps your family so busy that no one has time to cook?" Ursula asked as she began cutting the strudel into slightly crooked strips and then dropping them onto the matching blue dessert plates.

"My mother has a skincare line. I'm in charge of the marketing. It's great! I get to work on television commercials and advertising deals. I get to travel all over the States," Maria explained happily.

"What's the name of your company?" Ursula asked.

"Suavolino." Maria said.

"No kidding! I know it! It was in that movie … The Ideal You!" Ursula looked at her proudly.

"Wow! You noticed it!" Maria was thrilled.

"Of course! That was such a funny movie. You must be very talented," Ursula said in admiration.

"Thank you. But I have to admit it's not always easy working for my mother. She can be hard on me. And I get mad at myself for never finishing college. You see, I got pregnant and had to drop out," Maria confided.

"That must have been a tough decision," Ursula said sympathetically.

"Every once in a while, I wonder if I should go back and finish. But then, I'd have to stop working. And I'm already doing so well ... So, why ..." Maria trailed off, as her mother's words about being a college dropout began to sting again.

Ursula took a good look at Maria and pursed her lips. "You know, before I was allowed to marry Klaus, my father had one stipulation and that was for me to go to secretarial school, so that I had at least some other skills and education. It was overwhelming to go off to school on my own, not knowing what to expect. But I ended up loving it. It felt good proving that I could do it, and I even took some extra accounting courses, which came in handy because I could help out with the farm accounting," Ursula confided. "I know it's not quite the same thing, but maybe it'd be good for you?"

"Yeah, maybe," Maria murmured.

"You're a very lovely person, Maria. I'm so glad Phil has met you. And I take back what I said earlier. You may be out of my boy's league, but I think you'll definitely make each other very happy." Ursula beamed with encouragement.

"Thank you. I'm lucky to have met him." Maria smiled happily. "May I ask you something a bit forward?"

"Sure, what is it?"

"Did you and Heather get along?"

"Oh! That's not what I was expecting. Um, yes, I guess we did. But just between you and me ... I was a bit scared of her," Ursula giggled.

"I don't believe you," Maria teased.

"Just a teensy bit." Ursula pinched her two fingers together and smiled.

"You mean because of her temper?" Maria asked, ignoring Phil's request to not say anything.

"How did you know about that? Oh, I guess Phil told you." Ursula guessed and Maria nodded.

"Is it really that bad?" Maria asked.

"Let's just say I'd try to stay out of her way whenever she came over here, and leave it at that." Ursula pursed her lips.

With those final words, Ursula took out a tub of Kawartha's vanilla ice cream from the freezer and added a dollop to each plate.

Ursula motioned for Maria to grab the dessert forks. "Although, she did always bring a delicious dessert with her whenever she came over. But I'm sure yours is just as delicious."

"I hope so," Maria smiled.

Ursula and Maria brought the plates of crookedly cut strudel topped with ice cream into the dining room and handed them out, along with the forks.

"If I Had a Million Dollars" by the Barenaked Ladies was playing quietly on the radio.

"So, Brian, I hear you're an artist," Maria said once she'd sat down.

Brian looked at her like she was asking him to solve a math equation.

"Um, artist. Yeah, I guess," he mumbled.

"The painting of our farmhouse that you may have seen in the living room, was done by Brian," Phil explained.

"Brian has some new pieces on exhibit at the art gallery in town. You and Maria should go see them tomorrow. It's been a while since you've seen some of his newest pieces, Phil," Ursula added.

"Oh my gosh, I'd love that!" Maria said excitedly but caught herself before blurting out that she'd told Martha that she'd help out at the shop until two. "I love art. You know, the most famous Colombian artist is Botero. He paints really fat people as a kind of political statement. Something like that, anyway."

"Oh, my," Ursula said, thinking how fat people were always unfairly blamed for everything. "Here in Canada, we're known for the Group of Seven. In my opinion, they knew how to turn landscapes into fairy tales. You know, one of their curators flirted with me at an art show once."

Ursula fluttered her eyes.

"Everyone flirts with you, darling. Why wouldn't they?" Klaus announced proudly.

"Brian's sculptures are more like Henry Moore's. That's his muse, I guess?" Ursula explained as if Brian wasn't in the room.

"Really?" Maria pretended to be impressed, despite not knowing who Henry Moore was.

"Actually, yes, I would like to go see his art. It has been a while." Phil said, answering Ursula's earlier question. "Brian, would you like to show us your pieces?"

"They all have my name plaques on them. You don't need me to point them out," Brian mumbled.

"Or, how about we go for lunch, just the two of us?" Phil nudged.

"Nah, not really feeling up to it." Brian shook his head.

Everyone fell silent.

"Well, it's getting late. I should walk Maria home, seeing as she may not be walking in a straight line after all your bonding." Phil teasingly put bonding in air quotes before gathering up the dessert plates and bringing them into the kitchen.

"Yes, good idea," Ursula said.

"Really lovely meeting all of you. Thank you for having me over on such short notice," Maria said politely to Klaus and Brian, who remained seated at the dining table.

"You're welcome back anytime," Klaus said, smiling.

Brian gave them a half-wave.

Ursula walked them to the door.

Once they were out of earshot, Ursula sighed and said, "I'm so sorry about Brian. He's in a slump. I don't know what else to do."

"Don't worry, Mum. I'll get him to talk, even if it means kidnapping him for lunch tomorrow," Phil said as he grabbed their coats, along with Maria's purse and big bag from the front hall closet.

"Yeah, I think you should take him out for lunch tomorrow," Maria said as she tried to put on Ursula's coat but was having trouble finding the armholes. Phil noticed and held the coat open for her.

"Oh, you don't mind me borrowing your coat for a bit longer?" Maria asked, suddenly remembering the coat wasn't hers.

"No, of course not. It looks nice on you. I hardly wear it. I think you should keep it," Ursula said warmly, "and Phil, if you want to stay with Maria tonight, I'm fine with that. I'm sure your father will be, too."

Phil looked puzzled, and then his expression changed to comprehension.

"Ah, so Maria told you the truth," he said, nodding and giving Maria a so-you-did look.

"Yes, she did, and it's all going to be fine," Ursula said as she patted his arm.

BOCA BONITA
SUNDAY, DECEMBER 22

After Jack had thoroughly enjoyed his dinner with Heather over at Maria's house and introduced her to Lars, he'd returned to Yolanda's where the Rodriguez family was sitting comfortably in the lavish outdoor dining area. Yolanda's house had a similar layout to Maria's with its high ceilings, open concept design and expansive backyard.

Abuelita had said she was tired and had gone to bed early, Gloria had gone home to be with her family and then their neighbour, Camilla, had unexpectedly dropped by with a bottle of wine.

They were happily swapping stories in Spanish, after having enjoyed a pleasant dinner of baked tilapia and tamales, finished off with a few small slices of yuca cake.

Gabriel was sharing his latest adventures with the Nicolás Pérez's food travel show. "I think Nicolás is going to keep pushing the show more and more into political and social arenas, which I'm all for."

"I'm so proud of you," Yolanda said as she patted his hand, "but I worry you put yourself in too much danger."

"Thanks, Mamacita, but you don't need to worry." Gabriel kissed the gold cross that was hanging on a chain around his neck and looked up at the sky.

"I'll never stop worrying about my children. Now tell me the truth, what do you really think of Maria's latest escapade?" Unlike other visits from Gabriel, Yolanda had been waiting somewhat impatiently for him to stop talking about his show so she could bring up the topic of Maria.

"I think it's hilarious. She, who only goes to California, Las Vegas and Arizona, has chosen to go to Canada in the middle of winter... And no, Aspen doesn't count .... She'll be back before you know it. Once her little tush freezes off," Camilla, the neighbour, giggled.

"Camilla!" Jorge jokingly wagged his finger at her.

Gabriel ignored them and said, "oh, Mamacita, I'm sorry she's done this right at Christmas. I was really looking forward to seeing her. I mean, I haven't seen her since Gloria's daughter's first communion in June, and I wanted her to meet Carlos."

Carlos comforted Gabriel, "she'll be back sooner than you think. At least Heather's turned out to be someone who understands a situation. She's made herself scarce and kept to herself as promised. I don't think you have to worry about her anymore."

"You know, I'm not as clued out as everyone thinks. I've known for a long time that Maria and Alonso weren't doing well. I'm not surprised that he's left her. I just don't like that he had to do it right at Christmas. It was embarrassing enough that she missed our company Christmas party," Yolanda said.

"Darling, you know they've both always done their own thing," Jorge said.

"I agree with Camilla. From what I've heard about Maria from you, Gabriel, she'll hate the cold and will be back before you know it. There's no way she'd miss Christmas with her daughter," Carlos said.

"Where is Olivia?" Camilla asked.

"Key West. Apparently, she's having a blast. Snorkeling and swimming with the dolphins," Gabriel said.

"Well, I suppose I shouldn't be surprised by all of this. It's Maria all over again. Never thinking things through. Have any of you heard from her?" Yolanda asked, feeling hurt as she thought about Maria's latest idea last Friday of "refreshing" her image on the packaging of their youth-targeted skincare line with that cheap pop star's face … Rubia Lopez, of all people. She had to wonder if Maria's next idea would be to stop using her image all together. She was the one who built this company. She was the face. Sure, the glossed over photo was from when she'd just started the company, but there was no way she'd be swapping it with that of a floozy.

Jorge winced and then admitted, "yes, I got one very, very short text from her."

"You did! Why didn't you say anything!" Yolanda exclaimed.

"You were still digesting the information, and I wanted to let you digest as much as … and for as long as you needed. Digest away!" Jorge teased.

"I'm well digested now." Yolanda pursed her lips.

"Let me find her text. Honestly, it was nothing earth-shattering." Jorge scrolled through his phone messages and then read it out loud:

"Hi, Papa, everything is fine. Don't worry. I'm in Canada and the little house is very pretty."

"See, nothing much, really. Typical Maria. Nothing to worry about. I'm sure she's having a good time," Jorge said.

"That is exactly what I'm worried about," Yolanda stated angrily, thinking about the rumours she'd heard around the office about just how much of a "good time" Maria had on her business trips. Honestly, it was a miracle that she hadn't ended up pregnant again. Her own parents would have disowned her for such nonsensical behaviour.

Life was very different in Colombia. She'd grown up with a constant watchful eye on her. Always being chaperoned by one of her older brothers to parties where the girls sat on plush chairs at the country club, pretending to nonchalantly sip on a soda, but desperately waiting for a boy to ask them to dance.

She'd just turned seventeen when handsome Jorge had sauntered over to her at one such dance and had gallantly held out his hand as he asked her to join him on the dance floor. He was confident in his dancing skills, and rightly so, as he effortlessly guided her amongst the less gifted dancers.

She'd found out later that he was twenty-one and was studying to be a plastic surgeon, so she had made sure to always be positioned near his table whenever he was around. Her parents had happily agreed to their marriage three months later.

Their move to Florida had been upsetting to her family at the time, but they understood that things were politically unstable and that Jorge simply wanted to create a better life for them. When Jorge's father had passed away a few years later, to the surprise of both of their families, his mother had decided to come live with them.

"Darling, you're going to have to let Maria make her own mistakes," Jorge pointed out.

"Sure, I mean look at where her big mistake led her last time," Yolanda said sarcastically, thinking how Maria had thrown away her chance at gaining a valuable education when she'd gotten herself pregnant at such a young age.

"Oh darling, Maria will always do what she wants and I wouldn't exactly call Olivia a mistake, would you?" Jorge asked.

"Well, no, I wouldn't. She's turned out lovely, despite it all," Yolanda agreed.

"And, you wouldn't want Maria any other way, would you?"

"Well, that's debatable." Yolanda pursed her lips.

"We love her, warts and all," Jorge joked.

Yolanda frowned at Jorge. He always had a way of making her see the lighter side of a situation, but she wasn't quite ready yet.

Before anyone could say anything else, Jack's phone started to ring, and he held up his hand in an apology gesture and then ran into the house before answering.

As Jack entered the house, he whispered into the phone, "Dolores, hi. Is everything set?"

KEY WEST
SUNDAY, DECEMBER 22

After JC's unsettling texts with his mother, Captain Waters had driven Olivia and her friends back to their Cadillac SUV that'd been sitting in a parking lot by the beach. They'd said their thank-yous and goodbyes with the captain and then had headed back to JC's parents' dreamy beach house. Along the way, they'd picked up pizzas to share.

Once they'd arrived at the beach house, Olivia had sprinted up the floating spiral staircase to the bedroom she was sharing with Oliver. In the privacy of the bedroom, she'd left a voice message for her mom telling her about her amazing day and how she'd bonded with a dolphin named Pippa that afternoon. She'd left out the part about the barracuda and ended the call by saying that she hoped her mother's trip was going well.

Now, Olivia looked over at her friends who were sprawled out among the many pillows on the sectional couch in the vaulted living room. After a long, hot day in the sun, they were in their comfy tanks and joggers lazily watching a cooking show while picking away at the last of the pizzas and avoiding any mention of JC's dad.

On the television, contestants were presenting the three judges with their signature dishes and one of the judges had a look of disgust on his face just as the show cut to a commercial break.

"I know none of you guys can cook, so I won't even ask, but my signature dish would be chicken casserole," Bianca bragged.

In a fake British accent, Olivia asked, "and how would you elevate that?"

"Hey, I take offense to that blatant assumption, Bianca. Just because you haven't seen me cook, doesn't mean I can't." JC defended himself.

"Haha! Yeah, right!" Bianca laughed at JC and then turned to Olivia, "how would I elevate it? Hmmm ... I guess I'd deconstruct it by coating the chicken breast with panko, lightly frying it and then making a celery purée to place underneath it. And then, instead of pasta, I'd make rice, and shape it into a nice, round circle with one of those molds."

"So, you haven't given this much thought at all," Olivia teased.

"That would definitely place you in the top three, darling," JC complimented her, "but I'd still kick your ass."

"What would you make? Mac'n cheese?" Bianca taunted him.

"Hey, I'll have you know, our housekeeper, Breanna, has taught me a few things. I'd make my famous spaghetti and meatballs with homemade marinara sauce," JC explained satisfactorily.

"Famous? Mmmmm ... And you think that would beat my deconstructed casserole?" Bianca asked skeptically.

"Damn right! It'd be a clean sweep with my killer recipes! See, no one would suspect me because I look so young and innocent. You didn't, right?" JC leaned over and nuzzled his head in Bianca's belly.

Olivia giggled and realized Bianca was right, JC was the forever optimist. As she looked at them, she felt a little sad that Bianca was planning on breaking up with him. She was thoroughly enjoying this trip and had been looking forward to taking more vacations together as a foursome.

"Well, I may have zero interest in cooking, but I tell ya, I loved helping Captain Waters on the boat today. I think I'm going to join the school's sailing club next spring," Oliver announced.

"Woah, that's unexpected!" JC stopped nuzzling Bianca and looked over at Oliver in surprise.

"Yeah, I've been looking up all the different nautical knots he taught me today. It's fascinating –" Oliver was explaining excitedly just as JC's phone began to ring.

JC looked down at the caller ID, frowned and then answered.

"Hey, Mom, what's going on? ... What? ... Are you sure? ... When did this happen? ... Um, yes, okay ... Okay, leaving now," JC said in a panicky voice and then hung up.

"What's happened?" Oliver frowned.

"My dad's had a heart attack. She wants me and my sister Carmen to come to the hospital right away." JC stood up and began to anxiously run his hands through his dark, curly hair.

"Oh my gosh!" Bianca exclaimed.

"You guys can stay here. I'll ... Uh ... I'll..." JC looked confused.

"What are you talking about? We're not letting you go back alone!" Oliver yelled.

"Babe, we're coming with you," Bianca said quietly as she turned off the television.

They all nodded in agreement and then sprang into action. They quickly cleaned up the house, packed up their stuff, threw it all into the trunk of the SUV and then began the long journey through the night from Key West to Miami with Oliver at the helm.

MUNICH
SUNDAY, DECEMBER 22

As Phil and Maria made their way through the neighbourhood streets, hand-in-hand, large snowflakes were falling down around them, and the air had become comfortably warm. Maria was tipsy from the martinis and despite her new boots, skidded in the snow every once in a while, but Phil was quick to catch her before she could fall.

"Well, that went way differently than I expected. Although, I knew my parents would love you," Phil said warmly, "and listen, I'm really sorry about thinking I had to lie about how we know each other. That was really dumb on my part. No more lies from now on. Besides, Brian needs to move on."

"Good. No more lies." Maria said, poking Phil in the arm.

They walked in silence for a while.

"Have you ever had special brownies?" Maria asked, giggling.

"Nope, can't say that I have." Phil was surprised at the question.

"Do you want to try some?" Maria asked, hopefully.

"You mean, tonight?" Phil wasn't sure where this request was coming from.

"I've never tried them, either. And this trip is all about trying new things, so I bought two brownies from Heather's shop today," Maria said excitedly as she danced around Phil in the snow.

Phil hesitated. He'd been thinking about trying some new things tonight, but pot brownies definitely weren't on the list. "I guess we can try them. What's going to happen to us?"

"I think they just relax you."

"I'm pretty relaxed from the wine already, but okay," Phil shrugged.

They arrived at Heather's snow-covered front porch and entered the quaint house. They smiled at each other as they took off their coats and boots and then shoved everything into the tiny closet under the stairs. They made their way into the kitchen, where Maria placed her bag on the kitchen table and took out the brownies.

"Can we have them with a glass of milk?" Phil asked.

"I don't see why not," Maria shrugged.

"How long does it take for them to kick in?" Phil asked.

"Not sure, let me look it up," Maria said and then tapped her phone, "it says that if you take them on a full stomach, it could take one to two hours to feel the full effect."

"What the heck, let's go for it." Phil shrugged.

She lifted the lid of the carton of brownies and picked one up. She broke off a piece and offered it to Phil, who ate it from her fingers. She broke off another piece and ate it.

"Damn, that's sooo good," Phil groaned with delight.

"Gosh, yes, sooo good!" Maria said, licking her fingers.

Phil embraced her from behind and began kissing her neck and ears. She turned around, and they kissed passionately for a while. Phil hooked his finger into the front belt buckle of Maria's wool pants and pulled her closer to him. Phil slowly lifted off her turtleneck and draped it over one of the chairs. Then he slid her silk camisole off, threw it onto the table, and brushed his fingertips along the top of her black lacy bra.

"Take it off," Phil said, his breath tickling her neck.

Maria unhooked her bra, and Phil gently cupped her breasts and ran his thumb over her nipples.

"That tickles," Maria said shyly.

"Good," Phil grinned.

They kissed deeply.

"Let's have another piece of brownie," Maria suggested as she picked up the other half of the brownie and broke a piece off. Once again, Phil ate from Maria's fingers, rolling his tongue around them.

Maria laughed and broke off another piece and ate it. She licked her fingers and began unbuttoning Phil's flannel shirt from the bottom up as far as she could reach. Phil finished unbuttoning the top buttons, slid it off, and hung it on the back of one of the kitchen chairs.

"Now we're even," Maria said, pointing at their nakedness.

"Feeling anything yet?" Phil asked.

Maria thought about it and said, "nope, not yet."

"Me neither," Phil whispered.

He stared at her. "How'd I get so lucky to end up sitting next to the most beautiful, funniest, kindest, sweetest person in the world?" Phil was kissing her body and slowly taking off her pants.

He ran his hands over her tiny hips.

"Your turn," Maria said, pointing to his jeans.

Phil took off his jeans, and Maria could see he was ready to go.

"Where do you want to, you know, do it this time?" Phil asked. He began speaking really quickly, "I really don't want to do it in Heather's bed ... that's where my brother and Heather have been. I was thinking about that today. Kinda weird."

"Eek, I never even thought about that," Maria said, slightly alarmed. "You know what, instead of milk, let's have some of that wine I bought at the market."

"Good idea," Phil agreed.

Maria took out the bottle of red wine from her purse, found a bottle opener in one of the drawers, and opened it. Phil watched her intently as she found two ceramic wine glasses and poured out two even levels of wine. Her toned muscles flexed with every movement. He looked down at his soft, slightly bulging stomach and sighed.

"When we get back to Miami, you're going to have to help me get into shape," Phil said, sighing again and patting his belly. "If you still like me by then, that is."

Maria handed him his glass of wine.

She half-smiled and said, "as long as you don't do anything stupid like whatever your brother did, we'll be fine."

"That, you definitely don't need to worry about." Phil looked into Maria's dark eyes.

"Good." Maria held up her glass.

"Salud," they both said and took big sips.

"So, to answer your question, it's going to be awkward no matter what because, let's face it, they've probably done it everywhere, like probably all over the house," Maria pointed out.

Phil made a pained face. "True enough."

"Let's go upstairs, then," he whispered into her ear, tickling her with his breath.

As they finished their glasses of wine, Maria looked at the second brownie and picked it up. She looked at Phil, and he shrugged.

"I'll just have a bit, and you can have the rest," Maria suggested as they ate the rest of the brownie.

Maria poured more wine into their glasses, and eventually they finished the bottle. Phil grabbed Maria's hand and put her fingers in his mouth, one by one. Maria was enjoying the sensual feeling, but soon it began to feel like her fingers were in his mouth for a very long time. She closed her eyes and then asked, "can I have my hand back?"

"You have it back." Phil pointed to her hand, and she noticed that it was resting on the back of the kitchen chair.

"Let's lie on the floor," Maria said, thinking this was the best idea in the world.

"The floor?" Phil looked down, wondering how uncomfortable and cold it would be.

"Yeah." Maria lowered herself to the floor. She was on her hands and knees and couldn't remember how to turn herself over.

"Are you okay?" Phil was looking at her, wondering why she was on her hands and knees.

Maria slowly figured out how to turn herself over, and once she was lying on her back, she held her hands up towards Phil. "I'm wonderful. It's wonderful down here. Come join me."

Phil slowly positioned himself beside her. Lying straight across the floor, he almost touched the entire width of the kitchen. He was startled at how cold it was and reached up and yanked his shirt off the table and brought it down beside them.

"Here, let me put my shirt underneath you, so it's not so cold." He tried to shove his shirt underneath her, but it got stuck and bunched up.

"Oh yeah, that's nice," she sighed, not realizing she was still lying on the cold floor.

He rested himself on his left arm and began running his right hand over Maria's body. He ran his hand across her collarbone, around her breasts, circling her nipples, down her stomach, and making his way slowly down to her black lace panties. He feathered his fingers across the rim of her panties, and Maria sighed with satisfaction.

"Take them off," Maria said languidly.

Phil off slid her panties and began kissing her between her legs. He could feel that she was getting wet as he kissed her more deeply, and her back arched in response to the pleasure.

A few minutes later, his tongue started to feel like it had grown. He looked down, and sure enough, his tongue had unexpectedly grown quite long. Phil was embarrassed by his long tongue and stopped. He leaned back down onto the floor. All of a sudden, there was a pounding noise in his ears.

"What's that?" Maria yelled.

"What's what?" Phil yelled back.

"There's a pounding noise!" Maria yelled again.

"I thought I was the only who could hear that!" Phil yelled.

The pounding continued.

"I think someone's trying to get in," Maria sighed.

"Oh, someone will let them in," Phil said flippantly.

"Yeah," Maria sighed again and turned over towards Phil. She began tracing her fingers along his chest and down to his stomach. She reached further and down began stroking him.

A muffled yelling began.

"Maybe I'm the someone who's supposed to let them in?" Phil suddenly realized.

"Maybe." Maria nodded in quiet agreement as she stopped stroking him.

Phil had to use all of his powers to push himself off the floor and onto his feet. "Where do you think the noise is coming from?"

"The chimney," Maria said, slurring.

"Oh, okay." Phil awkwardly leaned down, grabbed his pants and wrapped them sideways around his waist.

He then walked over to the living room and squatted in front of the red-bricked fireplace. Looking up into the chimney, he hollered, "hello? Santa? Is that you?"

"Hello! I can hear you in there. Please just open the door. I have something important to tell you!" The voice yelled again.

Phil went towards the voice and found himself at the front door. He looked down at the door handle, but couldn't remember how to open it.

"Open the door!" The voice yelled.

Phil finally noticed the lock and turned it.

"Santa?" Phil asked as he opened the door with his right hand, and with his other, reached out and touched his brother's face.

"What the hell are you doing?" Brian yelled, swatting his brother's hand away.

"Just checking to see if you're real," Phil said, his words slurring together.

"Of course, I'm real!" Brian yelled again, but then he paused and looked closely at Phil, inspecting his eyes, "are you high?"

Phil shrugged.

"I came over to talk to Heather! Where is she?" Brian stormed past Phil and started looking around the house, cursing Heather for taking her house key away from him.

Brian ran upstairs, and Phil and Maria could hear his boots stomping across the house. Forgetting to shut the front door, Phil went back into the kitchen.

"I think Brian is here," Phil said, still not sure of what was real and what wasn't, "not Santa."

"Yeah, I think so too," Maria said from the kitchen floor. "I'm making snow angels, but it's getting cold in here."

"I'm pretty sure you should get up off the floor," Phil said, watching as Maria swept her arms and legs across the floor.

"Yeah, maybe." Maria stopped moving, and her head tilted to one side, feeling heavy.

They could hear Brian's footsteps clanking down the narrow stairs.

"Why is the front door still open?" Brian yelled, and then they heard the front door slam shut.

Phil looked around in a hazed panic and threw Maria's clothes on top of her. Brian entered the kitchen and looked at Phil in bewilderment and then down at Maria.

"I don't understand. What are you guys doing here? Where's Heather?" Brian demanded.

Maria wrapped her bundle of clothes around her and slowly sat up, the reality of what was happening sluggishly settling into her brain.

"I think you should wait in the living room while Maria and I put our clothes back on," Phil said to Brian.

"Yeah, you're right. This is weird." Brian left the kitchen and went to sit on one of the red loveseats in the living room.

Phil held out his hand and helped Maria up.

"I can't deal with this right now. I'm stoned and drunk and … horny," Maria whispered as she grabbed at Phil.

"Don't do that," Phil whispered back, playfully slapping her hands away. "Let me do the talking."

They stumbled about as they put their clothes back on and then walked into the living room, where Brian was waiting for them. Charlotte, the tuxedo cat, was nestled on Brian's lap and purring happily while he massaged her head and chin.

"Can you guys please tell me what's going on?" Brian whined.

Despite his promise to Maria, Phil was having a hard time forming his thoughts coherently and blurted, "you scared Heather off."

"What do you mean, I scared her off?" Brian was confused.

"Whatever you did, made her run off to Florida," Phil accused Brian.

Maria gave Phil an exasperated look. "Brian, what Phil is trying to say is that … Heather just needed some time away … We've exchanged houses

... She's staying at my house in Florida, and I'm staying here for a bit."

"I don't understand." Brian abruptly stood up from the loveseat and Charlotte thumped to the floor, giving Brian a dirty look before hissing and slinking away. He began pacing back and forth, vigorously rubbing his face with his hands.

"Brian, please ..." Maria tried to reach for his hand to guide him back down to the loveseat, but missed.

"I don't believe you! Heather would never do that! You're lying!" Brian yelled, pointing his finger at them accusingly.

"Brian, calm down. Just sit back down, please," Phil demanded. "Tell us what happened between you and Heather. What did you do to her that was so bad?"

"Nothing! I've literally done nothing!" Brian yelled.

"You had to have done something!" Phil shouted.

"Guys, please calm down," Maria begged.

Brian glared at Maria and then sat back down on the loveseat, slumping.

"I'm so so so stupid. What I did was so stupid," Brian yelled while repeatedly slapping his forehead.

"You can tell us," Maria said, sitting down on the red loveseat across from Brian.

"No, I can't. I came here to tell Heather, not you guys," Brian whined.

"Brian, I think at this point, you really don't have a choice. You need to tell us," Phil demanded.

"I can't believe I'm telling you guys what I did." Brian rubbed his face and took a deep breath. "It all started when I posted an ad for someone to pose nude for me, so I could, you know, paint a portrait for the show. For a small payment," Brian mumbled and then stopped talking.

"And ..." Phil motioned for Brian to keep talking.

"And ... Elsa answered my ad. She sent me pictures," Brian said gloomily.

"Pictures?" Phil and Maria both said at the same time.

"Ah, yes, partially naked ones," Brian mumbled, "and she was drop-dead gorgeous. But then she kept asking for more money and changing the dates on me ... on when I'd get to paint her. I eventually ran out of money and told her I couldn't send her any more money. That's when she stopped texting me, and now her number doesn't exist anymore."

"What do you mean?" Phil asked, hazily.

"She's disappeared. There's no sign of her anywhere. As soon as I told her I had no more money, she stopped answering my texts," Brian explained sadly.

"You got ghosted!" Maria exclaimed.

"More like catfished," Phil sighed and sat down beside Brian.

"Yeah, I finally realized that yesterday. I've been trying to figure out how to explain this to Heather, but I'm so embarrassed," Brian said, covering his face with his hands.

"You mean that you've been sexting with some old hairy dude pretending to be a hot chick?" Phil chided, gently bumping shoulders with his brother.

"Hmph, basically," Brian half-laughed.

"So, let me guess, Heather saw all your texts?" Phil chastised Brian.

Brian sighed and slumped further into the couch, "yes, enough of them."

Phil lambasted Brian again. "How could this girl, Elsa, you say her name is, have so much power over you? How much money did you give her? How'd you even get talked into giving her money?"

"Because she's drop-dead gorgeous ..." Brian mumbled.

"And ..." Phil said, frustrated and motioning once again for Brian to keep explaining.

"Fine, I'll show you. But we'll have to go to the art gallery," Brian said defeatedly.

"Okay?" Phil said, confused.

Still feeling hazy, Phil and Maria slowly put their coats and boots back on and weaved their way through the snowy streets in silence. When they reached the art gallery, Brian pulled out a set of keys.

"How come you have the keys?" Phil asked.

"I'm one of the organizers," Brian explained flatly.

"Oh," Phil said, not totally convinced.

Brian turned off the security alarm and led them through the spacious white walls of the art gallery. Wide archways separated one room from the next. Each room displayed sculptures and paintings from one solo, local artist.

As they walked through one of the final archways, Brian mumbled, "this is my space."

Maria saw that there were several metal sculptures of curvaceous and sometimes contorted women's bodies with Brian's name on plaques beside them, as he'd mentioned, but mounted on the far wall was a large canvas. It was an oil painting of the most beautiful woman Maria had ever seen. All three of them approached the painting in awe. It had been carefully displayed in a dark wooden frame and, on closer inspection, she realized that Norse carvings had been layered into it.

"I used the bits and pieces from her texts to paint her," Brian whispered.

Maria stared at the contours of the woman's face. She drank in her wolf-like eyes, her high cheekbones, her strong jawbone, and small chin that was lifted upwards. Her soft pink lips were sealed shut as if she were defiantly keeping a secret. Her sunflower-coloured hair was shaved at the sides and then braided down the middle. Her curvaceous collarbone and sturdy shoulders gave her an alluring strength. Her breasts were round and high. Nipples, pink and erect.

Brian had positioned the naked woman on a hand-crafted bed. He had draped a white hygge blanket gingerly across her stomach and all the way down to the floor. Her soft skin glowed under the moonlight, and her fingertips were resting gently on a metallic sword that lay on her lap.

Brian had achieved an extraordinary balance of strength and delicacy.

"Until we meet again," Maria murmured.

MIAMI
MONDAY, DECEMBER 23

Late last night, when the four of them had finally arrived at the hospital in Miami, where they were to drop JC off, he'd texted his mother to ask what room they were in and she'd replied back by thanking them for bringing JC to the hospital so quickly and then mentioned that they could all stay at the Juárez's house for now, until she knew more.

When the three of them had arrived at JC's monstrosity of a house, they'd been shown to their individual rooms by the housekeeper, Breanna, and all three had gone straight to bed, too worried and exhausted to do anything else. It wasn't until the middle of the night that Olivia had felt Oliver squeeze into bed next to her, slinging his arm around her and holding onto her tight all night.

That morning, when they'd come downstairs, they'd discovered that breakfast had been laid out for them on the glistening kitchen island. A big spread of scrambled eggs, freshly cut fruit, toast, cereal, and coffee.

Now, they were sitting at the kitchen table, eating listlessly. Olivia noticed that the kitchen décor was very similar to hers, all white and stainless steel, but about twice the size. All three of them were wearing the same clothes as yesterday since they'd been too tired to unpack the car.

"Have you heard from JC?" Oliver asked Bianca.

"Just that his father's in bad shape. And that his sister, Carmen, is on her way," Bianca said, slowly picking at her food.

"Do you think we should go to the hospital?" Oliver asked as he took a sip of his coffee.

"No, he told me not to come yet. He'll let us know." Bianca looked at her phone sitting silently on the table beside her untouched plate of food. Her glance was rewarded as it began to ring.

"Hi, we're worried about you," Bianca answered, "can I put you on speaker, so we can all hear what you have to say?"

Bianca hit the speaker button and put her phone back down on the table.

"My mom says you guys can come if you want to, but it's going to be a lot of waiting," JC said quietly, "my sister, Carmen, is coming from Boston, but it's still going to be a while before she gets here."

"We're coming. We're not leaving you alone," Oliver stated.

"Okay, good. I feel so helpless. And besides, there's some creepy guy who showed up this morning. He's hanging around the waiting room and staring at me," JC said, relief flooding his voice.

"Well, I'll make sure he gets lost," Oliver reassured him.

"We're on our way, babe," Bianca said quietly and hung up the phone.

They were about to clean up the breakfast table when Breanna, the housekeeper, appeared seemingly out of nowhere and shooed them away.

"I'll start the car," Oliver offered.

Bianca and Olivia ran upstairs to grab their purses and then stood in front of the huge double doors.

"How do we lock the door? I don't remember having to unlock it last night?" Bianca asked.

Once again, the housekeeper reappeared unannounced.

"I'll lock it behind you," Breanna said, smiling at them.

Startled by the housekeeper's uncanny ability to appear without warning, the girls shuddered and ran down the steps.

Olivia slid into the passenger side seat and Bianca into the back. Oliver backed the SUV out of the wide driveway and then navigated through the gated community and out onto the main street.

"Do you know how to get there?" Olivia asked.

"Already put it in GPS," Oliver reassured her.

They took off towards the hospital and a few minutes later, they heard sirens behind them.

"Pull over to the side and let them pass!" Olivia cried out.

Oliver pulled over to the side of the road but to their astonishment, the cop car pulled in behind them.

"He's pulling us over? What did we do?" Bianca yelled.

"I have no idea!" Oliver exclaimed.

They watched as the officer got out of his car and approached them. As the officer stood outside of Oliver's window, he motioned for him to roll it down.

"Yes, Officer?" Oliver asked as he pushed the window's down button.

"Son, are you stoned or drunk?" The officer asked.

"No, sir." Oliver shook his head.

"Do you know what you're supposed to do at a red light?" The officer asked.

"Stop?" Oliver answered hesitantly.

"That's right," said the officer, nodding, "and what are you supposed to do at a green?"

"Go?" Oliver questioned.

"That's right, you're doing very well. Now, what are you supposed to do at a yellow?"

"Um …" Oliver wasn't sure what to say.

"Sorry Officer, but my boyfriend's father, Judge Juárez, is in the hospital," Bianca interrupted from the back seat, "he's had a heart attack and we're on our way to the hospital. Were we speeding?"

Just as Bianca had hoped, a flicker of recognition at the judge's name registered across the officer's face.

The officer looked at them and then said sternly, "well, you blew right through that yellow light. But I'll tell you what, I'll let you off with a warning this time. From now on, please mind your colours, son." The officer wrote up a warning ticket and as soon as he left, they let out a collective sigh.

"I'm sorry guys. I was just trying to get us there as quickly as possible," Oliver apologized.

"Don't worry about it," Olivia said.

"Didn't even notice," Bianca reassured Oliver.

A half hour later, they arrived at the entrance to the hospital's parking garage. Oliver navigated the SUV beside the cashier booth, punched a button and took a ticket. He handed it to Olivia who placed it on the dashboard. Once the gate lifted, Oliver began turning the vehicle into the garage.

"Wait! You're going the wrong way! Don't you see the big, red 'Do Not Enter' sign!" Olivia yelled.

"Oh my God, you're right! I'm all shaken up by that cop!" Oliver yelled as he backed the SUV up and then turned it into the correct laneway.

Bianca started giggling, "mind your colours."

"Who says that?" Oliver chuckled.

"Yeah, what are we, like, five?" Olivia giggled.

They kept giggling nervously as Oliver drove up and around a couple of levels until he found an empty spot. Once parked, they all jumped out with relief that they'd finally arrived.

"The elevator's over here!" Bianca pointed and they ran over to it.

They took the elevator to the ground floor and then crossed the pedestrian walkway over to the hospital's entrance.

Bianca looked down at her phone, "JC says they're on the sixth floor and it's room 6508."

Once inside the hospital, they hoofed it towards the bank of elevators that were stationed to the left of them. Already waiting by the elevators was a nurse who was holding onto the handles of a wheelchair with an elderly patient slumped inside. They could see that the elevator's "up" button was already lit, so they paced as they waited.

When it finally arrived, they let the nurse enter the elevator first and waited as she rolled her patient in and around so that he could face outwards. Once the rest of them had settled themselves in front of the wheelchair, Oliver pressed the button beside the number six.

"Which floor?" He asked the nurse.

"Eight, please." The nurse smiled.

He pressed eight and the doors closed.

The elevator jerked its way up to the sixth floor as they all stared straight ahead. The quiet tension was unexpectedly interrupted by a loud fart and the three of them eyed each other sideways in surprise, trying not to laugh. When the elevator stopped at the sixth floor, they exited without looking behind them.

"Wasn't me," Oliver said defensively once the elevator doors had sealed shut behind them.

"It was the guy in the wheelchair," Bianca said and they all burst out laughing.

"Rooms 6000 to 6600 are this way," Olivia giggled as she pointed to a sign on the wall.

They walked down the overly lit hallway, following the signs to the room. Eventually, the hallway opened up into a neatly arranged waiting room with newly upholstered chairs. A lone man was sitting in one of the chairs with his head hanging in his hands. Feeling their presence, he lifted up his head.

It took a few seconds for Olivia to register who it was.

"Dad?" Olivia was confused.

"Olivia?" Alonso's face reddened.

In unison, they both exclaimed, "what are you doing here?"

"The creepy guy is your dad?" Oliver asked in bewilderment.

"I guess so," Olivia hesitated, "I'm so confused right now. Why don't you guys give us a minute?"

Oliver nodded as he and Bianca left the waiting room in search of JC.

"What's this about a creepy guy?" Alonso asked indignantly.

Ignoring his question, Olivia asked again, "what are you doing here?"

Alonso sat up straight in his seat and motioned for Olivia to take the seat across from him. She walked over and sat down. Olivia looked into her dad's dark eyes and noticed how tired he looked.

"Have you talked to your mother?" Alonso asked.

"She sent me a strange text saying that she went on a trip." Olivia frowned.

"A trip? That is strange. She never misses the company Christmas party. Um, so nothing else?" Alonso asked.

"Nope," Olivia said in a clipped tone.

"Oh boy, this isn't how I wanted you to find out, but I guess this is the universe's way of getting back at me," Alonso sighed.

Olivia eyed her father with suspicion.

"Um, first of all, I want to say that I'm so sorry for all the times I wasn't there for you growing up," Alonso began.

Olivia was taken aback by this seemingly abrupt admission out of the blue. What Olivia didn't know was that during Alonso's tedious wait, he'd seen how quickly Josephine's husband's health had deteriorated. It had made him realize that he didn't want to unexpectedly die knowing Olivia could possibly hate him.

Olivia stayed silent.

"Well, you know how things between me and your mother have never been that great?" Alonso asked desperately.

Olivia felt her body grow tense as her mind raced to make sense of what was happening.

"I never meant for you to find out like this," Alonso sighed, "your mother and I have separated."

Olivia's mind flipped through all that had happened, clicking the pieces together until she could see the whole picture.

"That's why JC's dad had an anxiety attack. His mom was telling him that she was leaving him for you," she accused.

"We never meant for this to happen," Alonso pleaded.

"So, you keep saying. My friend's father is in there dying!" Olivia roared.

"Josephine and I have fallen in love," Alonso whispered.

Olivia stood up.

"I think you should leave," Olivia ordered.

"What?" Alonso looked at her in surprise.

"I don't think you should be here," Olivia stated.

"But Josephine wants me here as long as I stay out of the way of her family," Alonso explained.

"Exactly. Which is why you need to leave. You're in the way," Olivia said meanly.

"But we need to talk. The two of us. We've run into each other for a reason," Alonso said desperately.

At that moment, Josephine entered the waiting room.

"What's going on in here?" Josephine asked.

"I'm not really sure, but this is my daughter, Olivia," Alonso explained.

"Your daughter?"

"It seems that she's friends with your son," Alonso grimaced.

Josephine looked at Olivia and then back at Alonso, as if trying to catch the resemblance.

"I was just telling my dad that he needs to leave," Olivia said as she looked Josephine up and down, noticing her elegant clothing and pixie cut.

"He's here because I asked him to be. I want him here with me," Josephine explained patiently. "I was just waiting for my daughter, Carmen, to arrive before explaining everything."

Alonso held out his hand and Josephine grabbed it and he gave her a supportive squeeze.

"I'm here for you," he whispered.

Olivia saw a look pass between the two of them and realized it was a look he'd never shared with her mother. It was a look of deep love.

"I'm so sorry, about all of this. I really thought I was making the right decision by waiting until Carmen got here," Josephine explained.

"Then I guess I'm the one who should leave," Olivia said obstinately.

"Olivia, please don't. We need to talk," Alonso pleaded.

Olivia ignored her dad and walked over to the hospital room where her friends were.

"Hi," she said curtly as she entered the room.

She noticed that the hospital bed was empty.

"They've taken him into surgery," Oliver explained.

"What do we do now?" Olivia asked, briskly.

"I guess more waiting." Bianca was sitting on the armrest of JC's chair.

"I kind of want to leave if that's okay with you, JC?" Olivia asked.

"What's your dad doing here?" JC asked.

"I think you need to talk to your mom. She hasn't told you anything, yet?" Olivia asked.

"Nope," JC shook his head.

"My dad wants to talk to me, but I just want to leave," Olivia said sadly.

"Sorry, babe, but I need to stay with JC until his dad gets out of surgery. And maybe you should talk to your dad. This is your chance to find out what's going on," Oliver said quietly.

"You think so?" Olivia frowned.

"Yeah, I do. We'll be right here waiting for you," Oliver reassured her.

"Yeah, maybe you're right," Olivia sighed.

She walked back into the waiting room, where Josephine and Alonso were sitting huddled side by side.

"Okay, let's talk," Olivia said, looking straight at Alonso.

BOCA BONITA
MONDAY, DECEMBER 23

After their late night of dancing, Heather had planned on waking up early, but when she looked at the clock – after she'd finally convinced her eyes to *stay* open – the alarm clock read ten-thirty.

After she'd showered, put on a clean T-shirt and shorts, and pulled her hair up into a shorter-than-usual ponytail, she'd opened her bedroom door to find a traveller's mug with three mini arepas sitting beside it on a plate. The mug was filled with what turned out to be a delicious berry smoothie and tucked underneath it was a cheeky note that read, "I convinced them all to have breakfast at Yolanda's. You're welcome. – J.".

Heather had then taken Maria's red Alfa Romeo to the tennis club where she and Sofia had played a ruthless doubles match against identical Filipina twins, Jamila and Camila. Heather had discovered that thanks to her long legs and arms, she was quite good at the game, so they'd won. They'd already agreed before the game that the losers would buy lunch.

Now, the four of them were sitting at an outdoor table on the club's flagstone patio, still in their cute tennis outfits. The patio overlooked a few of the courts, which meant they could hear the gentle thwacking of tennis balls followed by the grunts of players. They were all feeling energized from the exertion.

"I don't believe that you've never played tennis before, Heather! If I didn't know you better, Sofia,

I'd think we'd been duped," Jamila joked as she picked at her fish and chips.

"Yeah, but you gave us a good run for the money," Sofia said before putting a forkful of salad in her mouth.

"I still can't believe that love means zero in tennis," Heather joked. "How can love be nothing?"

"Didn't Shakespeare say it himself? 'Love is a smoke made with the fumes of sighs.'" Camila joked.

"Falling in love is easy. It's the relationship that's hard." Jamila remarked.

"You don't have to say that again," Heather sighed.

"That's why you're here, isn't it?" Camila prodded Heather.

"Is it so easy to figure out?" Heather was startled.

"Breakups make people do crazy shit," Jamila remarked.

"Not all the time. I think it all depends on how the breakup went down and how long you've been going out," Camila disagreed.

"What happened?" Jamila asked.

"The guy I was dating cheated on me," Heather explained succinctly.

"Was it the first time?" Camila asked.

"Yeah," Heather shrugged.

"How'd you find out? You walk in on them?" Camila asked.

"They were sexting," Heather explained.

"How long had you guys been dating?" Jamila asked.

"A few months," Heather answered.

"Who was the ho?" Camila asked.

"Some girl who was supposed to pose nude for him," Heather explained matter-of-factly.

"Whaaaat?" Jamila exclaimed.

"He's a portrait artist. So, I was fine with it. But then I saw all these flirty texts between them. I told him to get the hell out of my house, and that was it," Heather explained bluntly.

Sofia was squirming in her seat. That morning, Maria had texted her the whole story of what Elsa had done to Brian.

"You got ants in your pants over there, woman?" Jamila asked Sofia.

Sofia stopped squirming.

"But he didn't actually do anything?" Camila asked.

"No." Heather frowned.

"So, he didn't physically cheat on you." Jamila looked confused.

Feeling defensive, Heather began to overexplain. "Listen, I had to get out of there. He kept showing up at my shop with flowers and sending me texts saying that he'd made a mistake and that nothing had happened and that nothing was going to happen, and that he wanted me back."

"You do realize how creepy that sounds, right?" Camila was appalled.

"I think it sounds sweet. Heather showed me his texts, and they're harmless. He doesn't say anything mean or nasty. Maybe you should give him the benefit of the doubt instead of jumping to conclusions," Sofia pointed out.

"Doesn't matter. If Heather's told him to stop texting and that it's over, he should respect that," Jamila declared.

"He's basically trying to force you to love him," Camila pointed out.

"But what if you knew for sure he didn't do anything? What if you gave him the chance to explain what really happened?" Sofia asked.

"There's nothing he could say at this point that would make me change my mind. Besides, what could he possibly say?" Heather asked defiantly.

"Maybe that he got fooled? She wasn't who she said she was?" Sofia offered in a roundabout way.

"Hmmm ... that's a pretty weak argument," Camila observed.

"Yeah, I agree with Camila. I've thought about it, and he and I were never right for each other. He's too young and immature," Heather said.

"I think you should take some time for yourself," Camila remarked – just as Jamila weighed in with an opposing argument, and said, "I think you should have a rebound fling."

"I don't know about all of that, but I have some incredible news! I told Sofia already. I'm going to meet Lars Borgen this afternoon at his test bakery!" Heather exclaimed.

They all gave her quizzical looks.

"Who?" Jamila asked.

"You guys don't know who he is?" Heather was surprised.

"To be honest, I don't either. I kind of pretended last night because you looked so happy," Sofia confessed, laughing.

"Some friend you are!" Heather teased.

"Who is he?" Jamila coaxed impatiently.

Heather took out her phone and began searching until she found a dapper picture of Lars standing in front of a media wall sporting a tuxedo and his familiar ruby-coloured goatee.

"This. Is. Lars." Heather enunciated slowly as she presented the picture to the women.

"Huh ... Well, he's ..." Jamila nudged her sister to help her out.

Heather reiterated, "he's a famous pastry chef!"

"Well, there you go. He's cute in a famous pastry chefy kinda way," Camila giggled.

"He's your rebound guy!" Jamila offered, giggling, but Heather fluffed her off.

MUNICH
MONDAY, DECEMBER 23

Last night, after Brian had shown her and Phil the breathtaking portrait, she was now calling Elsa the Catfisher, Brian had reset the art gallery's security alarm system and locked up. He'd then mumbled goodbye as he began his trek back home through the snowy streets.

Phil had come back with Maria to Heather's house, and they'd slowly made love in Heather's bed, no longer caring that it was Heather's bed.

That morning, they'd woken up early and loaded up on coffee and chocolate croissants she'd also purchased from Heather's shop, which had seemed to cure any threat of a hangover. Phil had then gone back home.

She'd told Phil that Martha had wholeheartedly agreed to letting her off at two as she'd smartly recruited her two kids to help out at the shop since they were home from university for the holidays and had nothing better to do. When they'd arrived, judging by the reluctant looks on their faces, Maria could definitely tell they thought they had better things to do.

Maria had also listened to an upbeat voicemail from her daughter, Olivia, about a dolphin and then a rushed one telling her that their friend's father had some sort of medical episode, so they were back in Miami staying at their friends' house and would be visiting the father at the hospital, but not to worry.

Now, Maria and Phil were standing on the sidewalk outside of the shop, the afternoon ahead of them, free to do as they pleased.

"Have you ever been on a sleigh ride?" Phil asked, smiling. He was wearing his Bills toque, the same black parka, but she noticed he was wearing blue snow pants.

"Um, no?" Maria thought it was a pretty obvious answer.

"Would you like to? The winter fair's on, and Brian and I used to go there as teenagers. I remember it being a lot of fun." Phil beamed at her.

"I've never been to a winter fair!" Maria giggled.

"Great! It's going to be so much fun! I borrowed my parents' car. It's just over there." Phil pointed to the silver Mercedes SUV parked on the other side of the street.

"They're okay with not having a car for the afternoon?" Maria looked at Phil in surprise. "And what about Brian? Did you guys go for lunch?"

"No, we didn't because actually, he'd like you to come over for dinner tonight. And of course, my mum and pop would, too. Brian's promised to make us a beef wellington. It's his way of apologizing for everything," Phil said brightly.

"I'm so relieved to hear that! That's so nice of him. I'd love to." Maria smiled warmly just as an elderly lady tried to enter the shop by going around them, but found herself unintentionally blocked.

Maria and Phil were trying to move out of the way just as the elderly lady looked at them in surprise, "oh, Phil! I didn't realize it was you!"

"Oh hi, Mrs. Nolan," Phil said, tilting his head hello, "Maria, Mrs. Nolan was my home economics teacher."

"Nice to meet you, although I think I may have served you yesterday? Pinwheel cookies?" Maria observed.

"You caught me. I do have a bit of a sweet tooth," Mrs. Nolan confided.

"But wait, you were Phil's home economics teacher? Tell me, what was Phil like as a student?" Maria asked cheekily.

"He did make a pillowcase once," Mrs. Nolan teased.

"Really stretching those creative boundaries!" Maria chided Phil.

Phil's face went red.

"Well, it certainly was a pleasure running into you, Mrs. Nolan," Phil grimaced, trying to cut the encounter short.

"My pleasure," Mrs. Nolan tittered and waved goodbye as she entered the shop.

"Huh, so sewing is not one of your strengths," Maria teased.

"I am a weathercaster for a reason," Phil grinned.

"What's the weather going to be like today?" Maria asked, leaning into Phil's warm body.

"I forecast a flurry of fun," Phil joked.

Maria rolled her eyes at the cheesy joke, but looked up at him fondly, and he leaned down and kissed her. After a bit, they slowly unraveled themselves, looked both ways, and then safely crossed the street. As soon as they were inside the SUV, Phil pushed a few buttons on the GPS screen and began the drive.

"How far is it?" Maria asked, as she looked out the window at the bundled-up tourists loaded down with shopping bags.

Phil looked down at the GPS screen and then back up at the road ahead, "GPS says eighteen minutes."

"Perfect. So, I kinda need to say something about what happened last night," Maria said quietly.

"Yeah, I figured you would. It was a weird night," Phil nodded.

"I feel so badly for Brian ... and Heather. I mean, she doesn't know. She needs to know." Maria frowned.

"Does she?" Phil didn't agree.

"Yeah, I think so. I'd want to know." Maria nodded.

"Hmm... knowing Heather, it might just piss her off even more." Phil was relieved that of all the things she'd chosen to talk about from last night, it wasn't that his mother had mentioned wanting grandkids.

Phil slowed down and turned off Main Street to make a right turn onto a bumpy, country road.

"Why?" Maria asked.

"Because Brian was stupid enough to fall for it," Phil said matter-of-factly.

"I guess I can see that." Maria frowned.

"You know, Brian was hounding me before I left to pick you up about where Heather was staying. He wants to know where your house is. Don't worry, I didn't tell him anything." Phil said.

"Of course, thank you. Oh, I texted Sofia and told her about our brownie experience, and apparently, Heather said we were only supposed to eat half a brownie each. Well, she said in my case, I probably should've just eaten a quarter of it," Maria giggled.

"Well, that explains it," Phil sighed, "still, I don't think I ever want to do that again."

"No, me neither." Maria laughed, and when she turned to look at Phil, she noticed a white plastic bag lying on the back seat.

"What's in the bag?" Maria asked.

"Oh, I brought you gloves, a hat and a scarf, and my mother's snow pants. The pants are very warm and comfortable. They're waterproof, so you won't get cold if you get wet from the snow," Phil explained.

Eventually, they could see the fair up ahead. It was set upon a vast expanse of land where there seemed to be thousands of people milling about its huge buildings. They turned into a snowy laneway, and Maria noticed a sign high above them that read "Welcome to Munich's Regal Winter Fair".

"Well, here we are," Phil said, stating the obvious, as he drove up to the cashier booth that guarded the entrance gates.

"Hello, it's fifty dollars per adult, so that'll be one hundred," the attendant said, smiling.

"Hello, here you go," Phil said as he took out his credit card and handed it to the attendant.

"Phil, please let me at least pay for myself," Maria whispered, and Phil shook his head, no.

"Have fun," the attendant said as he handed Phil's credit card back. The gate lifted and Phil followed the laneway over to the snowy parking lot.

"Well then, here's to another something new I'm about to experience on this trip! Thank you for inviting me!" Maria exclaimed happily.

"I don't remember it being this big." Phil peered worriedly at the massive buildings.

"You said you came here as teenagers. Things change when they're successful. I mean, Munich is Christmas Town, after all," Maria teased.

A parking lot attendant motioned them towards a spot, and Phil eased the SUV in.

"Yeah, but ... I had no idea." Phil continued to look worried.

"It's going to be okay," Maria patted his arm, "just give me a minute to put on the snow pants."

Phil put the SUV in park and got out. Maria grabbed the shopping bag from the back seat, opened her door, and stepped outside onto the parking lot. Keeping her door open, she leaned in and turned the bag over so that everything fell out onto her seat: a matching set of gloves, hat and scarf, and pink snow pants.

She held the snow pants up to her body to see if they'd fit. Satisfied that they weren't too long, she pushed the gloves, hat, and scarf over to one side, sat back down onto the passenger-side seat and with the snow pants in her lap, closed the door.

She bent down and pushed open her boots. As she pulled her feet out, she was careful to prevent her socked feet from getting a soaker from any of the wet spots on the floor. With her legs elevated in the air, she tucked her wool pants into her socks, then began tugging the snow pants over her feet, one foot at a time, then over her wool pants, alternating legs, and then towards her bum. She put her feet on the seat for leverage and lifted her bum up in the air to convince the pants to go up and over without bunching. After a few final tugs and a few curses towards her Latin bum, the pants relented and were all the way up.

She stretched her legs straight out towards the console and bunched her coat upwards and tried to blindly find the button to snap the pants shut. After a few tries, she heard and felt the snap, but as soon as she bent down to push her feet back into her boots, she felt the pants snap open. She knew better than to try again.

Letting out a big sigh, she sat up and grabbed the set of gloves, hat and scarf, opened her door and then jumped out of the SUV. She bent down and pulled the pants down over top of her boots. Standing up straight, she bunched the coat underneath her chin and snapped the snow pants back together, pulling her coat back over top of them.

"Ta-da!" Maria yelled, not daring to move an inch.

Phil was about to tease Maria about the so-called minute she'd promised it would take but then noticed how nicely the snow pants hugged her curves. "You look pretty spectacular!"

"Thank you!" Maria beamed, while pulling on the hat, scarf and gloves, and praying that the pants wouldn't snap open again.

As they approached the exit to the parking lot, the same attendant who had directed them in, now handed them a map.

"Enjoy yourselves," the man said, smiling.

"Thanks," Phil said as he smiled back.

Phil opened the map and held it out in front of him, scratching his chin in disbelief. Maria tried to peer over Phil's arms, but couldn't quite see.

"Look, there's an ice sculpture contest over here and a tree-cutting contest over there. Strolling carollers and a horse wagon competition. A band is playing on this stage. There are pony rides in the small animal pavilion, some cattle barns ... Oh, the sleigh rides are over here ... An ice slide, a tractor show, mechanical bull riding." Phil was pointing frantically at different areas on the map. "It's gotten so big. I had no idea. Wow, it says it's on four hundred acres of land. But I remember walking here as a kid. Our farm must've been just over there somewhere."

Maria saw how bewildered Phil was and had figured out by now that the secret to getting him to relax was through food.

"Why don't we get something to eat first, and then we can decide what to do? There must be a food court? My treat," she suggested.

"Oh yes! Great idea! I could go for a snack. And no, this day is all on me," Phil said, visibly relaxing.

Phil studied the map again and then pointed left.

"It's this way! Come, my lady." Phil led her by the hand.

They made their way along the snowy pathway through the crowds. The atmosphere was festive. They could hear people yelling as games were being played, and every once in a while, musical notes echoed from the buildings. Eventually, they found a building with a sign indicating that there was a food court inside.

"What do you feel like? Hopefully, they have beavertails. Have you ever had a beavertail?" Phil asked enthusiastically as he held the door open for her.

"Canadians eat beaver?" Maria teased.

"Haha. Yes, apparently so." Phil blushed, remembering last night. "No, seriously, it's like a donut, but long and flat. I always get the Avalanche. It's like a Skor cheesecake." Phil was practically salivating.

There were several food trucks arranged in a circle around a few white plastic tables that were already occupied by people talking and eating.

"Oh good! There is a Beavertail food truck!" Phil exclaimed happily.

They walked up to the Beavertail food truck window, and Maria looked at the sandwich board to see what her other options were. "I'll have the apple cinnamon Beavertail, please."

After Phil ordered and paid for them, they waited as the stall owner picked up the hot Beavertails with tongs, carefully wrapping them in paper and then handing them over.

"Have a nice day!" The owner said, smiling.

"You too!" Maria smiled back.

They found a place to stand where they could eat without being jostled by passersby. As they opened them up, hot steam escaped from the paper, so they blew on them before trying to take bites. Once the Beavertails had cooled down a bit, Phil ate his in four quick bites while Maria savoured the sweetness of each tiny bite.

After eating about half of hers, she nudged Phil, "hey, feeling kind of full, you want the rest of mine?"

"You sure?" Phil eyed her beavertail.

"Yes, please have it." Maria handed it over, and Phil finished it in seconds.

After Phil threw the wrappings in the garbage, he took out at the map from his coat pocket and held it out in front of them.

"What were you saying about an ice slide? That sounds kinda fun," Maria suggested.

"Sure, it's over here." Phil nodded, and then traced an outline with his finger of the best route.

They exited the food court and made their way through the winding, snowy footpath alongside other visitors, passing by several buildings until they reached another huge building. As Phil opened the door for Maria, a bitter cold lambasted them, similar to the one they'd experienced at the airport.

"Brrrr. It's cold in here!" Phil cringed.

"I feel like I just walked into a blast chiller," Maria said, shivering.

Maria looked up at the enormous U-shaped slide that coiled around the room like a frozen snake. The ice had been molded into a transparent thickness that provided glimpses of silhouettes and she could hear the occasional happy scream.

They joined the lineup of people that led to a table staffed by a grey-haired lady wearing a red sweater. Maria noticed that everyone in line was wearing big puffy coats and snow pants.

"What's the lineup for?" Phil asked the young man in front of them.

"Apparently, you have to sign a waiver before going down the slide." The man explained before shrugging and turning back to his girlfriend.

"A waiver? Are you sure you still want to do this?" Phil asked Maria.

Maria looked up at the massive ice structure again. "I have to admit my palms are sweaty, but it looks fun! I think I'd be upset with myself if we didn't do it!"

"Fair enough," Phil nodded.

As they drew closer to the table, they could see that the grey-haired lady's sweater depicted a Tabby cat draped in a tangled mess of Christmas lights of which several were blinking.

When they reached the table, before the grey-haired lady could say anything, Phil asked, "how tall is this slide?"

The lady answered in a musical voice. "Oh, what a great question! The slide is forty-two feet, and the ride will last about five minutes. If you come back at midnight, we're going for the world record number of people to descend an indoor ice slide in a twenty-four-hour period. Would you like to come back?" Phil shook his head no, and she looked disappointed, so she continued matter-of-factly, "for now, just sign here."

She put the waivers on the table, and they signed their names. They stood beside the table, not moving but staring up at the slide until the lady finally yelled at them, "it's not going to come to you. You have to go to it!"

They both flinched at her words and jostled their way towards the tall and winding metal staircase, joining the line of excited visitors. They gingerly walked up the steps while trying not to look down between the gaps as they climbed higher and higher. The line of people eventually slowed and then came to a halt as they waited for their turn near the final steps. A man wearing a yellow vest instructed them.

"Please wait behind the yellow line, and I'll let you know when it's your turn." He instructed as he helped the young couple who had been in line in front of them.

They watched nervously as the girlfriend sat at the lip of the slide and, with one giant push by her boyfriend, shot down the slide. They could hear her yells spiraling downwards. After a few minutes, they heard a whistle, and the man in the yellow vest nodded. The young man sat down and then quickly disappeared. A few minutes later, they heard the whistle again.

"Now, you can come." The man in the yellow vest said, motioning for Phil to sit down.

"Ladies, first," Phil said.

"Not this time. You go first." Maria shook her head.

Phil shook his head, no.

Maria hesitated, and then said, "you know what, I'll go first."

"Are you sure?" Phil asked.

"Would one of you just go first!" The man in the yellow vest yelled, exasperated.

Phil and Maria gave each other a "sheesh" look and Maria finally sat down on the lip of the entrance to the slide. To her horror, she heard the button of her snow pants pop open. There was nothing she could do about it at this point, so she just had to hope her pants would stay on.

She peered down into the slide, not seeing much past the first curve. The U-shaped walls of the slide were high above her head and curved upwards. For one last time, Maria looked over at Phil, and they gave each other the thumbs up, and then she pushed off.

Maria swooshed side-to-side as a frigid wind rushed at her face. The slide was slightly cold on her bum, but she decided it had been worth the effort of putting the snow pants on, as she wouldn't be completely soaked through … and so far, they were staying on.

Sloshing back and forth, she dipped and twisted around the quick corners. She felt a sudden uneasiness as if she could catapult over the sides of the slide at any second, so she placed her palms down on the ice beside her legs to try to stabilize herself. As she slid downwards, the ice below tickled her palms, and a chill seeped in.

Soon, the undulating curves of the slide took her up, down, and around. One minute she was high up near the ceiling, and then the next, she was careening down to the floor, twisting sideways like a carrier pigeon in mid-flight.

Every once in a while, she could see the people in line below. For one courageous second, she lifted her hands up in the air, let out a joyous scream, and then quickly put them back down.

Eventually, the slide shot her out onto a huge air cushion, where she landed with a soft thump. Maria leaned onto her left side, daintily rolled off the mattress and stood up. She looked down and was embarrassed to notice that the zipper on her snow pants was halfway down, so she discreetly zipped them up, hoping no one had noticed, and decided not to even try to button them up again.

A woman wearing a yellow vest came over and helped her over to the side where she could wait for Phil without the chance of getting hit. The woman then blew into her whistle to indicate that the coast was clear for the next person to come down the slide.

Because of his height, Phil's head was high above the sides of the slide, which meant Maria could keep track of his swift progression as his head bobbed up and down. Every so often, she saw one of his legs shoot straight up into the air and then an arm flop over the side, as if he was hanging on for dear life.

After a few minutes, Phil shot out of the slide and onto the air cushion, causing it to deflate all the way down to the floor. Squished down into the middle of the mattress, Phil struggled to extricate himself by kicking his legs up in the air. The lady with the whistle ran over and began tugging his arms and Maria joined in by pushing his legs towards the lady. After a few more tugs and pushes, Phil eventually fell onto the floor, headfirst. He pushed himself up with his arms.

"Thank you," he said to them as he stood up, brushing himself off.

"Are you okay?" The lady frowned.

"Oh yes, I'm fine," Phil said as he fixed his clothing.

The lady smiled and motioned for them to get out of the way, and then blew her whistle.

"Wow, that was amazing!" Maria hugged Phil once they were over to the side.

"Boy, that was scary! I thought I was going to fly over the edge." Phil was out of breath.

"But I'm so glad we did that!" Maria yelled happily. "Where to next?"

Phil examined the map again and suggested, "we could go to the equestrian building?"

"Anything with you sounds lovely." The adrenaline from going down the slide was making her feel warm and fuzzy, and Phil gave her a squeeze.

Phil led Maria out of the cold building, and they took the snowy path to the equestrian building. As soon as they opened the door, the musty smell of wet hay and horse manure assaulted their senses.

"Oh, my goodness, what's that smell?" Maria asked in surprise.

"It's the smell of horses," Phil grimaced.

"Ugh, I had no idea." Maria began yanking her scarf up over her nose.

They saw that the auditorium was barely a quarter full. Phil led Maria up the concrete stairs to an empty spot on the metal benches.

Maria watched as a lady dressed in an equestrian outfit rode her chestnut-coloured horse towards the obstacles and jumped elegantly up and over each one.

"You see how she holds the reins tight like that? She's guiding the horse, telling it where to go with her reins and with her legs," Phil explained.

"How do you know that?" Maria asked.

"We had two Morgans on our farm," Phil explained.

At first, Maria thought Phil meant both horses were named Morgan.

"Lucy and Charlie," Phil further explained.

"Oh, you mean Morgan is the breed ... but the horses were named after the comic strip?" Maria asked, smiling.

"You got it!" Phil exclaimed enthusiastically.

"My daughter and I loved watching 'A Charlie Brown Christmas' every year! Of course, she's too old, now." Maria reminisced bittersweetly.

"They were the gentlest of horses," Phil nodded, reminiscing in his own fond memories.

They watched for a bit until Maria could no longer help herself, and confessed, "you know, Phil, as lovely as this is, I really can't stand the smell."

"Oh, you want to leave?" Phil asked, disappointed.

"Yes, please," Maria nodded.

"Sure, no problem. We can go see the outdoor animals. That'll be better," Phil suggested.

"Thank you. Very kind." Maria kept holding her scarf over her nose.

They walked back down the concrete stairs and exited the building. Once outside, Maria inhaled deep breaths of crisp fresh air.

"Much better," she said, sighing with relief.

"Oh, yoo-hoo, Phil!" A female voice yodeled at them.

Phil turned around to see that it was Mrs. Harris, the busybody from the Probus club his parents were a part of, and his shoulders sagged.

"Hello, Mrs. Harris," Phil said flatly.

"I'm so sorry to hear about Heather and Brian. What happened, exactly? I heard she caught him with a lady of the night?" Mrs. Harris asked, whispering and pretending to look over her shoulder.

"No," Phil shook his head, "that's not what happened."

As if coming to their rescue, a voice boomed deafeningly from the loudspeakers above them.

"Ladies and gentlemen, it's not too late to sign up for polka lessons from our expert dance crew. Make your way over to the Dance Pavilion, right away!"

Maria saw that this was her chance to pull Phil away from this horrible lady and said excitedly, "polka lessons? Should we sign up? I've always wanted to polka!"

"You want to polka? I'd love to! Sorry, Mrs. Harris, looks like we're off to polka!" Phil gave her a half-wave.

Maria grinned and Mrs. Harris pursed her lips.

"Seeing you dance is going to make my day!" Phil began picturing Maria performing a very different type of dance.

"Let's go!" Maria grabbed Phil's hand.

They entered the indoor pavilion and saw that there were at least twenty couples already there, waiting on the dance floor and facing a small, oval stage. A polka band was stationed to the right of the stage.

An elderly woman dressed in a red sweater with a green Christmas tree on it and black slacks approached them with a clipboard.

"Are you here for the polka lessons?" She smiled benevolently at them.

"Yes, we are," Phil nodded.

"What are your names, please?" She raised her pen, ready to write them down.

"Phil Müller and Maria Rodriguez." Phil said as the lady began writing down their names.

"Does Rodriguez end with a 'zed' or an 'ess'?" She asked, hesitating at Maria's last name.

"Zed." Phil answered and the lady nodded.

"Please take off your coats and snow pants, hang them on the clothes rack, and then make your way over there." She pointed to an empty spot on the dance floor.

Since there was no bench to sit down on, they leaned on each other as they took off their boots. Then they took off their snow pants and coats, hung everything up, and leaned on each other once again to put their boots back on. Maria looked at her snow pants, hanging there limply and couldn't help but giggle.

As they waited at their designated spot on the dance floor in their regular clothes, Phil pointed to the polka band and asked, "have you ever seen a live polka band before?" and Maria shook her head.

"Can you see all of their different instruments?" Phil asked.

"Sort of," Maria shrugged.

"See, this polka band has an accordion player, a tuba player, a trombone player, and a clarinet player. But not all polka bands are the same," Phil explained.

Before Maria could ask Phil what he meant, two lithe, young dancers dressed in polka outfits pranced across the dance floor and bounced onto the oval stage. The boy was quite tall and skinny with long, curly reddish hair arranged in a man-bun and a well-kempt beard. The girl was a couple of inches shorter than the boy, and her sandy blond hair had been pulled into two tightly braided pigtails.

"Welcome, everyone! We're so excited you decided to join us!" The girl announced chirpily, and the two of them curtsied towards the participants.

The boy spoke. "I like to describe the polka as three quick steps and a hop. And then you simply circle your way around the dance floor."

"Please, try a few with us. We will show you, slowly." The girl said and then they slowly performed the movements, while facing the audience.

Along with the other participants in the room, Phil keenly watched the boy and girl, took a few steps, and then tried to hop but lost his balance. Maria giggled.

"Your turn," Phil chuckled.

Maria performed the steps with grace and nailed them after a few tries. Phil gave her the thumbs up.

"Now, let's show you in real time," the girl said.

The couple curtsied towards one another, and then the boy put his hand around the girl's waist as she laid her hand on his shoulder. The polka band began playing "Merry Christmas Polka" by Jim Reeves, and they clasped each other's hands.

The young boy led the girl daintily around the oval stage in quick steps and hops, circling dangerously close to the edge, causing the audience to gasp. The girl's pigtails flew up and down in unison with their jolly steps. As the music came to a halt, the couple stopped dancing and curtsied towards one another.

"Now it's your turn." The girl beamed at the participants.

"Please curtsy towards one another," the boy instructed. "All of you who wish to take the lead, please take your partner's hand like this and put your other hand around their waist like this."

"I guess I'll take the lead," Phil said, and Maria nodded in agreement.

Phil clasped Maria's hand with his left hand and circled her waist with his right hand. The young girl was walking around adjusting the hands of couples to make sure they were positioned properly. When she reached Phil and Maria, she paused.

"Well, there's a considerable height difference between you two. You might want to put your hand here, instead." The girl re-positioned Phil's hand so that it was a bit lower.

She backed away and gave a nod to the band, who resumed playing, but instead of playing "Merry Christmas Polka" by Jim Reeves, they began playing Frankie Yankovic's "She's Too Fat For Me".

Phil and Maria tried their best to step and hop in unison, but the length of their strides was so different that soon they were jumping instead of stepping.

Jump, jump, jump, hop.

Jump, jump, jump, hop.

Maria became distracted by the lyrics, wondering if she was hearing the words correctly.

We don't want her, you can have her
She's too fat for me
Yeah, she's too fat, much too fat
But she's just right for me.
She's so charming
And she's so winning
But it's alarming
When she goes in swimming
We don't want her, you can have her
She's too fat for me (ha)

Around and around in circles, they went to the seemingly never-ending lyrics. Their jumps eventually turned into hops, and their hops turned into skips.

Hop, hop, hop, skip.

Hop, hop, hop, skip.

Soon, instead of performing the skips, Phil began lifting Maria up in the air.

Hop, hop, hop, lift.

Hop, hop, hop, lift.

The music abruptly stopped just as Phil was lifting Maria up in the air. Everyone stopped and looked at them in disbelief.

"What?" Phil asked and then slowly realized that he was holding Maria way up in the air. Embarrassed, he quickly set her down on the floor.

"Oh! So sorry!" Phil apologized to Maria who began giggling.

Soon, the rest of the participants were giggling as well. One participant in particular kept staring at them, and Maria assumed it was because she looked silly trying to straighten out her pink V-neck sweater and wool pants. But then the tall blond woman began walking towards them, and her short, bald partner shuffled behind her.

"Well, hello, Phil," she said dryly when she reached them.

"Clara?" Phil frowned as he studied her face.

"Yes, it's me. Hi there, I'm Phil's ex-wife." The woman held out her hand for Maria to shake.

"Oh sorry, this is Maria. How are you doing? I wasn't expecting to run into you here. Especially on a Monday afternoon." Phil gave her a puzzled look.

"Oh well, you know, it's Christmas," she answered vaguely. "So, are you still in Miami?"

"Yep. How are things with you?" Phil smiled at her.

"Well, you know. I'm so glad I ran into you because I've been wanting to say this to you for a long time. I wasted a lot of time being angry at you because you took away some of the best years of my life, but I'm in a healthy place now. It's good to see you're still the same goofy Phil," Clara said haughtily.

Phil was dumbfounded. "I ... What? But ... We parted amicably?"

"Well, yes, that's what I told myself at the time too, but then I realized how unfair it all was. But that's all in the past now, so don't worry about it. Good seeing you. Let's hope he doesn't do the same to you, Maria." Clara gave them a strained smile and pulled her partner towards the door.

"Wait. What are you saying?" Phil had a stunned look on his face.

Clara ignored him and kept walking.

Maria touched his arm. "Hey, are you okay? That was totally uncalled for on her part."

"I'm ... confused." Phil kept staring at the door as the rest of the participants left.

"Phil! Forget about her." Maria tried to get him to look at her.

"I don't understand what just happened." He finally looked down at Maria.

Maria could see the hurt in his eyes and understood what it was like to have things from the past thrown at you in an instant. She strongly felt that in this case, Phil didn't deserve it one bit.

Maria looked straight at him and said, "well, if that's a healthy place for her, then I really don't want to see what an unhealthy place looks like. As for you and me? She doesn't know nada de mierda[22] about us. That woman is crazy."

Phil nodded, still in shock.

"Besides, Brian's making us a beef wellington. Remember? And I need to pick up a few things. Let's forget about her and go!" Maria encouraged Phil, and he nodded again.

***

After they'd left the fair, Maria had asked Phil to take her to the grocery store to pick up a few things that she needed to make margaritas and then to make a quick stop at Heather's house before going back to his parents' house for dinner.

She was now heading up the pathway to Heather's front porch while Phil stayed parked in the driveway with the motor running.

As she unlocked the front door, she grabbed the package that had been leaning up against it and once inside, she flung off her boots and coat and then headed towards the kitchen.

Finding scissors in one of the kitchen drawers, she sliced the package open and took out the Miami Dolphins hoodie she'd asked Jack to ship to her from her closet in Miami. The Bills were playing the

---

[22] She doesn't know shit about us.

Dolphins that night, and she thought it would be fun if she could wear it while they watched the game together.

As she was taking off her pink V-neck sweater and putting on the hoodie, her cellphone began to ring. She finished yanking the hoodie over her head and was happy to see that the caller was her daughter, Olivia.

"Olivia!" Maria answered, smiling. "How are you, my darling? I got your messages. I'm so sorry I haven't called you back!"

"Mom! I'm actually calling to see how you're doing," Olivia asked.

"Why is that?" Maria asked as Charlotte came trotting over to her and meowed. Maria bent down and began petting the cat behind her ears.

"Well, I ran into Dad and he told me everything. So now I understand why you left. I'm so sorry, Mom. Are you okay? Where are you, anyway?" Olivia asked, and Maria could hear the worry in her daughter's voice.

"Ah, so you know everything. I honestly was going to tell you, but the last few days here have just been so busy," Maria sighed.

"Where's here?" Olivia questioned.

"I'm in Canada. I know this is going to sound crazy, but I've exchanged houses with a lady who lives in Canada, and I'm helping out at her bakery. It's only for a few days." Maria hoped Olivia wouldn't be hurt that she'd left around Christmas time.

"Wait … what? You mean there's some strange lady staying at our house, right now? Oh, I'm sure Yolanda's loving that!" Olivia exclaimed.

"Yes, and um, no, Yolanda's probably not loving it. But I really don't care. Besides, Sofia's been showing her around, and apparently, she's very nice," Maria said defensively.

"What's this about a bakery?" Olivia was puzzled.

"Listen, don't worry about that. So, what exactly did Alonso tell you?" Maria felt anxiety spreading throughout her body.

"He said he's fallen in love with some other woman. Is this true?" Olivia demanded.

"I only just found out myself, sweetheart."

"Can you believe she's married, too? I mean, they're breaking up two families!"

"I'm so sorry you had to find out like this." Maria was surprised at this new information.

"He's so selfish."

"Don't be too hard on him."

"Well, he put my friend's father in the hospital!"

"What are you talking about?"

"The guy had a heart attack when he found out!"

"Okay, back up. How does this all fit together?" Maria was confused and then realized Phil was probably wondering what was taking her so long, so she quickly made her way to the front door and cracked it open a few inches. She gave Phil the "one-minute" finger and pointed to her phone. He smiled and gave her the thumbs up.

"Well, when we went to the hospital this morning to see JC's dad ... Dad was there in the waiting room," Olivia explained.

"Who's JC?" Maria asked.

"Oliver's best friend," Olivia explained, exasperated that her mother wasn't keeping up with the information.

"Oh, your new boyfriend's friend." Maria was astounded that her daughter had met Alonso's new woman in a strange web of coincidences. "So, let me get this straight. Alonso is leaving me for your boyfriend's friend's mother?"

"Yes! And he apologized for stuff he did ... To be honest, I really didn't want to hear it ... But I mean, we ended up talking about stuff ... And we sort of figured some things out ... But I'm still mad at him ..." Olivia trailed off.

"It's okay, sweetheart. Don't be so hard on your father. I've actually met a very nice gentleman here in Munich myself." Maria hoped this information might calm her daughter down.

"I thought you were in Canada?" Olivia asked.

"It's a town called Munich, but it's here in Canada, near Toronto," Maria explained.

"So, you met someone too? I knew you and dad weren't really close, but wow, that's fast ... Like super fast ... Sorry, no judging. You know what ... Good for you, Mom." Olivia was shocked at how quickly her parents had moved on.

"Sometimes these things just happen." Maria tried to explain.

"But what about the whole long-distance thing? You're not going to move there?" Olivia was immediately worried.

"No!" Maria shuddered at the thought of living somewhere so cold. "He's actually a weatherman in Miami. He's here visiting his family for Christmas."

"What do you mean, his family? He's not married too? Oh my God, I can't take this!" Olivia cried out.

"What? No! His parents and his brother!" Maria yelled back defensively.

"Oh, okay, good," Olivia sighed with relief.

"What about your guy? Oliver? How's it going with him?" Maria felt slightly worried that her daughter was travelling with a new boyfriend whom she'd yet to meet.

"It's going great. He's super sweet," Olivia said and then added, "Mom, you know you can talk to me about anything, right? We're here for each other. Always."

"Yes, I know. I don't like burdening you with my problems. I'm okay as long as you're okay, sweetie. I'm glad you called. Let's talk later. The guy I met is actually waiting for me outside in the car, so I better get going. I love you." Maria said quietly.

"Love you, too." Olivia said, and they hung up.

MIAMI
MONDAY, DECEMBER 23

While Maria was enjoying her afternoon at the winter fair, Heather was experiencing her own afternoon of fun.

Following the instructions Lars had texted her the night before, Heather left Maria's car at the parking lot he'd recommended and began walking towards the building. It turned out that Lars' test bakery was hidden away in an industrial area.

Because of the afternoon drizzle, she'd chosen to wear her light jacket over top of her sundress, and her small purse was swinging from her left shoulder.

She walked towards the back of the two-storey manufacturing building and knocked on the blue metal door. Within a few seconds, the door swung open, and Lars' handsome face and wide smile greeted her.

"Hi! Welcome! Come in, please." He was wearing a chef's jacket that fit snugly around his belly and a puffy chef's hat that sat at an angle on his head. There was a smudge of chocolate across his left breast.

"Hi, thank you so much for inviting me. I'm so honoured to be here," Heather gushed as she walked through the door.

Lars kept beaming as he shut the door behind her. The first thing that hit her was the sweet smell of what she guessed was sugar, chocolate, and yeast in the air. The ovens were hard at work, and the steam escaping from the various appliances created a sweet coziness.

The industrial space seemed like an endless array of stainless-steel ovens, fridges, cooling racks, and countertops. As she got closer, she realized that each station was essentially its own full-fledged kitchen with a stove, oven, sink, and fridge. And each chef was posted at their own assigned station, within which they were busy working at a well-choreographed pace. A photographer was hopping about trying to stay out of the way while taking photos, and a young girl was furiously taking notes.

"Let me introduce you to everyone," Lars said enthusiastically. "This is Laura, my editor," he said as he pointed to a woman leaning against a nearby dining table set for two.

Laura extended her hand, and Heather shook it, both of them smiling at one another. She was a tall, dramatic woman with a swept-up hairstyle, a colourful, silk scarf loosely tied around her neck, and decoratively-patterned eyeglasses.

Pointing to his pastry cooks, one by one, Lars introduced them, "Heather, I'm pleased to introduce you to Oscar, Daria, Ilya, and Lottie. I would be lost without them."

"Hi, it's a pleasure to meet all of you!" Heather exclaimed.

The pastry cooks lifted their heads momentarily to smile at her and then resumed putting the final touches on their creations.

"The photographer is Lance, and our intern, is Sheri-Lyn," Lars continued his introductions, and they gave quick nods.

"My editor, Laura, is here for an official tasting, so they are running against the clock. That's why I wanted you to come. I would love for you to taste some of our newest creations, some based on traditional Danish recipes. Please be honest with your feedback. I saw your impressive track record of awards on your website," Lars said excitedly.

"Thank you," Heather blushed, "it's nothing, really."

"Please, you two, make yourselves comfortable at the dining table." Lars motioned towards the table.

"Oscar has made a traditional Glögg for you. But of course, with a bit of a unique twist." Lars said as Oscar brought out a tray with two drinks in glass mugs and placed one at each of the place settings.

"A what?" Heather asked.

"A Glue‑gh. It's what the Danish drink at Christmas time. And that's all I'm going to say. Enjoy your drinks while you excuse me. I must do a final inspection before we bring out the delicious desserts." Lars went over to the test kitchens and made his rounds, demanding minor adjustments at each station.

Heather and Laura sat down across from each other at the wooden dining table and picked up their mugs. They both examined them. Along with a red and white striped candy cane straw, the espresso‑coloured drink also had a sprig of spruce and a stick of cinnamon peeking out of it. Heather stirred them all around and then removed the sprig of spruce and cinnamon stick so they wouldn't poke her in the eye. She noticed Laura did the same. The glass was rimmed with red and green sprinkles and there were triangular slices of orange floating in the drink. The whole effect was very playful.

"Cheers!" Heather held out the drink towards Laura.

"Cheers!" Laura echoed cheerily.

She took a sip through the candied straw, and the dark liquid was a spiced and spiked otherworldly deliciousness. When she was finally able to pull herself away from it, Heather noted, "hmmm ... I taste mulled wine, amaretto, dark rum, and bourbon? Cardamom? And, of course, a tang from the orange slices."

Laura smiled at her. "You have an impressive palate. Lars tells me you have a German bakery?"

"Yes, I do! We make all types of baked goods and chocolates." Heather wasn't quite sure if she should mention the edibles side of her business.

"And where's that?" Laura asked.

"In Canada, near Toronto," Heather explained.

"What's your shop called?" Laura asked.

"My Sweet Addiction," Heather answered.

"Clever. And do you write baking cookbooks as well?" Laura asked.

"No, I don't." Heather said emphatically and then wondered why she'd never thought of it before. "I guess it would be easy enough. I have all of my recipes written down, of course, but just for me."

Lars interrupted them. "Attention! Ladies! The tasting is about to begin. Please enjoy yourselves and make notes as you taste."

Heather looked down and realized there was a tiny pen and notepad sitting beside her on the table.

"What are we supposed to do?" Heather whispered to Laura.

"Write down whatever comes to your mind. There's no right or wrong answer," Laura explained.

Daria brought out a platter of oversized cookies that had been half-dipped in a layer of chocolate and sprinkles, while the other half remained pale.

"I present to you our Gemini cookies," Daria said as she placed the plate of cookies in the middle of the table.

Heather took one and smelled it. Looking at it more closely, she could see that it had been piped and swirled in tight circles. She bit into the pale part first. She was happy to find that it wasn't too sweet and was sure she tasted almond. She was also pleased that it melted in her mouth and reminded her of the almond cookies her mother used to bake for her and her sister, and she momentarily felt the familiar ache of missing her mother. Next, she bit into the rich, dark chocolate portion. The chocolate and the sprinkles gave the shortbread-like texture a bittersweet crunch.

Heather noticed that Laura was scribbling extensive notes and had finished half of her cookie, so she began writing down what she'd observed.

When she stopped writing, she watched as Laura closed her notepad and moved her plate to the side. Heather mimicked her. Lars immediately saw that they were ready, so he motioned for Ilya to bring over the next creation.

Ilya picked up two plates from his station and brought them over. He placed one in front of Heather and one in front of Laura.

"I'm pleased to present to you my Gleeful Globe," Ilya said.

Heather looked down at a chocolate globe balanced delicately on a gold plate. Sitting beside it was a small ceramic sauceboat.

"Please pour the sauce over the globe and enjoy!" Ilya explained, joyfully.

Its sensuous presentation seemed to flirt with her. Heather lifted up the sauceboat and sniffed it. She picked up notes of caramel, vanilla, and a pleasant floral scent. When she poured it over the globe, it melted the top and revealed a thick mousse within it. She set the sauceboat down and picked up the tiny spoon that was resting along the top of the gold plate.

Delicately, she took a spoonful of the mousse, mixed it in with the sauce, and placed it in her mouth. It was light and delicate. It made her feel happy and satisfied. It reminded her of a Mexican mole sauce. She took another larger spoonful and lost herself for a second. She closed her eyes and slowly sucked on the spoon, wrapping her tongue around it.

When she opened her eyes, she saw that Lars was staring at her. Their eyes locked, and she blushed. Embarrassed, she busied herself by writing in her notepad. She wrote down luxurious and satisfying. On a whim, she added lickable and explosive. She noticed that Laura's hand was trembling as she wrote down her own thoughts.

Ilya took the plates away, and Lottie brought over the final dessert.

"Hello, I've prepared for you my triple-layer cake which I've named Mexican Sunrise," Lottie said.

She placed the glass cake tray down on the table and lifted the lid to reveal a cake that had been carefully covered in chocolate icing, topped with tiny marshmallows and drizzled in caramel. She began cutting the cake into thick, evenly sliced pieces.

Once sliced, Lottie gently placed each piece on dainty white plates that had tiny roses dotting its edges.

Lottie placed a plate in front of Heather and then did the same for Laura. Looking at one another, Heather and Laura took deep breaths and then began their final indulgence.

Sitting upright on the plate, the layers of the cake revealed themselves. Yellow, orange, and then red. With thick layers of what Heather guessed was a dark buttercream in between. Heather picked up her fork and slid it easily through the entire piece of cake. She placed the heaping forkful into her mouth. The chocolate frosting happily stuck to the roof of her mouth so that she had to swirl it around with her tongue, making her think of a sweet, sticky kiss.

The layers were moist and delicate. She could detect differing flavours that came together into a pleasing balance that made her whole body feel both happy and relaxed. After she swallowed, she picked up a marshmallow with her fingers and popped it quickly into her mouth. She looked over at Laura and noticed her face was pink. Feeling the gaze, Laura looked up at Heather, and they shared a secret smile.

Wanting to try each layer on its own, Heather discovered that the yellow layer was a light and airy pistachio cake. She assumed the obvious about the orange layer and was proved right as she enjoyed its citrusy sweetness. When she placed a scoop of the red layer in her mouth, the flavours immediately announced themselves, as if to say, hey, we're here. The layer tasted of strawberries mixed with what she assumed was tajin. She took delight in the kick of chili and lime from the tajin. It reminded her of her favourite childhood Hot Lips candy but without the taste of cinnamon. She could feel Lars watching her as she fervently finished the piece of cake and then wrote down her thoughts.

Lottie cleared the table, and Lars came over and sat down.

"So, how was everything?" He asked, smiling.

"Absolutely divine," Laura said, pleased.

"I feel like Laura and I are now forever bonded over a shared out-of-body experience," Heather said, smiling at Laura.

Grinning, Laura reached across the table and squeezed Heather's hand.

"Haha! Music to my ears! And now, we can share our secret with you, Heather!" Lars said, and Laura smiled.

"Everything you tasted today was gluten-free and dairy-free. It's my first time I'm trying out recipes in this space. I figured it was about time I joined in. These are our first three creations so far for our new recipe book that's going to be available in time for next Christmas. And they'll be featured in our bakeries," Lars explained sneakily.

"Well, that makes it even more astonishing!" Heather was shocked. All of her gluten-free attempts had turned into cardboard-like disasters.

As if reading her thoughts, Lars explained, "the key is to add in xanthan gum and tapioca starch ... and of course, a few other important ingredients. That's what makes it all moist and delicate. Otherwise, it turns into cardboard."

"Do you have gluten-free options at your bakery?" Laura asked.

"No, but I do make and sell edibles," Heather shared, testing to see how Laura would react.

"Edibles? As in goodies that make you feel good?" Laura asked, jokingly. "I'm not sure how I feel about that. I'm all about the natural high sugar and chocolate give you. Like what we just experienced."

"I can understand that. But honestly, I don't think it's that much different from what you're trying to do here." Heather defended herself.

"Yeah, but you said your shop is called My Sweet Addiction. Isn't that setting it up?" Laura asked.

"Not really. It was called that way before ... My shop only got into edibles when they became legalized a little while ago," Heather said defensively.

"Yeah, but you can see how it could be misinterpreted?" Laura asked.

"Actually, no. It's not that different from what you're trying to do. You're trying to help people who can't eat gluten or dairy because they'll get sick. You're giving them a chance to enjoy some delicious baked goods. Many of my customers take my edibles for medicinal reasons like menopause, anxiety, depression, and sleeplessness. It's not just to get high," Heather explained.

"I had no idea. How did you learn to make those?" Laura asked.

Once again, Lars interrupted them. "Do you mind?" He asked, motioning towards the notepads, and Heather and Laura pushed them across the table and over to him.

"I visited the best place to learn, Amsterdam, and took a course there," Heather explained.

Lars interrupted them again. "Haha! Heather, I'm loving your comments. You have an exceptional palate. How did you figure out some of my unusual ingredients? And your comments are so honest and keenly observant. Do you mind if I put them in our book or on our social media?"

"Are you sure?" Heather hesitated.

"Of course, I'm sure," Lars reassured her.

"May I see?" Laura asked, and Lars handed her the notebook.

After reading through Heather's comments, Laura said brashly, "well then, Heather, with a palate like that, perhaps we should talk about doing a baking cookbook for you, too?"

"You're just messing with me!" Heather teased.

"I kind of am. But I love your energy and enthusiasm. Why the heck not? Maybe we should at least explore the idea? You'll have to make some of your favourite baked goods for me to try. Not your edibles, just your regular baked goods. Maybe Lars will lend you his test kitchen while you're here?" Laura said smiling and thinking to herself that she'd never been so spontaneous in her life, and blamed the chocolate high she was experiencing. And yet, she could tell that Heather was craving something new in her life and for some crazy reason that Laura couldn't quite rationalize, she wanted to give that to her.

"I would love that! Use my kitchen, please!" Lars exclaimed.

"Wow, this is all so amazing. I can't believe this is really happening. Thank you both so much. For everything." Heather beamed at them, really hoping Laura wouldn't change her mind.

MUNICH
MONDAY, DECEMBER 23

Phil opened the front door to his parents' house and yelled into the vast front entrance.

"Hi! We're back!"

"We're in the kitchen!" Ursula yelled out to them.

Maria stepped inside and closed the front door.

"I have no idea why you needed to bring this huge bag over –" Phil began as he dropped a bulky duffle bag onto the floor.

"You'll see why soon. But first, I have a surprise for you." Maria said as she set the shopping bag and Pyrex dish with the leftover chicken stew on the bench by the door and then slowly began to unzip Ursula's fuchsia parka.

"Well, I like where this is going, but –" Phil watched intently as she revealed her well-fitting Dolphins hoodie.

"I had Jack ship a few things to me. Surprise!" Maria did a little dance.

"Oh! Haha! Now we definitely have a Dolphins fan in the house!" Phil laughed and wrapped his arms around her.

He leaned down and kissed her.

"I thought you'd like it." Maria smiled up at him.

"Promise you'll do more of that modelling for me later." Phil wiggled his eyebrows up and down.

"Promise," Maria beamed.

"Well, are you guys coming or not?" Ursula yelled at them from the kitchen.

"Geez ... yes, we're coming!" Phil yelled back.

They took off their winter boots, and Phil took off his snow pants. They shoved everything into the front hall closet.

"What do you want me to do with this bag?" Phil asked.

"Don't worry about it. Just leave it there. I'll take care of it." Maria said as she gently pushed it under the bench with her foot.

"Pop doesn't like clutter. Make sure he doesn't see it, or it might disappear."

"What? You're joking, right?"

"No, I'm serious. Look around. Do you see any clutter anywhere in this house?"

Maria stopped and thought about the tour she'd taken of the house yesterday and remembered thinking how sparse everything was. There was no clutter. No old newspapers hanging around. No food wrappers. No empty coffee cups. Her own house was clean but not clutter-free. She always had hand creams and body lotions lying around within arm's reach, plus magazines piled up on tables and towels hanging off chairs. And because of Jack, the kitchen and dining areas were in constant states of organized chaos.

"Pop used to throw out my toys if I left them lying around too long," Phil explained.

"Wow, okay, I'll take care of it." She nodded and quickly grabbed the shopping bag and Pyrex container off the bench.

They made their way down the hallway towards the kitchen, following the rich smell of beef wellington baking in the oven. As they passed through the dining room, she happily noticed the table was set and that it still had her chair from the dinette sitting at it. They ultimately turned left into the colourful and spacious kitchen.

"It has to come out of the oven in five minutes; otherwise, it's going to be overcooked." Brian was explaining impatiently to Ursula, who was sitting on a kitchen barstool, nursing a martini.

Maria noticed that Brian was wearing an apron over a dark blue Buffalo Bills T-shirt and grey sweatpants that had the words "Your opinion wasn't in the recipe" printed on it, and she smiled to herself.

"Well, they're here now, so we're good." Ursula rolled her eyes and motioned for Maria to come over.

"What's the matter?" Phil looked back and forth between Brian and Ursula.

"Nothing. Brian was getting a bit anxious about the timing, that's all. He was expecting you two earlier. Everything's fine." Ursula explained as she and Maria exchanged awkward air kisses because Maria was still holding the shopping bag and Pyrex container in front of her.

Ursula smelled of a lovely floral scent and was wearing a pink blouse with the collar popped up over a pair of slim fitting jeans.

Brian muttered something under his breath as he placed a cutting board onto the island. Next to it were several serving bowls waiting to be filled with vegetables from the various pots and pans simmering on the stove.

"Sorry, Brian, it took longer than we thought. I'm going downstairs to see Pop." Phil announced as he gave Maria a quick kiss on the top of her head.

"You have fifteen minutes!" Brian yelled as Phil ducked out of the kitchen, and then he looked at Maria and Ursula in exasperation. "Once it comes out, I can only let it rest for ten minutes; otherwise, it'll be ruined."

"It's all my fault, Brian. I had a few errands to run, and then my daughter called me. I'm sure it's going to be fine." Maria felt guilty, but didn't quite think it was all her fault since Phil had never even mentioned once that they were on a tight schedule.

"Exactly. They're here now." Ursula said, trying to appease Brian.

Brian nodded and kept working.

With her shopping bags getting heavier by the minute, Maria couldn't wait any longer for instructions as to where to put them, so she asked, "where can I put this stuff?"

"What *is* all that?" Ursula asked as she took a sip of her martini.

"I have a surprise for you!" Maria said happily.

"Let's move to the dinette." Ursula stood up with her martini in hand, and they made their way over to the dinette that overlooked the screened-in porch.

Maria placed the shopping bag and the Pyrex container on top of the table and then whispered to Ursula. "This is leftover chicken stew Heather's friend Pam left for me. I brought it over here since it's just going to go bad if I leave it at Heather's. And her tiny freezer was full of zip-locked bags with I-don't-know-what inside."

"How thoughtful of you. You can put it in the freezer downstairs. Brian's going to be making a huge turkey dinner tomorrow night with dumplings and red cabbage. We'll be eating leftovers for days." Ursula explained.

"Oh, right, of course!" Maria exclaimed, suddenly remembering tomorrow was Christmas Eve.

"Wait a minute. What are you wearing?" Ursula grabbed Maria's arm and extended it out to get a better look at Maria's teal blue and orange-sleeved hoodie. "I couldn't see it because you were holding all that stuff in front of you. Very cute."

"Thank you." Maria smiled.

"So, what's in the shopping bag?"

"I had Phil take me to the grocery store to buy the ingredients to make margaritas from scratch," Maria explained happily. "I wanted to do something nice for you."

"How sweet of you. But I'm fine with my martinis." Ursula said matter-of-factly while taking another sip.

"Oh," Maria felt disappointed, and Ursula noticed.

"I'm sorry, sweetie. I'm just not a fan of sweet drinks."

"But that's why I'm making it from scratch. We can make it however sweet or not sweet as we want. I can make it tart and rim it with salt?"

"Hmmm ... well, you'll have to show me then."

"And can I just ask? What's the deal with grocery stores not selling liquor?"

"What do you mean?"

"I asked Phil to take me to the grocery store to buy everything I needed. When I got there, I asked one of the clerks where the liquor aisle was. He looked all confused and said there wasn't one."

"Don't be silly! Of course, you can't buy liquor at the grocery store. Although, it would be nice. There are a few chains who carry beer and wine, but that's it."

"That's crazy! Well then, when you come visit us, I'm taking you to a proper liquor store. Your L-A-B-C ... or whatever it's called... is ridiculous compared to what we have in Florida. You will die."

"Can't wait!" Ursula giggled.

Maria took out the bottles of tequila and Triple Sec, three fresh limes, a packet of Stevia, a box of Kosher salt, and a carton of coconut water from her shopping bag and placed them on the dinette table.

"I'll put the chicken stew in the freezer, and when I come back, I'm going to make you the best margarita you've ever had in your life," Maria teased.

Maria turned around and saw that Brian was filling up a serving bowl with mashed potatoes. He was so focused on making it look nice that he didn't look up at her. She left the kitchen and made her way to the stairs that led to the basement. She was just about to take her first step when she overheard Phil talking.

"Pop, it was so awkward. Clara was accusing me of taking away the best years of her life. Right there, in front of Maria. I didn't know what to say. I was in a state of shock. I still can't believe that happened."

"Ah, I'm sure Maria understands." Klaus tried to reassure Phil.

"Yeah, but why would she say all of those things?" Phil sounded defeated.

"Sometimes people need someone to lash out at, and you were the nearest thing."

"Yeah, but Clara seems to remember things quite differently than I do. How can I explain that to Maria?" Phil sighed.

"I'm sure Maria understands. Did she even ask you about it?"

"No, she told me not to worry about it."

"See, she understands," Klaus emphasized.

"But, why did Clara say those things? Do you think I should call her? Talk to her about it?" Phil sounded desperate.

"No! That's a very bad idea. Definitely don't do that."

"Right." Phil sighed again.

"Just be thankful Maria's completely different than Clara."

The two men stopped talking, and she could hear the volume of the television begin to rise. She decided to knock on the wall to announce her presence.

"Hello! Dolphins' fan coming through!" She yelled as she made her way down the stairs. The basement ceiling was higher than she'd expected, and the two men were sitting on a dark leather sectional couch with their feet propped up on a low coffee table in front of a huge, flat-screen television that was mounted to the wall. She noticed they'd been watching the pre-game show. There was a dart board on the wall to their left, and the wall to their right was lined with floor-to-ceiling, built-in white cupboards.

"Maria, welcome! So nice to see you again!" Klaus said as he smiled and pushed himself off the couch. She saw that he was wearing the same dark blue Buffalo Bills T-shirt as Brian.

Klaus opened his arms to hug her, but stopped, "oh! What are you wearing?"

"I hope you don't mind." Maria teased.

"Nah, I'm just happy you're a football fan. I don't think any of Phil's other entanglements even liked football." Klaus said happily, and she saw Phil's face redden with embarrassment.

"Um, Ursula said I could put this leftover chicken stew in the freezer down here." Maria explained awkwardly.

"It's just over there." Klaus pointed.

Maria walked in between the sectional couch and television and made her way to the white, stand-up freezer that was beside a small sink. On the other side of the sink was a tall bar fridge filled with wine, beer, and liquor bottles. She opened the freezer door and was startled by how many buckets of Kawartha ice cream were stacked inside. Were they not worried about heart disease, she wondered? She put the Pyrex container inside the freezer and shut the door.

"I'll see you upstairs!" Maria said brightly and then hopped back up the steps.

This time, as she walked back towards the kitchen through the dining room, she noticed a beautifully decorated Christmas tree standing beside the buffet table. It stood about three feet higher than the buffet table.

Strange, it hadn't been there yesterday, but it's perfect, Maria thought to herself and quietly tiptoed to the front hall, where she grabbed the duffle bag and dragged it back to the dining room. She noticed there were a few small gifts already under the tree, and she carefully placed the gifts she'd asked Jack to send her beside them. He'd said no problem and that he'd even have them professionally wrapped.

She'd asked for two matching Buffalo Bills tracksuits for Klaus and Brian, figuring they could never have too many, an Apple Watch for Phil – partially because he'd said he wanted to get into shape and it would track his steps and partially so they could keep in touch while he was off covering the weather wherever the heck that took him – and finally, a box of skin and hair care products from her mother's company for Ursula.

When she re-entered the kitchen, she noticed a few things had changed. The beef wellington was now resting on the cutting board, which meant she had approximately ten minutes to make a batch of margaritas, or she'd be in Brian's bad books. Ursula was still sitting at the dinette but had turned on her wireless speakers and was swaying to "Margaritaville" by Jimmy Buffet. Ursula's martini glass was empty, but there were two margarita glasses on the table waiting to be filled and a roll of paper towels.

Maria took out her phone and scrolled to the margarita recipe she'd received from Jack. "Do you have a pitcher? And can I use that shaker?"

"Yep, right here." Ursula lifted a pitcher from the bottom shelf of the bar cart and placed it on the dinette and brought the shaker over.

"I need lots of ice," Maria said as she picked up the pitcher and shaker.

Ursula pointed to the ice maker on the fridge. Brian was washing something in the sink, so Maria was careful to stay out of his way and placed the martini shaker on the counter beside the sink and then pressed the pitcher against the knob on the fridge and ice clunked into it. Every once in a while, she stopped the ice maker and shook the pitcher to force the pieces of ice to rearrange themselves. Once it was filled halfway, she pranced over to the dinette and quickly placed the pitcher on the table, and then came back into the kitchen.

Brian was finishing washing his hands in the sink, so they did a bit of a waltz as she switched places with him so she could rinse out the martini shaker. Brian began placing the mashed potatoes, grilled white asparagus that had been carefully wrapped in bacon, and a medley of red and green peppers and shitake mushrooms onto the platters.

He looked at the timer on the stove, and Maria's eyes followed. She had seven minutes.

As she finished washing the pitcher, she yelled out, "can you pass me the limes?"

Ursula tossed them over, and Maria caught them and then quickly washed them. She squished herself against the sink to stay out of Brian's way as he stood at the kitchen island behind her, their bums almost touching.

When she was done, she squeezed past Brian and hopped back over to the dinette. Using the cap of the shaker, Maria measured out three ounces of tequila, two ounces of Triple Sec and, poured in a bit of coconut water, a dash of Stevia, and threw in three ice cubes from the pitcher. She rolled one of the limes on the cutting board to get it nice and juicy, as she'd seen Jack do so many times, cut it in half, and then squeezed it into the mixture, using her hand as a sifter to stop the seeds from going in. Securing the strainer and cap back onto the shaker, she began to shake it.

"You have to dance while you shake." Maria giggled as she twirled about to "Margaritaville" and Ursula giggled along.

She poured it into the pitcher and used a glass stir stick to mix it all together. She sliced up one of the other limes and threw a few slices in. She ripped a paper towel off the rack, took out a spoonful of the mixture to sprinkle on the towel to get it a bit wet, poured some salt onto the wetness, and then turned the glasses over and rimmed them.

"Okay, now we taste test!" Maria exclaimed happily as she poured a little bit into each of their glasses.

They clinked glasses and took sips.

They both paused.

"Hmmm ... not quite what I was expecting," Maria frowned.

"There's a strange texture. But on the upside, it's not too sweet." Ursula wasn't sure if she should take another sip.

"I think it could be the coconut water?" Maria said.

Ursula hesitated and then took another sip and nodded, "could be."

Maria took another sip as well and then grimaced. "Oh no, don't tell me. That's what it is! I couldn't find coconut nectar, so I grabbed coconut water. I thought it would be the same thing." She was embarrassed by her mistake.

"Don't worry about it. We'll just add more tequila, and it'll be fine!" Ursula exclaimed, and Maria giggled.

"But you said it's not sweet?" Maria asked.

"It's more tart than sweet." Ursula smiled.

"I'm calling them up now," Brian announced, and Maria and Ursula looked at each other.

Giggling, Maria began dumping the bottle of tequila into the pitcher and then threw in a few pinches of salt and the rest of the lime slices and mixed it all up.

Brian picked up the phone and hit the intercom button.

Phil answered right away with his usual, "coming!"

Maria poured a bit of the mixture into both of their glasses.

"Oof, that's strong!" Ursula exclaimed.

"And that's coming from you!" Maria teased, and Ursula chuckled. "Jack will never let me live this one down."

"Well then, he doesn't need to know." Ursula winked.

"Let's take a selfie, and I'll send it to him," Maria exclaimed.

"He can't taste it through the photo," Ursula giggled.

Holding their margarita glasses, they posed by the window so that the snowy background would be behind them.

"Hold your glass like this. No. Higher. Perfect." Maria ordered, and when she was happy with how they looked, she yelled, "cheers!" so the voice command would automatically take the photo.

They inspected the picture and saw that the snow had made the tall pine trees heavy, and the branches swung low behind them. They both had silly grins on their faces. Maria wrote "Going to Margaritaville in a snow globe" in the caption and sent it to Jack.

"Oh, I meant to tell you that your Christmas tree is gorgeous!" Maria gushed.

"Aw, thank you. I wanted to make it a bit more Christmassy around here for you. The boys don't care about these things, but I thought you would appreciate it." Ursula said as she turned off her wireless speakers.

While Maria and Ursula had been tampering with the margarita recipe, Brian had brought all of the platters and gravy boat trays into the dining room and had placed them on the trivets in the middle of the table. He'd sliced the beef wellington into slabs and had placed one on each plate.

Afterwards, he'd taken a moment to sigh with satisfaction at seeing each slab was a perfect medium-rare and then had filled up everyone's wine glass with chianti.

As they stood in the dining room doorway, Ursula gave him a look of approval. "Well done, Brian. Everything looks and smells delicious."

"Thanks, Mum!" Brian smiled.

Just then, they heard two sets of feet coming up the stairs.

Phil and Klaus entered the living room with beers in their hands, and she noticed that Phil was now wearing a Buffalo Bills sweatshirt. Klaus wandered over to the stereo system, and the duet by Gwen Stefani and Blake Shelton, "You Make it Feel like Christmas," began playing quietly over the speakers.

"Looking good, Phil. Let's hope your team looks just as good on the field tonight," Maria teased.

"Ooh, dem's fighting words. I like the spirit," Phil teased back.

"Everyone sit down, please," Brian ordered, and they all sat down at their usual seats, while he remained standing.

Maria leaned into Phil and whispered, "is this his first time making beef wellington?"

"I think so." Phil answered, and Maria gave him a "no wonder" look, but then remembered that none of them knew how to cook, so it wasn't her place to judge.

"Please help yourselves. Along with the beef wellington, I've made garlic mashed potatoes, grilled white asparagus wrapped in bacon, and a medley of bell peppers and shitake mushrooms. And, of course, a gravy." Brian announced dramatically and then sat down.

Everyone began passing the platters around and loading up their plates. There was a long moment of silence as they dug into the meal.

Eventually, Maria couldn't help but break the silence.

"Brian, if this is your first time making beef wellington, then you're a genius in the kitchen. This is truly amazing. Thank you so much for making this for us. It's such a complicated recipe. Such a treat. I've only ever seen it on television –" Maria gushed.

"Okay, woah, his head's going to get way too big at the rate you're going." Phil stopped her.

"Thank you, Maria." Brian smiled shyly at her, ignoring Phil.

"Okay, everyone, kudos to the chef!" Klaus exclaimed.

"Kudos to Brian!" They all yelled.

Afterwards, Ursula got up from the table, went into the kitchen, and reappeared with their two margarita glasses, placing one in front of Maria.

"What are you two drinking now?" Phil chided.

"Maria taught me how to make margaritas from scratch." Ursula giggled and shared a look with Maria.

Phil frowned. "You do know that margaritas, in no way, shape or form, go with beef wellington?"

"Of course, we know that!" Ursula laughed. "How was your day at the fair?"

"It was so much fun! We went down the ice slide, and then we danced the polka!" Maria exclaimed.

"You learned the polka!" Klaus exclaimed, and Maria pretended to curtsy while still sitting in her chair.

"Maria had her first Beavertail!" Phil blurted to change the subject away from his embarrassing lack of dance skills, and it surprisingly worked.

"What did you think of it?" Klaus asked.

"They're sort of similar to buñuelos, which is funny because that's what we eat during Christmas," Maria said.

"What else do you normally eat for Christmas dinner?" Klaus asked.

"A chicken soup called Ajiaco." Maria smiled, recollecting the smells that filled the house from its savoury flavours.

"A-what?" Klaus asked.

"A-hia-ko," Maria enunciated slowly. "It has potatoes and corn in it, sometimes avocado, and it's delicious. Ursula, you said something about dumplings? As in dim sum dumplings?"

"Haha! No, they are potato dumplings," Klaus said. "Explain to Maria how you make them, Brian."

Brian had been shovelling mashed potatoes into his mouth and now paused. He swallowed and said, "I used to grate the potatoes myself, but now I use the boxed version. You mix the powder with water and form them into balls and then simmer them. Pretty easy peasy," Brian explained.

Maria nodded politely, thinking that it sounded kind of bland and mushy.

"Have you two seen Brian's exhibit?" Maria looked at Ursula and Klaus.

"No, not yet. Why? Did you two have time to go?" Klaus asked, surprised.

"Um, sort of … We saw his painting. It was quite stunning." Maria explained and saw that Brian was shifting uncomfortably in his chair, and she smiled at him as if to say, don't worry, I won't mention Elsa, and he stopped squirming.

"Great. More praise for my brother," Phil teased.

"What did you mean by what you said?" Brian frowned.

"What did I say?" Maria asked, trying to remember.

"You said something about meeting again," Brian explained.

"Oh, right!" Maria remembered and smiled. "It's from that show, Vikings. My daughter and I loved watching it together. It's when Lagertha is saying goodbye to her husband, who just died, but really, she's saying it's not goodbye because they'll see each other again in Valhalla. So, she says, 'Until we meet again.'"

"That just sent chills down my spine," Ursula said.

MIAMI
MONDAY, DECEMBER 23

The day had settled into dusk, and with it came a light sprinkling of rain. Olivia and Bianca were curled up in their casual but cute T-shirts and joggers on the powder blue couch in the high-ceilinged living room of JC's parents' mansion.

"What am I going to do now?" Bianca whispered to Olivia while she had the chance as no one was around.

Oliver was upstairs in the bathroom, JC and his sister, Carmen, were on their way home from the hospital to get some rest, and JC's mother, Josephine, was staying at the hospital with Alonso. Meanwhile, Breanna, the housekeeper, was busy in the kitchen getting dinner ready.

"What do you mean?" Olivia asked.

"I was going to break up with JC, remember? I can't exactly break up with him now?" Bianca whispered.

"You were serious about that?" Olivia still didn't quite believe that Bianca was going to break up with him so soon.

"Of course, I was! I can't date someone who's always on their phone. And he mumbles. I have to keep asking him to repeat what he's saying. It's annoying," Bianca whispered.

"Well, if you think it's the right thing to do," Olivia said, thinking it was the wrong thing to do and hadn't ever noticed any mumbling. It seemed to her that Bianca's list of complaints against JC were getting suspiciously longer by the minute. Truth be told, she actually felt sorry for JC, knowing he was about to inherit her dad, despite Alonso's assurances that he'd changed.

At that moment, Max, the family's Chocolate Lab, came bounding into the room and whined at them. He ran back to the front door and then back into the living room, staring at them intently as if trying to send a telepathic message.

"You wanna go for a walk?" Olivia asked Max in a high-pitched, goofy voice and the dog barked back at her in response.

"You wanna come with me?" Olivia asked Bianca.

"Nah, you go ahead," Bianca responded listlessly, now flipping through a fashion magazine that had been lying on the coffee table.

Olivia decided to run upstairs to grab her sweatshirt from the bedroom she was staying in and Max pushed his way up the stairs beside her. He barked impatiently at her while she flung about her clothes, looking for her sweatshirt until she finally found it. As she was about to run back downstairs, the bathroom door swung open and Oliver stuck his head out.

"What's going on out here?" He asked, slumped against the doorframe.

"I'm taking Max for a walk," Olivia explained as she pulled the sweatshirt on over her head and then looked more closely at Oliver and asked, "are you okay?"

"Yes. No. I don't know ... I think I ate something bad at the hospital." Oliver said as he ran back inside the bathroom, slamming the door shut behind him.

"What'd you eat?" Olivia asked, trying not to listen to the noises coming from inside the bathroom.

"Uh, oh God ... Don't be mad at me. I was so hungry."

"Do you want to go to the hospital?"

"No!"

"What did you eat?" Olivia asked again.

"Okay ... Okay ... I ate an egg salad sandwich out of the vending machine," Oliver shamefully admitted.

"What? When did you do that? You know those things have expiry dates!"

"Uh ... Oh God ... I do now. When you were talking to your dad."

"Do you want me to ask Breanna to bring you a soda?"

"No, no. Please, go. I'll be fine. Just go." Oliver begged through the door.

Shaking her head at Oliver's foolishness, Olivia made her way down the stairs to the front foyer. She popped her head into the living room and saw that it was empty. She could hear Bianca and Breanna's combined laughter coming from the kitchen and decided not to disturb them, so she found Max's leash hanging nearby and snapped it onto his collar. From the front hall closet, she grabbed the first rain jacket she could find and then slipped into her sneakers.

To shield herself from the light rain, she pulled the hood of the jacket over her head as she stepped outside. Max was so happy to be out of the house that he bolted down the slab steps, across the expansive three-car driveway, and onto the wide sidewalk, pulling her behind him.

"Woah, Max. Take it easy, boy." Olivia laughed as she tried to control Max by tightening her hold on his leash and he eventually slowed down to a walking pace.

Olivia let Max take the lead as they wandered the sidewalks alongside the manicured mansions spread throughout the upscale neighbourhood. Max stopped and sniffed one lawn in particular until he found just the right spot to take care of his business. As he did so, he happily looked up at her, tongue hanging sideways out of his mouth, oblivious to the rain.

"Good boy, Max," Olivia cooed as she picked up his business with a poop bag.

Walking along the quiet sidewalks, Olivia felt at peace as she admired the beautiful homes, until she abruptly realized that she should be paying better attention as to where Max was taking her – the image of her phone sitting on the living room coffee table popping into her head. That's when she noticed a crosswalk leading to a park across the road and thought it might be nice to give Max a bit of a run without venturing too far from JC's.

"You wanna go to the park?" Olivia asked Max and his ears perked up at the word, "park".

Olivia looked up and down the road and even though it was empty, she pushed the crosswalk button and the lights began to flash. In his excitement, Max pulled Olivia onto the crosswalk just as a lone car turned down the road.

***

And so, it was an unfortunate fluke that the passenger in the lone car was none other than Carmen's childhood frenemy, Mila Moreno, who'd just been picked up from her parents' house for a dinner date by her latest boyfriend, Logan.

As they neared the crosswalk, Mila studied the figure crossing the road and the dog that was pulling her. She saw a figure who shared the same stature as Carmen, was wearing Carmen's college rain jacket and was being pulled by a dog that she assumed was Max.

"What's *she* doing home? She told me she was going to be in Boston for Christmas with her boyfriend's family!" Mila exclaimed in a shrill voice.

"Who?"

"Carmen!"

"What are you talking about?" Logan looked over at her and then sighed. He'd been looking forward to an evening with Mila in which he didn't have to hear another word about this Carmen person.

"That's her crossing the street." Mila pointed at Olivia's figure as she made her way across the road.

"You sure it's her?" Logan clenched his jaw.

"Of course, it's her! I can see her smugness from here."

"You can't even see her face." Logan rolled his eyes as he prepared himself for another list of complaints against Carmen.

"Fine. I can feel her smugness from here," Mila said, huffily.

"You shouldn't let her get to you." Logan offered his meagre two cents.

"I'm so tired of everything always going her way," Mila scowled, her olive skin turning pink. "She stole that job placement from me and you know it. It was supposed to be mine. She wasn't even interested!"

Logan had heard all about the stolen job placement over the past few days during several tearful phone calls. During previous dates with Mila, she'd droned on about how the two girls had grown up in the same neighbourhood together and had developed an on-again, off-again, tense and competitive friendship over the years. He'd heard how Mila felt Carmen had things handed to her too easily in life and he'd felt useless in trying to console her. And now, in some strange twist of fate, he felt that he was finally being presented with an opportunity to make things right for Mila.

"Why can't something go wrong for her, just once?" Mila whined.

"I can do that, right now." Logan snarled at the figure crossing the road.

"What do you mean?" Mila asked tearfully.

"Well, I could take a go at her. Not hit her. Just give her a bit of a scare. No one's around." Logan smirked.

"Run her down! I don't want you to do that!" Mila yelled.

"Not really run her down! Who do you think I am! Just scare her." Logan revved his engine as they watched Olivia make her way across the crosswalk behind Max. "Don't tell me you weren't fantasizing about that right now."

"Well …"

"That's all I needed to hear." Logan said as he floored the car towards Olivia just as she was about to take her last few steps towards the other side of the road.

The jarring roar of the engine broke the quiet of the night, causing Olivia to look up at them in alarm.

They watched as Olivia tried to leap for the safety of the sidewalk, but the loud noise had also startled Max who started to run, yanking the leash out of Olivia's hand and throwing her off balance.

As they sped towards her, they watched in horror as Olivia stumbled backwards and then cringed as they heard the passenger side mirror catch the right side of Olivia's body. They watched her body twist up through the air and then land a few feet away as they whizzed by.

Mila felt like she was watching a sickening, slow-motion nightmare and whispered in shock, "oh my God, what have we done?"

"Oh God, I didn't mean to hit her!" Logan yelled as he kept speeding down the road.

"We have to call 9-1-1!" Mila yelled, trying to look back at the body slumped by the road.

"No! No one saw anything. We have to get out of here!" Logan yelled as they kept speeding away from the body.

***

The rain had subsided, leaving dark, wet blotches along the streets and sidewalks.

"Do you think we made the right decision? Leaving the hospital while Dad is still really sick?" Carmen asked JC as they made their way through the neighbourhood.

JC was about to reassure his sister when he noticed a familiar shape peeing on a tree and remarked, "geez, that dog looks a lot like Max."

Then the dog vigorously kicked up dirt behind him, and JC screeched the brakes.

"That is Max!" JC abruptly stopped the Range Rover, causing Carmen to lurch forward and clutch the console so she wouldn't hit her forehead.

"Jesus!" Carmen yelled.

JC put the SUV in park and ran outside towards Max.

"Max! Here boy!" He bent down and yelled out to Max who had been sniffing the grass quite contently. The dog lifted his head in recognition of the voice and bounded towards JC.

"Why are you out here all alone? How'd you get out?" JC asked as the dog bounced around in his arms and licked his face. "Okay, okay, take it easy."

After finally calming the dog down, JC opened the back door of the Range Rover, and Max jumped inside, panting.

"Holy kamole, it is Max!" Carmen yelled. "Why was he out there all alone?"

"I have no clue. But he's got his leash on!" JC exclaimed.

His Spidey senses going haywire, JC revved the engine, sped through the neighbourhood towards the house, and swerved the SUV into the driveway. He opened the back passenger door, grabbed Max by the leash, and then burst through the front door.

"Hello? Does anyone know why Max was outside all on his own?" JC yelled into the vast house.

Bianca, who had been helping Breanna, the housekeeper, set the table for dinner, came running into the front hall.

"What's going on?" Bianca asked anxiously.

"We found Max walking the neighbourhood by himself." JC explained, feeling selfishly relieved to see Bianca as he'd feared something had happened to her.

"Oh my gosh! Olivia! Olivia was walking him!" Bianca yelled.

"Are you sure?" Carmen asked.

"Of course, I'm sure!" Bianca yelled. "What do you think happened to her?" All the colour had drained from Bianca's face.

Oliver, who had been making his way slowly down the stairs, stumbled into the front hall and whispered, "do you want me to call her phone?"

They all nodded, but to their disappointment, Bianca followed the ringtone to the coffee table in the living room. She pocketed Olivia's phone.

"Maybe she got hurt … Hit by a car? Is there any blood on Max? We have to go find her!" Bianca yelled as she ran over to Max and began inspecting him, but he kept wriggling away from her in protest.

"Okay, you two go look for her by foot. Carmen and I will take the car." JC said hurriedly and then turned to the housekeeper, "Breanna, please stay here and call us if she shows up?" Breanna nodded, wringing her hands in despair.

"Do you have a flashlight?" Bianca asked.

"Yep, right in that box with Max's coats." JC pointed towards a decorative box by the front door.

Bianca shoved her feet into her running shoes and then grabbed a flashlight while Oliver tried his best to keep up, wishing he'd insisted on going with JC in the Range Rover.

MIAMI
MONDAY, DECEMBER 23

Late that afternoon, while Heather had been packing up to leave Lars' test kitchen, he'd asked her to come over to his house for take-out sushi and had told her to bring a bathing suit. And she'd happily agreed.

Now, as the sun was setting, Heather was pulling into the driveway of a modest bungalow with a peaked roof and two bay windows that flanked the front door. As she parked in the driveway, she admired the orange Corvette that was sitting underneath the carport directly in front of her.

Before exiting the car, she grabbed her big purse that contained a bottle of wine, a bathing suit, a beach towel, and a few other things she'd carefully chosen with the hopes of their dinner date turning into the overnight kind.

On Jack's recommendation, she'd stopped at a Total Wine Shop and had been astounded at how massive the store was, feeling like she could get lost at any moment, and marvelling at how cheaply priced the wine was compared to Canada. She'd felt like a kid in a candy store and vowed to return. Another thing that had put her in a good mood was that she hadn't heard from Brian all day.

As she knocked on the front door, she was surprised to hear loud barking. Lars hadn't told her he had a dog. She could hear muffled yelling ordering the dog to quiet down, sit and stay. The door opened and she was greeted with a warm smile from Lars but was startled at the size of the dog sitting next to him. It was the biggest German Shepherd she'd ever seen in her life.

"Hi, Heather! Welcome! I'm so glad you could make it." Lars said, and Heather noted that he was no longer wearing his chef's jacket, but had changed into a long-sleeved, black polo shirt and dark plaid shorts which suited him nicely.

Then she eyed the dog.

"Um. Is your dog, friendly?" She asked nervously.

"Lucy? Yes, harmless. Just let her sniff your hand and she'll be fine," Lars assured her.

"Sniff my hand? She won't bite me?" Heather didn't budge from the doorway.

"No! Come inside. Trust me, you'll be fine." Lars beckoned her in.

"I'm not used to dogs. Don't judge me. I have a cat," Heather jokingly cringed.

"I won't hold it against you," Lars teased.

Heather hesitantly stepped inside while keeping an eye on Lucy. Once inside, with the door closed behind her, Lars gave Lucy a nod and she trotted over to Heather and sniffed her hands and legs. Heather stayed very still. Eventually, Lucy licked Heather's hand, looked up at Lars, and then trotted over to a nearby oversized dog bed with several stuffed animals spilling out of it. She turned around in a circle three times before finally flopping down and letting out a heavy sigh.

"See, nothing to worry about. She already likes you," Lars beamed. "Come in, come in."

Relieved, Heather stepped deeper inside.

"You have a beautiful home," Heather said as she glanced around.

"Thank you. I love this old Floridian neighbourhood. They'll have to carry me out of here," Lars joked.

Heather chuckled at his joke while taking in the open-concept bungalow with its oak kitchen and dining area, a sunken living room with a U-shaped couch in front of her, and hallways to the right and left that presumably led to the bedrooms and bathrooms. She noticed the colour scheme of the bungalow was predominantly black and tan. The back of the house was lined with sliding glass doors that opened up into a lush backyard with an abundance of grass and vegetation. She was surprised to see that there was no pool, but did spot a hot tub, and guessed the grassy vegetation was for the dog's benefit. And then realized, smiling to herself, that even the dog was black and tan.

"Do you mind if I wash my hands?" Heather pointed towards the sink, wanting to wash the dog's saliva off her hands before touching anything.

"Please, go ahead," Lars nodded.

After washing her hands, Heather took out the bottle of wine from her purse. "I brought this wine for you."

"Ah, this is one of my favourites!" Lars exclaimed, seeing that it was a fine bottle of New Zealand Pinot Noir.

"I know," Heather smirked.

"Haha! Of course, you do!" Lars guffawed. "I do have a few secrets I don't put in my books. I'll have you know."

"Well, hopefully I'll find out some of them tonight," Heather said flirtatiously. "I really love your Corvette."

"Thank you. It's all original. Well, no, I shouldn't say that ... I did have to get it painted when I first bought it. The Florida sun had done its damage, which is why I keep it under the carport. And only drive it in the winter. I got it at one of those car auctions," Lars overexplained, feeling a bit nervous now that Heather was in his home.

He looked out the bay window and remarked, "But, you've got a nice set of wheels, yourself."

"Oh, that's not mine. It came with the house swap. Back home, I drive a beast of a truck because of the insane winters we get up north." Heather was going to say more but then realized she was talking about the weather again.

"Oh yeah? What's that?"

"An F-150."

"Woah, that's a steady one for sure," Lars chuckled and then looked Heather up and down, noticing how nicely her sundress hugged her body. "You look very beautiful."

"Oh, thank you," Heather smiled, "you clean up well yourself."

"Ah, you're very kind. Is it okay if we eat outside on the patio?" Lars asked.

"Of course! It's the perfect night for it, the rain's cooled everything down," Heather said and then rolled her eyes at her own weather comments. "Is there anything I can help bring outside?"

"No, no. The outdoor table is already set. I just have to take the sushi out of the fridge ... Actually, on second thought, you could bring out the wine and I have a bottle of sake too," Lars pointed out.

"No problem." Heather smiled.

Lars handed back her bottle of pinot and then took out the bottle of sake from the fridge and handed it to her as well. As he took out the tray of sushi, he saw Heather's eyes widen in awe at the size of the tray and explained sheepishly, "I wasn't sure what you liked, so I got a bunch of everything ..."

"That's a lot of sushi, but very sweet of you," Heather chuckled.

Lucy watched as they made their way through the sunken living room and towards the sliding glass doors. She got up lazily from her bed to follow them until she found her outdoor dog bed and flumped down again. The patio table had been set for two and classic rock music was playing quietly over the wireless speakers.

"Please choose a seat." Lars motioned towards the table.

Heather walked over to the patio table and as she got closer, she could see the table settings more clearly. She was impressed at the care in which both place settings had been arranged. Sitting on top of the two opposing black placements were mindfully arranged traditional sushi plates and bowls. She put the two bottles on the table and then picked up the intricately patterned bamboo chopsticks.

"Where'd you get these?" She was astonished at their beauty.

"You mean the chopsticks or the whole set?" Lars asked.

"Well, the whole set is beautiful, but I mean the chopsticks. I've never seen anything like them." Heather rolled them around in her fingers, admiring their floral designs.

"Ah, I borrowed them from the set of some cooking show," Lars chuckled. "We kind of shared studio space with them while I was doing my 'Bake it or Leave It' show."

"So, you do have a secretive past as a klepto," Heather teased.

Lars chuckled as he set the sushi tray down in the middle of the table. Since Heather hadn't yet sat down, he pulled out one of the patio chairs and motioned for her to sit down. As she sat down, he pulled the chair towards the table for her. This was something that Heather had never let anyone do for her before, and she found it surprisingly charming.

Lars opened the bottle of sake, filled up the two miniature glasses and sat down on the opposing chair.

She held up her glass and announced, "May your coffee and your slanders always be alike – without grounds."

"Haha! Love it!" Lars laughed. "In Denmark, they say Skål!"

"Skål!" Heather repeated happily, and they both drank.

Lars began to explain dramatically, "skål means skull. The Vikings used to drink out of the skulls of their enemies to intimidate guests at their table."

"I'm glad these are just sake glasses then," Heather laughed.

"Me too! Please help yourself," Lars urged her.

They began picking up various pieces of sushi, sashimi and maki rolls and adding them to their plates. They also began to slowly make their way through a small basket of crab tempura, a bowl of edamame, a bowl of seaweed salad and two bowls of miso soup.

Lars watched as Heather poured a trickle of soy sauce into one of the little bowls and then took a dab of wasabi with the opposite end of her chopstick. She mixed it all together until it turned into a mushy, brownish mixture.

"I do the same!" Lars chuckled.

"Only way to do it!" Heather laughed and then picked up a Dynamite roll. She smooshed it around the little bowl so that it mopped up the pungent, salty mixture and then carefully placed it in her mouth.

After she finished savouring it, she exclaimed, "Wow, this is beyond delicious. But I'm not surprised. You know your food."

"Yes, it's my absolute favourite take-out sushi place. I'm lucky that it's just around the corner from here," Lars explained.

"So, you're seriously never going to leave this house? I mean, people in your position usually have houses all over the world." Heather pointed out.

"What can I say? I'm a simple man," Lars shrugged.

"Who comes up with complicated recipes," Heather teased.

"Exactly. That's where complicated belongs." Lars smiled satisfactorily.

"Ha! Yeah, your recipes are definitely not for the faint of heart!" Heather laughed.

There was a moment of silence as they enjoyed the sushi and sake.

"Well, all I can say is that I'm glad you and Jack visit the same tattoo studio!" Heather beamed.

"Me too!" Lars beamed back.

"I've always wondered, how do you choose a tattoo?" Heather asked as she took a spoonful of her miso soup.

"I choose things that I want to remember forever. Like this one," Lars pointed to the back of his calf, "she was my first love."

Heather peered at the face of a similar looking German Shepherd to Lucy and noticed that she'd been given yet another female name tied to light as "Dawn" had been transcribed underneath the face.

"You don't have any tattoos?" Lars asked, looking her up and down again.

"Nope. Never really had the desire." Heather said, thinking how putting something so permanent on one's body didn't appeal to her at all.

"To each their own," Lars chuckled.

"I have to say. I'm loving the Latin vibe down here. The music, the beautiful vegetation, it all puts me in a fabulous mood," Heather remarked as she took a sip of sake.

"That's what I love about living here, too," Lars said as he added more pieces of sushi to his plate.

"You put tajin in your recipe today. That's a Mexican spice," Heather pointed out.

"I know. I read your notes. You have an incredible sense of taste," Lars said with admiration.

"Thank you," Heather blushed. "You know, I really appreciate everything you've shared with me today. It's been an unbelievable day."

"The pleasure is all mine." Lars smiled.

"I can't believe I'm sharing sushi with the face I've stared at so many times on the cover of your books," Heather grinned.

"And does the real one measure up?" Lars asked cheekily.

"More than ever," Heather smiled.

"Good to know," Lars smiled back. "And you know, Laura is very perceptive. If she wants to explore a book with you, go for it."

"Ever since she asked me, I've had ideas swirling around in my head," Heather said happily.

"I knew it. I love your confidence," Lars said in true admiration.

Heather placed a few more pieces of sushi onto her plate and they ate in silence while listening to the conflicting sounds of Lucy's wheezy snoring and the guitar riffs of classic rock.

"I saw from your website that your shop is in a small town called Munich. Do you like living there? I think I'd miss the big city," Lars remarked.

"Sure, it's a small town, but it's my home, you know. And it kind of feels like a big city 'cause it's a tourist destination. I love that I get to meet different people every day," Heather mused, secretly wondering what tall tales the gossip mill was spinning about her absence from the shop.

"I imagine the community looks up to you. Winning Best New Bakery and all your other awards. Impressive." Lars gave her an appreciative nod.

"But that doesn't compare to a Michelin star. Congrats on that," Heather nodded back at him.

"Thank you," Lars blushed.

They both took a sip of their sake.

"Do you have family?" Lars asked, happily knowing she was single as Jack had filled him in on the situation.

"I have a sister who lives in Montreal. She's married with two kids," Heather explained.

"What does she do?" Lars asked.

"She's quite different from me. She's a screenwriter for a children's television network," Heather said.

"Wow, I wasn't expecting that!" Lars exclaimed.

"Haha! She was always putting on plays as a kid. But her husband's an engineer," Heather explained.

"And your parents?" Lars asked.

"Oh, that's another story for another time. Our parents died about two years ago," Heather explained quietly.

"Sorry to hear that." Lars looked at her with surprise and sympathy.

"It's still hard to believe," Heather said sadly.

"May I ask what happened?" Lars asked quietly.

"You don't want to hear about it. It's too depressing." Heather couldn't believe that she'd brought it up, she never let herself unload onto strangers.

"You can tell me," Lars urged gently.

"You know, I haven't talked about it in a while. Everyone has their own busy lives to worry about. And no one really knows what to say. It just makes people feel uncomfortable," Heather explained.

"I guess so, but you can talk to me about it," Lars said encouragingly.

Heather hesitated and then decided to tell the story as succinctly as possible. "Um, well, they were coming back from an Oktoberfest festival at a nearby town, two years ago this past October. A tractor trailer jack-knifed in front of them on an off-ramp, and they had nowhere to go."

"So sorry to hear this. That must've been an awful shock." Lars was taken aback by the story.

Heather took a deep breath and continued, "yeah, I mean, they were good people. I miss them every day. They ran a bookshop in town. That's kind of how I learned about running a shop. My sister and I would go there after school to do our homework. And once there, we'd get lost in reading whatever grabbed our attention. We were both voracious readers. My sister loved Shakespeare. I loved autobiographies. Actually, that's how I got interested in baking. I read Cheryl Heaventhrow's autobiography –"

Lars excitedly interrupted her, "she's a pretty effin amazing baker! And a lovely person! I had the pleasure of meeting her at a bake-off once."

"Lucky you! I fell in love with how she described baking with such precision. I've always been great at math and fascinated with chemistry and realized how they all came together so naturally. I'd bake cookies with my mother ..." Heather trailed off.

"I saw your comment about the cookies today reminding you of your mother," Lars said sympathetically.

"Ah, yes. My parents were like best friends to me. There have been so many times, especially over the past year, when I wished I could've run to them for advice and comfort. I'd reach for the phone to call them and then this ache would hit me. Right, they're gone. I can't talk to them anymore." Heather said sadly.

"That must've been so hard," Lars sympathized.

"You know, they laid charges against the driver and we're supposed to get compensation, but this whole thing has been tied up in the court system for so long ..." Heather said.

"That's really awful. So, you can't even really move on?" Lars pointed out, sympathetically.

"I don't like burdening people with it, but I do have my best friend Pam to lean on. She's like another sister to me," Heather said.

"I'm glad to hear that." Lars smiled.

"You know, I met Pam at a high school dance. We both liked the same boy and had to watch him dance with another girl all night," Heather giggled.

"Interesting. So, you bonded through mutual jealously," Lars teased and Heather blushed. "What does Pam do?"

"She runs her own deli in the farmers' market."

"Does everyone in your town have their own shop?"

"Haha! Pretty much! I guess growing up in a town like Munich, I always knew I was going to have my own shop. I never saw myself doing anything else."

"And you weren't going to run your parents' bookshop?"

"Blooming hell, no! That wasn't for me and it was a dying business. My sister and I sold our parents' house, and I used my portion of the money to turn the bookshop into my bakery. My sister wasn't interested in it and was happy for me to have it."

Heather continued explaining, "you see, I already had my own house at that point. When our grandparents died, they'd left my parents quite a bit of money. So, our parents helped me buy my own house and to make things fair, they opened an RESP for my sister's kids."

“The good and the bad are forever intertwined,” Lars mused.

“Who said that?” Heather asked.

“I just made it up,” Lars chuckled, and Heather raised her eyebrow at him, and he added, “by the way, what’s an RESP?”

“Oh right, you don’t have those here. A tax-sheltered investment to help parents pay for their kid’s university tuition,” Heather explained as if reading from a textbook.

“Another benefit to being a Canadian,” Lars chuckled and then noticed they’d finished the bottle of sake, so he poured some wine into their wine glasses, and they both took a sip.

“So, I have to ask. Why do you sell edibles?” Lars raised his eyebrow.

“I knew that question was coming!” Heather chuckled, “I started selling them because after my parents died, I couldn’t sleep. I’d wake up to the sound of a phone ringing, even though it wasn’t.”

“Because that’s how you found out your parents had died. A phone call in the middle of the night,” Lars empathized.

“Yep.”

“That must’ve been exhausting.”

“I tried everything to fall asleep. Melatonin at first sort of worked, but then I did some research and found out that by mixing certain cannabis oils together, along with melatonin, it can help you fall asleep. And with the right mix, you don’t feel groggy the next day.”

“So, you’re like me. You like to mix odd things together,” Lars chuckled, “But have you ever, you know, taken them just for fun?”

"I knew that's where you were going. Of course! A few times, but my rule is that I generally don't. I want to stay focused on my business and not get strayed by having too much fun. Not that I don't like having fun," Heather chuckled.

"Oh, I know you like to have fun, especially from some of your comments!" Lars chuckled and Heather blushed.

"Haha! And, I have to admit, when I was playing around at the beginning with the ratios ... Oof, I had a few unexpected trips."

They both started giggling.

"Please, let's talk about you." Heather said as she took a sip of her wine.

"No, no. I want to first hear what you already know about me," Lars teased.

Heather gladly took on the challenge and began rattling off some facts, "let's see, I know you were born in Denmark. You moved to Florida to work under a mentor, Trinika, who helped you open your first bakery at twenty-two."

Lars nodded but didn't want to interrupt this time.

"You got into the reality show business, but then got out of it. Were on the cover of a few tabloids because of some of your dating exploits," Heather giggled, and Lars pretended to look ashamed.

"You currently own several bakeries in the southern part of the States. You have a Michelin star. And now I know you're working on recipes in the gluten-free space – don't worry, your secret is safe with me – and, after spending the day with you, I can genuinely say that you are your true self on and off screen."

"That's an impressive list," Lars smiled. "And, thank you, but truth be told, I got out of the reality show business because I felt like I was becoming a parody of myself. But that's a story for another time. What do you want to know about me?"

"I told you about my parents. Why don't you tell me about yours? You never talk about them," Heather pointed out.

"That's true for good reason. Sounds like mine weren't anything like yours. Mine were very self-absorbed," Lars began, "you see, I was an oops. My parents were old. I had a sister and a brother who were twins and twenty years older than me. My parents thought they were done and then all of a sudden, I came along."

"That would definitely be a surprise," Heather remarked.

"They kind of just left me to my own devices. My dad was an inventor. He was always busy tinkering. He'd built this huge garage, or rather workshop, on our property where he had tons of tools and different types of machinery. He'd stay there all day, working on his ideas," Lars continued.

"Kind of like you. What did he invent?" Heather asked curiously.

"I know, I know. There are similarities. But that's where the similarities end. I hope, anyway." Lars looked at Heather for reassurance.

"Hey, I'm still getting to know you. And I've never met your father," Heather teased.

"Ha! Fair enough. But you did just call me genuine, or rather, true to myself?" Lars teased back. "Anyway, my dad was inventing stuff all the time, but only a few ideas got patented. He mainly invented small kitchen appliances. Early versions of what we now know as the instant pot, rice cookers, toaster ovens. That sort of thing. I remember things exploding or catching on fire in his workshop."

"Dangerous! Any baking related appliances?"

"Probably."

"And your mother?"

"My mother was sort of an eccentric, too. She worked at a nursery and that's where she spent most of her time. She was a grafter. She created hybrid plants that were more sustainable. Needed less water, less sun."

"Both of your parents sound impressive," Heather said, enthralled by the details he was willing to share with her.

"Sure, they do. To you. But to me, it meant I was alone all the time," Lars explained.

"But isn't that kind of what teens want? To be left alone? I know I did," Heather said.

"Yeah, as a teenager. But I was alone even as a young child," Lars explained.

"Oh, sorry, didn't realize that. What about your older siblings? Were they never around?" Heather asked.

"They were so much older, you know, independent and off on their own adventures at school and in the real world. On top of that, I always sort of felt like a misfit you know, with my ruby hair and green eyes when everyone else around me had blond hair and blue eyes. No one bothered to explain to me back then where I could've gotten it from ... now I know these things can just happen.

"When I finally had the courage to leave home at sixteen, I knew my sister was living in Paris working for some food company. So, I packed a bag, got some money for the train and left for Paris. Long story short, I slept on my sister's couch for a while and found work in different restaurants.

"And then one day, I showed up and there was a Creole woman working the pastry station. So loud and boisterous among all those serious Parisiens. But she was the boss. She took one look at me and from day one, treated me like a long-lost son. I'd never been hugged so much in my life. She's the one who made me fall in love with pastry." Lars smiled bittersweetly at the memory.

"Seriously? Trinika worked as a pastry chef in Paris?" Heather was astonished.

"Haha! True story. Head Pastry Chef. Sure, she didn't quite fit in among all those serious, uptight chefs, but she was the best. I worked under Trinika's wing for a while, but sleeping on my sister's couch in her tiny house with her husband and two kids was beginning to be a problem." Lars frowned.

"I can imagine," Heather murmured.

"When she came to me one day and said that her time in Paris was up and that she'd been offered a job as Head Pastry Chef at a pop star's hotel in Miami and that I had a choice to make. I could stay here with the wolves, or I could come with her –"

"Who was the pop star?"

"Diva V –"

"You're kidding!"

"Haha! No, not at all … Of course, I said yes, and then she said that there were two conditions. As soon as we got to America, she was taking me to a dentist and to a proper barber."

"Why's that?"

"I had buck teeth and I'd been cutting my own hair. She said in America, looks mattered and I'd better get used to it. She helped me get a passport and all the paperwork done. We got on a plane and that was it. That's how I ended up coming to America. You know, her favourite saying was 'Sak vid pa kanp'. An empty sack can't stand up." Lars smiled, feeling sentimental.

"Food is fuel," Heather nodded.

"Sure thing," Lars smiled.

"And dessert is love," Heather teased.

"Haha! True enough," Lars smiled.

"Now I understand why earlier you said, 'they say Skål'. You really don't feel Danish, do you?" Heather observed.

"Not completely, no." Lars admitted.

"Interesting. I guess we all feel a little lost sometimes when it comes to our roots. Who we are is a mix of where our ancestors came from, where we grow up and where we end up as adults. We're never just one thing," Heather mused.

"And we take what we need from each place we've been," Lars agreed.

"The best parts," Heather laughed.

"The simplest parts," Lars joked.

They both paused to enjoy some more sushi and sips of wine.

"Okay, now back to Diva V. That must've been soooo much fun working at a pop star's hotel?" Heather teased.

"There may have been a few parties I may have attended underage," Lars grinned.

"What about your sister? Do you ever see her? And your brother?" Heather asked.

"I do keep in touch with my sister and my nephews. It's so much easier now with social media. But they never come to the States. She moved to London, a few years ago, doing product development for a food company. My brother's in Vienna."

"You talk about your parents in the past."

"Yes, they died a few years ago."

"Didn't they ever reach out once you became successful?"

"Nope."

"So, you're an orphan too."

"Been one my whole life."

They stared at each other in silence for a while.

Lars broke the silence. "So, I have to ask ... when you wrote down 'lickable' as one of your comments. What exactly did you mean by that?"

"Haha! I did, didn't I? I think I wrote that down in a moment of complete happiness —" Heather began.

"Right ... an out-of-body experience." Lars let out a big sigh.

"I think you know what it means." Heather's face reddened.

"I have a pretty good idea," Lars smiled.

"Maybe we can discuss it in the hot tub? I think I'm ready to go in," Heather said flirtatiously.

Lars smiled. "You go change. I got this."

"Well, let me at least bring some stuff in."

"Sure."

Heather helped Lars carry some of the plates back into the kitchen.

"The bathroom is that way, correct?" Heather pointed down the hallway as Lars put the leftovers into the fridge.

"Yep." He nodded.

Heather brought her bag into the small bathroom and began to change into the sexy black bathing suit she'd bought with Sofia. She thought about all the little coincidences that had led her to meeting Lars and couldn't help but feel that despite how different their lives were, they shared similar philosophical views on life, and she was grateful for it. She also contemplated how they both craved that missing relationship with their parents and were perhaps searching to fill that void.

When she came out of the bathroom, Lars was no longer inside the bungalow, but she could hear the whirring of the hot tub and see his head bobbing up and down. She went through the sliding glass doors, closing them behind her, and then made her way over to the hot tub. She threw her colourful beach towel onto a nearby lounge chair. Lars admired her as she stepped inside the tub.

"It's quite hot in here, but I think it just got hotter." He teased, and Heather rolled her eyes, but secretly liked the cheesy compliment.

Sitting across from each other, Heather watched as Lars filled up her champagne glass. He handed it to her and then filled up his own. They each took a sip of their champagne and then sank back into their comfy ergonomic seats.

"This is the life. Maybe I should move here and open up a bakery." Heather sighed and Lars chuckled.

"I think that's a wonderful idea, but come closer, you feel too far away," Lars motioned for her to move closer.

Even though Heather had seen for herself that Lucy was indeed mild-mannered, but from the little she knew about dogs, Heather still felt that her every move was being scrutinized. With one eye on Lucy, Heather put her champagne glass down and crossed through the steamy, bubbling water over to Lars until their faces were inches apart.

Heather glanced over at Lucy one more time and noticed the dog's eyebrows were quivering up and down, as if worried, but otherwise the dog didn't move. Thankful that Lucy didn't start to bark at her in a protective jealousy, she looked into Lars' green eyes and affectionately rubbed his ruby-coloured goatee with her thumb, leaving a streak of bubbles.

Lars cupped his hand around the back of Heather's neck and pulled her into him. His goatee tickled her lips, at first distracting her, but she soon forgot about the goatee as they kissed deeply. He widened his legs and Heather fell up against him, the current pushing her towards him. As she leaned further into him, she could feel his happiness growing through his Hawaiian-patterned trunks. She pulled away so she could stare at him again.

"I can't believe I'm making out with the face I've stared at all these years on the cover of your books." Heather said, laughing.

"Yes, you said that before. Are you still happy with it?" Lars teased.

"Most definitely," she said.

She moved closer to him and they kissed some more. As they pressed up against each other, Heather's breathing grew heavier and Lars kissed her harder. For a moment, they stopped kissing and looked at one another. She could see sweat forming under his eyes and above his upper lip, and briefly wondered if she looked sweaty, too.

"What do you want to do?" Lars asked.

"What do you mean?" Heather asked.

"Well, do you want to go inside or continue out here?" Lars asked.

"Let's go inside," Heather said.

"Good idea. Don't want to get too overheated," Lars teased.

They lifted themselves out of the hot tub.

"Here, come over here and take a quick shower to rinse off," Lars said as he motioned her over.

Heather was surprised that she hadn't noticed the showerhead that was sticking out of the wall above a garden hose that was coiled around a tap. Lars turned on the tap and held his hand underneath it until the water temperature warmed up. He stepped under the water and motioned for her to join him. She squeezed in beside him.

After a few seconds, Lars said, "okay, that's good," and shut the water off.

Heather wrapped her colourful beach towel snugly around her body and then pressed it against herself, trying to squeeze as much water as possible out of her bathing suit before going inside.

Lars wrapped a nearby towel around his waist and walked over to the sliding doors and opened them for her. As she stepped inside and crossed the bungalow's sunken living room, she felt a slight chill from the air conditioning.

Lucy followed them inside, picked up a plush toy bear that was on the floor, dropped it on her indoor bed, and plunked herself down again while letting out another big sigh.

Lars took Heather's hand and led her down the hallway to the main bedroom. He closed the door behind them. She noticed it was very tidy, but also noticed once again, that the colour scheme was black and tan. Lars tried to pull down the straps of her bathing suit, but it was sticking to her skin now that it was partially dry.

"Let me do it." Heather said and then struggled to remove it, feeling a little ridiculous as she did so, and Lars looked away to be polite.

When she finally was able to peel off her bathing suit, she stood there naked in front of him and was glad she was slightly tipsy from the sake and wine.

"Well, what do we have here?" Lars exclaimed, admiring Dolores' handiwork.

Heather been so focused on their conversation throughout the night that she'd completely forgotten about the tiny vajazzle heart that Dolores had placed on her.

"Do you like it?" Heather chuckled.

"Yes, very much so," Lars grinned.

Heather smiled shyly and then shivered from the air conditioning.

Lars pulled back the duvet from the King-sized bed and told her kindly, "get in. I'll warm you up."

Lars peeled off his Hawaiian-patterned bathing suit trunks and they snuggled in the bed, facing each other. He rubbed the outside of the duvet along her body to warm her up.

"Are you warm, now?" Lars asked.

"Getting there, thank you." Heather smiled at him.

"Let me get a condom. Just one sec." Lars opened the drawer to the bedside table and took one out. He ripped it open and pulled it on quite expertly, and Heather wondered how many times he'd done this before.

They began kissing and Lars moved himself on top of Heather.

"Am I too heavy for you? I'm not squishing you, am I?" Lars asked.

"No, not at all." Heather looked up at him, smiling.

"God, you're sexy." Lars said, smiling back at her.

MIAMI
MONDAY, DECEMBER 23

While JC and Carmen were driving around the outskirts of the neighbourhood looking for Olivia, Bianca and Oliver were heading towards the park where JC and Carmen had found Max wandering on his own, as Bianca felt a strong pull towards that area.

Every once in a while, as they made their way towards the park, Bianca pointed the flashlight into random bushes for any sign of hope. Oliver kept praying that Olivia would simply pop out of a bush, laughing and yelling … *Gotcha!*

"The park's just up here," Bianca said as she began to break into a slight jog.

"Oh, finally," Oliver sighed, and then realized with relief that he had the energy to walk a bit faster. The food poisoning from the unfortunate egg salad sandwich had finally worked its way out of his system.

Bianca kept the flashlight pointed in front of them as they neared the park.

"I see something!" Bianca yelled.

Oliver squinted towards the area Bianca was shining the flashlight at and yelled, "so do I", as he noticed a lump lying near a thicket.

They both ran towards the thicket and as they grew closer, they could see that the lump was a body. They stopped just in front of the body and peered down.

"What should we do?" Bianca asked desperately.

Oliver knelt down in front of the body and began to gently tug at the hood of the rain jacket.

"Try not to move her. They say that's bad. We don't know what's happened to her," Bianca instructed.

"I know, I know. I wasn't born yesterday," Oliver snapped impatiently.

Bianca knelt down beside him and held onto the rest of the body as Oliver continued to gently tug. The hood finally fell backwards and they could see that it was indeed Olivia.

"Oh, thank God! It's her! What's happened? Why is she like this? She still feels warm." Oliver said, feeling agitated.

"I honestly think she's been hit by a car. We need to get her to the hospital. Call JC now." Bianca ordered as she began inspecting Olivia for broken bones. "Tell him we're at the east end of the park."

Oliver nodded and took his phone out of his pocket.

"JC! We found her! ... Yes, we think so ... Yes, hospital. We're at the east end of the park." Oliver shouted into his phone and then hung up. "He'll be here soon."

"She has a strong pulse," Bianca reassured him.

"I don't want this to come out the wrong way, but why was she out walking Max alone? Why weren't you with her?" Oliver asked, accusingly.

"No reason. I felt like helping Breanna with dinner, that's all." Bianca shrugged.

"As long as you guys weren't arguing about something?" Oliver prodded.

"Arguing? Not at all." Bianca defended herself, thinking how upset she'd been that Olivia wasn't taking what she was saying about breaking up with JC seriously.

"Good. Do you feel any broken bones in your pediatric opinion?"

"Well, it's going to be a while before I'm any kind of pediatrician. Honestly, it's hard to tell through this jacket. But she's definitely unconscious," Bianca frowned.

"Can I move her head so it's in my lap where it's more comfortable? Not on the cold ground?" Oliver asked.

"I'm really not sure about moving her," Bianca argued, "besides, why weren't you out walking with her?"

"Uh, I wasn't feeling well," Oliver mumbled.

"Not feeling well?" Bianca raised an eyebrow.

"Fine. I had food poisoning." Oliver snapped, embarrassed.

"Would you guys quit arguing?" Olivia whispered.

"You're awake! Are you hurt? What happened to you? I'm never letting you out of my sight again!" Oliver exclaimed, relieved.

"Ugh. I feel like I'm gonna puke." Olivia struggled to sit up.

"Try not to move too quickly! What hurts? We need to know what's wrong!" Bianca shrieked.

"Bianca, she's going to have to move eventually to get into JC's car," Oliver pointed out.

"Guys, can you please be quiet for like thirty seconds?" Olivia whispered.

"Sorry," Bianca said, feeling badly again about letting Olivia go for a walk by herself.

"Sure, babe," Oliver scowled.

They carefully helped her sit up as she held onto her right side, wincing in pain. Once she was sitting up, Olivia turned to her left and began puking into the bushes.

"Let it all out," Oliver said as he rubbed Olivia's back.

Bouncing headlights shone at them as JC's Range Rover approached and then slowed to a stop and eventually parked by the side of the road. JC and Carmen jumped out.

"How badly hurt is she?" JC asked.

"We're not sure yet," Bianca said.

"I'm done." Olivia said as she wiped her mouth with the back of her sleeve.

"Can you stand up?" Oliver asked.

"I think it's my right side that hurts," Olivia said, trying to assess the pain that was throbbing throughout her body.

"Do you remember what happened?" JC asked.

"Um, not really. Just that I wanted to take Max across the street to the – oh my God! Where is he? Is he okay?" Olivia panicked.

"Don't worry, he's okay. We found him wandering the neighbourhood on his own," JC reassured her, "which was a good thing, because that's how we knew to go looking for you."

"Oh, good." Olivia sighed with relief at the thought of Max back at home, safe and sound.

"We can worry about what happened later. Let's get you in the car and to the hospital right away," Oliver demanded.

"You can explain everything at the hospital," Bianca echoed, finally agreeing with something Oliver said.

"Can we lift you?" JC asked.

"I guess so," Olivia whispered.

JC and Oliver positioned themselves on either side of Olivia. Oliver lifted her left arm over top of him while JC hooked his arm around her right side so she could lean into him for support. They walked awkwardly, the three of them, stumbling with each step towards the backseat. Every once in a while, Olivia let out a high-pitched yelp in pain and they paused to give her a break.

When they finally reached the SUV, Bianca was already in the back, ready to help with getting Olivia inside. Slowly and methodically, they helped her into the backseat. Oliver joined Bianca in the backseat so that Olivia was sandwiched in between the two of them for extra support.

"I'll drive as carefully but also as fast as I can." JC promised as he sat down in the driver's seat and Carmen joined him up front.

"Olivia?"

"Yes, JC?"

"Can you tell us now, what happened?"

"Um ... the car stopped. And then sped up," Olivia mumbled.

None of them knew what to make of this explanation and then Oliver and Bianca watched in fear as Olivia lost consciousness again.

"She's passed out!" Bianca yelled.

"Hurry up and get to the hospital!" Oliver yelled.

"I'm going as fast as I can!" JC yelled as they sped through the city towards the nearest hospital, which he sadly realized also happened to be the same hospital his dad was currently being treated at.

"I can't believe we have to go back there already," Carmen sighed, as if reading his thoughts.

A few minutes later, JC swerved into the Emergency Room entranceway, right behind an ambulance that was just pulling out.

"I'll go get a wheelchair," Carmen offered.

"Thank you," Oliver said.

While they waited for Carmen to come back, Oliver looked sympathetically at JC and said, "honestly, JC, you and Carmen can go home. I know you were on your way home to get some rest. I got it from here."

"Yeah, you two, go home. I'm staying with Oliver. You've had enough of hospitals for today," Bianca nodded.

"You sure?" JC sounded relieved.

"Yeah, for sure," Oliver nodded.

Carmen came back with the wheelchair and they carefully loaded the unconscious Olivia onto it.

"We were just telling JC that you guys should go home and get some rest. We got it from here," Bianca said sympathetically.

"Thanks. Let us know how it goes." Carmen smiled compassionately at Bianca.

As JC and Carmen sped away, Bianca leaned her body over Olivia's to prevent her from falling off the wheelchair as they wheeled her through the hospital's automatic doors. Soon, they were both leaning into the wheelchair to keep Olivia from sliding onto the floor.

They looked around the ER and saw that it was bustling with activity. In front of them was a receptionist desk with nurses stationed behind it, who seemed to be either on the phone or typing at a computer. The desk had been hastily decorated for Christmas with garland draped and taped around its edges. To their right, was a bank of hospital beds separated by cubicle curtains, some of the curtains were draped all the way around for privacy, while others had been left open and they could see patients in various stages of examination. Only a couple of the beds were empty.

"Have you ever been to the ER before?" Oliver asked.

"No. Not sure what to do," Bianca admitted.

A triage nurse wearing a headband of reindeer ears approached them.

"Hi there, you guys seem to be having a bit of trouble. Why don't we put the legs up and that'll help keep her steady," he suggested.

He bent down and pushed on a lever until the legs of the wheelchair were straight out in front of Olivia and he gently positioned Olivia's legs in front of her so as to keep her body upright.

"Oh my gosh. Thank you so much!" Bianca gushed at the nurse.

"We think my girlfriend's been hit by a car and we need to get her looked at right away," Oliver explained, anxiously.

"Why don't we bring her over here?" The nurse pointed to an empty bed.

All four of them crowded into the small area beside the bed – the wheelchair taking up most of the space – and the nurse pulled the cubicle curtain around them for privacy. The nurse took out a tiny flashlight and lifted up Olivia's lids to check her eyes, and then asked, "what do you mean, you think she's been hit by a car?"

"We found her by the side of the road, unconscious. But then she woke up and puked and then said something about a car stopping and then …" Bianca began to explain.

"Going?" Oliver offered.

"What do you mean found her?" The nurse asked.

"She was out walking the dog by herself. The dog came back but she didn't," Oliver explained.

"So, we went out looking for her," Bianca added.

"And there was no car around when you found her?" The nurse asked.

"Nope," Oliver shook his head.

The nursed nodded but didn't offer an opinion. "I'll have them run some tests. She has a bad concussion, but most likely she'll need an MRI or CT scan. It may be a while as we're quite busy. For now, we'll put her on some oxygen. But we'll need her insurance information first. Do you have that?"

"Ah, no. Maybe Alonso, has it? I'll have to call him to find out. Bianca, do you have his number?" Oliver asked.

"I have her phone. It'll be in there." Bianca took Olivia's phone out of her pocket and handed it to Oliver.

"Great. Let's get her into this bed." The nurse smiled.

"I can help," Oliver offered.

"No, let us do it." The nurse shook his head.

He pulled back the curtain and motioned for another nurse to come help them. The nurse came over and they lifted and placed Olivia delicately onto the bed and then pulled the covers over her. Once Olivia was comfortably in bed, the other nurse left with the wheelchair.

"Should we be worried?" Oliver asked.

The nurse smiled at Oliver. "Make your phone calls and I'll be back with the oxygen. We're going to do everything we can to make sure she's okay."

After the nurse left, and now that the wheelchair was out of the way, they noticed that there was only one chair and Oliver motioned for Bianca to sit down.

"Here I thought we were done with hospitals," she sighed as she sat down, and then impulsively grabbed Olivia's hand and said loudly, "we're in a hospital. It's going to be okay. They're going to look after you."

"What's her passcode?" Oliver asked, unable to unlock the phone.

"She always uses the year she was born, 2005," Bianca explained.

Oliver smiled at its practicality, entered it and then scrolled through her recent calls to find Alonso's number. "What do I tell him?"

"You're going to need to tell him everything so he understands how serious this is," Bianca explained, knowing how absent Alonso had been all of Olivia's life, but hoping he'd keep his promise to make it up to her now. Too little, too late in her opinion, but who was she to say anything.

MUNICH
MONDAY, DECEMBER 23

In the basement of Phil's parents' house, Maria was snuggled on the couch beside Phil as the Bills vs. Dolphins' game was coming to a close. It had been an exciting game to watch as both teams had fought for every point, but it seemed the final score was going to settle at thirty-four to thirty-one for the Bills. The other three members of the Müller family were spread out across the rest of the sectional couch.

Maria and Ursula hadn't been able to finish the pitcher of margaritas but had consumed enough to make them giddy and were still feeling quite relaxed.

Maria's cellphone began to vibrate.

She looked down at her phone and saw that it was Alonso. She almost didn't answer because she assumed he was butt-dialing her, but then something told her it was important, so she answered.

"Hello?" She asked quietly into the phone, so she wouldn't disturb the others.

"Maria?" Alonso's voice cracked with emotion.

"¿Qué ha pasado?"[23] Alarmed at the unusual emotion in Alonso's voice, Maria's voice came out loud.

"Que no cunda el pánico, pero Olivia está en el hospital."[24] Alonso began.

---

[23] What's happened?

[24] Don't panic, but Olivia's in the hospital.

"¡Al hospital! ¿Qué quieres decir con que está en el hospital?"[25] Maria yelled as she quickly unraveled herself from Phil and he looked down at her with concern.

Even more concerned by the repetition of the word "hospital", he pressed pause on the remote and Brian started to protest, but Phil gave him a don't-you-dare look.

"Oliver y Bianca se apresuraron a llevarla al hospital de inmediato."[26] Alonso explained as he tried to regain his composure.

Phil motioned for her to put it on speaker and it took her a few seconds to find the button. "Can you tell me exactly what's happened? And please speak in English. I'm putting you on speaker," Maria explained.

"English? Um, okay." Alonso frowned at the request, but wasn't about to argue as it had been a long day. "The kids were all at JC's house and I guess Olivia went to take their dog for a walk and the dog came back, but she didn't, so they went to look for her and found her by the side of the road, hurt." Alonso felt his face crumple.

"By the side of the road? Hurt?" Maria asked anxiously.

"I'm so sorry to have to tell you all of this. They think it was a hit and run," Alonso said in despair.

"How badly hurt is she?" Maria felt panic taking over her body.

---

[25] Hospital! What do you mean she's in the hospital?

[26] Oliver and Bianca were quick to take her to the hospital right away.

"We're not sure yet. They've taken her to get a CT scan and an MRI. I'm guessing she's going to need surgery," Alonso explained despondently.

"Surgery?" Maria cried. "Oh, my poor baby! This is all your fault! If you hadn't left, this would never have happened!" Maria yelled, momentarily forgetting that the Müller family was watching and listening.

And there it was, Alonso thought to himself, the blame. He knew it would come, so he said in a calmer tone, trying to regain his own emotions. "Maria, please, calm down. She's a strong girl."

"Have you seen her yet?" Maria asked.

"Well, no, not exactly. I'm at the hospital with Oliver and Bianca, but they took her to get a CT scan and an MRI before I got to her room." Alonso said, leaving out the fact that he'd been in another part of the hospital with Josephine and it had taken him a while to make his way to Olivia's room. "Maria, you know she's going to need her mother."

"I know." Maria took some deep breaths, and then having forgotten all about Olivia's convoluted explanations about who'd she'd been travelling with, asked, "who's JC?"

"Ah, Josephine's son," Alonso gulped.

"Who's Josephine?" Maria asked innocently.

Alonso paused and cleared his throat. "My, um, friend."

"Oh." Maria said quietly, hurt at the reminder that he was leaving her for another woman, "tu nueva mujer,"[27] she added bitterly, being in too

---

[27] your new woman

much shock at the moment to recognize the hypocrisy as she sat beside Phil.

"Please don't do that," Alonso sighed.

"Why was Olivia out walking their dog alone?" Maria asked.

"I'm not sure. Listen, Olivia's a resilient girl. She's going to be okay," Alonso reassured her.

"Let's hope so," Maria said, knowing all they could do right now was pray for Olivia.

"Where are you, anyway?" Alonso asked.

"I'm in Canada," Maria explained.

"Canada? How quickly can you get here?" Alonso wasn't about to point out that it was perhaps her leaving that had also contributed to the situation.

"I'm not sure. I'll have to check flights." Maria said as all four members of the Müller family continued to stare at her with worry.

"Okay, keep me posted," Alonso said and then added, quietly, "she's a strong girl, but she'll need you."

"I know." Maria felt tears well up in her eyes. "Can you please call Yolanda? I really don't feel up to it."

Alonso wasn't surprised at the request. "Sure, but I'll wait until morning. No quiero molestar al oso demasiado pronto."[28]

As soon as Maria hung up, Ursula moved closer to her on the couch and grabbed her hand. She looked at Maria and said reassuringly, "she's going to be okay."

---

[28] Don't want to disturb the bear too soon.

"Let's look up flights," Phil said as he stood up from the couch.

"Good idea. You're going to need a clear head. I'll make some tea," Ursula said.

"Thanks, guys," Maria said as she stood up.

As the three of them made their way upstairs, Maria could hear the post-game commentary on the television, and she didn't blame them as there wasn't anything Klaus or Brian could do about the situation. Once they entered the kitchen, Ursula grabbed the kettle, filled it up and placed it on one of the burners.

"I'll get the laptop so we can look up flights." Phil said as he ducked out of the kitchen.

Feeling drained and overwhelmed, Maria sat down on one of the stools at the kitchen island and buried her face in her hands.

"My poor baby. She must be in so much pain. And so scared," Maria cried out.

Ursula came over and hugged her sideways.

"It's going to be okay. The hospital will know what to do," Ursula reassured her, knowing that if it was her daughter, she'd want to be right by her side as soon as possible.

"Who does that? Just leaves someone by the side of the road like that?" Maria cried out.

"I'm sure they'll find out whoever did this," Ursula said consolingly.

"We're going to make sure you get home," Phil said adamantly as he re-entered the kitchen and booted up the laptop.

He typed in the date and searched several airports, but to their dismay, not one airport in all of southern Florida had seats available on any direct flights.

"What are we going to do? I want to leave right away. She needs me." Maria was trembling.

"We'll figure something out," Ursula reassured her, thinking to herself that there had to be more to the story, more than what they'd heard, based on how Maria had reacted to the mention of a Josephine.

"Hang on a second," Phil said as he left the kitchen and jogged to the front hall closet. He rummaged through his coat pockets until he produced the map of the Regal Winter Fair. He brought it back into the kitchen and spread it across the dinette table.

"Yes! I thought so!" Phil jabbed his finger at a spot on the map.

"What are you pointing at?" Maria walked over to the dinette table and peered at the map.

"I thought I remembered seeing a hangar on the map."

"How is that relevant?"

"Your brother's a pilot, right? He has his own plane?"

"Well, yes. But you're not thinking he can come get us?"

"Yes, why not?"

"Seriously? But how would we even get in there? The hangar's got to be all locked up?"

"Yes! I'm serious. I have an idea. I'll be back. Call your brother!" Phil yelled over his shoulder as he left the kitchen and made his way back downstairs to the basement.

Standing in front of his dad and his brother, Phil bent down and picked up the converter that was lying on the couch beside his dad and paused the television again.

Klaus looked at him anxiously. "How's Maria holding up? Have you found flights? Is there anything we can do?"

"Well, Pop, that's what I wanted to talk to you about. Did you know that there's an airstrip hangar on the grounds of the fair?" Phil asked.

"Sure ..."

"Do you know if we could use it?"

"Use it? What do you mean use it?"

"Well, there aren't any available flights. Maria wants to leave ASAP and she's on the phone with her brother, seeing if he can come get us. He flies a jet. Didn't you say your friend at the Probus club ... What's his name ... Martin? Is part owner of the fair?"

"Maria's brother has his own jet?" Brian asked, dumbfounded.

"Yes, for work," Phil said curtly. "Maria's going to see if he can come get us. But we need a place for him to land. Can you call your friend?"

"You want me to call Martin and ask him to let us use the landing strip? I understand the situation, but are you sure there's no other option? This seems a little extreme," Klaus said worriedly.

"We're desperate. What would you do if it was one of us?" Phil asked.

"Pop, you gotta do this. A daughter always needs her mother," Brian said and they both gave him a strange look.

"Okay, yes, you're right. Anything to help." Klaus took his eyeglasses out of his pocket, picked up the phone and dialed.

"Hey Martin, sorry for the late call," Klaus said as soon as it was picked up. Phil motioned for Klaus to put it on speaker and right away they could hear loud background noises, so Klaus began to shout. "We're having a bit of an emergency! My son and his girlfriend —"

Phil raised an eyebrow at the term "girlfriend" while Martin interrupted enthusiastically. "Girlfriend? I heard Phil was spotted with some real exotic looker at the farmers' market and then here at the fair!"

"Well, yes. What's all that background noise?" Klaus frowned.

"I'm at the fair. We're getting set up for our shot at the Guinness Book of World Records!" Martin exclaimed and Phil perked up.

"Guinness Book of World Records? For what?" Klaus asked.

"For the record number of people to descend an indoor ice slide in a twenty-four-hour period. It starts right at midnight tonight. We've got camera crews here already and people lined up all the way around the building!" Martin yelled excitedly.

"So, the fair's open!" Klaus gave Phil the thumbs up.

"Oh yes, we're open!" Martin said happily.

"Do you think we could borrow the airstrip at the hangar?" Klaus asked and Phil secretly crossed his fingers behind his back.

"What for?" Martin sounded puzzled.

"Well, that's what I was trying to explain. My son's girlfriend's daughter has been in a terrible accident –"

Phil interrupted, and deciding to embrace the term "girlfriend", he explained, "actually, she's in the hospital and will be needing surgery, and we need to get back down to Miami as soon as possible. My girlfriend's brother flies a jet and has agreed to come get us."

Phil kept his fingers crossed as he explained the last part, hoping Maria had indeed convinced her brother to come.

"Oh Lord Almighty! So sorry, to hear this. Yes, of course! After all, it's the least I can do for you, Klaus. You know I owe you big time," Martin chuckled. "I'll tell Peter to call you. He's in charge of the hangar."

"Thank you, Martin. You're a real lifesaver," Klaus said and then hung up. "I guess we just wait for Peter to call us."

"Thanks, Pop." Phil said and then frowned, wondering what type of favour his Pop had done for Martin.

Phil returned to the kitchen where he found Ursula and Maria sitting at the island drinking martinis. He gave them the hairy eyeball.

"What? We needed something stronger than tea," Ursula said shamelessly.

"Did you talk to your brother?" Phil asked.

"Yes, there's good news and bad. The good news is that my brother has agreed to come get us. The bad news is that he won't be here until the morning, around nine. Something about regulations and flight plans." Maria explained, leaving out the fact that not only had her brother been upset about Olivia, but had also grilled her on who exactly this Phil person was and how had she met someone so soon and if she truly trusted him. She'd been glad that she'd gone into a different room to call him, away from Ursula's prying ears.

"Okay, well, it's all falling into place. Pop's friend Martin is going to have his friend Peter call us. He's in charge of the hangar. It's all going to be fine," Phil said as he embraced Maria in his arms. "By the way, this a strange coincidence … Remember how the lady at the ice slide asked us to come back at midnight because they're going after a spot in the Guinness Book of World Records?"

"Yes, the lady with the musical voice," Maria nodded, looking up at him.

Phil frowned at Maria's odd comment. "Well, that's why the fair is open and we're able to use the hangar! I think it's a sign. A good one."

"Let's hope so," Maria whispered into Phil's belly.

MIAMI
TUESDAY, DECEMBER 24

It was two o'clock in the morning and Carmen was lying wide awake in her bed. She was unable to sleep because of the shock and grief she was feeling at the death of her father that evening. Their mother, Josephine, had called her and JC from the hospital to tell them the news and they'd both felt tremendous guilt for not being there.

She hadn't yet been able to muster the strength to call her boyfriend, Dylan, to tell him. How different she'd pictured this Christmas being. She'd been so happy when her mother had told her she could spend it in Boston with her boyfriend's family who she felt more at home with than her own. She'd been so relieved that she'd be as far away as possible from whatever family drama she had a feeling was playing out at her own house, but then her mother had called her in Boston with the news about their dad and her whole life had changed in an instant.

Her cellphone began to ring.

"Hello?"

"Oh! I wasn't expecting you to answer!" Mila's slurred voice rang in her ear.

"I can't sleep," Carmen sighed, wondering what drama Mila was about to instigate.

"I'm calling to say I'm so sorry," Mila slurred.

"Thanks Mila, but I'm still processing everything," Carmen said, relieved it was a condolence call, but wondered why Mila sounded so drunk.

"I'm so sorry," Mila repeated.

"How did you hear about it so quickly, anyway?" Carmen asked.

"I hope you can forgive me. I swear I never meant for it to happen," Mila murmured.

"It has nothing to do with you," Carmen frowned.

"It wasn't my idea," Mila said defensively.

"It's okay, Mila, it wasn't your fault." Carmen was getting annoyed.

"Oh, I'm so glad to hear you say that. It was all Logan's idea," Mila slurred accusingly.

"Logan?" Carmen asked.

"My boyfriend … I think you met him," Mila mumbled, "but I broke up with him."

"Okay?" Carmen was confused.

"I hope you're not too hurt. He just meant to scare you with the car, not hit you," Mila said.

Carmen paused and then began to realize that Mila wasn't calling about her dad's death after all.

"I thought you were calling about my dad dying?" Carmen asked, confused.

"Is that why you're home? I'm so sorry for that too," Mila said and then hung up.

Putting on her lawyer's cap, Carmen reviewed the conversation in her head, and after a few minutes – after having a flashback to seeing Olivia in *her* college rain jacket, and then remembering what Olivia had mumbled about the car stopping and starting again – she put two and two together.

With a jolt, Carmen suddenly felt sick to her stomach at the realization that the car had meant to hit her, and not Olivia.

After a few more minutes of reflection, she knew exactly how she was going to deal with Mila in the morning.

MIAMI
TUESDAY, DECEMBER 24

Heather woke up to a panting dog staring at her.

"Ugh, you need to get your teeth brushed," Heather scolded Lucy.

Heather turned over and saw that Lars was no longer in bed with her. She looked at the bedside alarm clock and saw that it was six-thirty.

She also noticed that he'd brought her big purse with her clothes that she'd left in the bathroom into the bedroom for her. Digging into her bag, she pulled out her white capris and sky-blue tank top and changed into them. She was happy that she'd added them to her bag in hopes the night would end exactly like it had.

Lucy closely followed behind her as she walked from the bedroom into the kitchen that overlooked the sunken living room. She could smell coffee.

"Good morning! I see someone has a new friend!" Lars said, happily.

"Morning! More like a stalker!" Heather joked and then cheerfully noticed that he was wearing a long-sleeved, sky-blue polo shirt over a pair of light-coloured khakis.

"Would you like a cup of coffee?" Lars asked.

"Yes, please. With milk and sugar," Heather said, "and look at us, we're mirroring each other."

"Oh yes we are!" Lars laughed, looking at Heather's outfit and then down at his, "but aren't you cold?"

"Not at all," Heather scoffed.

"But it's only sixty-eight degrees out," Lars frowned.

Heather smirked, but let it go.

"Do you have to work today?" Heather asked, hoping the answer was, no.

"Yes, I'm meeting Laura this morning to go over some ideas for the new recipe book. I know it's Christmas Eve, but that's what gets me inspired since the book is coming out next Christmas. It just puts me in the right mood," Lars chuckled.

"Now I get it. I thought maybe Laura was the one pushing you to get started on your cookbook so early."

"No, no. You'll need to be prepared if you end up working on a baking cookbook with her. She'll want to start as soon as possible. It can take up to eight months to complete one." Lars warned.

"That long? I had no idea. I just thought you were being super diligent," Heather laughed.

Lars chuckled as he handed Heather a cup of coffee. "Well, I wasn't planning on working all day and it would be nice to see you later. Unless you have plans?" He asked.

"I actually have no plans. I haven't been to the beach yet, so maybe I'll do that this morning. Is it far?"

"No, no. It's a ten-minute drive. It'll be windy though, so you'll want to bring a jacket. And it's partially closed from the tornado that touched down last week," Lars explained.

"Right," Heather said, remembering Phil's video and memes, and then she thought about how much her luck had changed over the last few days and briefly wondered what Maria was up to.

At that, the doorbell rang, waking her up from her thoughts. Lucy ran to the door, tail happily wagging.

"Oh, that'll be my dog walker. I'm usually out the door by now," Lars said, cheerily.

"I'm so sorry. I should get going. I can find the beach on my own." Heather instantly felt like she'd overstayed.

"No, no. Take your time. Let's meet somewhere this afternoon and then tonight you're coming with me to Chef Juarcito's house for a Christmas dinner party. I was missing a plus one," Lars said, smiling, as he opened the front door.

"Hi. I saw two cars in the driveway and wasn't sure who was here. Do you still need me to walk Lucy?" A girl's voice asked.

"Oh, right! Heather, I'll have to move your car," Lars said.

Heather was lost in her own thoughts again, stunned that she'd just been invited to a famous chef's house for dinner and began wondering what she had to wear ... the pleather pants?

"Heather?" The girl's voice asked.

Heather turned around and it took her a few seconds to register the face.

"Dolores?" Heather peered at her.

"You two know each other? How is that possible?" Lars was confused.

"Heather was a client of mine on Sunday at the salon," Dolores said, smiling.

"Well, lucky me." Lars smirked and Heather blushed.

"You walk dogs, too?" Heather asked.

"Yep, and rescue them," Dolores said, proudly.

"That's amazing!" Heather exclaimed.

"Just picked up two more rescues yesterday. Oh, you probably know Jack, if you know Sofia. Do you know Maria?" Dolores asked as she approached Heather.

"Um, well yes, long story short, I've exchanged houses with Maria for the holidays. So no, I don't know Maria, but Sofia and I have become quite close," Heather explained.

"I help Gabriel and Jack bring in rescue dogs from South America. And then we find them good homes," Dolores explained.

And that's when Heather realized that Dolores was one of those close talkers, the ones who invade your personal space without a clue. The ones who are so close, you can feel their words coming out of their mouths. She hadn't noticed the other day because, well ...

"You do all of that!" Heather exclaimed as she took a step backwards, only to have Dolores follow her.

"Yes, as I said, Jack gave me two more dogs yesterday," Dolores said in Heather's face.

"That explains it!" Heather exclaimed before she could stop herself. So, it wasn't anything sketchy that she'd overheard, they were bringing in dogs not drugs, she giggled to herself.

"Explains what?" Dolores frowned.

"Forget I said anything." Heather waved her hand as if to wipe her and Dolores' words away.

Lucy started to whine.

"Sorry girl!" Dolores exclaimed. "I better take her. Nice to bump into you again, Heather."

"Yes, you too," Heather nodded, relieved that Dolores was bumping away from her.

Dolores snapped a leash onto Lucy's collar and yelled out "Merry Christmas!" as she left.

"Merry Christmas!" Heather and Lars yelled cheerily back.

"I'm going now, but we'll text, later?" Lars said as kissed her. "Don't worry about locking up. Dolores can do that. If you want to give me your keys, I'll move your car to the side of the road?"

"Yes, for sure." Heather said, digging the keys out of her purse and handing them over.

They kissed one more time before he left. Not wanting to impose any longer, Heather hurried back to Lars' bedroom, quickly packed up her things, and then got back into Maria's car that was now parked on the side of the road with the keys inside. Giddy with excitement, she decided to text her sister. She took out her phone and saw that there was a text from Sofia.

Sofia's text read:

Hi Heather, I have some unexpected news, Maria and Phil are coming home today. Can you call me when you have a chance? How's it going with Lars?

Heather was startled at the news and wondered what would make them come back early.

"Hi, Sofia." Heather said into the phone when Sofia picked up.

"Hi, Heather. I guess you got my text," Sofia said.

"Yes, and I'm kind of confused," Heather said.

"I know. It's not how the house swap was supposed to go."

"What's happened? Why are they coming back so soon? Is it because of Yolanda?"

"No! Nothing like that. It's actually because Olivia, Maria's daughter, was hit by a car last night –" Sofia began to explain.

"Blooming hell! Is she okay?" Heather interrupted.

"She's okay, but from the text Maria sent me late last night, Olivia's broken her arm and has a few cracked ribs. She had to have surgery, and Maria wants to be home so she can look after her," Sofia explained.

"Yes, of course. Totally understandable!" Heather exclaimed.

"I'm so sorry it's cut your stay at Maria's short. I'd say you could stay here with us but we've got a full house," Sofia said, apologetically.

"Oh Sofia, please don't worry. I'll figure something out. I'm just glad it's a few broken bones and nothing more serious. Please pass on my best wishes for a speedy recovery to Maria and her daughter," Heather said.

"I will. How did it go with Lars last night by the way?" Sofia giggled.

"I was about to text you to tell you that everything went amazingly well and that he's asked me to go to a dinner party tonight, so I'll probably be staying over there again, anyway!" Heather announced happily.

"That's wonderful! I'm so happy for you! Let me know how everything goes," Sofia gushed.

"I will. And thank you so much for everything you've done for me over the past few days," Heather said happily.

"Oh, it was my pleasure. I promised Maria that I'd show you the meaning of 'mi casa es su casa' and I really hope I did," Sofia giggled.

"Blooming right you did! I know you think of Maria as a sister from another mister, but maybe we can be honorary sisters," Heather suggested jovially.

"I love it!" Sofia exclaimed happily. "That's what we are and will be, from now on."

"Well then, Merry Christmas and all the best to you and your family and I'm sure we'll see each other before I go back to Canada," Heather said warmly.

"I'm sure we will. Merry Christmas to you and all the best with Lars," Sofia echoed Heather's happiness.

After Heather hung up, she put her phone on speaker and started up the car as she headed back to Maria's.

"Call Sara!" She yelled, and her phone began dialing.

"Heather!" Sara answered happily.

"Hey, Merry Christmas! How are things at the in-laws?" Heather asked cheerily.

"We're having so much fun! I mean, it's a packed house, so a little hectic, but yesterday we took the kids to a local theatre to see The Nutcracker and they loved it! So far this morning, we've baked cookies and are making tourtières for tonight's dinner. And then we're going tobogganing this afternoon," Sara said cheerily.

"Oof, that's a lot. Make sure you have time to relax. You deserve it," Heather said.

"How's Florida?" Sara asked.

"Oh my God, I love it here! I've been out dancing. I tried some Colombian food. I played tennis and found out I'm actually good at it! And I have some other absolutely unexpected news!" Heather was glowing with excitement.

"Okay, who is this new Heather?" Sara was puzzled.

"Honestly, I feel like a different person down here. I don't know if it's the sunshine or all the beautiful vegetation and food ... but it's just so different from being in a cold, grey place."

"I'm loving the new Heather!"

"Oh my God, I have so much to tell you! You know that chef ... Lars Borgen ... the one whose cookbooks I buy all the time?"

"Yes. What about him? And when did you start saying 'oh my God' so much?" Sara laughed.

"I met him! He invited me to his test kitchen yesterday and well, one thing led to another ... and I might be doing my own cookbook!"

"Oh, thank goodness! I thought you were going to say something else!" Sara laughed at her silly thought.

"Well, that too!" Heather blushed and giggled to herself thinking how she'd judged Maria for having a 'good time' with Phil after just one night, and here she'd pretty much done the same thing.

"Aha! Really? Good for you! Moving on so quickly! No wonder you sound so different." Sara wasn't sure how to deal with this information.

Heather let out a happy sigh. "You know, I went over to his place last night and we had so much to talk about. It was so easy and natural between us. Well, maybe it was a bit awkward at first. But that's normal, right? He's just so confident and funny and sexy. I think it's because he's older than me. Brian was too young and immature for me. I need to be with an older man. And someone who's successful but still grounded. You know?"

Sara frowned. "Okay, but don't rush into anything. Nothing wrong with taking things slow."

"Yeah, yeah." Heather dismissed her sister and then changed her mind about telling her about the dinner party invitation.

"Are you going to keep staying at Maria's?"

"Oh, actually she's coming back. Her daughter's been in an accident and she has to come back. I'm on my way there now to pack up my stuff and maybe find a motel."

"Oh dear, I'm so sorry to hear that. Okay, text me where you end up staying. And Merry Christmas!" Sara said, relieved Heather hadn't said she would be staying with Lars.

"Will do. Love to all!" Heather hung up the phone, secretly knowing that she'd end up at Lars' again tonight.

***

Heather slowly opened the front door to Maria's house and looked around. Seeing that for once the house was empty, she whispered thank you.

She tiptoed to her bedroom, removed her clothes and took a long shower in the ensuite bathroom. She dried herself off and picked out the sundress with the blue flowers.

She picked up her carry-on from the closet floor and packed up all of her belongings. While doing so, she abruptly realized that with Maria's unexpected return, she could no longer use Maria's Alfa Romeo, so she ordered a ride to come pick her up. Then she realized that she'd have to tell Pam that Maria was no longer staying at her house.

She texted Pam:

Hi Pam! Having an amazing time with Lars! FYI – Maria has a family emergency and is coming back to Florida today. Ttyl 😊

With her sunglasses sitting atop of her head to hold her hair back and her purse around her left shoulder, she slowly opened the bedroom door and exited. She pulled her carry-on beside her as she made her way to the front door. To her dismay, she saw that Yolanda was on her own in the kitchen.

Yolanda eyed her carry-on and observed, sarcastically, "You're leaving so soon?"

Heather was still on a high and wasn't going to let Yolanda ruin her mood, so she retorted, "yes, you'll have the pleasure of never seeing me again."

"You know, it's nothing against you. I just don't like strangers in my daughter's house," Yolanda countered.

"Really? That's not how it felt," Heather snapped.

Heather studied Yolanda and decided to lay into her a bit more. "You know, I have to say, what really confused me was that I've always been under the impression that Latinas are warm and welcoming."

Heather could sense a shift in Yolanda's mood.

"It really wasn't anything against you. I was just taken off guard," Yolanda said with less anger.

"Well, you have your wish, I'm leaving," Heather said stiffly.

"Thank you for following the rules. No boys and Maria's car is in one piece," Yolanda said.

"I always keep my promises," Heather half-smiled as she looked at Yolanda, and then said in a more compassionate tone, "just talk to Maria when she gets back today. Hear what she has to say."

"She's coming back today?" Yolanda exclaimed.

"You didn't know?" Heather was surprised.

"No, I didn't." Yolanda shook her head.

Feeling there was nothing more to say, Heather continued towards the front door. She could feel Yolanda's hard gaze as she closed the door behind her, and then heard Yolanda's phone ringing.

Once outside, waiting for her ride, Heather decided to let Lars know the situation and see if she could sweet talk her way into an invite to stay at his place. Lars' phone rang three times before he picked up.

"Heather!" Lars yelled happily.

"Hi! Just thought I'd see how things are going," Heather said.

"Magnificently! I'd say we'll be wrapping up in a few hours."

"Great!"

"Is everything okay?"

"Um, well, no, not really."

"What's happened?"

"Maria's coming home today unexpectedly. So, I don't have a place to stay. But don't worry, I'll find a motel."

"No, no. You can stay with me. When do you need to be out by?"

At that moment, her ride pulled into the driveway.

"Um, like, right now." Heather said as the driver popped open the trunk, so she could put her carry-on inside and then she slid into the backseat.

"Go to my place. My neighbour to the north of me has a house key." Lars kindly offered.

"Are you sure?" Heather made a silent fist pumping motion.

"Yes, of course, not a problem." Lars said.

"Okay, I really appreciate it and promise I won't overstay my welcome."

"Haha! I'm looking forward to sharing more hot tubs with you!"

"Haha!"

"Why don't we meet at my place around two? The party starts at four. I'm picking up my tux and then I'll meet you."

"Sure, I think I'm going to do some shopping. Skip the beach." Heather said, gulping at the word "tux", as she realized her pleather pants and sparkly top from the other night wouldn't cut it – she'd have to trek back to the outlet mall and find something more suitable to wear.

"Okay, see you at two."

"See you then."

MUNICH
TUESDAY, DECEMBER 24

Last night, Ursula had insisted that Maria spend the night at their house; saying there was no way she was going to let Maria sleep alone at Heather's. So, while Phil had driven her back to Heather's to pack up all of her stuff, Ursula had made up the spare room. Later that night, Maria had called Sofia to tell her what had happened and Sofia had said she'd let Heather know. Then Maria had left a message for Martha, the shop manager, thanking her for everything while explaining she had a family emergency and had to go back to Florida.

Right before she'd gone to bed, she'd received a text from Alonso letting her know that the results from the CT scan and MRI showed that Olivia had broken her arm in several places and would be going into a three-hour surgery. She'd sent Sofia a quick text to let her know.

That morning, when she'd woken up, she'd been expecting to see a text from Alonso with an update on how the surgery went, but there was nothing. Frustrated by his lack of communication, she'd sent him a feisty text.

After a breakfast of fried eggs and Oktoberfest sausage that Brian had cooked for them, Klaus had then driven the three of them – Brian had insisted on coming along – to the airport hangar where they'd met up with Martin and Peter.

Now, it was closing in on nine o'clock in the morning and Maria was standing beside Phil just outside of the hangar at the Regal Winter Fair. Warmly dressed in Ursula's fuchsia coat, she was shielding her eyes from the large snowflakes that were steadily falling down around them from the moody sky.

"He can see through the falling snow, right?" Maria asked.

"Yes, he'll be able to see," Phil reassured her.

Despite Phil's reassurances, she was worried. Very worried. She knew her brother had never even come close to flying in this type of weather before, but kept reminding herself that he was a seasoned pilot.

They could hear it before they could see it. The roar of the engine grew louder and more deafening as it closed in on them. Eventually, the jet came into view and she clasped her right hand tightly around Phil's left hand as she watched her brother, Gabriel, begin his descent towards the well-lit airstrip that had been cleared off just for him.

A sudden gust of wind came in strong from the west and her anxiety piqued when the wings of the jet began to wobble. The snow seemed to be falling harder. Large flakes that she convinced herself would be making it difficult for her brother to see through the windshield. Phil was saying something, but it was too loud for her to hear.

To her relief, she saw the wings straighten out as Gabriel made his final approach toward the airstrip.

As the gap between plane and airstrip narrowed by the second, the plane soon bounced onto the asphalt. She watched tensely as it bounced angrily a few times before coming to a screeching halt in front of the Regal Winter Fair's hangar. Finally, Maria felt she could let out the breath she'd been holding the entire time.

Once Gabriel finished switching off all of the controls, he and Carlos opened the door of the jet and jumped out.

"Hola! That was an adventure! Let's get you guys out of here and back to Miami!" Gabriel yelled as he shivered. They were both wearing light nylon jackets over tight jeans.

Maria ran and hugged her brother.

"You made it!" She yelled before realizing it would sound like she hadn't thought they would.

"Of course, we did! You didn't doubt us, did you?" Gabriel smiled.

"Of course not! Gabriel, this is my friend, Phil." Maria said, quickly changing the subject.

"Mucho gusto."[29] Phil said, towering over Gabriel as the two men shook hands.

"Likewise," Gabriel said as he scrutinized Phil. "This is Carlos."

"Thank you for accompanying my brother," Maria said to Carlos.

"Sí, por supuesto,"[30] Carlos said.

Gabriel's enthusiasm cut into the formalities. "Wow our first-time seeing snow! I'm sorry, Maria, crappy circumstances! But this is crazy! So, this is what snow is like!"

"Apologies for Gabriel. We never shoot in winter. Our crew is allergic to the cold," Carlos joked.

Maria couldn't help but smile at her brother's enthusiasm. "It's okay. I get it, believe me," she said.

---

[29] Pleased to meet you.
[30] Yes, of course.

Klaus, Martin, Peter and Brian had been waiting inside the hangar and were now making their way over to the group.

"Hello, I'm Klaus," Klaus said to Gabriel and Carlos. "This is my other son, Brian."

They all shook hands.

"Hello. Nice to meet you, despite the circumstances," Gabriel said.

"Yes, exactly," Klaus said and then motioned towards Peter. "Peter will help you fuel up."

Peter nodded and said, "let's get you fueled up, so you can get back up in the air as soon as possible."

"Carlos will get your suitcases onto the plane, right Carlos?" Gabriel said.

"You bet." Carlos said as he grabbed Maria's suitcase and Phil's carry-on. He went to grab Maria's tennis bag, but she shook her head, no.

"Do you mind if I watch you get the plane ready?" Brian asked and Gabriel shrugged.

After Gabriel, Carlos, Brian and Peter left to get the plane ready for take off, Phil and Maria waited inside the hangar with Klaus and Martin.

"I'm so sorry to hear about your daughter. I'm sure the hospital is taking great care of her," Martin said to Maria.

"Thank you," Maria said, noticing he was wearing a parka similar to Phil's.

"I'll wait until you guys are up in the air before heading back home." Klaus said. He'd also bundled himself up in a dark blue parka over a pair of brown corduroy pants.

"How's your try at the Guinness Book of World Records going?" Phil asked, hoping to butter him up and find out what favour his Pop had done Martin to make him feel like he owed him.

"It's going really well. We've got lineups all around the building. If it keeps up like this, I think we're going to make it," Martin said excitedly.

"Glad to hear that," Phil said, "we actually went down the slide yesterday."

"You did? And how did you like it?" Martin asked excitedly.

"We found it exhilarating, right Maria?" Phil asked.

"Yes, we did." Maria said wishing her greatest worry right now was how high a slide was and not her daughter's health.

"So, it was really generous of you to ask Peter to open up the hangar for us," Phil prodded.

"Oh, you know, it was the least I could do," Martin answered vaguely.

Phil was about to say that he didn't know, but then thought better of it as Klaus was hovering over them.

"Where are you flying into?" Martin asked.

"My brother keeps his plane at a small hangar like this one just outside of Miami," Maria explained, "but this weather worries me."

"It's going to be okay. I talked to Stuart at the weather network, and I know which areas to avoid," Phil reassured her.

"I appreciate that," Maria said

"Guys! The plane is ready! Let's go!" Gabriel yelled into the hangar.

"Thank you so much for arranging this for us, Martin," Maria said.

"It was the right thing to do. Best of luck, but I'm sure it'll all work out," Martin said.

Klaus, Brian and Martin stood back as Phil and Maria exited the protection of the hangar and continued toward the plane sitting in the heavily falling snow.

Carlos opened the door of the jet and motioned for them to step inside. Phil held out his hand and Maria slipped hers into his as she daintily stepped up and into the plane. She walked over to the left-side passenger seat and sat down. Phil heaved himself up the steps, ducking his head and buckling his knees as he entered, trying his best to fit inside the small plane. Once they were seated somewhat comfortably for Maria and somewhat uncomfortably for Phil, Carlos jumped back into his co-pilot seat.

Gabriel had already turned the plane around, so they were in position to head down the runway and back up in the air. He picked up the cross hanging around his neck, kissed it and then whispered something before letting it go.

Gabriel gunned the plane and it hurtled down the runway, picking up speed as they approached the end. Maria clutched Phil's hand and squeezed it hard as the plane nosed up into the air.

"Hey, I kinda need that hand." Phil flinched.

Land and aircraft said their quick goodbyes as the plane continued to pitch upwards and they ascended into the frosty sky. Up and up they went into the snowy sky. The plane nosed through the clouds and dismissed the snowflakes as if they were but small nuisances in its urgent quest. Maria's ears popped with the drastic change in altitude.

Once they reached the appropriate altitude, Gabriel leveled the plane out. Maria let out another deep breath and tried to un-pop her ears. It was a smooth ride, but she was too nervous to look out the window at the clouds floating below them.

"Gabriel, I know you probably have your route all mapped out, but I talked to my coworkers, and I can help you, if you like?" Phil yelled into the cockpit.

"Sure!" Gabriel yelled back.

Maria ignored them as they discussed flight paths and weather patterns and began thinking about Olivia. She wondered about the surgery and hoped that Olivia wasn't in too much pain, cursing Alonso for not yet responding to her, and not regretting her feisty text, one bit.

Interrupting her thoughts, Gabriel asked, "have you heard any more news?"

"Nope!" Maria yelled bitterly above the engine noise.

What Maria didn't realize about Alonso's lack of communication, was that he'd been busy spending the night comforting Josephine, whose husband had just passed away.

"Olivia is a strong, resilient girl. She's going to be okay," Gabriel said vehemently.

"By the way, what are these cages for back here?" Phil pointed to the small cages behind them. He saw that there was bedding lined at the bottom of each cage.

Before anyone could answer, snow squalls picked up and shoved the plane back and forth. The plane bumped around for a few seconds and then with a sudden brute force, hit an air pocket. As the planed dropped down several feet before coming to an aggressive halt, Maria and Phil instinctively grabbed onto their armrests, whispering prayers under their breaths. Phil's question forgotten.

MIAMI
TUESDAY, DECEMBER 24

It was ten o'clock in the morning and Alonso, Oliver and Bianca were hovering over Olivia as she rested in her bed in her shared hospital room. They'd drawn the curtain around them for privacy from the two other patients in the room who had their own visitors. With all of the curtains closed, a low hum from the voices of visiting family members permeated the room.

"Are you comfortable?" Oliver asked.

"Not really, but please stop fussing," Olivia grimaced.

"Did they give you breakfast?" Alonso asked.

"Ugh, it was some type of watery egg thing," Olivia said.

"Have the police interviewed you yet?" Bianca asked.

"Geezes, what's with the twenty questions? But yeah, they came by early this morning when I was trying to sleep. I guess the good thing is they filed my statement right away." Olivia said.

"Did you at least remember some more details?" Alonso asked, feeling protective.

"Not really. I still can't remember much. But the main thing that sticks out in my mind, that I can't quite shake, is that the car stopped and then all of a sudden revved up again. I can't be imagining that, can I?" Olivia asked, her face looking up at them with a childish innocence.

"I guess not." Oliver frowned.

"Honestly, it was almost like it was speeding at us on purpose," Olivia explained.

"That's scary and strange," Oliver frowned.

"You still don't remember what the car looked like? And you didn't see their faces?" Bianca asked.

"Nope. I told the police I can't remember." Olivia frowned.

"Don't stress yourself out, Olivia. It's better you get some rest. Your mother's going to be waiting for you at home," Alonso said, leaving out the fact that Maria was flying home in Gabriel's jet. Maria didn't want to worry Olivia – as she'd explained in the feisty text she'd left him that morning.

"She's home?" Olivia asked.

"Not yet, but soon. You understand that I need to be with Josephine for a little while to help sort out funeral arrangements, right?" Alonso asked, looking at her with worry, not wanting to break his promise that things were going to be different.

"Yes, I understand. Don't worry about it," Olivia smiled.

There was a quick rapping at the door and then a surgeon entered the room.

"Is the Rodriguez family in here?" The surgeon yelled into the room.

"Yes, over here," Alonso said as he pulled back the curtain.

"Hello, you're the father?" He looked at Alonso who nodded and the surgeon smiled. "Good, you have a very strong daughter here. You should be proud of her. So, her arm was broken in three places, but the good news is that we were able to put it back together using some screws and plates. You should be as good as new in a few months. But, no going through any metal detectors, any time soon," he joked.

Olivia smiled. "Not planning on it."

"Now, for the not-so-good news," the surgeon continued, and they all looked at him with worry. "Don't worry, it's treatable. As you know, we had to run a bunch of tests. While we're happy that she won't have any long-term effects from the concussion, in doing so, we discovered that Olivia could possibly have juvenile diabetes."

"Diabetes? What does that mean?" Alonso asked, anxiously.

"You mean there's something wrong with me?" Olivia asked, her brows furrowed.

"Well, unfortunately it's been left undetected for a while, so I recommend following up with your family doctor who can explain everything to you and order more tests to be sure." The surgeon explained just as his pager went off, and he looked at it and frowned.

"Undetected?" Alonso questioned.

"Well, I really don't want to worry you, but it's important that you do get it checked out. As I said, you'll have to follow up with your family doctor." His pager went off again and the surgeon looked at them apologetically.

"Why can't you explain everything to her now?" Alonso asked, knowing Maria would grill him, having already avoided responding to her message from this morning.

"Honestly, I wish I could, but it's Christmas Eve and we just don't have the resources or capacity right now, unless it's an emergency. But, if she's feeling dizzy or faint, she should definitely come back to the ER. She's free to go. And I have to stress that she's going to need someone's help getting dressed and with bathing. Even though I know she's a tough girl," the surgeon said, smiling.

"Free to go?" Alonso scowled at the surgeon.

"Listen, she's lucky that she only has a broken arm and a few cracked ribs. It could've been much worse. I'm sorry, but I really have to go. They'll give you a printout of all of your test results when you get discharged. And a nurse will show you how to take care of your cast. Good luck with everything," the surgeon said and then quickly left the room.

"Lucky? Your mother isn't going to see it that way," Alonso sighed.

"It's okay, Alonso. I'm glad I'm getting out of here. The food sucks and this bed is horrible. Let's not worry about what we don't know." Olivia tried to shift her bum to a more comfortable position in the bed.

"Yeah, maybe, don't mention this to your mother just yet. You won't be able to see your family doctor until after the holidays anyway, right?" Alonso said.

"Exactly. Let's wait until after the holidays. There's too much going on right now." Olivia said and couldn't help but notice the relief on Alonso's face.

As Bianca watched the exchange, she bit her tongue, judging for herself that Alonso was already trying to get out of family obligations.

Oliver kissed the top of Olivia's head and said, "we'll grab our stuff from JC's and then get you home."

"Sounds wonderful," Olivia smiled gratefully.

MIAMI
TUESDAY, DECEMBER 24

As Mila lifted the wrought iron knocker and wacked it three times against Carmen's front door, her knees involuntarily trembled in fear.

Last night, after the unintentional hit and run, she'd spent the evening at Logan's house drinking and trying to forget about what they'd just done. But the drunker they got, the crazier the thoughts, and they'd eventually hurled accusations at one another until she'd told him she never wanted to see him again and had ordered herself a ride home.

When she'd arrived home, her guilt was too pressing, and she'd drunkenly called Carmen's cellphone.

The thing was, when she woke up this morning, she couldn't quite remember what she'd said to Carmen during that drunken phone call and was terrified she'd revealed too much.

But then, she'd received a text early that morning from Carmen thanking her for the condolence call about her father's passing, admitting that she could really use the emotional support, and asked if Mila could come by the house that morning.

It was now eleven-thirty in the morning and Mila waited nervously as Breanna opened the heavy wooden door. She watched as Breanna face changed into a forced, polite smile. "Hello Mila, what can we do for you?"

"Carmen told me about her dad's passing and asked me to come over," Mila said as she held up a bouquet of flowers and a box of chocolates.

"Come inside then," Breanna said briskly as she opened the door wider.

Mila stepped inside the foyer.

"Wait here while I get her," Breanna instructed and then left.

While she waited, Mila shifted nervously in place, trying to think of the right things to say. She wondered how badly hurt Carmen was and began picturing her on crutches with her leg in a cast and her head wrapped in bandages; which meant, she was completely dumbfounded when Carmen did finally appear within her sight, walking down the hallway towards her without a single bruise, bandage, or scratch.

"Hi Mila, thanks so much for coming," Carmen smiled mischievously.

"I'm just so sorry … I brought these for you. I know, they don't make up for anything, but …" Mila trailed off as she handed the flowers and box of chocolates to Carmen, not too sure how to take Carmen's strange smile.

"Thanks," Carmen said coolly as she took them.

"How are you doing?" Mila asked, looking Carmen up and down for any sign of injury.

"Actually, there's someone else you should be asking about. Follow me," Carmen motioned for her to come inside and then placed the flowers and chocolates on a nearby console.

Mila felt tricked but slipped off her shoes and followed Carmen down the hallway and into the high-ceilinged living room. She saw that there was a young girl sitting on the powder blue couch with her arm set in a serious looking cast. Max was lying on the couch beside the girl with his head in her lap. His tail wagged when he saw Mila but otherwise, he didn't move. Mila felt her whole body grow cold.

"Mila, this is Olivia, my soon-to-be stepsister. She was run over by a car last night. An apparent hit and run. You wouldn't happen to know anything about that, would you?" Carmen looked steadily at Mila.

Mila swallowed hard and stammered, "no."

Olivia looked back and forth between the two girls, trying to understand what was transpiring and could feel the tension mounting.

"Olivia just happened to be wearing my college jacket and walking our dog, Max. Still doesn't ring any bells?" Carmen grilled her.

Mila crumpled. "I'm so sorry. It wasn't my idea. I thought she was you! I was so mad at you about the job placement. And Logan ... He has such a temper ... He charged the car at you before I could do anything!"

"Wait a minute. Are you saying that *you* ran me down?" Olivia scowled. "So, it wasn't a random hit and run? Now it's all starting to make sense ..."

"Yeah but ... He didn't mean to actually hit you, just scare you ..." Mila said, agitated.

"What job placement?" Carmen scowled.

"You took my job placement away from me! You didn't even want it!" Mila cried out.

"Is that what this is about? Oh, for God's sake, I didn't take your placement! Who told you that?" Carmen exclaimed.

"You didn't? Um, Gary did." Mila stammered.

"Gary? You believe the crap that comes out of his mouth? You know he loves to fuel the fire between us, right?" Carmen rolled her eyes.

"You mean, it isn't true?" Mila put her hand to her mouth in embarrassment. "Oh, I'm such an idiot. You never wanted my placement."

"No, I didn't." Carmen shook her head. "Why didn't you just ask me?"

"I was too upset," Mila admitted.

"You can be such a pain in my ass, you know that!" Carmen yelled.

"Yeah, well, I'm tired of everything always going your way! You get everything handed to you!" Mila yelled back.

"What are you talking about? You know that's not true!" Carmen defended herself.

"Yes, it is! And the worst part is, you're so smug about it!" Mila said.

"You know what your problem is, you never think about anyone else but yourself! And you're always feeling sorry for yourself!" Carmen yelled.

Olivia felt like she was living her worst nightmare, and blamed Alonso. Ever since he'd left her mother for JC's, her life had been upended. Feeling angry and bitter, she interrupted, "can you two just shut up for a minute! I'm still trying to figure out what happened because I don't remember everything!"

Mila stopped yelling and suddenly asked Carmen in a panicky voice, "you're not going to report us to the cops, are you?"

"No, don't worry, no cops." Carmen said, her mischievous smile reappearing, once again.

"Oh, thank God," Mila exhaled.

"Please just tell me," Olivia whined.

"What do you want to know?" Mila asked.

"I want to know what happened!" Olivia cried out.

Mila shivered and then began explaining, "I guess the noise from Logan revving the engine scared Max ... He must've pulled away from you, ripped the leash out of your hands and then you lost your balance ... I'll never get the image out of my head of you falling backwards ... or the sound of you hitting the passenger side mirror and then flying through the air ... I am truly sorry."

Mila and Olivia stared at each other, letting her words sink in.

Carmen winced at the thought that it was meant to be her flying through the air and meanly hoped Mila's job placement was a crappy one, and asked, "if you didn't get the placement you wanted, where'd you end up?"

"Ugh. I'm going to be articling for Laithy, Wadkins and Parvey," Mila groaned.

"Hahaha ... You mean, Lazy, Waddles and Pervy?" Carmen couldn't stop herself from laughing as she corrected Mila with the nickname the law firm had been given after a few students had shared hilarious horror stories about their time articling for the firm.

"I guess I deserve it now," Mila smirked.

"You so deserve it." Carmen grinned.

"Yeah, I really do," Mila sighed

Carmen looked at Olivia. "In all seriousness, we need to come up with a plan on how you're going to make it up to Olivia. She's going to need a lot of help."

"Yeah but, back up. You said Olivia's going to be your stepsister? Didn't your dad pass away just last night? What the heck is going on?" Mila asked.

"Ugh. Long story," Carmen sighed.

"My dad and her mom have fallen in love," Olivia said in an exaggerated tone, "she's the love of his life."

"Seriously?" Mila asked.

"I guess my dad didn't take the news very well," Carmen said.

"That's the understatement of the year." Mila snorted and Carmen sighed.

"We're guessing they're going to get married before the ink is even dry on the divorce," Olivia murmured bitterly.

"I'm so sorry, Carmen. I really am. I really liked your dad," Mila said sympathetically.

"I can't believe he's gone. I never thought it would happen like this. I hadn't seen him since Thanksgiving and he was looking fine." Carmen said.

"You know, I'm here for you, if you need anything," Mila said kindly. "I know you tricked me into coming over because of Olivia, but I really am here for you."

"I'm still in a bit of shock at how it all happened so quickly," Carmen said.

"You know, when I saw you, or rather Olivia, walking across the street, I was so upset that you hadn't told me that you were coming home for Christmas. I thought you were trying to avoid me because you'd stolen my placement. But now, I understand everything. I am really sorry for being such a horrible person," Mila said.

"I really wish you'd just asked me, but that's all in the past now. We have to think about Olivia. You need to make it up to Olivia," Carmen reiterated.

"Sure, anything. What can I do?" Mila asked, looking over at Olivia with concern.

"How long do you have to keep your cast on?" Carmen asked.

"About six weeks," Olivia answered quietly.

"She's going to need a lot of help getting dressed and doing her schoolwork," Carmen said.

"Yes, I realize that. But how can I help with that?" Mila asked.

"Well, you're going to be her nurse and assistant." Carmen demanded.

"Me? I won't have time for that! You know those firms work us to the bone. I'll be living there 24/7!" Mila cried out.

"Then you're going to have to hire someone to look after her," Carmen said matter-of-factly.

"Hire someone? I can't afford that! How am I going to pay for that?" Mila yelled.

"You should've thought of that before you launched a car at her!" Carmen yelled back.

"Let me think!" Mila cried out and they all stayed quiet. After a few minutes, Mila's face lit up. "I know! You know how they have those message boards with students looking for volunteer hours, or offering tutoring lessons? Why don't we get one of them to help you? Like a student aide?"

"Maybe somebody who's studying to be a doctor or something similar?" Carmen suggested. "Are you okay with that, Olivia?"

"Yeah, I guess that sounds okay," Olivia sighed, wondering how the two girls could go from hating each other one minute to acting like best friends.

"You know what we need to do? We need to make a pact," Carmen announced.

"About what?" Olivia asked.

"Oh, you're right," Mila nodded.

"We can't tell any of our parents about what actually happened," Carmen stated.

"Pinky swear." Mila nodded.

"Let's do it," Olivia nodded, suddenly realizing that if her mother knew what had actually happened, she'd somehow twist the whole thing around and never let her see Carmen, which would then include, Oliver and JC, by association.

Mila and Carmen stood up and hovered over Olivia. The three of them hooked their pinky fingers around each other's, Olivia using her left hand.

"On three ... one, two, three," Carmen instructed.

"Earth, sea, water, air. I declare a pinky-swear." Carmen and Mila chanted as Olivia murmured along, and then they threw their pinkies up in the air, giggling.

"I guess you'll never borrow my college jacket again," Carmen teased.

Olivia raised an eyebrow at Carmen and then realized that teasing was her way of welcoming her into the fold.

"Learned my lesson there," Olivia giggled.

The three of them giggled and then quieted down, each lost in their own serious thoughts. In the stillness, they could hear thumping noises coming from the stairs, and then eventually Oliver stuck his head into the living room.

"I've packed up all of our luggage and brought it downstairs. You ready to go?" Oliver said, and then looked quizzically at Mila.

Mila waved from her spot on the couch beside Carmen. "I'm Mila. I live down the street," she said, smiling.

"Oliver. Olivia's other half," he said.

"Where are JC and Bianca, by the way?" Carmen asked.

"Ah, not sure." Oliver blushed as he wasn't about to admit that he'd heard arguing coming from JC's bedroom, and then eventually other, more amorous noises.

"Oh!" Carmen caught onto Oliver's thoughts by the flushed look on his face and giggled.

"What time is the car coming?" Olivia asked, wondering if Bianca had finally broken up with JC.

"It should be here soon," Oliver said just as his phone dinged, indicating that the driver was waiting for them outside. "Oh, it's here! Let me help you up."

As Oliver and Olivia slowly made their way to the front door, Mila turned to Carmen and whispered, "do you seriously want me to stay here with you for a bit because of your dad?"

"Sure, that would be nice," Carmen nodded as they both stood up from the couch so they could see the couple off.

"Where is your job placement, anyway?" Mila asked quietly.

"With Dylan's ... well, his family's firm," Carmen answered, proudly.

MIAMI
TUESDAY, DECEMBER 24

After those first few terrifying moments of being tossed around in the heavy snow, the rest of the plane ride had been relatively uneventful, much to Phil and Maria's relief, and they were now approaching Miami.

Looking out the window beside him, Phil stared down below at Florida's eastern coastline. Nothing looked real and it felt like he was looking at a pretend world so far away from him. He looked at the tiny houses below and watched as miniature boats sped through the sparkling water as if already late to their destination. He looked over at Maria who was staring out her window as well.

"The hangar is just up ahead, so we're going to be making our descent a little bit at a time. Keep your seatbelts on, please," Gabriel announced.

Phil grabbed Maria's hand. "How are you doing?"

Maria smiled. "I'm okay. She's a strong, resilient girl. We need to stay positive for her."

"Of course." Phil nodded.

They felt the plane lurch downwards and begin turning to the right. Maria squeezed Phil's hand. The runway now appeared within their sights as Gabriel guided the jet towards it. Gabriel was barking commands at Carlos as the plane swayed to the left, its outside flaps creakily opening and closing. After a few seconds, it straightened out and they were heading directly onto the runway. Gabriel aggressively slowed the plane down, and in anxious anticipation, they finally felt the wheels bounce onto the airstrip.

Maria let out a sigh of relief as the plane screeched to its final halt at the end of the runway. Gabriel switched off the plane and his radio crackled.

"I'll grab all of your suitcases from the back. You guys go wait on the tarmac," Carlos yelled.

Once they were all safely standing on the tarmac, Phil asked Gabriel, "so, which one's your car?"

"It's that one over there," Gabriel said, pointing to a convertible Mustang.

"Fantastic." Phil sighed with relief.

Maria looked down at her phone and saw that there was a voice message, so she immediately dialed her voicemail and was grateful to hear Alonso's voice: "Maria, I have good news. Olivia's surgery went well last night and she's being discharged from the hospital this morning. She'll meet you at home in Boca Bonita."

Maria felt relief wash over her as she'd been imaging all types of unbearable scenarios during the flight. She relayed the message.

"Oh, thank God!" Phil yelled and Gabriel kissed his necklace.

Maria ran over to Phil and hugged him.

"Does that mean I have to go back to Canada?" Phil joked.

"Very funny," Maria giggled.

BOCA BONITA
TUESDAY, DECEMBER 24

"Please try to avoid any bumps or hard turns," Oliver instructed the driver as they made their way towards Boca Bonita.

Olivia was sitting in the centre rear seat to ensure she was able to lean her left side against Oliver's right side for support as they sped through traffic.

"How are you doing?" Oliver asked with concern.

"I've been better. Not how I pictured my Christmas break going," Olivia muttered.

"How are you and Carmen getting along? You guys were so quiet when I came into the room," Oliver observed.

Olivia was about to brush Oliver off, but then realized that the pact she'd made with Carmen and Mila only included parents, which meant she could tell Oliver the truth. In fact, she'd have to tell Oliver the truth in order to honour the pact, so he would know not to say anything to her mother – and the sooner the better as the driver continued to speed towards her house.

"There is actually something I need to tell you, but you have to promise not to freak out," she said in a serious voice.

"Sure, I guess," Oliver frowned.

"I'm serious. You can't freak out and you can't tell anyone." Olivia gave him a steady look.

"Okay!" Oliver said defensively.

"I found out who hit me," Olivia began.

"You did! From the cops? Did they call you while I was upstairs?" Oliver asked excitedly.

"No. Not from the cops." Olivia swallowed hard with nervousness.

"Then who? How?" He asked.

"Well, you know how Carmen's friend Mila was sitting in the living room with us when you came downstairs to get me?"

"Yeah, who is she?"

"Apparently they're long-time childhood friends," Olivia explained, not knowing what other word to use to describe their strange relationship.

Oliver waited for her to continue explaining.

"Well, remember how I said that the only thing I truly remembered was the car stopping to wait for me to cross the street, but then all of a sudden starting up again and coming towards me?"

"Yes, of course, I do."

"Well, I guess it was Mila and her boyfriend who were in the car," Olivia began.

"Okay?" Oliver was startled.

"Let me explain everything." Olivia said and then carefully moved herself every so slightly sideways so she could look directly into Oliver's eyes.

Olivia then launched into a detailed explanation of everything that Mila had told her, and some of what Carmen had said, making sure Oliver was getting a clear picture of everything that had happened.

"Mila admitted all of this to you!" Oliver yelled, once Olivia had finished explaining.

"I know it's a lot." Olivia pursed her lips.

"I wish I'd known all of this when we were back at the house!" Oliver yelled.

"Please, you promised not to freak out."

"That was before I knew what you were going to tell me! This is crazy. They're friends." Oliver frowned.

"They have a complicated relationship, okay? Can we just leave it at that?" Olivia sighed.

"I really don't understand women." Oliver shook his head.

"You understand me." Olivia tried to lighten the conversation and Oliver rolled his eyes.

"We have to tell the cops," Oliver reiterated.

"No cops. In return, she's going to arrange for someone to come help me while I'm stuck in this cast," Olivia explained.

"She has the money to do that?" Oliver frowned.

"Well, we figured out a cheap way to do it. But, don't worry about that right now. And, we can't tell my parents," Olivia begged.

"Seriously? So, what are we going to tell your family when they ask?" Oliver glowered.

"I need to do this for Carmen. She's going to be my stepsister and I need her to know I'll always have her back," Olivia begged.

"You do realize how ridiculous that sounds? She's the reason you're hurt," Oliver scolded.

"Yeah but, if I hadn't gotten hurt, we wouldn't have found out about my diabetes, right?" Olivia pointed out.

"True, but are you going to at least tell your mom about that?" Oliver asked.

"Like Alonso said, let's wait until after the holidays. There's nothing we can do about it now, anyway. I have to get my family doctor to run more tests. And who knows, it could be nothing." Olivia looked steadily at Oliver.

"So, basically, we can't tell your mom anything," Oliver frowned.

"I know it's not ideal. For now, let's just say the cops are still looking into the matter, which is true." Olivia kept looking into Oliver's eyes.

"Fine. Can you at least promise me one thing?" Oliver asked.

"What's that?"

"To never leave my sight again. That's how all of this started in the first place." Oliver looked steadily back at Olivia.

"Actually, I think it all started with you eating a bad sandwich, but sure, I promise," Olivia giggled, knowing full well how silly such a promise was.

BOCA BONITA
TUESDAY, DECEMBER 24

Phil had been sporting a goofy grin ever since they'd found out Olivia was okay and kept repeating how happy he was that everything had worked out and how excited he was to be meeting her family.

As soon as Phil had sat down in the front passenger seat of Gabriel's convertible Mustang, he'd asked if he could move the seat all the way back and Carlos, who was sitting behind him, had said no problem. So, while Phil had been fiddling with his seat, Gabriel had quietly asked Maria if Yolanda knew about Phil and she'd shaken her head, no.

Now, Phil was enjoying the freedom of having the space to stretch out in the front seat. With the roof retracted, his head towered miles above everyone else's as they breezed along the highway towards Boca Bonita.

As they approached Maria's lavish house, Phil's eyes widened at the statuesque endlessness of it. He took in its beautiful rose-colored stucco with white trimmings underneath a wave of terracotta roof tiles, its endless turrets and its delicate white shutters announcing beautifully arched windows, some with Juliet balconies.

"This is your house?" Phil asked in astonishment.

"Yes, don't you just love it?" Maria beamed.

Gabriel parked beside Maria's Alfa Romeo.

"This is your car?"

"I have great taste, don't I?" Maria giggled and leaned forward into the front to pat Phil's arm.

Phil chuckled at the cheeky joke.

"You guys go on ahead and say hello. We'll bring in your suitcases and stuff," Gabriel said to Phil and Maria.

"Gracias, Gabe." Maria said happily.

Maria knew Yolanda wouldn't be impressed that she was bringing a strange man home, but she had a good feeling that Yolanda would fall in love with his goofy charm and good looks.

Maria opened the front door and shouted, "We're here!"

The first thing she noticed was the upbeat Latin music and then the familiar and pleasant aroma of ajiaco simmering on the stove. She saw that the amount of presents under the white Christmas tree in the corner had grown exponentially. Jack and his sous chefs were in full hustle, working hard at getting the Rodriguez's family Christmas dinner ready.

"¡Hola!" Jack yelled from the kitchen and then ran over to give Maria a quick hug, "So happy to hear Olivia's okay!"

"Jack, I'd like you to meet Phil," Maria beamed and noticed that Jack was wearing his short-sleeved chef's jacket over a pair of skinny jeans.

"Don't worry, we aren't making alligator soup," Jack teased and Phil grimaced.

"How did you know about that?" Maria exclaimed.

"Gabriel and I wanted to see exactly who you were bringing home. So, we looked him up!" Jack chuckled.

"Much appreciated. About the soup." Phil chuckled as he towered over Jack.

Abuelita had been sitting and drinking coffee in her favourite chair in the living room. She was now slowly making her way over to the front entrance.

"Abuelita, this is Phil," Maria said and watched as Abuelita looked up at Phil in awe.

"Mucho gusto de conocerte,"[31] Phil said, and Maria thought she saw Abuelita blush.

"Abuelita, you look so elegant!" Maria said, taking in her grandmother's graceful figure in her powder blue pantsuit and saw that she had pinned a Christmas brooch to her left lapel.

"Yolanda is getting her hair done. She'll be back soon," Jack explained as he made his way back to the kitchen.

The front door opened and in came Gabriel and Carlos, bringing in the winter coats and suitcases.

While Phil was distracted with helping Abuelita walk back to her seat, Gabriel discretely leaned into Maria's ear and whispered, "Where should I put Phil's carry-on?"

"Has Heather left?" Maria whispered back.

"Let me check." Gabriel peered into the guest bedroom and saw that the closet was empty and the bed was made, "looks like it."

"Maybe it's best you put it in that room for now," Maria said.

"Good idea," Gabriel said.

As Gabriel left to put the suitcases away, Phil returned from the living room.

"Should we help Jack?" Phil asked.

"No! He definitely doesn't want our help," Maria giggled, "he's got his helpers."

---

[31] Nice to meet you.

"Listen to Maria! Please go outside and enjoy yourselves! There are appetizers and drinks in the outdoor fridge!" Jack yelled.

With the suitcases now put away, the four of them walked through the patio doors, across the pool area and exited through the screen door of the lanai and into the outdoor dining area along the back of the house.

"You have a beautiful home!" Phil exclaimed.

"Thank you!" Maria smiled.

Phil followed Maria to the outdoor kitchen. She opened the fridge door and began passing him plates of tortilla chips and salsa, chicken empanadas, shrimp ceviche and palitos de queso <cheese sticks>. He placed everything on the table. There were small plates and napkins already laid out on the table.

"What would everyone like to drink?" Maria asked as she took out a bottle of Rosé for herself from the fridge.

"¡Cervezas, por favor!" Gabriel yelled and everyone nodded, so Maria grabbed some bottles from the beer fridge and brought them over.

"It's been a long day," Gabriel sighed as he unscrewed the bottle cap.

"Thank you for coming to get us," Phil said, tipping his bottle towards Gabriel.

"If you want to go up again, let me know," Gabriel said politely.

"No offense, but that experience will last me a lifetime," Phil said.

"Fair enough," Gabriel chuckled.

"Phil, do you know what all of these appetizers are?" Carlos asked.

"Actually, I do. These palitos de queso are my favourite! On second thought, maybe the ceviche. Sorry, no, can't choose, everything's fantastic!" Phil exclaimed. "Although, I have to admit that I'd always incorrectly assumed all South American food was spicy like Mexican food, but I've learned my lesson that this is not the case."

"We get that a lot! People are always surprised at that!" Carlos exclaimed.

At that moment, they heard the slam of the screen door shutting and then Oliver and Olivia appeared.

"My baby! Look at you!" Maria shrieked at the site of Olivia's right arm in a cast and wrapped Olivia gently in her arms. "I'm here now. I'm going to take care of you."

"I know," Olivia whispered.

"I'm so glad we didn't lose you. I don't know what I would've done," Maria whispered back.

"I love you, mom," Olivia said.

"Love you too, darling," Maria said.

When they finally broke free of each other, Olivia said, "Mom, I want you to meet Oliver, the best boyfriend in the world!"

Oliver grimaced in embarrassment, and they shook hands.

"So nice to meet you. I'm so glad you could be there for my daughter," Maria said.

"She's a brave one. Nice to meet you as well," Oliver said politely.

"Olivia, this is Phil," Maria said, smiling.

Olivia craned her neck to look up at Phil and took in his thick blond hair and bright blue eyes.

"Well, you're certainly quite different from Alonso. Like, complete opposite. I'd say you're a tall drink of water," Olivia said in awe.

"Um, thank you," Phil blushed.

"Olivia! What a thing to say!" Maria was embarrassed, but Phil chuckled.

"So nice to meet you and so glad you're okay," Phil added gallantly.

"What did happen to you? Why were you walking their dog on your own and how could it be a hit and run?" Maria asked.

"Listen Mom, I'm fine. It's a long story and I'm really tired. I hardly slept in that horrible hospital bed and I need to wash my hair." Olivia exaggerated her words to play up how tired she was.

"Okay, honey. I understand." Maria smiled.

"I've invited Oliver over for Christmas dinner. Is that okay?" Olivia added in a sweet voice.

"Of course! But won't your parents miss you?" Maria asked.

"I have four younger sisters. They won't even notice," Oliver joked.

"You know what they say about boys who have younger sisters?" Gabriel said.

"No?" Oliver looked at him quizzically.

"They're good husband material," Gabriel said cheekily.

Oliver blushed and Olivia giggled.

"Well, on that note, Oliver's going to help me wash my hair," Olivia said, smiling.

"I am?" Oliver asked, surprised.

"Yes, you are," Olivia giggled.

"¡Dios mío! I can help you with that! And, don't you want anything to eat?" Maria asked and Olivia shook her head.

"I don't mind," Oliver said.

"Actually, we're going to go too," Gabriel said, draining the last of his beer. "We just wanted to make sure Olivia got home safely, but Carlos and I are going to shower up at the hotel and then we'll be back for the party."

"I could use some freshening up too," Phil agreed.

"We just brought out all of this food!" Maria exclaimed.

"We need to save room for the main event," Gabriel joked as he patted his stomach.

"I'll help you put everything away," Phil offered.

"You're the best," Maria smiled.

MIAMI
TUESDAY, DECEMBER 24

Later that afternoon, Heather was relaxing in one of Lars' outdoor patio chairs while enjoying a glass of Chardonnay from one of the bottles she'd bought at the Total Wine Shop and nibbling on some cheese and crackers from the charcuterie board she'd picked up. Lars had told her where he kept the dog treats and Heather had given Lucy a rawhide, so she had something to nibble on as well.

She decided to call Pam.

"Hello!" Pam answered on the third ring.

"Hi! Just wanted to wish you a Merry Christmas!" Heather said.

"Thank you! You too! How's it going?" Pam asked.

"I'm having a blast. Honestly, I'm pinching myself. I can't believe I'm going to a famous chef's house for a dinner party tonight. Never in a million years would I have thought this would happen. Kind of nervous, actually," Heather admitted.

"You got this! Just picture those celebrities in their underwear," Pam giggled, "remember, without the money, they're all just regular people like you and me."

"Haha, true enough," Heather chuckled.

"I still can't believe you're hanging out with your idol," Pam said.

"I know! Crazy, right? I mean, I'm not naive. I know this is probably some sort of a fling for him. He's a celebrity, I'm sure he can get whoever he wants," Heather said.

"You never know, he seems to really enjoy your company. Don't discount it yet. I mean, he's letting you stay at his house." Pam said.

"Yeah, for now. And I definitely don't want to overstay my welcome. But we do get along quite well. I'm going to enjoy it, however long it lasts," Heather said.

"And I was so relieved to hear that Olivia is okay," Pam said

"Oh, I know! What a scare," Heather said.

At that moment, Heather could hear the loud roar of Lars' Corvette pulling into the driveway. Lucy barked and bounded towards the closed patio doors.

"Lars is back. We'll talk later?" Heather asked.

"Sure thing. You're going to have a great time tonight." Pam reassured her.

After Heather hung up, she opened the patio doors for Lucy who ran to the front door. Heather sat back down and a few minutes later, Lars came out the patio doors with Lucy following closely behind.

"Hi, Heather!" Lars happily greeted her.

Heather got up and they gave each other a quick smooch on the lips.

"How's your book coming along?" Heather asked.

"Our creativity is exploding!" Lars exclaimed as he popped open the beer he'd grabbed from the fridge.

"Amazing!" Heather giggled.

"Oh, food! I'm starving!" Lars grabbed some meat and cheese from the charcuterie board and gulped them down.

Heather laughed and said, "I have something for you, but don't worry, you didn't have to get me anything."

"A present?" Lars smiled.

"Yes, for letting me stay here." Heather presented him with a large, gift-wrapped, rectangular object.

Lars picked it up, jokingly shook it, and then began ripping off the wrapping paper.

It soon revealed itself to be an ethereal painting of a rustic crab shack nestled under a trove of mangrove trees by the banks of a river deep in the Everglades. The crab shack's corrugated metal and wooden structure had been textured in an artful mix of muted and vibrant colours set against a powder blue sky.

"As soon as I saw it, I knew I had to get it for you!" Heather beamed.

"It's beautiful. I love it! Thank you so much, but I hope you didn't spend too much on it." Lars smiled as he admired it.

Heather chuckled as she admitted, "I actually bought it at the flea market set up in the mall parking lot. It's painted by a local artist."

"That makes me love it even more! I know exactly where it should go," Lars said as he carried it inside and Heather and Lucy followed him. He held it against the far wall in the living room, and asked, "What do you think?"

"Perfect!" Heather exclaimed happily as it had the exact effect she'd been hoping for. The colourful painting brightened up the black and tan house.

Lars rested the painting against the wall, took Heather's hand and pulled her towards him. They stared at each other and then began to kiss.

Lars pulled away and chuckled, "I'm feeling kinda frisky. Are you? What do you say we take this to the bedroom?"

Heather laughed and said, "Good idea," and then followed him to the bedroom where they closed the door behind them.

***

"Our ride is going to be here in six minutes," Lars announced, looking at his phone. He was only half-dressed in a white dress shirt over blue boxer briefs and Heather giggled at what Pam had said earlier about picturing celebrities in their underwear.

"I'm almost ready," Heather said. They'd both showered and she was slipping into the burnt orange halter top dress she'd bought at the outlet mall. It was ankle length and had a long slit down the right side, flirtatiously revealing bits of leg as she walked about.

"Not quite. You're just missing one thing," Lars said amusingly.

"Oh?"

Lars went to his dresser and picked up a black velvet box.

"You really didn't have to get me anything," Heather said as he handed it to her.

"It's Christmas!" Lars exclaimed.

She opened the box and saw that it was a gold pendant necklace.

"It's gorgeous!"

"Let me put it on for you!" Lars exclaimed happily.

Heather took it out of the box and he clasped it around her neck.

"You look stunning!" Lars beamed.

"Blooming hell, you have great taste!" Heather was amazed at how nicely it fell within the halter top.

"I know when I like what I see," Lars teased, not wanting to admit that his assistant, Tammy, had approached him that day with several necklaces to choose from.

Once Lars had let Tammy know that he was bringing a plus one to dinner that evening, news had travelled in electrifying speed around the office about Heather. His team was ecstatic to hear about this new love interest as it'd been a long time since he'd dated anyone, let alone shown interest in dating anyone. So, that morning, Tammy had rushed out to the store to buy a few necklaces and he'd chosen the gold pendant.

"Merry Christmas! I'm so glad I get to spend it with you," Lars said, smiling.

"It's one of my best ones so far," Heather said, blushing.

They both finished getting dressed and then made their way to the front door to wait for their ride. A few seconds later, a black sedan pulled up to the house and they slid into the backseat.

"Good evening," the driver greeted them.

"It sure is," Lars beamed, and Heather chuckled.

The driver smiled and began the drive to South Beach.

"So, what should I know about these people I'm about to meet?" Heather asked.

"You have nothing to worry about. They're all very nice. Well, some might be a bit stuffy, but we'll ignore those ones," Lars reassured her.

"Fair enough," Heather chuckled.

"I'm looking forward to you meeting my good friends, Rocco and Kiki. They're going to love you!" Lars exclaimed.

"And what do they do?" Heather asked.

"They're in the entertainment business."

"Then I'm sure I'll love them!" Heather exclaimed happily.

"And my good friend, Chef Grudo," Lars said.

"The one who hosts Grudo's Game House? He seems like a fun but intense guy."

"Ah, you'll love him! Don't worry, you're going to fit right in."

"And what about the food?"

"They always hire up-and-coming chefs who are trying to make a name for themselves in the community."

"That's generous."

"And we never know what the menu is. It's all part of the allure. Sometimes it's a traditional turkey dinner, but last year they had massive seafood towers. It all depends on the chef."

"Seafood towers! That sounds heavenly!" Heather giggled.

After weaving in and out of traffic like an F1 driver, their driver soon announced they'd arrived. As they pulled up to the mansion, Heather was relieved to see that the women exiting the cars ahead of them were wearing similar dresses to hers.

BOCA BONITA
TUESDAY, DECEMBER 24

Inspired by the upbeat Latin music playing over the speakers, Maria had convinced Phil to give cumbia dancing a try. They were now dancing in the open portion of the outdoor dining area and Maria was giggling as she attempted to show Phil how to move his hips. Abuelita joined in the laughter from the comforts of the sofa, sipping on a glass of red wine.

Maria had changed into a shapely red dress and Phil had put on a collared, blue shirt over top of a pair of khakis. The dining table had been set for twelve and the appetizers were now scattered across the bar's countertop.

"I don't think I'm ever going to get the hang of this, my dear," Phil said as he began to exaggerate his movements to make them laugh even more, "You'll just have to put up with dancing next to a gorilla."

"Hey, I'm never giving up on you!" Maria giggled.

They heard the screen door open and shut and soon Olivia and Oliver appeared from around the corner.

"Look at you guys! Practicing your moves!" Olivia yelled, laughing.

With Maria's help, Olivia had changed into a long floral dress and Oliver had put on a black polo shirt over a pair of dark plaid shorts.

"And I'd say we all cleaned up well," Oliver announced cheekily.

Olivia gave Abuelita a kiss on the cheek.

"Let's dance!" Olivia said to Oliver.

"Are you sure you're not in too much pain?" Oliver asked.

"Ah, it's okay. The doctor prescribed me the good stuff," Olivia joked and then added, "as long as we take it slow."

Since Olivia's right arm was in a cast and she had limited movement because of her cracked ribs, they struggled to find the best way to hold onto each other, but eventually they figured it out and began to slowly dance to the music. Abuelita applauded as the couples tried to match their moves to the rhythm of the music. By this point, they were all giggling quite loudly and didn't hear the screen door slam shut.

As Maria performed a twirling motion, she turned to see Yolanda's puzzled face as she watched her daughter and granddaughter dancing with two strangers in her daughter's house.

"What on earth is going on in here!" Yolanda hollered over the music with one eyebrow raised in disapproval.

She was wearing an elegant emerald green dress with a necklace encrusted in diamonds. Jorge was positioned behind her in a chic red and green checkered blazer over a dark shirt and dress pants.

"Yolanda! You knew I was going away with my boyfriend for Christmas! This is Oliver." Olivia giggled and motioned for Oliver to give her grandmother an air kiss.

"Mucho gusto, Yolanda," Oliver said as he air-kissed her gallantly on both cheeks.

Yolanda enjoyed the attention and then looked up at Phil, taking in his bright blue eyes, mass of blond hair and substantial height.

"Who are you?" Yolanda asked.

"Mamá, this is my wonderful friend, Phil." Maria said, as she patted Phil's stomach.

"Fill? ¿Llena?" Yolanda asked.

"No, como Felipe."[32] Maria explained.

"¿De dónde has sacado éste?"[33] Yolanda asked.

"Cálmate,[34] Yolanda." Jorge touched her arm.

Maria had known her mother would be angry about a few things that had happened over the past few days, particularly the Rubia Lopez pitch, but her words still felt like a slap in the face.

To Yolanda's surprise, it was Phil who answered her in his limited Spanish.

"En realidad yo la recoger. Cuando en cola en el aeropuerto. No pudo resistir sus encantas latinas."[35] Phil explained hesitantly and Yolanda was taken aback that he'd not only understood what she'd said, but was able to reply somewhat coherently in broken Spanish.

Jorge extended his hand towards Phil, and they shared a sturdy handshake.

"María dime mucho de todos vosotros. Pero especialmente de ti, Yolanda."[36] Phil said slowly.

Last night, Ursula had taken Phil aside and had given him advice on what he should say to Yolanda when he met her. Ursula had explained that she had a feeling something had happened between the

---

[32] No, like Philip

[33] Where did you get this one?

[34] Calm down

[35] Actually, I pick it up. When in line at the airport. I couldn't resist her Latin charms

[36] Maria tell me so much about all of you. But especially you, Yolanda

mother and daughter that had led to Maria's last-minute escape, and perhaps whatever it was needed a gentle push towards repair.

"¿De verdad?"[37] Yolanda asked.

"Sí, me dijo tan orgullosa es de ti por creer tu propio negocio."[38] Phil explained in broken Spanish.

"She did?" Yolanda frowned.

Phil switched back to English and stated, "Scouts honour. And I take that stuff very seriously. I'm Canadian."

Yolanda pursed her lips, not quite knowing how to take Phil.

"Yes, and that you gave her the career she has. That she'd be lost without the opportunities you've given her," Phil added.

"Well, I wouldn't go that far," Maria mumbled.

Yolanda kept staring at Phil.

"I don't mean to be so bold, Jorge don't mind me, but you are strikingly beautiful. It's obvious where Maria gets her good looks from," Phil said, putting on his boyish charm. "Maria always accuses me of being cheesy, but I mean all of this from the best of places."

"I get it, my friend. That's why I picked Yolanda out of a whole roomful of girls." Jorge smiled.

"Ew, that sounds so creepy." Olivia cringed.

"By best of places, you mean Canada?" Yolanda asked.

"Yes, Phil is from there, but works in Miami." Maria explained quickly, before Yolanda could jump

---

[37] For real?

[38] Yes, she told me so proud of you for creating your own business.

to conclusions that she was planning a spontaneous move to Canada.

"And what do you do?" Yolanda asked suspiciously.

"Do you know what topic of conversation the average person spends at least thirty-five minutes a week discussing?" Phil asked and Oliver and Olivia shouted out some guesses.

"What's for dinner?"

"Whose turn is it to pay?"

"What should we watch?"

"Who left this mess?"

"Nope. The weather." Phil said proudly.

"And what does that have to do with you?" Yolanda asked.

"I'm a weather forecaster. I predict and follow weather patterns. I studied meteorology," Phil explained proudly.

"You're on television! That's so cool!" Oliver exclaimed.

"Hmmm. I guess that's a nice, safe job." Yolanda said.

"Not really. Phil reports on tornados and hurricanes, he almost got squashed by an alligator last week!" Maria pointed out.

"Squashed by an alligator?" Yolanda was puzzled.

"That's a story for another time," Phil said, embarrassed.

"Now, more importantly, Olivia. Tell me. What happened to you? How could a car hit you and then take off?" Yolanda asked, wanting to hear every detail.

"Oh, I'm going to copy Phil on this one. Let's save my story for another time." Olivia said, praying they'd leave her alone for now.

Yolanda was about to ask more questions, but was interrupted by the appearance of Gabriel and Carlos.

"¡Hola! ¡Feliz Navidad!" Gabriel yelled.

The family air kissed and hugged each other.

"Let's put everything aside for now. It's Christmas and I'm happy that everyone is here to celebrate with us as family and extended family," Jorge said.

Next to appear in the backyard party was Sofia and her husband Kevin.

"Sofia! What are you doing here!" Maria was shocked to see her as Sofia's daughter usually hosted a family-only Christmas Eve dinner.

Sofia hugged Maria tightly and whispered, "Yolanda invited me. And I had to come and see you! I'm so glad everything worked out. I was so worried."

"She did?" Maria was surprised at this revelation and then added as they left each other's arms, "you look beautiful," taking in Sofia's red ruffle blouse and black leather pants.

"Thank you, so do you," Sofia smiled, admiring how pretty Maria looked.

"Phil, I'd like you to meet my best friend Sofia and her husband, Kevin." Maria announced.

"The one Maria sent the picture of her wearing my Bills toque and Heather's parka! So nice to finally meet you!" Phil exclaimed.

"Oh, that picture was hilarious! I'm so happy to finally meet you!" Sofia beamed.

The last family to arrive was Gloria and her husband Nick, as well as their four kids who immediately ran over to a separate folding table set up just for them, upon which Jack had laid out kid-friendly snacks.

The noise level began to increase as conversations became more amiable and the drinks flowed. Jorge had to clink his beer glass with a spoon quite loudly several times before everyone finally stopped talking and turned to look at him.

"Everyone, thank you for coming! We are truly blessed that we are all here today safe and sound on this very special Christmas Eve ... A toast to my dear family and a special toast to the friends we've made during this adventure we call life!" Jorge smiled warmly.

Everyone raised their glasses and yelled, "¡Brindis!", except for Phil who yelled, "¡Salud!"

Maria giggled when Phil gave her an embarrassed look. "I thought it was 'Salud'?" Phil whispered.

"Sometimes we say 'Brindis'." Maria whispered back.

"Now, please take your seats and enjoy the meal," Jorge continued.

Phil and Maria happily noticed they'd been placed beside each other right across from Sofia and Kevin. Phil held out the chair for Maria as she sat down and Sofia winked at her.

Right on time, Jack's sous chefs appeared with a trolley filled with bowls of ajiaco and began setting them down at each place setting.

"Looks and smells delicious!" Phil exclaimed as he bent down and took in its rich and savoury aroma.

"Have you ever had ajiaco before?" Maria asked.

"No, I've never had the chance to." Phil admitted.

"It's chicken with potato, avocado and corn," Maria explained.

"Yes, I remember you telling my parents about it," Phil said.

"Oh yeah, that's right," Maria said, smiling.

"You met Phil's parents?" Yolanda was surprised.

"Yes, I went there for dinner a couple of times." Maria smiled warmly at the memories.

"And where exactly was there?" Nick asked.

"Yes, where were you?" Gloria asked.

"I was in a small town near Toronto called Munich. It's very cute. Phil took me to the farmers' market," Maria explained.

"You mean like a flea market?" Gloria asked.

"Way bigger. We ate sausages and beavertail," Maria giggled.

"What the heck is beavertail?" Gabriel asked, chuckling.

"It's like a big churro but with toppings." Phil explained, his mouth watering at the memory.

"Ay Maria, you know what I always tell you." Yolanda wagged her finger at Maria.

"Yes, I know. A moment on the lips, a lifetime on the hips." Maria rolled her eyes.

"No wonder you eat very little," Phil remarked.

"How exactly did you two meet?" Gloria asked.

"We met on the plane ..." Maria began, unsure of how much to reveal.

"Actually, I think it was more like Maria took full advantage of my height," Phil teased.

"Haha! I guess I did!" Maria giggled as she remembered how Phil had offered to put her carry-on in the above head compartment, and then later on take it down. She smiled warmly at the thought that his chivalry had now become their meet-cute moment.

"What does that mean?" Gabriel chuckled.

"Phil helped me with my luggage and then it became one of those strange coincidences where Phil knew Heather and we just started talking. By the way, how is Heather? How come she's not here?" Maria asked.

"Um, she was invited to another Christmas party," Sofia answered vaguely.

Maria looked over at her mother who was sitting to her right at the head of the table – across from Jorge who sat at the foot of the table – and wondered what Yolanda had done to offend Heather.

"Bueno, ¿cómo están todos esta noche?"[39] Jack asked, appearing with his sous chefs who began filling the trolley back up with everyone's empty bowls.

"¡Enhorabuena al chef! ¡Bien hecho, Jack!"[40] Jorge yelled and everyone clapped enthusiastically.

"My pleasure," Jack said, taking a small bow.

After all of the bowls had been cleared off the dining table, conversations started up again and the sound of boisterous laughs and competing voices expanded into the night.

"What else did you do when you were there?" Carlos asked Maria.

"We went down an ice slide. Oh, Phil you should find out if they made it into the Guinness Book of

---

[39] Well, how is everyone doing tonight?
[40] Compliments to the chef! Well done, Jack!

World Records!" Maria exclaimed and her family gave her puzzled looks.

"Wasn't it cold on your butt?" Sofia giggled.

"Yeah, but I borrowed Ursula's snow pants," Maria giggled.

"Who's Ursula?" Gloria asked.

"Phil's mom." Maria explained warmly.

"So, you live in a town called Munich and your mother is Ursula. Let me take a wild guess, you're German?" Kevin teased.

"Most of the people in my town are," Phil nodded.

"But they get tourists from all over the world," Maria added.

"What do Germans usually eat for Christmas dinner?" Carlos asked.

"I don't think it's that much different from what anyone else eats ... roast turkey, potato dumplings, warm sauerkraut and red cabbage," Phil grinned.

"Sounds delicious," Nick commented.

On time as usual, Jack's sous chefs came back with the trolley filled with dinner plates, each loaded with roast turkey, peas and rice.

While they were passing out the plates, Yolanda and Maria decided to have a quiet side conversation in Spanish solely between the two of them.

"How could you leave just like that without telling me?" Yolanda asked.

"I wasn't gone that long," Maria said defensively.

"You missed the company Christmas party!" Yolanda whispered harshly.

"I am sorry for missing the party. I truly am," Maria said, and she could see the hurt behind the anger in Yolanda's eyes.

Maria said hesitantly, "You know, I was thinking of maybe going back to school part time and finishing my marketing degree?"

"Really?" Yolanda looked at her in surprise.

"Take fewer business trips. Stay here, work hard, study," Maria said pointedly.

Yolanda studied Maria's face for a few seconds and understood the underlying meaning, "I think that's a smart idea. Maybe this Phil is a good influence on you."

"And my idea about Rubia Lopez ..." Maria began.

"I see this trip has finally knocked some sense into you. But we can talk about all that later." Yolanda said.

"And, Yolanda, Phil is a super sweetheart. Give him a chance." Maria smiled, but was hurt by Yolanda's harsh words once again.

Their side conversation was interrupted by Gloria asking, "Maria, have the police found out who hit Olivia?"

"I think the police are still looking into it," Phil said.

Maria looked over at Olivia and Oliver and studied them as they stayed huddled together on the sofa, giggling and whispering. She knew they were hiding something to do with Olivia's accident, but couldn't figure out what or why.

***

As there were no more seats available for them to sit together at the outdoor dining table, Oliver and

446

Olivia had opted to sit on the sofas by the bar and have their Christmas dinner there.

"Can you believe JC's going to be your stepbrother? I mean, how weird is that?" Oliver teased Olivia as they snuggled together on the sofa, having finished eating their Christmas dinner.

"It's a good thing I like him," Olivia giggled.

"But not too much," Oliver pretended to scold Olivia.

"Don't worry, you'll be invited to all family gatherings and vacations," Olivia smirked.

"Good! Because I'm hoping they'll be very lavish and expensive," Oliver laughed.

"Well, we'll see if Alonso keeps his promise about being a better father from now on," Olivia grimaced.

"I guess, time will tell. Um, do you feel up to meeting my parents tomorrow? My mom sent me a text asking if you wanted to come over for a late lunch." Oliver held his two hands together in a plea motion.

"That's so sweet of her. Of course, I'd love to! Can we exchange presents tomorrow, then? In all this chaos, I can't remember where I packed away your presents," Olivia giggled.

"Presents? Who said anything about presents? Was I supposed to get you something?" Oliver teased.

"Haha. Very funny." Olivia beamed.

SOUTH BEACH
TUESDAY, DECEMBER 31

It had all been Lar's idea. And it would turn out to be one they would never forget.

A few days after Christmas, during a late-night dinner of pizza and a few bottles of wine, Heather had unintentionally opened up to Lars about what had led to the house exchange with Maria and all of the adventures that had ensued during her time in the Sunshine State.

In response, Lars had enthusiastically exclaimed that there was no better way to celebrate new friendships and discard old ones than during a New Year's Eve extravaganza.

He'd decided to use his connections to snag six tickets to one of the country's biggest New Year's Eve bashes to be televised in South Beach, Florida, and had arranged for a limo.

When it had come time to choosing their outfits for the evening, the women had happily slipped into sparkly outfits perfect for dancing.

And so, on New Year's Eve, once they were all settled in the limo – Lars, Phil and Kevin squished into one bench and Sofia, Maria and Heather squished into the other – it was Sofia who picked up her champagne glass and led the three couples in a toast to Lars.

"To Lars! The best guy in the world for arranging this evening!" She shouted and they all clinked glasses.

When the limo approached the venue, the three women daintily entered the lavish main entrance, with the men trailing behind them.

They were then greeted by a friend of Lars' and the three women cheered enthusiastically as it became apparent that they were being directed to one of the private booths to the side of the stage.

"We can dance all night and not worry about blocking the people behind us!" Maria exclaimed, and Sofia and Heather giggled in appreciation.

The venue was partially outdoors and partially indoors thanks to a covered pavilion. Its different classes of seating areas were partitioned off with stanchions. Bodyguards were stationed at each entrance and exit, as well as around the stage, to ensure crowd control. Lights twinkled from various areas and there was an electric attitude emanating from the crowd.

Once they were settled in their booth, strobe lights flashed onto the stage, and a few minutes later, a tall, skinny figure ran into the spotlight.

"Welcome to tonight's New Year's Eve bash, live from South Beach, Florida! We've got a tremendous line up of star power and celebrities for a jam-packed evening of fun as we count down to the New Year! We're so glad you've decided to join us this evening! Now, back to you, Chris!" The host yelled into his microphone as the crowd went wild.

Many in the crowd were dressed in their shiniest of outfits, some wearing tiaras and oversized glasses, as partygoers typically do on New Year's Eve. In their anticipation for the evening ahead, some of the partygoers began waving sparklers and blowing metallic squawkers and noisemakers, unable to stop themselves.

Throughout the evening, as one act followed the other – along with celebrity interviews and entertaining video clips of notable events from the past year – Sofia, Maria and Heather danced to the entertainment. They enjoyed a steady supply of Cosmos and shots of Sex on the Beach, while Lars, Phil and Kevin bonded over beers and a few glasses of whiskey.

The men not only enjoyed watching the musical acts strut their stuff on stage – except for a few they'd both agreed they could do without – they also appreciatively and proudly watched their women dance sexily, right in front of them.

"Where did you learn moves like that, Heather?" Maria asked in admiration.

Heather giggled, "From Sofia."

"She's the best teacher!" Maria screamed and the three of them giggled even more.

Soon, as the New Year's Eve bash came to close, the act that the three women had been anxiously awaiting was finally about to appear on stage.

"She's on next! She's on next!" Maria shouted as she jumped up and down excitedly.

"Woo-hoo!" Heather and Sofia both screamed.

The lights dimmed and they watched as a dark figure bounced lightly onto the stage and then noticed something drop down from the ceiling.

As the lights came back up, the audience gasped as they saw that Rubia Lopez was sitting on an aerial hoop. In her skimpy, leather halter top and gold sequined tights that glittered, she daringly swung energetically back and forth, and then way up high.

Without needing to be prompted, the crowd sang along as she belted out her hit song, "Bail·la·la Conmigo·go"[41] and then threw herself into an aerial acrobatic routine that she meticulously performed while never missing a beat.

The three women looked at one another with wide, giddy smiles on their faces.

"Isn't she amazing?" Maria exclaimed.

"She really is," Sofia nodded.

"The absolute best," Heather agreed.

"Wait. Let's take some selfies!" Maria screamed.

"Great idea!" Sofia yelled.

The three girls positioned themselves along the booth's railing with Rubia Lopez in the background. The singer was way up high in the air, the size of a walnut, as they snapped the photos. When they reviewed the photos, they began to giggle … their heads were slightly cut off and Heather's eyes were closed in most of them, but they didn't care, they were just happy to have shared the moment together.

As Rubia Lopez's performance sadly came to a close, the host of the televised show rushed back onto the stage.

"Ladies and gentlemen, it is nearing that time in the evening when we're getting close to the midnight hour. Everyone, please join me in welcoming our final act of the year who will lead us in the countdown." The host announced and the crowd cheered.

---

41 Dance with Me

A lithe female singer joined him on stage, and together, they began the countdown. In a mix of excitement and sentimentality, the entire audience screamed:

"Ten, nine, eight, seven, six, five, four, three, two, and one … Happy New Year!"

Confetti and fireworks erupted.

The host and his lithe co-host then led the giddy and well-inebriated audience in a rendition of "Auld Lang Syne".

As for the three couples, in those final moments of their Christmas holiday, they took turns kissing and hugging one another in delight, while whispering "Happy New Year".

Heather took it one step further and yelled out:

"Out with the old, in with the new, cheers to the future, and all that we do!"

EPILOGUE

Gloria & Maria

A few days after Christmas, Gloria had taken Maria aside and had confessed that she'd overheard her and Yolanda yelling in the boardroom on the Friday before Maria had left for Canada. She confided in Maria that she would put in a good word with Yolanda about the Rubia Lopez pitch in the New Year; to which Maria had wrapped her arms around her and given her a big, happy hug.

Yolanda & Maria

In the months that followed, things were moving in the right direction towards repair between the two. Yolanda even dangled the possibility of promoting Maria to Chief Brand Officer – once she'd completed her marketing degree. And of course, thanks to Gloria, Yolanda promised (albeit irritatingly smugly) to reconsider the Rubia Lopez pitch.

Oliver & Olivia

As promised, the two were able to stay tight-lipped about who the real driver of the "hit and run" was and Olivia and Carmen had solidified themselves as steadfast stepsisters.

Olivia and Oliver were both disappointed to learn that Bianca had broken up with JC after the judge's funeral. Apparently, she was leaving him for an old high school flame she'd reconnected with over Christmas; after he'd liked some of her social media posts of her sporting a bikini.

Olivia & Maria

It was only once Christmas break was over that Olivia revealed to her mother that she could possibly have juvenile diabetes. And, after her mother had hugged her and shed a few tears, they made an appointment with her family doctor to get the ball rolling on the necessary follow-up tests and treatment options.

When Maria questioned as to who was paying for the student aide while she was in a cast, she'd answered, without thinking, that it was Alonso. Afterwards, Olivia had made a panicky phone call to her dad asking him to please pretend he was paying for the aide and to not ask any questions, to which he'd agreed – simply grateful that Olivia was still talking to him.

Heather & Lars

Despite Heather's skepticism that Lars was a hot commodity who could have anyone he wanted, they became their own hot item. They appeared on Page Six of the gossip columns after killing it at the Christmas Eve dinner party; during which Lars had been roped into hosting another reality TV baking show.

Learning how much Heather loved hiking, Lars took her to Corkscrew Sanctuary where they thoroughly enjoyed each other's company. Over the next few months, they easily travelled back and forth, visiting each other. And, a few months later, Heather used Lars' test kitchen to impress Laura and she found herself poring over the fine print of her own book deal.

Alonso & Josephine

Knowing how exhausted Josephine was after dealing with the judge's funeral, Alonso had presented her with a pair of re-booked tickets to Paris. They'd found solace in the cafés tucked far away from the tourist areas where they could nuzzle together.

Klaus & Ursula

According to Klaus, and to their delight but not surprise, Martin made it into the Guinness Book of World Records for the record number of people to descend an indoor ice slide in a twenty-four-hour period. Phil still wasn't quite able to figure out what favour Martin owed Klaus.

And, as fortunate as life can be at times, a security guard found a note stuck to the empty wall where *Elsa the Catfisher* had been hanging in the art gallery. The note from Brian explained that he'd left for South America so he could see these Botero paintings for himself. Apparently, his painting had sold for a substantial sum of money.

Maria & Phil

Fondness turned to love between the two, but Yolanda made it quite clear that she'd only allow them to live together once married. So, on a blustery spring day, Phil knelt down on one knee in front of Maria's whole family and asked for her hand in marriage. Her answer was "Si, como no."[42]

---

[42] Yes, of course.